# the WOLF'S HOWL

# the WOLF'S HOWL

## ARCHIVES OF THE WARDEN
### Book Five

## V. K. DIXON

XHP
xenia house press

*For Anna.*
*Imagining your reactions kept me going.*
*So thankful for you!*

# Porthaven Township

*The salt-swept shores of serenity*

# Table of Contents

*Author's Note*


*The spirit world referenced in this novel is inspired by the truth.*
*It is not, however, the real truth.*
*In making the truth fantastic, it is my hope to stir up questions within reality.*

*Ten years ago*

In the small town of Porthaven, Maine, Cait Lewan lived with the stain of her father's rumored curse. After her parents' murders, she and her sisters were brought to Porthaven and placed under protective custody, though young Cait never knew from whom or what they were being protected.

Living as a social outcast, seventeen-year-old Cait feared the rumors that plagued her family history. Tales of witches and demons had besmirched her beloved father's reputation, and now, one of his daughters was said to be the heir to his curse. Worse, Cait was convinced that she was the one the demon chose, haunted as she was by dreams of beasts and a creature that stalked her.

Desmond Simon was the Varon heir and the golden child of Porthaven High. Popular, intelligent, and destined for greatness, he didn't want any of it. Burdened by the weight of responsibility, Desmond acted out, pretending to be rebellious and irreverent when in truth, all he wanted was to live up to the demanding expectations put in place for him. But Desmond had a secret: He was in love with the Lewan girl.

Cultivating a hidden and forbidden friendship, Cait and Desmond would do anything for each other. Even if that included letting go of their dreams of being together.

But when beasts of the spirit world started randomly appearing out of the Veil in Porthaven, Desmond discovered that the rumored Lewan family curse was not as idle of gossip as he thought. He and his father, William, the town mayor and leader of the Warden, learned that the Veil was damaged and producing these beasts on its own—a seemingly impossible feat.

During their investigation, they spoke with Timothy Faulk, a potential Vessel, and Lilith Drake, an ex-Druid who came to the town for protection. While neither could offer answers for the Veil's damage, Timothy informed them there may be more than one Veil in the town, and Desmond felt there was more Lilith wanted to say despite his father's distrust of the woman.

As an honorary member of the Warden, Desmond had always known more about Cait's parents' untimely demise than he let on since, after all, it was a result of their ties to the spirit world.

Cait's father, Owen, was no witch, and he hadn't sold his soul to a demon. He was a Vessel, a Wielder of great power tied to a spirit-being—a creature of unknown power and origin that the Warden was desperate to control—called the Wolf. Porthaven itself had been built to house another Vessel in the Faulk family and their spirit-being, the Leviathan. Upon the instruction of the Raven, Corva—another spirit-being whose prophecies are infallible—the Lewan daughters were brought to Porthaven not for their protection but for the protection of the new Vessel: whichever daughter the Wolf chose.

Worried that Cait's family "curse" might impact her, Desmond worked to find the truth behind the damaged Veil. He uncovered another prophecy from Corva, one his father had hidden from him his entire life. He discovered that the Warden knew of the danger to Cait's father's life and hadn't done anything to stop it. Even more troubling, the prophecy itself put Cait in potential danger, stating, "Our success shall come only at her great sacrifice."

But when Cait's dreams took a turn for the worse with the appearance of a raven who harkened Desmond's death, Desmond realized the truth: Cait was the Wolf's new Vessel.

Desperate to save her from this fate, Desmond returned to the Veil, determined to fix it. Before he could enact his plan, Cait appeared on the Veil's island seemingly out of thin air, just before twelve beasts emerged from the Veil. While Desmond tried to use his powers to send the beasts back into the spirit world, it was Cait who, wielding for the first time in her life, managed to control them, returning them to the ether and sealing the Veil herself. Then she collapsed.

When Desmond returned Cait to her home, she dreamed a new dream. One with the raven, the damaged Veil, and a strange, redheaded woman . . .

Two years ago . . .

Upon an unexpected inheritance, brothers and co-authors Peter and Spencer Collins moved to the small town of DeVerre, Washington, to accept the grand estate of their estranged great-aunt, Diane Larkin, and pursue their lifelong dream of being full-time authors. Along with their inheritance of a new house—called the House of Occasus—two dogs, and the townspeople's suspicions, they found themselves drawn into the mysterious past of their great-aunt and the reason for her move to DeVerre over thirty years ago.

With the help of Diane's closest friend, Cassandra Clement—who, to their surprise, was a young and attractive woman their own age—the brothers discovered that they were not biological Collins as they believed. Their ancestors originated from DeVerre. Cassandra taught them about Diane's search for the parents she'd lost and introduced them to the spirit world that the two women had discovered together. A world filled with ghosts, phantoms, and beasts.

Together, the trio sought out the truth of the brothers' past and the secrets held in the town. Their pursuit of answers led them to Owen Bernard, a Wielder of the spirit world and agent of the Warden sent to DeVerre to ensure its safety. Owen taught them about the Warden—an organization dedicated to protecting the spirit world from the machinations of the Druids—and about the Veil hidden within DeVerre—a space where the line between the spirit world and physical world was thinnest.

As a team of four, Peter, Spencer, Cassandra, and Owen discovered the presence of Druids within the town, working to take over the Veil. Their investigation led them to the discovery that Cassandra's cousin,

xiii

Debbie Mercier, was one of these Druids intent on taking control of the Veil.

Through weeks of trial and error and two near-death run-ins with the Druids, they finally found the key to the secrets they were so desperate to uncover. The brothers learned that they were Varons and discovered a list with the names of the Druids within DeVerre.

Armed with the knowledge, they prepared to rid the town of Druids. But before they could enact their plan, the cultists attacked their home, twenty against four. Only through a feat of extreme, unknown power did Cassandra drive the Druids back, saving their lives.

After their survival, the team prepared to face the remaining threat of Druids in their town, desperate to earn the townspeople's trust. However, before they could convince the town of anything, Peter stumbled upon a meeting with the Druid leader, Alexander Frossard. Unable to get away in time, Alexander took Peter captive.

Spencer was desperate to find his missing brother. Along with their friends, Spencer, Cassandra, and Owen worked to stop the Druids and save Peter, even bringing in Silas Varon, a distant relative of the brothers. But the Druids had a firmer hold on the town than they'd ever realized.

Fighting the leadership of the town, Spencer was stalled in recovering his brother, leaving Peter the captive of Alexander Frossard, subject to the thrall of a valravn, a bird-like beast with the power to manipulate the mind. For four days, Peter was subjected to nightmares, watching Spencer die and hearing his family call for his help. Suddenly, his dreams began to change when a raven interrupted the nightmares, bringing the visage of a mysterious redhead with it.

After being freed by Connor Frossard, Alexander's son, ready to throw off his father's abusive control, Peter was returned to Spencer and Occasus. With Connor's help, they prepared to bring down the Druids before they could enact their ultimate plans within DeVerre: Unleashing the Spectral from the Veil.

In the midst of their planning, Silas revealed to Peter that he was the "true Varon" of Matthias's line, marking him as the primary leader of the Varon bloodline. They also learned that Cassandra was a potential Vessel, a wielder of extraordinary power that the Druids wanted to control.

In a battle at the lake, the brothers and their friends fought to stop the Druids, but while they removed the Vessel prepared by the Druids to house the Spectral, they couldn't stop them from tearing the Veil. The Spectral was freed, the Druids forfeiting their lives in a fight to take Cassandra, the presumed Vessel.

With the removal of the Druids from DeVerre, the town was presumably safe and back under Warden control.

Now, our story leads us back to Porthaven, where Cait and Desmond face the consequences of her burden as the Vessel for the Wolf . . .

# PROLOGUE

# Cait

*Present Day*

"So . . ." Peter held the door open with his back, glancing down at the dog by Cait's side as she walked into Porthaven's town hall. "Do people know?"

Catching his meaning, Cait let her fingers brush against the soft fur on Ludus's pointed ears. "Some do," she replied, then dropped her voice. "But this *is* a Warden town. Secrets are inevitable, aren't they?"

Peter let out a knowing scoff.

They entered the government building, her sneakers almost silent while his boots echoed with every step and Ludus's nails clicked on the tiled floor. After a brief conversation at Rese's coffee shop, Cait suggested that Peter join her for the next inevitable meeting. Changes were coming; that's what Peter had told her, and actions needed to be taken.

Cait and Peter walked past the receptionist's desk and moved toward the staircase. Initially, no one paid them any special attention. Cait and Ludus frequently visited the mayor. Why would they question her presence?

But then, the abstracted glances turned into double takes as several of the workers thought they recognized the man at her side. Jaws dropped, and a murmur rose to fill the space. It sounded quite similar to the hum radiating through her head, filling her mind with the awareness of his importance.

Cait could tell the difference now. The hum she heard around Peter had a comforting, bassy tone, an almost familial recognition. The one *he* elicited—the unique sound that belonged solely to *him*—was far stronger, its vibrations occurring in a tighter, more intense pattern. It felt like a predator locking in on its prey.

Peter leaned down to whisper to Cait, causing the rumble to spike. "This guy I resemble . . ." He paused, tipping his chin toward the many staring workers. "I take it he was well known."

A rueful grin tugged at Cait's lips. "You could say that."

"And they all think I'm him?"

"Most likely." Cait moved up the staircase in the direction of the mayor's office. "It doesn't help that you're with me."

He followed, glancing over his shoulder. "Because you hung out with this guy?"

Ludus let out a small snort that might have been a laugh or could have simply been a dog sneeze.

Cait decided she could be brave enough to give Peter clarity. "His name was Desmond," she said, the words tight in her throat. "And yes, it's because of our past . . . relationship."

Peter nodded but didn't have the opportunity to ask more questions as they neared the mayor's office. The receptionist's desk stood several feet from the cherry wood door, with a handful of chairs lined against the far wall. The wavy-haired blonde woman seated behind it looked up from her book, a smile illuminating her whole face.

"Oh, hi, Cait. Here to see—?" The receptionist's words rolled merrily off her tongue until she noticed the other visitor. Her eyes widened. "Uhhh?"

Cait stopped at the desk while Ludus sat promptly beside her. "Melissa, this is my friend, Peter."

He stood partially behind Cait, leaning forward to offer his hand. "Nice to meet you, Melissa."

Melissa gaped at him, clearly unconvinced. "P—Pete—Peter?"

"You got it," Peter replied, a hint of amusement playing on his lips. He gestured toward her desk. "That's a great book you have there. Have you read any of his other works?"

Melissa blinked in a daze. "Uhhh," she repeated.

Cait decided to save her friend. "Mel, I need to talk to him," she said with a tip of her head toward the mayor's door.

"Uh-huh." Melissa picked up the phone receiver, absentmindedly pushing buttons as she tried not to stare at Peter. After a moment, she spoke into the phone. "Uh, Cait—Cait is here to see you. She, uh—she brought a, uh—a friend." A few seconds passed as she listened to the response and then muttered, "Okay."

Hanging up the phone, Melissa's eyes darted between Cait and Peter. "Go ahead."

Cait thanked her and led the way to the mayor's office. Little had changed over the years. The white walls displayed different pictures, but the layout remained the same. Basic file cabinets and a credenza lined the walls, while the cherry wood desk occupied the back of the room. Two chairs for visitors stood before it. The mayor rose from his seat as they approached.

A lighthearted tinge lit Hunter's voice as he greeted Cait with a cheerful, "What did you do to spook—?"

His words cut off just like Melissa's the instant he saw Peter, his eyes widening.

"Oh." Behind his glasses, Hunter's sharp gaze darted to Cait as she shut the door, then returned to Peter. "You're back."

Peter looked at Cait with a wry smile.

Ludus waited by the door as Cait moved ahead, gesturing to Peter.

"Hunter, this is Peter Varon," she said. "Peter, this is our mayor, Hunter Varon."

"Ah." Peter held out his hand instantly. "Always nice to meet a cousin. Or whatever we are to each other."

Hunter scratched his jaw, surveying his newfound relative. "Peter?"

"Yep."

His eyes flashed to Cait. "You're sure?"

Cait sat in one of the chairs, working to maintain a casual tone as she remarked, "I think I'd know."

Hunter's mouth twitched in a grimace before he redirected his attention to studying Peter.

Taking the inspection in stride, Peter gestured to the room. "You're the mayor?"

Hunter straightened his shoulders, drawing himself up to take on his officious role. "Yes."

"That's cool." Peter rested his hands casually on the back of a chair. "You're younger than I'd have expected."

"My dad retired last year," Hunter explained.

"Warden town, through and through, huh?" Peter brushed his fingers through his hair. "I know something about that."

Hunter's eyes narrowed at the sight of the ring on Peter's right hand as he dropped it onto the chair's arm. "Is that what I think it is?" he asked.

Without a need for clarification, Peter smirked. "Seeing as you're a Varon, I'd assume so. I'm still kind of new to the role, myself."

Hunter blanched. "I'm not—I mean, we lost ours years ago," he said, a thrum of annoyance in his tone. He cleared his throat. "Matthias or Henry?"

"Matthias," Peter answered.

"Courage, then." Hunter tapped his knuckles on the desk. "We're of Edmond's line here in Porthaven. But like I said, we lost our—" His jaw tightened, and Cait could tell he was trying not to look at her. "We lost our *you* years ago."

Peter adjusted his gold signet ring. "I take it that was this Desmond guy I keep getting mistaken for?"

Hunter's eyebrows raised. "It's quite the coincidence."

The locket around Cait's neck felt particularly heavy, yet she held her head high. "I didn't just bring Peter here to meet his family, Hunter," she said, redirecting his attention back to her.

"Right." Hunter motioned for Peter to take a seat while he dropped onto his own. "What's up, Cait?"

"I need to leave town for a while."

Hunter's eyes went wide again. "Leave?" He shook his head. "Cait, it's my job to protect you. I can't do that if you leave."

"It seems that her protection is my job now," Peter interjected, digging into his pocket. He produced an envelope. "My brother and I received this a week ago today, actually."

Hunter accepted the proffered letter. He opened and unfolded the page, adjusting his glasses to read it. He began wearing the glasses at Liz's insistence a few years ago. She had noticed him squinting while reading and told him she wouldn't let her husband go blind when her uncle was an ophthalmologist. They gave him a scholarly air that Cait thought suited his new role as mayor.

Once he finished reading the letter, Hunter glanced at Peter. "This is from the Raven," he deduced.

Peter dipped his chin in confirmation. "Through her Vessel. It's the first correspondence our family has had with her since nineteen-forty." He paused, a curious gleam in his eyes. "Would you happen to know what the signature H.H. stands for?"

Hunter handed the letter back to him. "No. The last Vessel we knew of was Sylvia. This one must prefer some anonymity. Though I suppose that could be due to, uh—" He glanced at Cait. "Past events."

"You mean the whole reason for the fifty-man detail and insane levels of training for Vessels?" Peter asked sarcastically.

"You're familiar with it?" Hunter asked.

"Intimately."

Cait leaned forward in her seat. "He showed me the letter too," she said. "This is what we've been preparing for, Hunter. Peter and I need to leave immediately."

A worried look crossed Hunter's face. "I understand." He opened his mouth to continue but paused to take a deep breath. He rested his elbows on the desk, holding Cait's gaze. "Have you told William?"

Cait's stomach clenched. "Not yet."

Hunter dipped his chin. "Will you leave today?"

"Oh, uh—" Peter cut in. "The morning would be preferable. I've been driving for almost a week straight. It'd be nice to have a break."

"Driving?" Hunter frowned. "Why didn't you fly?"

Peter brandished the letter. "She told me not to travel by air, remember? Something about picking up some friends on the way."

Hunter nodded. "Right. Well, you're welcome to stay with my wife and me, or. . . ." He stopped, turning to Cait.

"He'll stay with us," she confirmed.

"I—Cait, I don't want to overstep, but . . ." Hunter lowered his voice, concern evident in his expression. "Are you going to be all right with that?"

"Because of his resemblance?" Cait stated it bluntly, knowing that was what he meant.

Hunter tipped his head in confirmation.

Fingers tingling to touch the locket, Cait gripped the arms of her chair instead. "They don't look *that* much alike, Hunter."

A sudden scoff burst out of the mayor. "Sorry," he apologized. "It's just—I mean, I wouldn't have been able to tell them apart."

"It's been ten years," she challenged. "You don't remember him as well as you think."

Hunter dropped her gaze, abashed.

Peter squirmed in his seat next to her.

"I appreciate your concern," she promised. "But their similarities don't affect me like that."

A low rumble echoed in Cait's mind, calling out her lie. The resemblance between Peter and Desmond affected her far more than she wanted to admit. The hum of Peter's presence, though less alluring and demanding, reminded her of every moment spent with Desmond. It dredged up the memories she'd kept locked behind the door of her dreams for the past decade.

After a brief exchange of plans and Hunter's invitation to dine with his family that evening, Cait and Peter left. Ludus brushed against her leg as they passed through the hallways of the government building. Workers stopped and stared once more, peering out from office doors and windows to catch a glimpse of the man they believed they had known as a teenager.

When they were outside the building and back in the afternoon sunshine, Cait turned toward the docks. "We have one more stop," she told Peter, keeping her eyes on Aster Island. The sea glinted with blinding white flashes, the lighthouse patiently awaiting them in the distance.

Peter tucked his hands into his jeans pockets. "Can I ask you a question?"

Confident that she knew what he wanted to ask, Cait tamped down the nerves tingling in her chest. "Of course."

"This Desmond," he began. "Why are you the only one who can tell us apart?"

Cait sensed his gaze on her as they walked, and he waited for her response. A pulse came through the hum, comforting and encouraging. Her fingers instinctively wove into Ludus's fur, the wolf dog standing almost to her waist. He'd become her strength over the years, ever since he'd broken into her life.

But that didn't make Cait's throat any less dry, nor did it steady her pulse as she prepared to speak the truth that everyone else chose to ignore. Memories flashed through her mind, whirling together to disrupt her calm. His callous smirk, his dark eyes flecked with green, his melodramatic façade, and his secretive nature. Those two freckles that created a line down his left cheek. The warmth of his arms wrapped firmly around her. The scent of him, the feel of him, the tingle that his presence ignited under her skin.

Cait let out a heavy sigh, her eyes fixed on the lighthouse as if it could anchor her in the present instead of drifting into the past that haunted her.

Why was she the only one who would know Desmond from a sea of look-alikes?

"Because he's my husband," she answered.

# CHAPTER ONE

# Rese

*Ten years ago . . .*

A subtle *thump* drew Rese out of the pages of her novel. At first, she thought it was the heater kicking on. But she could have sworn the sound came from outside the house.

Rese furrowed her brow, looking up from the page. The only lights in her room were from the book light that sent a single beam onto her book and the glow of moonlight that shone in a halo around her curtains. It was late. Too late for her to be up reading after an early morning at the coffee shop. But she'd needed a distraction from her memories.

It was the twenty-third of September, the twelfth anniversary of her parents' deaths. A day that would haunt her and her sisters in perpetuity.

So, there she was: Awake at 1:00 a.m. and reading a gothic fantasy romance just creepy enough to make her startle needlessly at nothing.

With a sigh, Rese burrowed deeper under the covers and turned back to her book.

Then, she heard the faintest *creak*.

Rese dropped her book entirely, sitting up in bed. The cold night air nipped at her bare shoulders. *That* had sounded like a window opening. But who would be stupid enough to open a window during an already frigid Maine night? If her sense of sound was on point, the culprit was Cait.

That made less sense than ordering a decaf double shot of espresso.

Staring at the wall she shared with her sister, Rese listened dubiously. Cait wasn't the sort to sneak out or . . . well, to do anything wrong. But there would be no good reason for her to open her window at this time of night.

Of course, the creak might have been anything else. Maybe the latch on the shed had finally broken. The one door always did hang at a funny angle, sliding open if it wasn't kept latched. Or it could have been the settling of the house. The place was old as dirt. It was basically dilapidated at this point.

Having convinced herself, Rese grumbled about creaky old houses, checked how many pages she had left in the chapter, and decided it'd be best to call it quits before she really let her imagination run wild.

Then, the subtle squeak of Cait's bedroom door made Rese jolt back up in her bed. So, Cait *was* up. But why?

Rese rolled her eyes at herself. She'd let the book make her paranoid. Likely, Cait simply needed to use the bathroom. That earlier creak was the shed door, which must have woken her sister.

Rese began to shuffle beneath the blankets when she heard another, more sure sound that made her freeze: the telltale creak of the staircase.

Eyes narrowing, Rese stared at her bedroom door. The bathroom was right next to Cait's room. Why would she need to go downstairs? For a cup of water, maybe?

But after the previous noises, Rese couldn't shake the feeling that something was off. Maybe it was just the book's nefarious plotline, but her gut told her to check it out.

As quietly as she could, Rese rose from the bed and darted for her door. Carefully and ever so slowly, she opened the door to peek out.

Through the sliver of the door and the jamb, she looked past the shadowy hall to the staircase. And her breath caught in her throat.

It wasn't Cait cautiously sneaking down the stairs. It was a boy!

Despite the low light, the boy's dark, messy hair and trim figure were nearly unidentifiable. Maybe it was Matt. What other boy did Cait hang out with?

Rese fought the scoff that worked its way up her throat. She couldn't decide whether to be proud of Cait's gumption or annoyed by her indiscretion. Though Rese wasn't known as the model of modesty around town, she'd never snuck a boy into her room. And besides, her flirtatious demeanor and tastefully seductive clothing choices were all for a purpose. Rese had always known that if she could secure the affection of a founding son—like Ryan Greene—then she'd never have to worry about her sisters or their futures. If Rese married well, her sisters would be brought into the highest ranks of Porthaven society with her. And they would be safe.

So, yes. Rese was less than discreet about her feminine charms. But at least she had the delicacy not to invite a boy over so late at night.

The stairs creaked under Matt's weight again, and his shoulders visibly cringed inward. Cautiously, he glanced over his shoulder to ensure his secret escape. And that's when Rese's jaw dropped into a very unladylike gape.

No matter how thick the shadows were, there was no mistaking *that* boy's face.

Cait hadn't invited Matt into her room.

She'd invited *Desmond freaking Simon,* the prick of all pricks. The spoiled brat who treated their whole family like they didn't even exist. Rese had seen how he'd blatantly ignored Cait at school for three years. There was no way one semester after Rese's graduation had changed that.

Rese was irate, shocked, and appalled that Cait would waste any time on that arrogant, horrid boy, let alone invite him to her room.

But as Desmond disappeared down the stairs, the thought occurred to Rese that Cait might not even know. Maybe he'd snuck in to pull a prank. Perhaps the boys at school had put him up to some weird bet. After all, she wasn't deaf. She'd worked her way into the social scene at Porthaven High early in her freshman year, affording her the unique opportunity to hear how the popular boys all spoke about her and her sister.

They were the Lewan girls—the mysterious, beautiful, strange Irish girls whose names had dark rumors attached to them. Rumors that made them somewhat of a challenge for the boys to try to win.

Rese used it to her advantage. However, Cait's self-isolation made her somewhat impossible to woo. But that only seemed to make the challenge all the more appealing. And now, perhaps the schoolboys had egged Desmond into something worse than Rese would ever expect.

Instantly, she felt the urge to check on her sister as Desmond descended slowly, working to avoid the creaking stairs. And doing a decent job at it, she realized. Somehow, he figured out just where to put his weight to miss all but the most sensitive warps. Rese watched as his messy-haired head disappeared from view. Their terrier, Red, slept in the living room. What would happen if Desmond woke him? Would that be the best thing? If Cait *had* invited the boy over herself, Rese didn't want their nan to find out. She'd make a big deal about it, and Cait didn't need that.

And even if Cait hadn't invited him—if it was some foolish prank, Rese wanted to stop it before anyone found out. She held her breath, waiting for any sound of Red stirring. No sound came.

Carefully, Rese slipped out of her room, shutting the door behind her. Should Desmond come back, she wanted to catch him in the act. In only her tank top and pajama bottoms, she shivered but quickly tiptoed the few inches to Cait's bedroom, finding that Desmond had left the door wide open.

Rese glanced back at the stairs once before entering her sister's room. Moonlight streamed through the windows, washing the space in a pale white like spilled milk. The lavender walls turned silver, the sketches pinned to them reflecting the light. But it was the empty bed that grabbed Rese's attention.

Empty.

Her lips parted as she surveyed the bed. The rumpled covers suggested that someone had been sleeping there at one point that night. Cait was orderly, making her bed most mornings. The bed's state of undress might make sense if this were Genni's room, but Cait's?

So, where was her sister?

A flash of movement drew Rese's attention to the window seat. One curtain had been drawn back, but in the shadow of the other, two neon yellow eyes blinked at her.

With a gasp, Rese jumped back.

The eyes blinked again.

Heart pounding, Rese nearly bolted from the room. But her curiosity kept her in place long enough to get a better look at the shadow. A slow twitch of movement cut gracefully through the darkness. A tail, she thought. And it struck her. Those eyes, now closing as the creature yawned, were distinctly feline.

Had Desmond left a cat in Cait's room? Why? Cait wasn't afraid of cats, nor was she allergic. A cat would be a sad excuse for a prank. Did that make it a gift? But why would Desmond Simon, of all people, give Cait a gift?

And where *was* her sister in the first place?

The cat showed no signs of moving from its lounge on the bench, so Rese turned her attention back to the room. Whatever the point of the cat, she wanted to be sure that Desmond hadn't stolen or ruined anything. And she needed to know if he'd left anything besides that animal.

Rese shifted to Cait's desk. There wasn't much to look at. A jar of pens and pencils, a small mirror with a smattering of makeup products beside it, an organized stack of schoolwork, and a framed sketch of their family of five—Da, Mum, and the three sisters as little girls.

Rese recognized the picture. Cait had drawn it years ago, based on memory alone. They'd left everything in Ireland thanks to their rapid flight to the States after the fire that set their childhood home ablaze. What little they did have, their nan had locked in the attic in a small trunk. Rese had snuck up there to look into it years ago. She'd found keepsakes, letters, and pictures—one of which strongly resembled the one on Cait's desk—but nothing of great value beyond sentiment. Rese had filched some of the photos for her own secret stash but left the rest.

The sharp whine of the stairs pierced the air. Rese whirled around, her pulse pounding as she inched forward to peer out of the room. The top of Desmond's unruly hair came into view as he slowly returned up the staircase.

Rese muttered the softest curse under her breath. She didn't have time to run back into her bedroom. He'd see her. She cast her eyes around the room, looking for a place to hide. She hurried to the only one she could see: the closet.

Pulling the bifold door closed behind her, Rese pressed in amongst her sister's tees, blouses, jackets, and dresses. Nearly all the items had once belonged to Rese, but now they carried the distinct smell of Cait: the florals and citrus of her soft perfume—a Christmas gift from Rese just last year—and the remnants of salt air and forest trees.

Carefully shutting the closet door, Rese held her breath. The slats of the doors gave her a limited view of the bedroom. The bright moon flooded past the black cat, providing plenty of light. The stairs continued to creak as Desmond made his painfully slow ascent. She had no doubts that he was up to something nefarious now. Why else would he be sneaking *back* into the house?

It took what felt like hours for Desmond to reappear, and Rese had to cover her mouth with both hands to keep herself from crying out. Draped over his shoulder, he carried the unmistakable and unconscious form of her sister. Her straight, bright blonde hair swayed with each of Desmond's steps. He shuffled cautiously to the narrow bed, fumbling as he worked to lift her off his shoulder. He made sure not to jostle her too much as she hit the mattress, then dashed back out of sight.

Rese thought perhaps he was making his break for freedom, having done whatever he'd done to her sister. Had he gotten her drunk? Or had he struck her into unconsciousness, whether accidentally or not? Whatever the case, Rese's jaw tightened with fury. Next time she got the chance, she'd slug Desmond Simon right in the nose and hope she had enough strength to break it.

She heard the door latch, then a heavy, masculine sigh of relief.

So, he hadn't left.

Rese narrowed her eyes, trying to get a better view of the room as Desmond approached the bed again. The closet door slats made everything into narrow lines of an image. She caught him lifting a hand to his head, presumably running his fingers through his hair. Then, he bent to adjust Cait on the mattress. He pushed back some of the blankets, clearing a spot before gathering her into his arms.

Gently, Desmond carried her around the bed and laid her onto the spot he'd cleared, thoughtfully resting her head on the pillow and brushing the hair out of her face. Rese watched, completely bemused by the caring way he drew the blankets up and around Cait's shoulders, tucking her in. He paused, but Rese couldn't see the expression on his face as he stood there. She worried he would climb into the bed next to her sister as he pushed the blankets back again. Then, he guided Cait's arm out over the covers as if to ensure she didn't get too hot.

Rese's jaw went slack, her head swimming with confusion. She recognized this sort of tenderness, this affection. She'd seen it in how her da cared for her mum during her pregnancy with Genni. Those final months were difficult; her mum was regularly exhausted by the task of growing and carrying a child while caring for two others. On the hardest days, even after his own long days at work, Owen Lewan would come home and graciously and gently care for his beloved wife, Sabine.

The memory came clearly into Rese's mind, her da helping his wife to the couch, insisting that she let him put the girls to bed while she rested. He'd brushed some of her dark blonde hair from her forehead in the same fashion that Desmond had just done for Cait.

Rese couldn't decide whether to sneer or gag. It wasn't possible. Desmond Simon didn't care about Cait that way. He wasn't capable of that sort of tender feeling. Rese had watched him for twelve years, assured time and again of his rude and flippant behavior, not only toward her and her sisters but toward the entirety of life. He lived selfishly, in defiance of anyone who got in his way.

He *couldn't* care for Cait like that.

But Rese heard it, the sad and almost longing sigh that escaped Desmond just before he drew away to the window seat. She watched through the slats as he sat down, the cat padding around him into the light. His blue-black fur nearly glowed as his large nose sniffed Desmond's jacket. She couldn't see what Desmond was doing, her view too obscured by the slats and the bed, so she focused on the abnormally large cat. It had to be even bigger than Red—who was an admittedly small dog. Still, there was something off about the feline. Something Rese couldn't quite put her finger on. Maybe it had to do with its tall, pointed ears. Or those too-wise eyes.

Suddenly, Desmond stood again, Rese's gaze going back to him. He stepped back over to the bed, his footsteps slightly heavier now. But rather than reaching for Cait, he turned to the nightstand, reaching for something there. Rese watched as he scribbled, then returned to the cat and the window seat. He opened the casement window, giving Cait one last look over his shoulder, before climbing onto the roof. Then, the cat vanished.

Rese froze in shock. The cat . . . The cat had disappeared. Animals didn't blip out of existence.

A chill swept down Rese's bare arms as a memory resurfaced. On her sixth birthday, Owen had taken her on one of his long walks. *"Yer old enough now, Terry-girl,"* he'd said as his massive wolfhound, Conroy, walked alongside them. *"Yeh need to understand jest how important our family is."*

He'd told her the secret of their family. He'd taught her what she needed to know should it be her who took his place. He had explained the spirit world, what wielding was, the danger of the Druids, and the spirit-being they were divinely called to protect. And that cat . . .

*"There are creatures that live within the spirit world,"* Owen's voice whispered in her memory. *"Not good or bad but waiting to be given their purpose. They are called beasts."*

Rese wasn't well-versed in the wielding etiquette of Porthaven, but she was rather certain summoning beasts wasn't considered acceptable. Especially if your last name wasn't Lavigne.

Assured that Desmond wouldn't return, Rese left her hiding place. Cait lay on the bed peacefully and safely, so Rese marched to the window first, locking it and yanking the curtain back in place. Whatever Cait and Desmond's relationship entailed, the knowledge that he was wielding negligently was another assurance for her that Cait should stay as far from him as possible.

With the curtain now blocking most of the moonlight, Rese turned back to the dim room. She moved to Cait's side, worried by her heavily unconscious state. But Cait's expression was calm, and her breathing was steady. Whatever brought her to this state, it didn't seem she was in any danger.

Pursing her lips, Rese drew back. Gooseflesh spread down her arm as she contemplated what to do. There wasn't much she *could* do, she supposed. Cait was safe. She was asleep in her own bed. And Desmond was gone, seemingly without a trace. Whatever the pair had been up to, it wasn't something Rese could deal with now.

And honestly, Rese wasn't sure she could handle it later either. Talking to Cait, in general, was difficult. When they were girls, they had been best friends. But somewhere along the way, as Rese grew popular in school and Cait hid in the shadows, their paths irrevocably diverged. Any time Rese tried to talk with her sister, they inevitably ended up in an argument.

Even if she tried to warn Cait of Desmond's negative influence, her sister wouldn't listen.

Peering down at Cait's nightstand, Rese found her sketchbook propped open. A short note lined the top of the page: *"I'll explain everything - Des"*

Rese grimaced. Des? Seriously? She glanced at Cait. What sort of relationship did they have that she called him *Des*?

Turning back to the sketchbook, Rese scanned the drawing beneath the note. A dark, stormy scene with a boy standing before a churning sea. A rather impressive work, if Rese was being honest. She could feel the emotion in the weight of each stroke. Cait had always had an uncanny level of skill with a pencil. But this was beyond the sketches she'd seen in the past.

Rese's eyes were drawn to the right page, away from the ocean scene and to the twisting coils of . . . something. She couldn't tell what the drawing was meant to be. There was so much detail, so many intricate features, that she struggled to know where to focus. The coils all pulled together, dozens of them overlapping.

Cait's steady, heavy breaths reassured Rese that her sister wasn't going to wake, so she leaned closer to catch the drawing's details in the darkness. Each coil bore tiny, diamond-like patterns. Almost like scales, Rese thought. She followed the twisting tendrils to the center, where they amassed heavily into an angular shape with slitted white ovals that nearly glowed amongst all the dark shading around them. And that's when Rese realized it wasn't just some random twisting pattern drawn for practice or out of boredom. It was a creature of horrifying design.

Her sister had drawn a *monster*.

It didn't make sense. Cait was quiet and distant, yes, but she wasn't crazy, and she certainly didn't enjoy frightening things. She thought Rese's gothic romances with ghosts and paranormal creatures were on par with horror stories. She wouldn't watch a scary movie if it saved her life. How could she draw such a terrifying creature?

After checking on Cait, still deep in sleep, Rese couldn't help herself. She turned back the page, looking for more of Cait's sketches. She gave a cursory glance to the right page—some sort of wild-eyed bear creature—before her eyes latched onto the other.

Her heart stuttered, her body chilling to the bone.

Rese had to tilt her head to get the full picture, but she recognized it in an instant.

Her hands began to shake. The beast was giant, its broad body enshrouded in shadow-black fur. A great, powerful maw snarling to show off its sharp fangs. Some might mistake the creature for a wolf or even a large dog, but Rese knew it. That hulking figure was larger than any canine. It had the height of a man and the breadth of two. Nothing about it could be considered normal.

Rese's whole body trembled. Her brain went fuzzy, her mind flashing back to her childhood, to the moment Owen had taken her to the woods— to the monster he'd revealed to her there.

Rese shut the sketchbook in horror, backing away as though it had snapped at her.

Without thought, she rushed back to her bedroom, fighting off tears. Her throat closed up, and her mind reeled. She shoved herself back into her room, managing just enough control of her actions to shut the door without too much noise. Yet, the second it latched behind her, her knees gave way.

Dropping to the floor, Rese let the tears fall.

Rese had tried—she'd tried so, so hard. For twelve years, she'd done all she could to protect her sisters. That was her job as the oldest. Without their parents to care for them, it fell to Rese. She'd done everything in her power to help them leave Ireland in the past and the spirit world with it. She'd given up her accent, she'd locked away her memories, and she'd ignored every question about her family's sordid history. Even when her friends asked about her life before Porthaven, she'd dismissed it with the lie, *"I don't remember."*

She'd tried in every way she knew. She'd done her best to become a new person in Porthaven. She'd remade herself into the girl that everyone either wanted to be like or to be with. She'd gained the adoration of her peers and her seniors. Every teacher praised her in school. Her boss at the coffee shop loved her. She'd even won the attention of Ryan Greene.

Every day, Rese did everything she knew to protect her sisters from their past. And every night since she was seven years old, Rese had prayed. She prayed that if there was one thing God would give her, that he would let the curse fall to her.

It hadn't been enough.

Through the haze of her tears, Rese glared at the halo of moonlight around her curtains. Her da had warned her, *"Most often, it falls to the firstborn."* And she'd hoped he was right.

Because he'd taught her, he'd prepared her. Rese could handle the Wolf. Cait? Genni? They couldn't. Genni was too flighty, too impetuous. And Cait . . . She didn't have the strength for something so damning.

But Rese had the strength. She had the determination. And she'd built her life to support it. She'd made a name for herself. She'd created a perfect life where she'd marry Ryan and put herself at the top of Porthaven's elite, where her sisters could find their own husbands. Then, it wouldn't matter if she were the host of some monster. They'd all be safe. They'd all be together.

But she'd been wrong.

The Wolf hadn't chosen her. It'd chosen to prey on the weakest of them. It'd chosen Cait.

If Rese could figure this out through Cait's sketches, then Desmond had certainly figured it out too. And no matter his strange feelings toward her, it was inevitable—the Warden would find out. They'd put Cait in a cage like they had the Faulks.

And then, all of Rese's efforts to protect her sister would mean nothing.

# CHAPTER TWO

# Cait

Thunder rumbled, the clouds swirling overhead, while the figure stood waiting in the shadows.

And then, Cait woke.

A gentle tinkle of music caused Cait to bolt up in bed. Her heart filled her throat, her lungs struggling for air as though she'd been holding her breath. A dull morning light passed through her curtains and blended with the purple of her walls to create a grayscale haze in the room. What time was it? She'd thought it was night, the storm obscuring all but the moon. . . .

Cait looked down at her nightstand, the chime of her alarm still singing its merry tune. She blinked, reaching over on instinct to turn it off. The storm, the tree, the shadow—they had been a dream. The redhead and Sterling, they'd been just as much a dream as the rest of it.

But she'd had another dream, hadn't she? Or was it two additional dreams?

Sitting up fully, Cait tried to reconcile the night. She'd been dreaming, that much she knew. She'd dreamed of her childhood room and the door that held the demon at bay. The raven had come, taking her to the cove where Desmond waited. She'd gone to Desmond, desperate to save him, and then . . . he'd kissed her.

A slight shiver brought gooseflesh to Cait's skin, the subtlest hum tingling along her spine. Desmond had kissed her in the dream just before the waves crashed into them. And he'd dissolved into sand. The wave carried Cait to the pebbled beach, tossing her out before a horde of monsters—all twelve of the monsters that had haunted her dreams for the last dozen years.

Then, Cait had woken up on the forest floor, cold and disoriented. She'd found Desmond and Brady there, standing before a behemoth of a tree with a large gash in its trunk. The monsters had appeared again— beasts of the spirit world forming from smoke that tumbled from that tree. Together, along with an old man named Fish, the boys had fought off the beasts. But they weren't strong enough. And suddenly, Cait found herself stepping forward to save them.

She'd saved them.

Cait glanced at the journal on her nightstand. The monsters of her dreams—these beasts of the spirit world—she'd controlled them, commanding them to return to the tree. And then she'd sealed that gash.

Or had she?

Shaking her head, Cait couldn't clarify the blurred lines between dream and reality. Everything she'd experienced last night felt real. The cove and the kiss. The tree and the beasts. The raven and the storm. Everything felt so real. Yet, with the strangeness of every event last night, she couldn't fathom that *any* of it truly was.

It must have been some grief-addled nightmare fueled by the anniversary of her parents' deaths.

Cait tossed the covers back. She didn't have time to dwell on her dreams. School awaited her—reality awaited her.

Slipping her feet out from under the sheets, Cait paused. She wiggled her toes, feeling a gritty dryness sticking between them. She reached for her feet, finding particles of grass and dirt. Then, she saw her fingers.

Cait held them up in the dim morning light. Dark brown half-moons of dirt were embedded under her nails too. A memory of curling her fingers into the earth as she rose from the forest floor flashed through her mind.

*"Cait?"* Desmond's voice rang in her head. *"What are you doing here?"*

It came clearly to her then. The island and that tree with its gash. The smoke and the beasts they'd fought. The surge of power and the amber. Yes, that part of the night must have been real. But how did she get there? And how did she get home?

Cait lifted her phone from the nightstand. No notifications awaited her.

Frowning, Cait tried not to be disappointed. She didn't know why she'd expected a text from Desmond in the first place. Even if he had been the one who got her back home safely, he probably didn't know what to say any more than she did. Not only had she magically appeared on the island, but she'd also taken control of those beasts and somehow sealed that gash in the tree. Maybe he'd played some role in getting her home, but there was an equally good chance that he was frightened of this new version of her.

Cait was frightened of herself.

How had she done it? What had given her the idea to try it in the first place? She couldn't say. She'd simply known that Desmond, Brady, and Fish needed saving. So, she'd saved them. And by some miracle, the beasts had listened.

The memory of the beasts sparked a surge of irritation within Cait. All these years, Desmond had lied to her about them. Or rather, he'd lied about the monsters in her dreams, playing them off as some oddity. But he'd known—he *had* to have known they were the beasts of the spirit world. Why hide that from her? Why lie?

Desmond had told her about beasts years ago when he explained Hades, his cat-beast. She should have suspected then, with how vague he'd been. Creatures of the spirit world, he'd said. Wielders summoned them to do their bidding. Or, in Hades's case, to be their companions. But it wasn't approved behavior by the Warden, so no one knew about the cat but her.

Cait supposed she couldn't be too angry with Desmond. He wasn't supposed to tell her anything about the spirit world, and she didn't want him to. The spirit world scared Cait. She knew it had something to do with her parents' deaths, and she wanted nothing more to do with it.

Now, she realized that the danger of the spirit world was even greater than she could ever have imagined. It was clear: She'd inherited her da's curse, the very thing that got him killed. Whatever was happening to her—whatever this demon was doing to her—the danger was only beginning. If she'd wielded the spirit world so easily last night without any knowledge or training, of what else might she be capable?

But perhaps that was the problem. Cait didn't know what she was doing. She didn't know how to fight off this demon inside of her. She was becoming dangerous because of her lack of knowledge.

The surging tempest of Cait's final dream swirled in her vision. The massive, gnarled tree, the raven and the redhead, Sterling Faulk's appearance, and the shadowy, unidentified figure on the far side of the clearing—they all haunted her in the daylight.

In the past twelve years, she'd had the same dream each night. The raven's appearance and subsequent arrival at the cove was the first exception. The divergence to that tree . . . It was something altogether new.

Cait didn't know what that meant, but she knew one thing: It had something to do with the spirit world. It had something to do with her inheritance.

Cait jumped out of bed at the thought. She hurried to her closet, grabbing the first sweater and pair of jeans she found. Whatever these changing dreams implied, Cait couldn't leave it alone anymore. She couldn't stay in the background, hiding away from the rest of Porthaven in hopes that they wouldn't notice her connection to the darkness. She needed answers. And she would find them.

She couldn't go to Desmond—Cait knew that much. It wasn't that he'd been lying to her. No, that wouldn't have stopped her. She was the one person who knew how to force honesty out of Desmond. But after last night, Cait was more convinced than ever that she couldn't handle being around him anymore. Not if she wanted to move on and find some semblance of happiness in her life.

She'd decided three days ago: She couldn't be friends with Desmond Simon any longer. And she was going to stick to that decision.

Cait grabbed her backpack from the floor beside her desk. It already held her schoolwork and textbooks, but she slipped around her bed to grab her sketchbook, lying closed on her nightstand. She dropped the book into her bag, zipped it up, and slung it over her shoulder.

Today, she resolved, she'd get answers.

And she had a good idea of who to ask.

~

"Do you like baseball?" Matt asked as they waited for their history class to begin.

Cait looked at him, bewildered. "Huh?" she muttered, forcing her brain to recenter on reality.

She'd been staring at the middle row, where Hunter Varon and Sterling Faulk were engaged in what appeared to be a highly secretive conversation. Hunter usually sat in the front of the class next to his girlfriend, Elizabeth. But today, the boys had walked in together, murmuring under their breath, Hunter following Sterling to his seat in the middle row.

Whenever someone came near them, they'd pause to glare at the person until it was clear they weren't eavesdropping.

As she watched their odd behavior, Cait pondered the greatest question she had after her dream last night: Why Sterling Faulk? She didn't think she'd ever shared so much as a "hello" with the boy. So, why had *he* shown up in her dreams?

"Baseball," Matt clarified, drawing her divided attention. "Do you like it?" He was back to his old self, their conversation the previous afternoon removing all his suspicions regarding Cait's disappearance at the Greene party over the weekend. His animated expressions were full of the good humor she'd grown used to seeing.

Cait tried to see it as a good thing. But engaging in silly, meandering conversation felt wrong after the night she'd experienced.

Twirling her pencil between her fingers, Cait shrugged. "I dunno. Can't say I've ever seen a game."

Matt's upper lip curled in disbelief. "Really? We have a team."

Cait was more than aware of this. Desmond was the captain of the Porthaven Trident's basketball and baseball teams.

She didn't bother to inform Matt of this. Instead, she said, "I've never gone to a game."

"Why not?" Matt asked, then shook his head. "Never mind, I can guess. Anyway, I was only asking because I'm thinking of joining in the spring."

Cait felt her eyebrows draw together in confusion. "Are you—I mean, did you play at your old school?"

"No," he admitted. "Like, I tossed the ball around with Dad dozens of times, but I'm not much of an athlete."

"Then, why join?"

"I told you yesterday—ya know, about Mom wanting me to join some kind of extracurricular thing?"

Cait nodded, though she didn't remember.

"Yeah, well, the thing is," Matt frowned, "Porthaven doesn't really have anything but sports. I mean, there's the debate team and the theater downtown, but those aren't my thing. It's too late to join the basketball team this year, and I didn't think I'd be much good at that anyway, which leaves the baseball team."

"Oh. Okay, good luck, then," Cait offered, assuming that would end the conversation.

Matt tapped his pencil on the desktop, a shy smile tilting up the corner of his lips. "Would you come to a game if I made the team?"

Having a reason to go to one of Porthaven High's games had never crossed Cait's mind. She'd have gone for Desmond, of course. She regularly heard reports of his fantastic leadership and gameplay and would have loved to see him in action. She could have sat with Genni and her friends—they attended almost all the games. But Cait had never had the bravery to go.

Now, she felt even less inclined.

If she were to go to the games, she'd not only have to watch Matt play, she'd have to watch Desmond. And she needed to find ways to avoid him, not ways to be around him more.

But the hope in Matt's eyes, the sincerity of his desire for her to be there, struck Cait with the ugly realization that if she wanted to move on from Desmond, she needed to foster the singular friendship she had.

With a nod, Cait forced herself to return Matt's smile. "Yeah," she confirmed. "Yeah, I would."

Matt practically beamed at her, though his eyes dropped to his notebook, the edges of his temples turning the slightest shade of pink.

Before Cait could fully comprehend the reason behind this behavior, the hum welled up at the back of her head, spreading into her skull and across her shoulders.

Desmond entered the classroom, Brady and Garrett with him. He was dressed the same as ever in his cool yet lazy style: black jeans and a hunter-green long-sleeved tee that she just knew would set off the green flecks in his eyes. His dark, wavy hair was fashionably disheveled, and he moved with his usual confident stride.

Yet, dark circles marred his otherwise perfect appearance, and his jaw held a tension that wasn't usually there.

Desmond dropped his backpack next to his seat, his gaze flashing to stare straight at Cait. He didn't even pretend to hide it behind a glance at Garrett. He just stared at her expectantly.

Brow furrowing, Cait intentionally turned away from Desmond. What was he doing? If anyone saw him looking at her, they might begin to ask questions. And just what was he expecting anyway? It wasn't as though she could give him answers about last night. He was likely more knowledgeable on the subject than she.

"Oh!" Matt reached over to nudge her arm. "I can't believe I forgot. Guess what?"

Cait relaxed her expression, allowing herself to forget Desmond Simon and focus on her friend. "What?"

Matt's wide grin caused his eyes to squint. "My grandpa's giving me his old truck."

Unsure what else to say, Cait simply replied, "That's great."

"Yeah, especially because it's getting so cold." Matt shivered as though remembering their bike ride to school that morning. "It's not working right now," he admitted, "but Grandpa said that if I help him get it running, I can have it. So, we're going to start working on that tonight after school. Then, once it's ready, I'll be able to drive us to school . . . And anywhere else we want to go!"

Cait smiled, happy for Matt, just as the bell rang, announcing the start of class.

Penny Davis, Matt's mom and the history teacher, rose from behind her desk. She straightened the collar of her blouse, smiling knowingly at her bleary-eyed students. "Good morning, everyone," she said in her chipper tone. "Today, I've got a special announcement. As you all know, next month, our town will be celebrating the end of the season with our annual Fisher's Festival. Do any of you know how the Festival began?"

The entire classroom remained silent until a heavy sigh came from the far side of the room, drawing everyone's attention to Desmond, who lazily slumped in his chair. "The Festival first began on October 17,

1783," he began, his deep voice carrying a disinterested quality. "It went through the weekend, ending on the nineteenth. James Varon, the mayor at the time, instituted the Festival to celebrate the Revolutionary War's end. And, like everything else Varon, it's stuck around."

Back in his seat at the front of the class, Hunter Varon huffed, but Penny raised her brow, impressed. "Very good, Mr. Simon," she praised. "Seems you'll do just fine with the essay I'm assigning you all."

The whole class groaned except for Matt and Cait. She didn't know if this was due to Matt's interest in writing the essay or if he'd expected it from his mom. Cait refrained because she simply didn't want to draw attention to herself.

And really, how hard could it be to write an essay about a festival?

"Over the next week," Penny continued, "we'll take some time to study the history of Porthaven, particularly relating to the history of the Festival. Then, on Friday, we'll take a quick trip to the library to gather our research." She picked up a stack of papers from her desk, brandishing them pointedly. "You'll need to have your parents or guardians sign these waivers by then."

Dividing the stacks into small groups, she handed them to the students to pass to each other. "One final note," she added. "This will be a partner project. Before we head off to the library on Friday, I'll pair you up to work on the essays together. It will be a joint grade, so make sure you give your partner your best, yes?"

After the last two waivers were passed to Matt, he leaned over to Cait to whisper, "She'll pair us up."

Still unused to having a classmate to mutter conversation with throughout class, Cait cautiously glanced at Penny before replying. "Really?"

Matt gave her a firm nod as she accepted the waiver from him. "For sure. I'll pretty much nag her about it until she gives in."

Somehow, Cait felt both gratified and disappointed by this. Of course, it was preferable to have a partner who wouldn't be put off by being paired with the outcast. But at the same time, she worried about what people would think of her and Matt being put together all the time.

Unwillingly, Cait's eyes drifted toward Desmond. She found him staring at her again, his expression lifting slightly when she met his gaze. She immediately averted her own. Why did he keep doing that?

Tightening her grip on her pencil, Cait stared straight ahead, attempting to listen to Penny's lesson on the Fisher's Festival. She should be taking notes to prepare for the upcoming essay. Just because she and Matt would work together didn't mean she could slack off.

In her distracted state, Cait caught Sterling casually adjusting on his seat, tucking some of his long black-brown hair behind an ear. The slight movement was enough to revert her thoughts to the dream and his presence in it. Why him? She knew his family had connections within the Warden, something that made them equal parts oddities and insiders. Desmond had never explained it to her. He'd simply said that the Faulk family made a deal with the Warden a couple of centuries ago, leading to the development of Porthaven. Yet, they weren't considered a founding family, nor were they technical members of the Warden.

Cait didn't understand it, and she hadn't cared to.

Until now.

Chewing on the inside of her cheek, Cait fixed her eyes on the back of Sterling's head. He was her answer. Sterling was an outsider like her. Granted, he'd *chosen* that role while she'd been thrust into it. Which led her to believe he must have a good reason for wanting to be on the outside.

She'd thought about going to Brady for answers, but he was absolutely loyal to Desmond. Chances were, if she approached Brady, Desmond would leverage it as an opportunity to talk with Cait. She couldn't take that risk.

That left her with one path.

Whatever the Faulks' relationship with the Warden, Sterling was in her dreams. That alone was reason enough to point her in his direction.

What was more, he was close to Hunter, so close that they were sharing secretive conversations.

Cait had no doubts. If she wanted answers, Sterling Faulk was the person she needed to talk to. . . .

A sudden knock on the classroom door made Cait jump. Penny stopped her lecture midsentence as the principal opened the door halfway.

"Pardon me, Mrs. Davis," he said, giving her an apologetic, pressed-lipped smile. He gave the class a curious glance before turning back to her. "I'm afraid I need to borrow Mr. Faulk, please."

Every student whipped their head around to stare at Sterling. He sat stock-still in surprise.

At the front of the class, Hunter's brow furrowed, his jaw growing tense.

"Of course," Penny said, then motioned to Sterling. "You're excused, Mr. Faulk."

Slowly, Sterling rose from his seat, grabbing his backpack and notebook as he went. As he passed Hunter's desk, the boys exchanged tight looks, but no words were passed between them.

While Sterling left with the principal, Cait instinctively looked to Desmond. He was frowning as Brady whispered to him and gave a subtle shake of his head that Cait interpreted to mean: No, he didn't know what was going on.

With the men gone, Penny returned to her lesson. But Cait couldn't pay any more attention now than she had before the interruption. Why had the principal come for Sterling? Would he be in the next class? Or was he gone for the day?

Cait frowned at the thought. She'd hoped to approach Sterling today. She wasn't sure how or when, but as soon as she found an opportunity. Now, she worried she wouldn't get the chance, and she'd be left to face another night of dreams with no more answers than before.

# William

George Faulk passed away in the night, sending William's morning into a flurry. A normal mayor might not have had such burdens laid on his shoulders. But William was not a normal mayor, and Porthaven was not a normal town.

Neither had George Faulk been a normal townsperson. The Faulk family held a far more unique role within Porthaven. A role of which nearly none of the other residents knew. It was one that gave them both great respect and created great fear. And with George dead, it brought on a new set of worries.

As the head of the Warden within Porthaven, William was given manifold responsibilities, each of great importance and demand.

The death of George brought one of those responsibilities to the immediate forefront. Loraine Roberts, the younger sister of Kenneth Greene and the head doctor at Sunset Seniors' Home—the assisted living facility in town—had called William to inform him of the man's passing. Due to George's presumed status as the Vessel, William was listed as his emergency contact rather than the man's son. This placed William in the unusual position of having to deliver the news. Now, not only did William have to offer his condolences to Timothy, Sahila, and Sterling Faulk—the son, daughter-in-law, and grandson—but he also needed to adjust the strength of the blocks placed upon both surviving men.

Which reminded William. . . .

After placing a quick phone call to the principal of Porthaven High, William ensured Sterling's prompt return home from school. He'd not informed the man of the whys, thinking it best that Sterling be told of his grandfather's death with his parents by his side. Sahila was William's next call. He suggested that she go pick up her son and bring him home.

"He drives himself to school, but I'll let him know. Can you tell me why?" Sahila asked, her tone curious rather than concerned.

William hesitated. This wasn't news to be delivered over the phone. Nor could he expect her not to tell Timothy or Sterling. But perhaps that would be for the best. Let the wife and mother inform the family of their loss.

Recognizing his desire to get out of a difficult task, William accepted his duty. "I'm afraid I can't say at the moment," he replied. He informed her that he'd already called the principal and that he would meet the family at their house in half an hour.

Sahila agreed, her curiosity finally turning to discomfort. He couldn't blame her. He knew he was withholding, but he felt it was for the best.

Next, William called the reverend, Ben Lavigne. "I need you to meet me at the Faulks," he informed his best friend.

"Mm, yes," Ben murmured, "I heard about George from Rick. I hate this for Tim and his family."

"Is Rick already telling everyone?" William asked with no small edge in his tone. As the sheriff, Rick Edgars was called to the senior's home to ensure there was no foul play. But that didn't give him the right to announce the man's death readily.

"Don't worry," Ben immediately replied. "He just told me because he knew I'd need to help out. He's keeping it to himself until after the family's been informed."

"He's the sheriff. He should know to keep it to himself no matter who's involved."

Ben acquiesced, promising to meet him at the Faulks', and they said their goodbyes. Only then did William leave his mayoral office, letting his receptionist know he'd be out most of the day.

Leaving the town hall, William tried to settle the frustrations welling up within him. It was poor timing, George's death. Not that death was ever in good timing. But this was particularly troublesome. They were already dealing with the strange damage to the Veil and the beasts it—or someone through it—was summoning. What was more, Timothy had just dropped the bombshell that a second Veil might be in play. Something William had failed to confirm or deny over the weekend.

He'd tried studying all the books he had on the subject, knowing that it was useless. They'd been studying all the Warden texts in Porthaven ever since they learned about the problem with the first Veil. The idea that there might be a second worried him. If someone had tampered with the one, who was to say they hadn't tampered with the other?

But then, William wasn't convinced that Timothy was right. They had no proof that there was a secondary Veil. As far as they knew, the spirit-beings shared the thing.

Regardless, Porthaven's troubles were spiraling, and William felt his family's inheritance slipping through his fingers. He'd made too many mistakes. He'd been too proud, too determined to prove his father wrong. And now, it was coming back to haunt him.

*"You're weak,"* was Charles Simon's favorite refrain to his only son. *"And you're sloppy. You don't have what it takes to make the hard decisions this town needs in order to keep it safe."*

For years, William had promised himself that his father's abuse hadn't affected him. He worked hard to keep a firm grip on the Warden and Porthaven while striving to be equally caring to its residents. He didn't have to be cruel and calculating like Charles to earn people's respect. He could simply prove himself by being a good, faithful leader who wasn't afraid to make the hard choices as they came.

But his failures seemed to be proving his father right. He was weak. He was sloppy. He couldn't control the Veil. He couldn't even control his own son.

Pulling up to the Faulk house, William let go of all his nagging doubts. He had work to do here. And he would be the strong, caring leader that the Faulks needed.

Sahila let William in, a cautious expression on her face as she offered him a cup of coffee. He declined, noting Ben sitting on the couch across from Timothy and Sterling. As the last to arrive, he wouldn't keep the family waiting.

They took the news as well as might be expected. Timothy got teary-eyed, and Sahila wrapped her arm around her husband's shoulders. Sterling just sat there, staring into nothingness. They didn't have many questions about how it had happened. George had been in poor health for the last several years. His mind had gone first. The medical diagnosis was dementia. William and the Warden suspected otherwise. They'd seen this pattern with the previous Vessels. The block helped suppress the spirit-beings, but it took its toll on the individual. That sort of power had strong demands, and the fight between human and creature never ended well.

A thread of guilt tugged at William as he addressed Timothy and Sterling. "I have to ask: Have either of you experienced anything strange in the last twelve hours? A sense or awareness of a presence. Odd dreams, perhaps. Anything that might suggest which of you inherited?"

"I thought we didn't know whether Grandpa carried the thing in the first place," Sterling muttered tensely.

"We don't," William conceded, though the dementia was a likely sign. "But we can't be too careful."

Timothy sighed, running a hand over his face. "No," he said. "I've not experienced anything like that."

Sterling remained silent, hands clasped tightly between his knees as he glared at the coffee table.

William studied him a second, working to deduce if the boy's behavior was due to grief or secrets. There weren't many tells in the boy. He'd drawn his shoulders in and kept fidgeting, but those could be simple coping mechanisms with near strangers in his house. Finally, William prompted, "What about you, son?"

Dark brown eyes shot up to meet William's with a sharpness that reminded him too much of the edge that Desmond's gaze often carried when turned his way. A twinge of regret tugged at William's heart, but he forced himself to remember his job.

"No," Sterling replied, the word biting. "Nothing."

William struggled to believe him. He was too caustic, too guarded to be truly honest. Yet, William reminded himself to give the boy the benefit of the doubt. He'd just lost his grandfather, and grief often masqueraded as anger.

With the formalities out of the way, Ben prayed for the family's strength in their difficult time. He laid his hands on both Timothy and Sterling's shoulders during the prayer, and William knew he was taking the chance to channel the spirit world, tightening the blocks in their minds.

The Warden had learned how to apply blocks centuries ago. It was a complicated, intensely intimate process that went into a person's spirit and altered their ability to connect to the spirit world. That's how William knew George's "dementia" had nothing to do with the mind. It came from his spirit, dampened all these years.

The Faulks knew what they were agreeing to, even back in 1775 when Porthaven was founded. The family had willingly taken on the mantle of the Leviathan, sacrificing their bloodline to carry the creature safely and protect the world from its power. Any understanding the Faulks had of their responsibility stemmed from their long-term relationship with the Warden, established well before they accepted this burden. When

Archibald Faulk volunteered to become the Leviathan's host, he accepted the first block in their family line. Each descendant had also received one of these blocks over the following two hundred thirty-eight years.

It was necessary, the Warden claimed, to keep both the Vessel and the extended populace safe from the unknowable, vast power of the spirit-being tethered within. There were four Vessels under the Warden's control—only one of them didn't have a block.

Most of the Warden wasn't aware of that Vessel. William only knew because the prophecy charging the Lewans to Porthaven's care had come from the young woman's predecessor. He understood why they kept her a secret. Many Warden members would have been outraged to learn of her. But the Warden had determined centuries ago that she was a necessary evil, hosting as she did the spirit-being who could see the future. The Raven, they called her. Corva, once carried by Sylvia Lyon and now hosted by a nameless young woman safely hidden away. Not even William knew of that Vessel's location.

William always felt a surge of resentment when he thought of the Raven's Vessel. Not that he resented the young woman's freedom. No, he resented that while this singular Vessel got to live without the oppression of a block, he was forced to institute them at birth for the Faulk children. He'd had to do the same with all three Lewan girls, not knowing which of them the spirit-being had connected to.

He hated that part of his job. He hated many parts of his job, but that one—he thought he hated that one the most.

William's meandering, self-pitying thoughts were redirected by the resurgence of Timothy's tears while Ben concluded his prayer. He rebuked himself for thinking of his own problems rather than this family's loss. He hadn't felt the same pain when his father died. But George had been a loving parent, and the Faulks' sorrow would run deep.

Once the prayer reinstating the Faulk men's blocks was complete, William and Ben said their goodbyes and stepped onto the porch. Sky-blue Adirondack chairs rested by the front window, a large flower box of yellow mums underneath. Ben set a hand on the porch rail as he looked at William.

"Do you ever get the feeling that this could all be different?" the reverend asked, a hint of distaste in his tone.

William didn't respond but held his best friend's steady gaze.

Ben nodded. "Me too."

"We're doing our jobs," William reminded them both. "We're protecting the spirit world and the people of this town."

"By repressing two families out of no fault of their own."

Desmond had accused William of something similar not even a month ago. *"Guess it's our job to be hypocrites too."*

His son had no idea.

William moved for his sedan, disappointed in himself even as he defended his actions. "This is what the Warden requires," he told Ben. "We don't know what these creatures want or what they're willing to do to get it. It's better to keep them locked away—untouchable—than to give them complete access and have a potential crisis on our hands."

"We already have a potential crisis," Ben returned. Then, he waved off the comment with a grimace. "Don't mind me. I'm being ornery. It always happens after this sort of thing."

William wanted to tell his friend that he was right, that he had reason to be much more than ornery. But he kept his mouth shut, reminding himself that this was one of those hard decisions his father had told him he was incapable of making.

The sudden vibration of his phone drew William's attention. He pulled it out of his jacket pocket, checking the caller ID. He lifted the phone toward Ben, saying, "I've got to take this. I'll talk to you later."

Ben offered his goodbye, and both men got into their cars.

Once William had the door shut, he answered the call. "How can I help you, Fischer?"

"You don't sound so pleasant this morning, William," Fischer Lavigne replied, the gravel of his voice amplified by the phone call. "Should I call back at a better time?"

"No, your timing is just fine." William started the car, preparing to back out of the driveway after Ben. "What did you need? Is everything all right with the Veil?"

Fischer, also known as Fish, took his time before saying, "To the best of my knowledge. I just had a favor to ask of you."

"What's that?"

"With all these patrols keeping me up at night, I've let the care of the lighthouse go," Fish explained. "It's not in bad shape, of course. But there's a pile of repairs I need to make before the winter. With the cold weather, my old bones, and the lack of sleep I've been getting, I could use some help."

William frowned, trying to figure out why Fish was coming to him with this matter. "Do you want me to send someone to help you?" he asked.

"Not someone," Fish replied. "Your son. And my great-nephew."

"Ah." William nodded, understanding. Desmond and Brady had often gone to Aster Island in their youth to help the lightkeeper on his property. The three had a strange camaraderie that William could admit made him slightly jealous. However, he'd also noticed the good influence that Fish had over his son. After time on the island, Desmond always had a renewed sense of purpose that William could only attribute to the presence of Fish. And despite his envy, William couldn't refute or find fault in the lightkeeper's success.

However, that didn't negate Desmond's grounding, which was intended to last another week.

After explaining as much to Fish, the lightkeeper grunted as though it were a nonissue. "This isn't some picnic I'm inviting him to, William. He'll be working his fingers to the bone. Don't you think that's a punishment of its own kind?"

Though the man had a point, William struggled to approve. He knew how much Desmond liked being with Fish on the island. The work would hardly be a deterrent.

"Fish, I'm trying to teach him responsibility," William said. "He needs to understand that his actions have consequences."

"I'm not arguing with your method of discipline," Fish insisted. "I'm simply saying, this isn't exactly a break from it either. Besides, the kid listens to me. Maybe I can talk some sense into him."

William initially bristled at the remark but reminded himself not to give in to his pride. Fish wasn't attacking his ability as a parent. He was trying to help him out.

With a sigh, William finally agreed. "All right. Just be sure Brady gets him home by nine."

"You have my word," Fish promised.

"Thank you."

"And, William?"

"Yes?"

Fish hesitated, grumbling to himself in an incoherent whisper. Then, he said, "I'll tell you if there's anything you oughta know."

William felt himself frown. He didn't know whether to be grateful or suspicious. He settled for the former, hanging up with Fish.

He didn't have time to wonder what his son might be up to with the lightkeeper. He had a Veil to find.

# CHAPTER FOUR

# Desmond

Cait was ignoring him. That much was obvious.

The reason wasn't quite so clear to Desmond.

He knew last night was a crazy, weird, and even terrifying experience. She'd appeared out of nowhere, none of them having any clue how she'd gotten on the island in the first place. Then, they'd been attacked by twelve beasts of the spirit world. They'd nearly died, only her sudden and unexpected powers breaking through the block to save them. And to top it all off, she'd passed out.

If that hadn't scared her, he thought it should.

But he was sure his note would remove some of that fear. He'd promised her answers, and if nothing else, she'd be desperate for those, right? Yet, all school day long, she pointedly avoided him. She hadn't texted him either.

He'd considered texting first. Even a short *"You okay?"* would be an effort. But no matter how many times he typed a message, it felt too paltry, too false to send. No text would be enough. She'd ignore them as she ignored his presence. The cold way she turned away all day made her decision painfully clear: She'd meant it when she said they were over, and she wouldn't be changing her mind.

*"I don't need you anymore."*

Desmond still felt the barb of her declaration slicing into his chest every time he remembered it. Even worse was the memory of her following words: *"And you've never needed me."*

It wasn't true. Desmond had always needed Cait. He always would. But even if he wanted to tell her the truth, she wouldn't give him the chance anymore.

The cruel reality made Desmond even more desperate to talk to her. He needed to find a way to force her to listen. If he could just explain . . .

He'd, what? Tell her about her connection to the Wolf? Warn her that she would have to sacrifice herself if he didn't break her free?

Desmond didn't have time to dwell on "what-if" scenarios. A miracle had happened.

Or rather, Fish had happened.

After last night's debacle, Fish had made Desmond promise to come over and explain everything. The alternative was clear—he'd tell the Warden about the whole event, including Desmond's relationship with Cait and her evident connection to the Wolf.

Desmond had readily agreed.

The inconvenience of his grounding was a detail he hadn't remembered until the cold light of the morning.

Thankfully, Brady contacted his great-uncle on Desmond's behalf, explaining the situation, and Fish managed to convince William to send Desmond and Brady to the island to help him out with "caring for the lighthouse."

Now, Brady pulled his sedan into the parking lot at the docks. "What's the plan?" he asked as they headed for the slick rock bridge that adjoined Aster Island to the mainland.

Desmond watched his step on the uneven surface. "What do you mean?"

"I *mean*," Brady tucked his hands into his jacket against the cutting wind, "what do you plan to tell Fish?"

With a nonchalant shrug that he didn't feel, Desmond said, "The truth."

"Like, the *whole* truth?" Brady asked, incredulous.

"Yeah."

"As in, the *entire*, unembellished, no-holds-barred truth?"

Desmond sent him an annoyed glance. "Yes."

"Wow."

"What?"

Brady smirked. "You think you're capable of it?"

"Don't make me push you off the bridge," Desmond said with a scowl.

Brady chuckled, and Desmond wished he could feel the same easy calm as his friend. But he had to admit he was nervous because Brady was right: He didn't tell the truth. He'd never really learned how. Telling the truth often meant that he had to be more vulnerable than he liked, and he only allowed one person to see that side of him. Even Brady didn't know the real him—not fully.

Now, that one safe person wanted nothing to do with him.

The boys stepped off the rock bridge and onto Aster Island as the salt spray of the ocean dampened the hem of their jeans. Drying golden-brown grass crunched under their boots. Reeds bowed to the biting wind. The white lighthouse loomed over them across the island's lawn, beams of sunlight reflecting off the lantern room as the clouds periodically revealed the sun.

Desmond kept his stride purposeful as they approached Fish and Laurel Lavigne's home. His gaze shot over to the forest, its massive trees already dropping their leaves to become skeletal sculptures. The previous night flashed through his mind—the beasts, Cait, and her powers. The usual sense of serenity he felt on the island attempted to soothe him, but his muscles remained tense and rigid, affected by the memories.

Standing outside the little cottage, Fish met the boys on the path to the door. The lightkeeper wore his fleece-lined jacket as always, his silver-streaked brown hair hanging to his shoulders. Despite his weathered and suntanned skin, he and Brady shared several features marking their relation: heavy brows, strong jawlines (though Fish's was covered in a thick gray beard), and those signature Lavigne cheekbones that created deep contours in the hollows of their cheeks.

"Afternoon," Fish greeted, his voice rumbling with an ominous tilt. His sharp eyes locked with Desmond's. "You ready to answer some questions?"

Desmond sucked in a deep breath. "Yeah."

Fish motioned for them to follow him, then headed down the path. "This way, then."

Realizing that Fish was headed away from his cottage and toward the lighthouse, Desmond frowned. He'd imagined sitting down with Fish at the kitchen table to tell this story with a cup of coffee and one of Laurel's famous cinnamon rolls before him. He supposed Fish didn't want his wife there though, ensuring Desmond more privacy to speak.

When they entered the lighthouse, Desmond realized he'd miscalculated the minute Fish flicked on the lights. The two small windows on each floor of the lighthouse offered minimal lighting on cloudy days such as this. The yellow haze of the overhead light revealed the number of tarps, toolboxes, and ladders ready and waiting for their arrival.

"I thought working on the lighthouse was an excuse," Desmond said.

Brady bore a grim expression as they both looked up at the lightkeeper. "I'm not a liar, kid," Fish said. "This place genuinely needs repairs, and I don't got time for them with the present situation on our hands. So, while you explain, you'll also help me get this place in order."

Alongside his primary role as keeper of the lighthouse, Fish watched over the island, acting almost like a game warden. He ensured the Veil's safety as he kept the lighthouse's lantern steadily shining. That kept him busy during routine life. With the Veil's damage and the beasts' presence, his work had doubled.

After Desmond and Brady shed their jackets, Fish went about showing them the primary work that needed doing, floor by floor. There were five floors altogether, including the lantern room. They'd all work together, of course, to facilitate the conversation, but there would be plenty of moving about throughout that time.

Equipped with a ladder, a bucket of spackle, and a putty knife, Desmond set to work sealing up the cracks and chips in the stone walls. Brady helped Fish deep clean and reorganize the shelves of the storeroom on the bottom floor.

Once they'd all settled into their tasks, Fish addressed Desmond again. "All right, let's hear it." His voice was firm even as he kept his eyes on his hands, tightening a bolt that kept the metal shelves affixed to the walls. His subtle Maine accent was stronger than anyone else in the Warden's—meaning he *had* an accent. Upon the creation of Porthaven, the Warden had intentionally chosen not to adopt the more lackadaisical tones of those from Down East, and with the leadership often leaving the state for college, it was rather easy for them to maintain their more neutral manners of speech.

Fish didn't care about those things, which Desmond took as a sign that he was more trustworthy than the rest of the pretentious Warden members.

Desmond pursed his lips, his mind tumbling through the millions of secrets he'd been hiding his whole life. What did Fish want to hear? "I'm not really sure where to begin," he admitted.

"Start with the beginning," Fish prompted. "What were you trying to accomplish last night?"

"Right." Desmond dipped the putty knife into the white paste in the bucket. "Well, the original goal was to, uh—to try to fix the Veil."

Brady furrowed his brow, looking up at Desmond. "You said you wanted to gather evidence before telling your dad about your theory."

Desmond shrugged. "That was a lie."

"Great," his friend grumbled.

Fish handed Brady a box of what looked like random junk. "Sort that," he ordered, then turned back to Desmond. "What made you think that you could fix the Veil?"

Studiously applying the spackle, Desmond avoided Fish's gaze. "I figured that if anyone would be strong enough, it'd be me."

"Because of your Varon blood?"

"Because I'm the heir of the Varon power," he corrected. "My dad and I have the potential for the most power in this town. Only the town rules keep us from living up to that potential."

Fish gave a firm nod. "And those rules don't mean much to you." It wasn't a question but a conclusion the man had come to for himself. "As you're not supposed to wield the spirit world, how did you learn to? Did your dad teach you?"

Desmond couldn't help his sardonic scoff. "Not a chance. If Dad knew I was wielding . . . well, I don't care to think how much extra work I'd be forced to endure at my internship."

"You're a Sage," Brady noted.

"Yeah. I'm a Varon." Desmond found it harder than normal to mean his flippant reply. "Connection to the spirit world is kind of our thing."

"And how long have you been wielding?" Fish prodded.

Desmond gathered another precise amount of spackle. "Since I was six."

Brady let out an annoyed gasp as though he'd been betrayed.

Fish simply continued his work, rewrapping a tangle of rope. "What all has that entailed?"

"If you're asking if I've done anything dangerous, the answer is no," Desmond assured him.

"You summoned a beast," Brady argued.

That got Fish to pause in his work and look up, one of his bushy eyebrows raised.

Desmond sighed. "It's no big deal. I—when I was a kid, I heard Dad talking to Uncle Rick about beasts, and I thought, heck, I'd always wanted a pet, but Dad is allergic to cats and said that dogs were too much work. As a goldfish seemed like a waste of space, I decided to make my own."

"So, you summoned a *beast*?" Brady demanded. "That's insane."

Rolling his eyes at his friend's melodrama, Desmond snapped his fingers, summoning Hades. The cat-like beast, known as a sith, appeared with a blip of dark blue light on the bottom stair leading up to the second floor. His blue-black fur had a perpetual ethereal quality, fuzzed like wisps of ivory smoke. Bright neon yellow eyes brimmed with otherworldly intelligence, and his two tails twitched merrily.

Brady started, wide-eyed at the cat-beast's arrival, while Fish narrowed his gaze.

"He's not dangerous," Desmond insisted. "I summoned him, so he does my bidding. And that means that he's my companion exclusively. There's nothing wrong with that."

Both Lavignes remained skeptical, but Fish returned to his work. "And your ability to summon the essence of the spirit world," he pressed, referring to the rift of light Desmond could wield, "when did you start that?"

"When I was twelve," Desmond admitted. "I'd heard so much about it—about how Varons were supposed to be so good at it, and I just thought . . . why not try?"

"Because it's against our laws in Porthaven," Fish offered.

"Laws don't mean much to me either."

"Mm."

"I don't do it often," Desmond said. "Only occasionally, and only to be sure I still have access to it. Never with any intention to use it."

A long silence stretched out, only the scrape of Desmond's knife and the jostle of Brady and Fish's work filling the space. He knew that the lightkeeper was working out what to think. Hades had curled up on the stair, watching them intently, the sith's presence a damning reminder of Desmond's guilt.

Finally, Fish broke the silence once more. "And what is your relationship with the Lewan girl?"

Tightening his grip on the putty knife, Desmond muttered, "Her name is Cait."

Another beat of silence passed, Brady's head down as Fish hesitated in thought. "What is your relationship with Cait?" he restated.

"She's—" Desmond stopped himself, wondering who she was to him anymore. Their "not-friendship" from the past ten years was dead. She'd made that perfectly clear. They'd always been nothing, but somehow, it hurt worse *knowing* they really were nothing now.

With a sigh, Desmond began again. "We don't have a relationship," he said honestly. "We were secretly friends for the last ten years, but she, uh . . . she ended that."

"Why?" Fish asked.

*"I don't need you anymore,"* Cait's memory reminded him. *"And you've never needed me."*

Desmond frowned into his bucket of spackle. "I wasn't brave enough to be the friend I should've been. She finally realized that . . . and she moved on."

A heavy hum came from Fish, considering the weight of all that was left unspoken in Desmond's words. Thankfully, he didn't push for a more specific answer. Instead, he asked, "Do you know how she wound up on the island?"

Readily, Desmond shook his head. He climbed down from the ladder, work complete. "I have no idea. She was simply there all of a sudden."

"There were amber wisps of light around her," Brady cut in. "Like she'd somehow used the spirit world to travel."

Desmond brushed off the idea. "That's not possible."

"In my time," Fish noted, "I've learned to never discount what's possible with the spirit world."

Raising his brow dubiously, Desmond held the man's stare. "If you ever figure out how to teleport, by all means, let me know."

"How else did she get there?" Brady asked.

Desmond turned to his friend. "Do you think the Varons wouldn't know if we could teleport?"

Brady shrugged, bashfully going back to his heap of junk.

"There's a good deal that the Warden, including the Varons, doesn't know," Fish said. "How a Veil gets damaged, for example. Or how a girl with a block on her spirit somehow managed to break through that block and wield the spirit world with more power and skill than anyone I've ever met."

Fish's remark reminded Desmond of a line from the prophecy about Cait: *"The bond of spirit and child will bring forth power like we've never seen."*

Maybe teleportation wasn't that far-fetched. . . .

While Desmond remained silent, Fish continued his line of questioning. "Were you aware that she had that sort of power?"

Desmond's gaze snapped up. "What? No—no, Cait—she doesn't even know that she's capable—I mean, I've hardly told her anything about the spirit world myself, and as you know, my dad isn't exactly sharing details with the Lewan family."

"She was old enough to remember her life in Ireland," Fish suggested. "Could be she remembers her father wielding and has tried it out for herself."

Desmond sent the man a hard glare. "Cait isn't behind this," he insisted, then realized that maybe he was wrong. Hadn't he concluded that Cait's dreams were tied to the beasts summoned from the Veil? He'd even considered that she was unwittingly the one summoning them herself. Perhaps it wasn't Cait directly behind the Veil's damage, but he knew enough to consider that the spirit-being attached to her *was* at fault.

"He's right," Brady offered, contradicting Desmond's new line of thinking. "She can't be directly involved in whatever's going on with the Veil."

"She can't?" Desmond asked.

Brady frowned as though surprised he was second-guessing him. "Yeah, I mean—like I told you, the beasts coming from the Veil aren't tethered to anyone," he explained. "Which means she can't be summoning them—no one is."

"They were looking to her for direction," Fish noted, reminding Desmond of how the twelve beasts that appeared the previous night had looked straight at Cait once they'd formed.

Brady shrugged the detail off. "I can't explain that, but I can tell you it isn't because she summoned them."

"Brade," Desmond interrupted, knowing it was time to come clean. "She dreams about them—the beasts. She has since her parents died. And I double-checked; each beast that showed up out of the Veil matched the beast in her dreams each night."

"Okay, that's weird, but so what?" Brady motioned toward the outside, in the direction that the Veil lay within Aster Island's forest. "She's been having dreams for, what? Twelve years? And these beasts only began showing up a month or two ago. If anything, that proves that she's not the one summoning them."

"Or," Fish cut in, "it proves that her powers are simply growing stronger. Strong enough to damage a Veil and summon beasts."

Brady sighed. He spoke again in Cait's defense, enunciating each word with marked annoyance. "The beasts weren't tethered." He held his great-uncle's stare, determined to make his point. "*No one* is summoning them. Plain and simple. The moment we accept that, we can stop pointing fingers at innocent people and begin to find a solution to the problem."

"I think Cait already solved that problem," Desmond reminded them. "She sealed the Veil. I don't think we have to worry about beasts coming through anymore."

"That remains to be seen," Fish countered, then switched gears. "These dreams—you said they started after her parents' deaths?"

Knowing the direction the conversation was headed, Desmond worked to calm his pulse. "Yes."

Fish's eyebrows rose, wrinkling his forehead. "Immediately after their deaths?"

"Yes."

The lightkeeper's nod said that he understood. "Do you believe her to be the Vessel?"

Desmond sighed, picking at some dry spackle on the side of the bucket. "Yes," he murmured.

Brady's chin dipped.

Fish drew his fingers through his beard. "Does she know?"

"No," Desmond admitted.

"Do you plan to tell her?"

"No."

Fish's eyes went wide.

Desmond drew his shoulders back. "It's her greatest fear—inheriting her father's . . . attachment. And like I said, she's ended our . . . So, I'd like better evidence before ruining her life."

"And you haven't told your dad?" Fish asked.

"Absolutely not," Desmond said, voice taut. "And he can't know. He won't wait for better evidence. She's almost eighteen. He'll follow protocol, tighten her block, and find some fanatical maniac from some other Warden town to come here and marry her the second she's old enough, all but locking her in a cage."

Fish tipped his head, a curious gleam in his eyes. "You think Sahila Faulk is a fanatical maniac?"

Desmond let out a huff. "I think she's a fanatic, yeah. A maniac, not so much," he said. "But she and Tim allowed themselves to enter into an arranged marriage for the sake of 'the cause.' It had nothing to do with love. And Cait doesn't deserve that."

Brady shuffled a golden gyroscope in his hands, the rings spinning randomly. He wore a sly grin, dark eyes locked with Desmond's. "There is another option," he offered.

Doubtful, Desmond quirked an eyebrow. "What?"

"*You* could marry her."

Shocked by his friend's suggestion—joke or not—Desmond glanced nervously at Fish. The old lightkeeper continued to stroke his beard, no sign of approval or disapproval on his face. Heat welled under Desmond's collar, and he began to laugh nervously. "That—that's ridiculous," he deflected. "I can't—I'm in high school."

"So?" Brady spun the gyroscope again. "Like you said, she's almost eighteen, and *you're* almost eighteen. If your dad pushed the matter, you could marry her before anyone else got the chance."

So, it wasn't a joke.

"Don't be stupid, Brady."

Brady's eyes narrowed mischievously. "Didn't you say something about her deserving a husband who loves her?"

Desmond's hands curled into fists, the heat spreading up his neck and onto his face. "That wouldn't matter, even if I did feel that way," he said. "I'm in line to lead Porthaven, which means my kid will inherit from me. Which further means my kid can't be a Vessel."

"And if you gave up the leadership?" Brady suggested. "You'd be free to do whatever you want then, right?"

The idea wasn't new to Desmond. He'd considered it many times. But each time, he knew he couldn't go through with it. He wanted the power too much—he wanted to prove to himself, to his dad, and to everyone else that he had what it took to lead.

On the far side of the room, Fish dropped a box back onto the shelves. "There's a lot in this town that could use remodeling," he remarked. "The old canning factory. This lighthouse. The government and the Warden's structure. The feud between the Varons and your family."

Desmond and Brady listened for whatever wisdom Fish would

inevitably give them. Their eyes locked onto the man's weathered features, and their heads tipped forward to hear every word.

"The handling of the Vessels," Fish concluded, "that could use the most remodeling, in my mind."

Desmond agreed.

"But," Fish held up a finger, "none of that has anything to do with what we're discussing today."

Taking a large step toward Desmond, Fish's piercing blue stare cut into him. "Whether or not you're in love with this girl, you have knowledge that can either keep this town safe or cause great harm. That Veil out there is torn. Dangers unknown to the Warden are creeping onto our shores. Maybe the girl stopped it, maybe she didn't. Regardless, she's got a creature tied to her that's trying to break free."

A deep fear welled up in Desmond's chest like the tide rising.

Fish's gaze felt damning as he spoke. "So, the question is, Desmond, what do you plan to do about it?"

Despite the shaking of his fists at his sides and the pressure that compressed his lungs, making breathing hard, a coolness settled over Desmond's mind. No matter all the things he didn't have answers to, all the questions that plagued him every second—*this* was the one answer he did have.

"I'm going to save her," he said. "I'm going to find a way to break the bond between Cait and that creature if it's the last thing I do."

# CHAPTER FIVE

# Cait

A raindrop, icy and startling, landed on Cait's cheek. She stood under a stormy sky, black-gray clouds blocking out the moon. Her back was to the woods, shadows filling the clearing before her, only a single, hulking tree in its center.

She was back on the island.

The hum filled her whole body, stronger and more aggressive than the sound that came with Desmond's presence. A pull in her gut drew her a step closer to the tree, and Cait wondered if this was reality—if she really was back on the island. Her skin tingled under her sweater, her body brimming with the energy she'd felt rush out of her when she'd commanded those beasts and done whatever she'd done to the tree.

Lightning split the sky, granting her a clear view of the massive sycamore, an unusual tree in the forests of Maine. Its giant trunk bulged, its gnarled bark strained by some interior pressure. The branches above reached to the sky in a spiderweb of tangled limbs. The whole thing groaned under the furious wind.

Reaching to brush back the hair blown into her face, Cait looked up again. The smoky clouds broke into wispy tendrils to reveal the moon's full, silvery face. Rain fell in her eyes, causing her to squint and look away.

Confusion drew Cait's attention away from her surroundings. For the past twelve years, her dreams always started in her childhood home. Yet, she'd even bypassed her time at the cove, arriving here on the island with no beasts, no smoke, and no pacing creature.

As if in response to her unspoken musing, a low rumble sounded behind Cait. She whirled to find a door wedged between the trees, a fissure marring its face from upper hinge to center. Inexplicably, she could see a shadow pacing through the crack at its base, with an orange glow emanating from beyond. Still, it remained surrounded by trees, an impossibility in the forest.

Heart pounding erratically, Cait turned back to the damaged tree. Three streaks of lightning burned paths through the clouds as if parting them to allow more moonlight to penetrate. A pale wash of light filled the clearing, revealing more of the sycamore. Its thick branches were so tangled that she could hardly see through them. However, a faint movement drew her attention to the shiny blue-black feathers of the raven perched on a bough.

It cried at her, a piercing "caw" rending the air.

Thunder rumbled like a growl in reply.

Then, the bird flew off its perch, the silver light flashing along its wings. It swooped low to land on the shoulder of the young woman who had just appeared, her figure gilded in the moon's beams. Her coppery hair drifted around her face, lifted as she stared at the tree. She stood in the clearing that encircled the sycamore, free of the forest's shadow. Something in Cait urged her a step toward the girl. Her expression was soft, almost inviting, as she considered the tree, and her light blue sweater and jeans gave her a friendly demeanor.

Last time, Cait wasn't brave enough to call out to the young woman, unsure of her allegiance. She'd never experienced strangers in her dreams. Only the visage of William Simon, a representation of some protective force, and the new arrival of Desmond over the past couple of weeks.

Now, they were both gone, replaced by this pretty, unknown woman.

A croon from the raven caught the redhead's attention, but it was quickly diverted to Cait across the clearing.

Cait didn't take a step back this time, though. She stood still, returning the young woman's gaze, wondering if she had the answers Cait needed. Maybe that was the point of these dreams. Perhaps if she could find the redhead, she could get her answers.

But Cait had never seen this woman in reality—in Porthaven or otherwise. She looked a couple of years older than Cait—perhaps twenty, at the oldest—which meant they would have been in school together, even for just a year. If she lived in the town, Cait would have seen her *somewhere*, surely.

Lightning flashed a third time, the raven cawing again.

Simultaneously, Cait and the young woman turned to look at the far side of the clearing. The tree limbs cast haunting shadows across the ground, skeletal fingers stretching out to grasp the boy standing within their reach. The hum rose higher, and the energy in her body rose with it.

Sterling Faulk was there, staring at the tree, his thick, shoulder-length hair wild in the wind. His rich brown skin took on a deeper shade in the darkness. His broad shoulders hunched forward, and he tucked his chin low as he surveyed the sycamore and took a single step toward the tree.

Cait tightened her jaw. Perhaps she didn't know the redhead in real life, but she *did* know Sterling.

Anticipation spiked within her, the hum howling through her ears and the energy snapping like electricity under her skin. If she'd had any hesitation left, she was decided now. Sterling Faulk would have the answers she needed; she knew it.

A sudden urgency filled Cait's chest, a dread that warned her of danger. The hum turned to a growl, tugging her eyes from Sterling and back to the redhead. She saw the young woman standing in the same place, staring into the shadows on the opposite side of the tree—the side that Cait couldn't see—and she was frowning.

Heartbeat rising, Cait shifted to her left, trying to glimpse the other side. Slowly, she stalked around the bulging tree trunk, straining to see. Another burning streak of light cut through the clouds. The rain matted her hair, soaking through her clothes. The winds burned her cheeks, sending a shiver through her bones.

Hollows of light and shadow obscured the other side of the clearing. A fourth figure stood there, shrouded by the night.

Cait narrowed her gaze, desperate to see who it was.

Then, she woke up.

~

When Cait opened her eyes, she was groggy and fuzzy-headed. However, she moved with renewed purpose as she prepared for school. No matter how exhausted the dream had left her, it had given her resolve and a task—one that she refused to put off.

Thankful that Genni and Matt carried the conversation during their bike ride, Cait let herself sink deep into her thoughts. She had to create a plan, some means of talking with Sterling alone. It would be harder than it should be. She'd have to catch him when Matt wasn't with her. And when Hunter wasn't with Sterling. She'd have to orchestrate some perfect moment—maybe in the halls or as they were preparing to leave for the day. Otherwise, there was no guarantee that Sterling would say so much as a word to her, let alone agree to answer her questions.

Cait continued to ruminate on her plans all through the morning classes. Normally, her eyes would drift to Desmond during school. Today, they found the back of Sterling's head. He wore his black hair back in a messy stub of a ponytail. He'd looped the cable of his headphones over his shoulders, ready to slip them back in the moment class ended. Cait never had learned what he listened to every day. Many kids speculated that it was probably heavy metal or emo music. Others joked that he listened to motivational speeches.

For some reason, Cait doubted all their guesses. Sterling struck her as the type to subvert stereotypes.

Cait watched for any and every chance to pull Sterling to the side. But class after class passed without providing any opportunity.

After overhearing one of Desmond's cousins—Monica—telling the other students about Sterling's grandfather passing away yesterday, Cait began to second-guess her plan. She was surprised that Sterling had shown up to school in the first place. If her nan died, she was sure she'd need to take the whole week off. But Sterling moved through the morning as though it were a normal day. She knew everyone grieved in their own way, but she had to believe it was a front, an attempt not to feel the grief.

Either way, Cait didn't feel right about approaching him after that. So, she reluctantly relegated herself to waiting another day . . . Or possibly longer.

Attempting to hide her dejection, Cait walked into the cafeteria with Matt. They parted ways as he joined the lunch line, and she walked to their usual table. Nearest the door, the table put them in the path of all the other students, which Cait had never liked. However, it did allow for quick entrances and exits, improving her opinion of the location.

Students cluttered the cafeteria, their voices an overwhelming cacophony of noise. Clutching her bagged lunch tightly in her hand, Cait wove through the bodies, trying not to draw attention to herself. It was a reasonably simple feat with her small frame and predisposition to remain unseen.

As she neared her table, she caught the snippet of a hushed conversation, Hunter's familiar voice grabbing her attention. "Two nights in a row?" he whispered, tone incredulous and worried.

"Yeah," a warm, smooth voice replied. "It's freaking me out."

Cait turned her head subtly just in time to see Hunter and Sterling walk near her, lunch trays in hand. She'd hardly recognized Sterling's voice, having only heard him speak when called on in class.

"It's not that weird," Hunter said as they passed. "I have this recurring dream about riding in a driverless car."

"That's not the same," Sterling said firmly.

They moved out of earshot.

Standing at the side of her table, Cait stared after Sterling and Hunter as they worked their way to the middle of the cafeteria. They sat down together, heads close, as they continued their conversation. Hunter's expression grew more and more pinched while Sterling's jaw tightened.

*The same dream, two nights in a row.*

Sterling was having dreams . . . Like Cait.

Frozen in place, Cait watched as Elizabeth Greene joined Hunter and Sterling at the table across the room, their other friends, Scott and Melissa, just behind. The boys drew apart, a clear, silent agreement between them to pause their conversation. They jumped into their normal camaraderie with their friends, Hunter draping his arm across the back of Elizabeth's chair. Cait watched as they all bowed their heads, and he prayed over their meal.

She wondered at the act, questioning its sincerity. She didn't know Hunter or any of his friends well, but she *had* seen them at the Greenes' party last weekend, and she wasn't so sure devout Christians would behave that way.

As though in punishment for her judgmental thoughts, Desmond walked past Hunter's table and into her sight line, reminding her of how she'd behaved with him that night. She'd allowed him to pull her into a room and then lain on the Greenes' guest bed with him. Though nothing of real significance happened, Cait knew that if he'd tried to kiss her, she wouldn't have stopped him.

Her eyes drifted back to Hunter and Sterling's table. They were all starting to eat the cafeteria's offering of the day, a singular seat left empty at the six-seater table. Cait's mind fixated on that chair, her eyes locked on its back.

The faint memory of Hunter's words at the start of the school year swept through her mind. *"I meant what I said,"* he'd assured her after apologizing for the embarrassing lunch debacle where Matt had called him out. *"You're welcome to sit with Liz and me in the future."*

Glancing at the lunch line, Cait spotted Matt nearing the end. She saw Genni lingering with her friends, Alexis and Jared, toward the middle. Then, she looked back at the empty chair and made her decision.

Before she could think through her choice, Cait grabbed her lunch bag from the table. She slipped into the center aisle, walking straight toward the middle of the cafeteria and Hunter Varon. She veered past a group of teens and came to a stop right next to the empty chair. Hunter and Elizabeth were busy laughing at something Scott had said, but Sterling noticed her presence right away. He stared up at her, thick eyebrows drawn together.

Cait's palms grew sweaty around her lunch bag, but she refused to back down. "Is this seat taken?" she asked.

That got the rest of the table's attention, as well as the attention of several people at the surrounding tables.

Scott and his girlfriend, Melissa, looked up at her with a mixture of shock and amusement. Hunter gaped at her. Elizabeth studied her as though she were an intriguing anomaly. Sterling continued to stare.

"Uh . . ." Hunter looked at Elizabeth for help.

"No, it's not," Elizabeth said for him, her light hair and timeless beauty softened by a polite smile. She had the same hooded eyes as her brother Ryan—Rese's new boyfriend—but there was a gentleness and consideration within them that he didn't share.

Cait gestured toward Hunter with her lunch bag. "Hunter invited me to join you . . . if I ever wanted to."

Clearing his throat, Hunter gave a hesitant nod. "I did." He almost sounded regretful about it.

"I'd like to," Cait clarified.

"Okay," Elizabeth replied with a simple acceptance.

Cait pointed toward her usual table. "Would it—would it be too much trouble if my friend and my sister joined us too?"

"The tables seat six," Scott noted.

"We can add two more seats," Elizabeth challenged, then set her hand on Hunter's arm, where it rested on the table. "Babe, why don't you and Scott get two more seats?"

"Uh-huh," Hunter mumbled, standing.

Scott let out a heavy sigh, following his friend's lead.

In their absence, Elizabeth motioned for Cait to sit. Both Melissa and Sterling continued to stare at her, but she bolstered her courage and sat down.

"I think your friend is looking for you," Elizabeth said.

Cait looked over to the lunch line, finding Matt with his lunch tray and a scrunched-up face as he scanned the cafeteria. Cait feared momentarily that she'd have to call across the room, but Hunter passed him just then, chair in hand, and did it for her. Matt gaped at him, then followed his direction toward the table, eyes going wide to match his mouth when he saw Cait there.

A collective murmur worked through the cafeteria, matching the hum thrumming through Cait's body. In the school, it was nearly constant with Desmond's presence in classes or the cafeteria. Every student cast not-so-subtle glances over as Scott set a chair at the end between Melissa and Elizabeth, taking it for himself. Hunter placed the other on the far side, next to Cait.

Intentionally keeping her gaze away from Desmond's table across the room, Cait gave Matt a shy smile at his approach. "I decided to take Hunter up on his offer to sit with them," she explained.

Matt took the seat at the head of the table, his shocked expression still untamed. "Uh—that's, um . . . cool," he mumbled.

Across from Cait, Sterling ignored them, dunking a piece of fried fish into tartar sauce.

A long silence stretched around the table while the murmurs in the cafeteria grew. They all settled in, the chair between Melissa and Cait open for Genni.

Cait began to question if she'd made the wrong choice. She'd drawn so much attention to them. Her head ached with the fight between the hum and the buzz of chatter. What had she hoped to accomplish in the first place? She couldn't ask Sterling about his dream in front of everyone. He and Hunter were obviously keeping it between themselves. They wouldn't appreciate her dragging their secrets into the light. Nor did she care to include the others in their conversation either.

But she was seated at their table now. No matter the stir she'd caused, Cait knew this was the only way. If she could insert herself into Sterling's friend group, *eventually*, she'd find a way to talk to him.

Settling into the awkwardness, Cait opened her lunch bag.

As the silence stretched, Elizabeth elbowed Hunter. He met her expectant stare with a baffled one. They had some wordless exchange before he sighed and turned to Cait. "I'm glad you decided to join us," he said, though his tight voice said otherwise.

Cait removed the lid of the plasticware in front of her. "Me too."

Sterling continued to dunk the same piece of fish into his sauce, eyeing her.

Cait met his stare and gave him a polite smile before digging into her own meal.

Slowly, the students around her relaxed, returning to their meals. Matt picked his fish apart, scanning the table. "So, uh . . . You guys are all on the basketball team," he remarked.

"Yeah," Hunter confirmed.

"Cool." Matt nodded, his expressive face filled with nervousness. "Are you on the baseball team too?"

Hunter shared a look with Scott. "Yeah," he said again. "I'm on first, Scott's got center field, and Sterling's our catcher."

"That's cool," Matt repeated, then furrowed his brow, recognizing the repetition. "I was thinking of trying to join in the spring. Ya know, if there's a position open."

"Technically, there's not," Hunter said. "But we can always use extra guys on the team. In case someone's sick or injured. Or if our captain gets grounded again."

The dig at Desmond made Scott and Sterling snicker. Cait bit the inside of her lip, keeping her eyes on her plate. It was like fighting the current, every instinct begging her to give in to its pull and find him. The hum trilled, reminding her that if she looked up, she would see the boy in question directly ahead of her at the table nearest the far wall.

Cait turned her gaze to Matt instead. The hum almost growled in disapproval as she listened to him talk.

"Oh, awesome," Matt was saying. "I know the season's kind of far away, but I figure it's best to be prepared. How has the basketball season gone for you guys so far?"

"We have our first game this weekend," Hunter said. "On Saturday. It's out of town, though. We travel pretty often, being so far out on the peninsula."

"Really? Is it the same with the baseball team?"

Hunter began to nod as Genni suddenly appeared at Cait's shoulder. The whole table looked up at her. Yet, she stood there completely still, lunch bag dangling at her side. Her bright blue eyes were wide, and her mouth was ajar as she stared directly at Sterling.

"Gen—" Cait began, but her sister cut her off.

"Are we sitting here now?" Genni asked, something between awe and incredulity in her tone.

"Seems that way," Hunter said, then motioned to the chair across from him. "We saved you a seat."

"Thanks," Genni said directly to Sterling.

Sterling frowned but turned back to his meal.

Baffled at Genni's odd behavior, Cait watched as she took the seat.

Matt remained oblivious and spoke to Hunter again. "You said that the baseball team *does* travel?"

"Uh—yeah." Hunter shook his head, clearing his thoughts. "Yeah, we do."

Matt appeared rather starry-eyed at the idea. "Where do you travel to? Like, there aren't a ton of cities this far up in Maine, so I didn't imagine there'd be a ton of schools either."

"We have about five other towns within four hours of us," Hunter explained. "We all take turns traveling."

The conversation devolved further into sports talk after that. Melissa and Scott drew Elizabeth into their own conversation, talking about people and situations in which Cait had no involvement. Genni worked up her courage and chimed in with Matt and Hunter. Cait and Sterling just sat across from one another, letting their friends carry on without input unless called upon.

Cait did her best to become comfortable with her new surroundings. It felt wrong to be amongst so many people at once. Not only at the table but also sitting in the middle of the cafeteria. She'd spent so much of her life in the corner at the back of the room.

And yet, even in the incongruity of her feelings, Cait found herself smiling and laughing as lunch progressed. She kept quiet for the most part, but she liked listening as the conversation twisted and evolved from sports to the nuisances of schoolwork, life in Porthaven, and Matt's history of traveling with his family for his dad's job in the military.

Strangely, Cait had a good time.

Even more strangely, she found herself disappointed when the bell rang, ending their meal.

"You know," Hunter said to Matt as they rose, gathering their trays.

"Tons of people travel with the team for the games. If you want, you could join us on Saturday. Lots of the guys on the basketball team are on the baseball team, so it'd be good for you to meet 'em all."

Matt's eyes went wide. "Seriously? That'd be awesome." He frowned as a thought struck him. "I'll have to ask my mom, though."

Hunter brushed a hand through the air. "No worries. Just lemme know."

As they walked out of the cafeteria for their next class, Matt nudged Cait's arm. "I'm glad you did that," he said. "Sitting with them, I mean."

Cait smiled. "So am I."

"What made you do it?"

She shrugged, not willing to tell him the truth. She tried to work out an answer that wouldn't be a complete lie. "I guess I'm just tired of letting my fear hold me back."

Matt grinned, something like pride twinkling in his brown eyes.

Before he could get another word out, Genni slammed into Cait's side. Her sister gripped her arm with a white-knuckled hold. "Cait," she whisper-hissed, "I can't believe you!"

Cait was about to defend her choice when Genni let out a small squeal, her face vibrant with giddiness. "He's so perfect," she crooned, a soft sigh escaping her before she began to gush. "His hair. His eyebrows. His eyes! Ugh, I could die. And the way he listens to music all the time. He *has* to be an intellectual. Maybe a poet. Oh, his poetry would be so emotional and heartbreaking."

Matt's whole face scrunched up in disgust.

"What are you talking about?" Cait asked, extricating herself from her sister's grip.

"Sterling," Genni whispered dramatically. She glanced around as though he would be lurking nearby. When he was nowhere to be seen, she turned back to Cait. "Did you do it on purpose?"

"Do what?" Cait asked.

Genni jabbed her in the side. "Sit with them so that I could meet him."

Cait frowned, realizing that an introduction had never happened. "You didn't meet him."

"You know what I mean."

"No," Cait replied. "I didn't even know you liked him."

"Who doesn't?" Genni let out another wistful sigh. "He's so dreamy."

Matt scowled. "Can we talk about something else? This is weird."

"Don't be such a boy," Genni said, twirling to walk backward before them. "I've gotta get to class. Thanks, Cait! You're the best!"

Then, she bounded off down the opposite hallway, leaving Cait and Matt staring at each other in disbelief.

"Is that it?" Matt whispered. "You decided to sit with them to set your sister up with Sterling?"

Cait rolled her eyes. "Come on," she said, pulling him off toward their next class.

# CHAPTER SIX

# Desmond

He couldn't believe it. He simply couldn't believe it.

Cait had gone to Hunter over him. She'd written Desmond off so completely that she'd chosen to befriend *Hunter*, of all people.

Desmond ground his teeth all afternoon. He'd be surprised if he had any enamel left at his next dentist visit. But he couldn't help it. Having Cait ignore him was one thing. Having her go to his public enemy felt like a betrayal.

He'd offered her answers, plain and simple. Why hadn't she come to him? Had he really been such a bad friend that it had driven her so far away?

It took all of Desmond's efforts not to constantly stare at Cait throughout the rest of the school day. The only thing that kept his sanity in check was the anticipation of his and Brady's plans. They would find a way to save Cait, and then she wouldn't have any more reason to shut him out. In fact, there wouldn't be any reason that Brady's ridiculous suggestion the day before would be ridiculous after all. If Cait weren't the Vessel, there'd be nothing to stand between Desmond and her.

Focusing on that fragment of hope, Desmond rehearsed how he'd convince his mom to allow Brady to come over after school. It'd been Brady's idea initially. After they left Aster Island the previous night, Brady mentioned that his dad, Ben, had some books in his office at the church that might be of interest to their efforts.

"As the reverend, he has to know pretty much everything about the spirit world," Brady explained. "I've only read a couple of them so far, but eventually, it'll be my job, so I'll have to read them at some point. I can swing by tomorrow and pick up a couple."

Desmond approved of the plan, though he wasn't sure when they'd actually be able to get together. His grounding meant no hanging out with friends. But that morning before school, Desmond overheard his dad on the phone with Uncle Rick. They were discussing the upcoming stakeout on the island—and William would be there, which meant that he'd be out all night.

Desmond wondered—and worried—about how long it would take the Warden to figure out that no more beasts would appear now that Cait had sealed the Veil. They already kept a hundred-yard perimeter from the Veil's clearing, not allowing the lower members to go near it—both for their safety and to maintain its secrecy. But when the beasts stopped emerging, William would eventually check the Veil and discover the amber that now encased the tear.

Regardless, Desmond knew tonight was a golden opportunity for him and Brady to enact their plans. First thing that morning, he'd told Brady to pick up the books after school and come over at seven, knowing his dad would be gone by then.

Desmond kept his hopes in check, knowing that the books wouldn't be likely to grant them some grand revelation immediately. The Warden's attempt at learning about the Veil's strange tear and the beasts it was producing told him that answers weren't nearly as easy to come by as one might wish. But he refused to give up without trying at all. There had to be information somewhere out there. If he could be patient and dedicated enough, he knew he'd find it eventually.

When Brady arrived at the Simon house, Desmond's mom immediately balked. "No," Robin insisted. "I'm sorry, boys, but you're grounded, Desmond. That means no friends."

"Dad never specified that as part of the punishment," Desmond argued, keeping his tone respectful and his words light. "He simply said no extracurriculars, and he took my keys away."

"Don't try to lawyer your way out of this," Robin said.

"I'm not," he promised. "Brady isn't even here to hang out."

"No?"

"No." Desmond held his mom's crystal clear blue eyes, preparing his rehearsed lie. "I'm helping him out. *Because* I'm grounded, Brady has to pick up my slack as team captain this Saturday. That's taking away some of his time from schoolwork, so I agreed to help him get ahead on our assignments."

Robin studied his face. Desmond kept his expression relaxed and sincere. But his mom was good at reading him—too good. Even when he worked his best lies, she could always spot their weaknesses.

Lifting her chin, her eyes narrowed knowingly. Perhaps this trait of hers, this ability to suss out his falsehoods, was why he found most girls vapid. Robin Simon was too smart. Without even trying, she could see through his best acts. It made life challenging, and it made Desmond try harder each time.

"Do you have a good reason?" Robin asked, calling out his lie.

Desmond gave her a derisive smirk. Then, he sighed, admitting, "He's not here to hang out, Mom. I promise."

"Why *is* he here?"

"I need help with something."

Her light brown eyebrows rose. "Something you don't want to tell me about."

Desmond tipped his head to the side, acknowledging her suspicion.

Robin glanced at Brady, who remained in the doorway while the two of them had stepped a handful of paces away to discuss the matter with *slightly* more privacy. She crossed her arms, the heather gray cardigan she wore bunching at the elbows. "Despite my better judgment," she began, turning those crisp blue eyes back on her son, "I'll allow it."

Desmond smiled. "Thanks."

She held up a hand to stall him momentarily from retrieving Brady. "I've told you before, seabird," she said, using her childhood nickname for him. "I trust you. Don't make me regret it."

Feeling a well of guilt, Desmond nodded. "I won't," he said, hoping that he could live up to that promise.

The boys ascended the stairs to his room, preparing for a night filled with laborious study. When they renovated the house last year, the remodel had included Desmond's room. He'd been immensely grateful, glad to be rid of his more childish decor from the past sixteen years.

At the time, Desmond hadn't fully understood why they would redo the room when he was only a couple of years away from graduating and leaving for college. But he'd come to understand: From generation to generation, the Simons had passed down this home. Desmond would live here until *his* kid was old enough to inherit and start a family. Just as his parents would live in the house until *he* married and then produced said child. At that time, his parents would move into the house next door—the house where his grandmother currently lived.

His room wasn't renovated to carry him through the next two years. It was renovated for Desmond to live in until his parents moved out. Whether that occurred in the next five or ten years, it didn't matter. This home was as much a part of his future as the entirety of Porthaven.

Brady dropped his backpack onto the desk, sitting in front of one of the room's two windows. "You've gotta learn not to lie," he said, retrieving the books from his bag.

Desmond shut the bedroom door, not wanting his mom to overhear their potential conversations. "It's a habit," he said offhandedly.

Brady didn't respond, instead holding up two thick books. "You pick," he said.

Desmond frowned. "You only brought two?"

"Dude," Brady said in a deadpanned tone. "We can only read so fast. And I didn't want my dad noticing a whole bunch of books on the spirit world suddenly missing."

Recognizing his friend's forethought, Desmond studied the volumes. One bore a green linen cover, gold embossed lettering and scrollwork across its front. The other looked older, bound in a worn brown leather with its title simply impressed with gold leafing. He recognized the authors of each, if only by name: Theodore Watson for the old, brown one and Marcus Lawrence for the other. If his recollection of all the information his dad fed him about the Warden was correct, Watson's book would be from the 1800s, while Lawrence's would be a century newer.

Desmond took the newer book, sure it would be the easier read. He let Brady use the desk while he rummaged through his bookcase until he found a blank notebook, then swiped a pen from the desk. Dropping onto the small gray couch that sat in front of his TV, he settled in for the start of his studies.

Turning to the back of the book, Desmond checked the index for all the subjects relevant to their research.

Vessels: nothing.

Spirit-beings: nothing.

Veils: a handful of pages.

Desmond jotted down the locations, beginning his search. The thin pages felt flimsy under his fingers, and he turned them all with care. The book was thick—thicker even than some of the novels collected on his built-in shelves. Its margins were narrow, the pages double-columned, and the words small.

Eventually, Desmond found the first entry on Veils: *"The start of our mission began with the most infamous event in our history: the Veil in Amesbury."* The entry went on to tell the condensed story of John William Lawrence and his experience in Amesbury, United Kingdom. A story Desmond knew perfectly well and didn't care to rehash.

After skimming the section and seeing no other reference to Veils there, he moved on to the next location toward the middle of the book. It started in a chapter entitled "The Great Rifts." The promising title piqued Desmond's interest, and he poised his pen, ready to take notes.

*"Our founder's life and discovery in Amesbury not only changed the course of history,"* he read, *"it revealed to us the great purpose of our organization: Protecting the Earth from the Druids and these Veils they'd hoped to control.*

*"For the Christian layman, Veils hold little purpose or significance. We ourselves were blind to their purposes for dozens of generations. Even Lawrence himself didn't fully understand their consequence. It wasn't until the 1600s, with Brigid O'Donnell's defection, that we began to gain an inkling of their purpose. Yet, even Ms. O'Donnell's contribution lacked the heart of the Veils' importance.*

*"Indeed, Veils are the rift between our physical world and the world of the spirit; they are wellsprings of spiritual activity; they make the presence of ghosts and phantoms possible, but is that all? The Druids don't seem to think so. They wield these Veils as conduits of power, as do the Sages of our people, but they also revere them, worshipping them as gods. They sacrifice their individual power to them and commune with them as though they are alive.*

*"Does that not suggest greater importance than we've given them before? Does it not beholden us to understand what power these Veils hold? If these cultists recognize their importance, should we not as well, not for the purpose of worship but of protection? If these Great Rifts in the fabric of our physical reality garner such awe and reverence, can we discount them as mere glimpses into another realm?"*

After the meandering introduction, Desmond began to skim the chapter. It developed into a diatribe of how the Druids worshipped the Veils, what little the Warden knew about them, and why they should study them more rather than providing any *actual* study on them. Clearly, this Lawrence hadn't followed his own suggestion. At least, not in this book.

Desmond scrubbed a hand over his face, turning to Brady. "Find anything?"

Brady raised his head, pieces of his floppy bangs falling onto his forehead. "It's been, like, thirty minutes."

"And . . . ?"

"I've just gotten halfway through the introduction."

Desmond scrunched up his nose. "You're reading it?"

"Well, yeah. It's part of the book."

"No, I mean: You're reading the *book*?" Desmond asked incredulously. "We don't have time for that."

Brady's dark eyebrows pulled together over his hooded eyes. "How else do you want to learn what information they have?"

"Check the index," Desmond instructed.

Brady wasn't impressed. "That'll only tell you small snippets of what *might* be in the books. Reading the whole book gives context. Don't you want to understand what we're reading?"

"I want answers," he retorted. "And if these books don't talk about damaged Veils or spirit-beings and Vessels, then I have no use for them."

Brady tapped his thumb along the edge of the desk. "Did you ever stop to ask: What if we have the wrong terms?"

"What?"

"Come on, Desmond. We both know that terminology has changed over the years—in the regular world and within the Warden. 'Spirit-beings' and 'beasts' were both called 'demons' in the early days. It wasn't until they figured out that the two were not only separate but that demons were completely different entities themselves—not even a part of the side of the spirit world that *we* wield—that the terms changed. Who's to say that in . . ." He paused to glance at the front of his book. "In 1872, the term for Vessel wasn't something completely different?"

With Brady's suggestions swimming in his head, Desmond frowned. "And you think the only way to know for sure is to read these books from cover to cover?"

Despite Brady's shrug, his face gave no signs of uncertainty. "We won't know for sure otherwise."

Desmond let out a dramatic sigh. "Fine." He lifted his book, opening it to the beginning. "Let me know if you find anything interesting."

"Oh, I already have."

Desmond sat up straight, eyes wide.

Brady pointed to the open book beside him. "Did you know that Heinrich Schwarz was best friends with this reverend in Amesbury, and that's why he moved there in the first place?"

Pressing his lips together, Desmond sucked in an annoyed breath through his nose. Count on Brady to find some anecdotal tidbit about some reverend's past to be interesting.

Desmond held his friend's bright-eyed stare with his bored one. "Anything *relevant* to our search," he clarified.

Brady scoffed in good humor and returned to his book.

They lost the rest of their night to deep concentration and complex theology. Brady left the book with Desmond, suggesting he take as much of the "free time" his grounding provided to read it. Desmond agreed, but after making it a mere fifty or so pages through the great tome, he began to question if there was any point to their research at all. It wasn't just the religious mumbo jumbo and grand references to the Warden's creation. He started wondering if their attempts would be in vain.

Even if they learned how to save Cait, would they have the power to do it? It'd been Cait's powers that healed the Veil, not his own. Varon blood or not, Desmond had felt inept after their experience on the island. His arcs of the spirit world weren't even as powerful as Fish's. And none of them had come close to the sort of power Cait so suddenly wielded.

What if Desmond wasn't strong enough to save her or separate her from that creature? Worse, what if her power continued to break free? The block was supposed to stop her connection to the spirit world, keeping the creature from surfacing. It was failing, and that meant time was short. Possibly too short for them to figure out the answer.

Alone in his room, Desmond picked up the book again. He determined to stay up, reading those narrow lines of ink until his eyes closed on their own accord. He *would* figure it out in time. He *would* save Cait. Because if he didn't, he'd lose her for good.

# CHAPTER SEVEN

# William

Age did terrible things to a man. What William once accomplished with minimal effort now took inordinate amounts of discomfort and difficulty. No longer was a night of sleep lost willingly. At forty-seven years of life, the exhaustion fought back with a furious rage that plagued him with an unrelenting headache and a dull pain at the back of his eyes.

William hadn't taken many shifts watching the Veil. As the mayor, he felt it was a part of his responsibilities. However, his brother-in-law, Rick, who manned the shifts per his role as sheriff, insisted that William's ability to uphold the day-to-day routine of Porthaven was far more important than a flexible patrol of the island.

Still, William insisted that Rick put him on the schedule at least once per week.

And so, last night, William went to Aster Island and patrolled with Ben Lavigne and Raymond Edgars. For ten hours, they'd walked the hundred-foot perimeter around the Veil. Through darkness and shadow, they kept their voices hushed and their movements cautious, all on guard since they'd not found any beasts the last two nights.

It was disconcerting, knowing that two beasts were roaming unhindered on the island. Or worse, perhaps they'd slipped past the patrol and onto the mainland. Tethered or not, aggressive or not, it wasn't safe to leave them wandering. Who was to stop someone from coming in and tethering any rogue beasts, using them as a weapon against the people of Porthaven? What if that was their purpose from the start?

No, the missing beasts couldn't be left alone. And that meant the patrol had to continue.

William rubbed a hand over his face, the exhaustion making the muscles in his shoulders and arms feel abnormally frail. He'd never been small or weak. Even as a kid, his broad-shouldered and barrel-chested build granted him a bulkier frame that his peers might've teased him for if it also hadn't made him especially strong—or if his last name hadn't been Simon. But today, it felt as though his age was catching up to him.

The computer screen glared with a pulsating blue-white glow. His eyes screamed in protest as he forced himself to stare at it. He'd swung by the house before coming to the town hall. The long night required a mind-clearing cold shower.

Returning at five that morning, he'd been cautious not to wake Robin, but she was a light sleeper. She'd sat up to greet him, holding out a hand for him to draw near. At her insistence, he'd told her of his evening, brushing down the rumpled back of her light brown hair.

As a young man, he'd admired Robin Edgars from afar. Their paths didn't cross much, her only entering high school the year he'd left. He'd known of her, of course. Her oldest brother, Rick, had been in William's class, and the boys were friends throughout that time. But it wasn't until William had joined Rick and his family to watch his younger brother, Raymond, in his final game on Porthaven High's baseball team that he actually met Robin.

That was the moment he'd fallen in love.

Robin, only fifteen at the time, was far more clever and confident than most girls—even the ones William's age. Of course, he didn't call it love at the time. He called it appreciation, or respect, or some other word that made his two-months-shy-of-nineteen-year-old self not feel strange for finding himself inexplicably drawn to such a young woman. Whatever the truth, William didn't seek out Robin or allow himself to dwell on her. He didn't wait around for her but took a half dozen other girls on dates occasionally to see if they had any potential. None of them did.

Then, Robin turned eighteen, and William, aged twenty-two, remained remarkably single. At which point, he'd asked her out. She'd replied with, "What took you so long?"

William always smiled at those memories. He'd done it that morning while he told her of his night, and he did it again in his office, distracted from his work. Robin had suggested—and that meant outright instructed—that William stay home and get some rest, but he'd foolishly shrugged off the order.

"I have too much work," he'd told her.

And he did.

As the mayor of Porthaven, William had a never-ending list of tasks. He glanced down at the physical manifestation of such to-dos written on a notepad beside his keyboard. Every day, he added more and more checkboxes to that list. A high number of the tasks had to do with the Fisher's Festival, only a handful of weeks away. Contacting vendors, approving the budget for hires, purchases, and rentals, and overseeing tourism were just some of his responsibilities.

Thousands of people visited Porthaven for the Fisher's Festival. They'd become widely known for it, the lighthouse and rocky shoreline an idyllic portrait of the northeast. Porthaven was the sort of place tourists liked to post on their social media, or so William had heard. Robin had suggested that Porthaven hire a social media manager to help develop tourism. William wasn't sold, but that was another item on his ongoing list: Look into social media management.

Beyond that, there were coded tasks that involved the operations of the Warden. William worked two jobs at all times. He was the leader of Porthaven and the leader of the Warden within Porthaven. The second title required him to complete such tasks as reevaluating the Veil patrol with Rick, searching for the second Veil, investigating the damage to the first Veil, visiting Maeve Lewan to check in on her granddaughters, and discussing new ways of researching the spirit world with Ben.

A deep tension pressed against the center of William's forehead. He glanced at the clock on his computer. Ten-thirty, and yet, he'd struggled to focus on any one task all morning.

Perhaps Robin had been right.

William corrected himself. Of course, she'd been right. He was too tired to choose a task, let alone complete one.

Pushing himself back from his desk, William decided that enough was enough. He was calling it a day.

"Mr. Mayor?" The voice of his receptionist came through the intercom.

Massaging the bridge of his nose, William pressed the return button. "Yes, Lori?"

"Fish is here to see you," Lori replied, a nervous edge to her words. "He says it's urgent."

William frowned. Fish was Lori's father-in-law. She'd married into the Warden, which meant she knew the basics, whether she personally chose to participate or not. With her husband on patrol, she was aware that something was wrong in the town. And when Fish said it was urgent, she clearly reasoned that it had something to do with the Veil and the beasts coming out of it.

Forcing himself to clear his aching mind, William pressed the button and replied, "Send him in."

The door to his office opened, and Fischer Lavigne appeared in the doorway. He looked his usual, wind-rumpled self. His silver-brown hair curled messily around his shoulders. "Mornin', William."

"Fischer," William said by way of greeting, gesturing to the chairs across from him.

Fish sat down heavily, his large frame filling the brown leather seat. His sharp blue gaze locked on William's face, but he said nothing.

"Is everything all right on the island?" William asked, taking up Lori's line of reasoning.

"'S far as I know," the lightkeeper replied, his gravelly Maine accent direct.

"And the Veil?"

Fish held up a hand. "Everything is fine, William. That's not why I'm here."

"Lori said it was urgent."

Fish nodded but remained silent. He clasped his hands in front of him, elbows pressed firmly against the arms of his chair. A pensive, hesitant glimmer filled his eyes, which were locked on William.

"What is it?" William prompted.

Settling back into his seat, Fish sighed. "I've thought on it for two days now," he began. "I gave my word, and I've stood by that. But after consideration . . . I feel you ought to know."

William narrowed his gaze on the lightkeeper. "I'm all ears."

With a resolute nod as though encouraging himself, Fish explained. "Three days ago, your son asked a favor of me. Well, really, it was Brady who asked, but it was on Desmond's behalf."

William set a hand on his jaw, listening intently.

"I trust those boys," Fish said, his words as unflinching as his posture. "Desmond may act like a punk, but he's got a good heart. And Brady only goes along with the foolishness because he'd rather be at his side, watching out for him, than let him get into trouble alone. So, when they asked for help, I said yes. I don't regret that, and I don't think I made the wrong choice. I stand by all my actions for the last few days as I stand by the choice to come to you now."

William nodded for him to continue.

"The favor the boys asked of me," the lightkeeper said, "was to help them get onto the island. They intended to go to the Veil on their own. I refused that but offered to go with them as protection. And it's a good thing I did."

A cool tingle broke out at the base of William's neck, his worry rising.

Fish continued, "Desmond wanted to attempt to fix the Veil. He thought he'd have the strength for it because . . . Well, because he's been wielding since he was six."

William felt his jaw slacken.

"He explained that to me the other night," Fish said. "He believed that because of his Varon ancestry and the inheritance the Simon family now carries, he might have the power to fix it. He didn't."

Somehow, none of this news surprised William. He felt he should have suspected it. After all, he'd been an impulsive teen once himself. He'd wielded the spirit world when he shouldn't have. For Desmond, who craved all things off-limits to him, it should have been expected that he'd try wielding the first chance he got.

But at *six*?

And to attempt something so dangerous and impossible as fixing a Veil?

"I appreciate you telling me this—" William began, but Fish cut him off.

"That's not all."

William's expression tightened in confusion and worry. There was more?

Fish leaned forward in his seat. His piercing gaze stood out sharply against his suntanned skin. There was a weight in that stare, an impending doom that William wasn't sure he was ready for.

The lightkeeper spoke, his deep voice blunt. "Are you aware that your son is spending time with the Lewan girl?"

William blinked. Perhaps it was due to his exhaustion, but his brain struggled to process the question. His son . . . spending time with . . . one of the Lewans? Why? When? How?

None of it made sense. William had seen the way Desmond acted with the Lewan girls. He ignored them. *If* he deigned to interact with any of them, it was in a taunting manner. Spending time with one of them . . . That didn't add up.

During William's extended silence, Fish gave a firm nod. "I didn't think so," he muttered.

The fog of denial still clung to William's brain. "He—he knows not to befriend them. Same as the Faulks. As leaders, our family's role is their protection, and we can't allow feelings—"

"It's a bit late for that, William," Fish interjected.

William lifted his head, the truth beginning to settle in. It felt like a rock bulging in his chest. He tried to look back to see the signs he'd missed. He tried to figure out how he'd been so blind to his son's behavior.

"Which one?" William asked, the answer coming to his mind before the question fully left his lungs. "Caitriona?"

Fish's bushy eyebrows rose. "You suspected?"

William shook his head. "Not once."

"Then, how—"

"He won't say her name." William almost laughed at his ignorance. "He'll say Therese's or Genevieve's, but Caitriona? He *always* calls her Lewan."

"Hm."

William felt a chagrined smile come to his lips. "How . . . how bad is it?"

Fish didn't hesitate. "He's in love with her."

William pinched the bridge of his nose. "He told you this?"

"He didn't have to." Fish paused, observing William's discomfort. "But that's hardly our biggest concern."

William met the lightkeeper's direct stare. "What *is*, then?"

Fish told him. He explained how the entirety of Monday night's events had gone down and how Desmond led them out under the false pretense of gathering information while his real intent was to fix the Veil. How Fish had stayed to watch the perimeter while the boys examined the tree. How Cait Lewan had appeared on the island with no apparent clue as to how she'd gotten there. He told him about the twelve beasts and their fight to return them to the spirit world. Then, he told him about Cait's interference, controlling the beasts without struggle and wielding the spirit world despite the block. She'd imposed an amber seal over the tear in the Veil, which explained the missing beasts from the past few nights. And about Desmond's conclusion that Cait was the one to inherit her father's connection to the spirit-being.

William worked to take it all in. He wasn't an angry man in general. His father had been, and he'd sworn never to become like him. So, he processed Fish's words silently, letting his frustrations roll through him for only a minute before allowing them to seep out of him in one long exhale.

"Thank you," William said, meeting Fish's patient stare, "for informing me. I will . . . consider the appropriate way to handle this."

"Whatever she did . . ." the lightkeeper pressed, his gaze adamant. "There may not be beasts coming through anymore, William, but I don't believe for a second that means she *fixed* anything."

William held up a hand. "I will visit the Veil tomorrow to inspect her . . . handiwork. Even if it isn't fixed, hopefully, it can give us more time to figure out our next step."

"And what will happen to her?"

The gruff tone of Fish's voice told William that he held certain expectations—ones of which he didn't approve.

Scratching his jaw, William considered the question. "I'm not sure," he admitted. "It needs to be confirmed before anything is decided."

"She's a kid," he noted.

William's brow furrowed. "I'm aware."

"She doesn't deserve to be a prisoner for something she had no control over."

"I understand your perspective. But we have protocols."

"I don't think your son will take well to those protocols," Fish warned. "And you know he isn't likely to let them pass. Not with how he feels about her."

William frowned in acceptance. "You have a point."

"And, William?"

He looked up.

Fish's sharp features had hardened. "*I* won't let them pass either. She's not an animal to be caged. She's a young woman carrying a burden she was forced to accept."

"I understand," William promised. "And I will do everything in my power to ensure her safety."

"This isn't about safety," Fish argued. "Survival means nothing if you have no will to live."

William shook his head. "Are you suggesting that I let my son have an affair with a Vessel?"

"I'm suggesting," he shot back, gaze fierce, "that you consider the danger of breaking her heart for the sake of your bloodline."

William was silent. He didn't have an answer to that. What could he say? Whatever the feelings between his son and Cait Lewan, they had no future together. They *couldn't* have a future together. Not with the responsibilities of the inheritances that fell to them both. But Fish's warning . . . it had a merit all its own.

The prophecy warned the Warden—they couldn't risk losing the Wolf or his Vessel. They needed her. If William didn't play this carefully, there was a chance that he'd drive her to hate the Warden. And that could lead to the loss of much more than a young woman's safety.

"I understand," William assured him. "And thank you again."

Fish stood, then paused. "One last thing," he said. "When we were on our way to the Veil . . . we overheard a conversation between Brett Varon and Kenneth Greene."

William's chin lifted.

The lightkeeper's tone held both apology and warning. "Brett called Jeremiah Rhader, bringing your leadership into question. I'd expect some uppity representative of the Warden in a matter of days if I were you."

A roar of fury echoed in William's brain. It was all too much. His son wielding behind his back and cavorting with the Lewan girl. The damage to the Veil and the discovery of the Wolf's Vessel. The danger of everything they were facing. And now, his own people were acting against him.

A final, unfelt "thank you" fell from William before Fish left his office. He knew the words came out clipped, but his head hurt, and his blood burned. His gratitude was running dangerously short in supply.

He had too many decisions to make. Too many things were at stake. The Varons were after his job. And Desmond. . . .

William pushed away from his desk. His office walls suffocated him, pressing in with all their demands and responsibilities. He grabbed his jacket, logged off his computer, and pushed out the door, telling Lori he'd be taking the rest of the day off. She wore a worried expression, surely disturbed by her assumptions about Fish's visit and William's terse manner as he left for the day.

But William didn't have time to worry about Lori's fears. He had far bigger issues at hand.

First on the list: What was he going to do about his son?

# Cait

"As we've spent the week overviewing the history of the Fisher's Festival," Penny Davis said, standing behind her desk, "today, we're going to get hands-on and research at the library. I told you that you'll be writing these essays in pairs, so let's get you teamed up and head out to the buses, all right?"

Matt gave Cait a confident grin, assured in their pairing. Yet, Cait didn't feel the fear she normally would at being paired up with one of the other students in the class. Everything had changed in the last four days. And all thanks to the one small, if terrifying, choice to sit with Hunter and his friends at lunch.

Cait was no longer isolated when she walked into school. Of course, she'd had Matt at her side over the last month, but it wasn't the same. He was as much of an outsider as she.

But now?

Now, it was all different.

Matt and his grandpa were still fixing the truck, so Cait, Genni, and he rode to school on their bikes. As they'd locked them at the bike stand that morning, Hunter and Elizabeth walked past, greeting them openly and pausing to wait—actually *wait*—for Cait and Matt to catch up so they could walk through the halls together.

Liz—she preferred to go by Liz, she'd told them—immediately abandoned Hunter to slip to Cait's other side. "I was wondering," she set a hand on Cait's arm, "would you have any recommendations for beginner art supplies? I've been wanting to try my hand at some fan art for my favorite book series, and when Matt mentioned that you sketch, I realized that you would be the perfect person to ask."

Cait readily offered up her favorite products. She didn't often purchase the fancy supplies she might have preferred, but she always asked for them on each birthday and holiday, so she had a handful still in her collection. And she knew that Liz wouldn't have any problem with the cost.

Soon, Scott and Melissa joined them in the classroom, readily hopping into the conversations. It'd taken a little longer, but they'd begun to warm up to Cait, Matt, and even Genni too. Scott found Genni's directness hilarious and Matt's chatter adequately engaging. Melissa, far more soft-spoken than her snarky boyfriend, enjoyed Cait's presence and easy conversation.

So far, neither Cait nor Matt had managed to break Sterling's hard shell, and he avoided even looking at Genni. While Genni took this in stride, Cait fought off her frustration that she hadn't found the opportunity to talk with him about his dreams or the spirit world. Each day, she reminded herself to be patient, sure that it would only be a matter of time.

The rest of the students still held Cait at a distance, watching the developing friendships with wary eyes, but Cait no longer felt the need to hide the second she stepped into the school. For the first time, she felt free. She felt seen without fear of disapproval.

Cait was locked in conversation with Liz and Melissa right up until

Penny stepped up to start the class. She had to hurry to her seat, a wide and strange smile on her lips. She wasn't used to smiling in school. She wasn't used to feeling *happy* in school.

"I'd like to give a note as to how I went about selecting the partners for this assignment," Penny continued, picking up a clipboard from her desk. "In determining each pair, I've observed you all closely to help make my selection. As such, I've chosen to pair you based on whom I've noticed has the least interaction in school."

Matt's expression fell, realizing his expectations were doomed to fail, but Cait found hope rising within her. She looked toward the seat two rows ahead of her, where Sterling sat. While there was a tinge of fear over working with someone she didn't know, her odds of being paired with Sterling had just gone up. And that would provide the exact opportunity she needed to discuss their dreams.

Granted, that also increased the odds for her to be paired with someone like Garrett, Desmond's cousin Miranda, or even Sydney. That thought sent a cold wave of discouragement over her momentary hope.

The rest of the class appeared equally as anxious about the predicament.

Penny stepped around her desk, clipboard tucked against her side. "This assignment is meant to teach you how to work with people you don't know," she explained. "There are times in life when you'll have to set aside differences to get a job done. Whether it's simply because you haven't taken the time to get to know your partner or because you have a prejudice against them, this is your opportunity to learn how to work with *anyone* and to set aside your assumptions about others."

Hunter raised his hand. At Penny's gesture of approval, he spoke in a respectful though incredulous tone. "No offense, but I fail to see what this has to do with history."

Penny smiled. "How many times in our history have individuals had to set aside differences for the greater good? The United States wouldn't exist without men and women who were willing to band together, no matter their differing beliefs and opinions. This is essential training for anyone hoping to help shape the history that the following generations will learn."

That answer squashed all remaining questions.

"Now," Penny brought the clipboard forward, "onto the pairings." She began to read from her list, the students glancing across the room at one another when their names were called.

Matt sighed in disappointment when his name was called along with Brady Lavigne's. "I knew it couldn't happen," he whispered to Cait. "But I'd kinda hoped she'd pair us up anyway."

Though Cait couldn't agree with his hopes—after all, people would *know* Penny Davis was playing favorites if she'd paired her son with his friend—she gave him an appreciative smile.

The smile immediately fell as Penny called out, "Cait Lewan and Desmond Simon."

A cold chill crawled over Cait's scalp, the hum at the back of her mind rising as she instinctively looked across the room. Her eyes met Desmond's. He looked as baffled as she felt.

A disbelieving laugh built in Cait's chest, but she managed to force it down. Of all the people for their teacher to pair them with, it was the most ironic and disappointing thing that could have happened. Penny couldn't know, just as no one knew. Desmond went out of his way to ignore her or even to prove his indifference to Cait in school. It made sense that Penny would think them strangers. Yet, she'd paired the two people who likely knew one another best.

Wisely, Desmond turned away from Cait, muttering something to Brady, who wore a funny smirk.

Cait's heart dropped. She'd been trying so hard to stay away from Desmond. She'd ended things, gaining the distance she needed. Just as she'd begun to grow happy without him, she'd be forced to bring him back into her life.

Penny completed her list of pairings, informing the students that she'd require them to sit together on the short bus ride to the library so they could get to know one another and devise a plan for the essay. The students began to rise, gathering their bags and books. Penny ushered them out into the hall. None of the correct pairs drew together, all of the teens sticking with their typical friends, muttering about the injustice of the pairings.

She heard Sterling grumble to Hunter. "Seriously? She put me with *Garrett*? I'm gonna have to carry the whole thing."

Even Matt complained, stating that Brady was notoriously standoffish and haughty, and he worried about his willingness to work together. "He's got to be the least friendly person in class," he lamented.

But Cait couldn't pay attention. She was too distracted, watching Desmond from a distance. He and Brady were whispering to one another, Garrett loping behind with Whitney at his side. Just a week ago, Cait would have been thrilled with this partnership. Spending time with Desmond publicly was something she'd dreamed of since they were eight and at the burgeoning of their "not-friendship."

Now, Cait only felt panic.

Why him? When she was finally getting her footing without him in her life, why did this have to happen?

Penny led them out the front doors of Porthaven High, a dingy yellow bus awaiting them under the soft blue sky. Their teacher positioned herself as a guard at the doors, making sure that the students boarded in their appropriate pairings. Most students ambled dejectedly along with their new partners, slowly making their way onto the bus. Cait lingered near the back, Hunter and Liz nearby.

Liz gave Cait's jacket sleeve a friendly tug. "Sorry you got paired with Desmond," she whispered. "But honestly, he's not that bad of a guy. And he knows more about Porthaven than anyone else."

"*Almost* anyone else," Hunter corrected defensively.

Liz ignored him. "He'll make a good partner."

"If you can put up with his arrogance," he grumbled.

Cait passed Liz the smallest, grateful smile. She couldn't quite bring herself to speak. Her heart thudded as Penny called for her, Desmond waiting at the bus's steps. While Matt, Hunter, and Liz watched with pitying looks, Cait approached, keeping her head down.

The cedar and musk scent of Desmond's cologne spiked the hum that raced through her as she passed. She bounded up the bus steps, desperate to escape him, yet knowing it would only be a temporary reprieve. What was she going to say? Not only had they never gone this long without speaking or texting, they'd yet to address the disaster of Monday night. They couldn't very well ignore that, could they?

Cait sat down at the back of the bus, as far from the rest of the students as possible. She made herself small, leaning against the walls and wrapping her arms around her backpack. When Desmond sat beside her, dropping his backpack on the ground between his legs, she realized that no amount of scrunching would keep her clear of his presence. His knee grazed hers, and their shoulders brushed.

Desmond didn't look at her but glared at any students who dared attempt to sit near them. Brady had conveniently chosen a row near the front, Matt glancing over his shoulder at them. Only once the bus doors were shut and the driver put the vehicle in gear did Desmond settle back in his seat.

"So," he said, voice low and words measured, "you're friends with Hunter now."

Out of the corner of her eye, Cait scanned him. After a week of silence—after their horrifying experience on Monday—*that* was what he chose to say to her. She couldn't believe it. He hadn't even attempted smoothing over the situation with a "Hey, Monday night was weird, right?" He'd simply ignored it as though it never happened at all.

Rather than vent her frustration, Cait crossed her arms and slumped deeper into the vinyl seat. "I guess so," she murmured.

Desmond's hand clenched between them on the bench. "Strange choice."

Cait shrugged. "It made plenty of sense to me."

The bus pulled onto the main road, and the dip down of the curb caused the whole vehicle to wobble. Desmond grabbed the seat in front of them to steady himself, but he still bumped into her. The vibration of the hum spiked within Cait, and she slid herself farther against the side of the bus, hugging her backpack tighter.

Desmond scoffed.

Cait's head involuntarily turned to look at him. His jaw was set while he kept his eyes on the front of the bus. His hand still rested on the back of the seat, fingers tapping an irritated rhythm.

Cait bristled. What did he have to be irritated about? *He'd* ghosted *her*. *He* was the one who needed to explain things. *He* was the one who'd lied.

"What?" Cait heard herself demand.

Desmond hardly spared a glance her way. "Nothing."

"Don't treat me like I'm stupid," she said quietly. "Unlike everyone else on this bus, I know when you're lying."

He rolled his eyes. "And unlike everyone else on this bus, dear ol' teach got our pairing wrong. Think I should tell her?"

"No." The word practically flew out of Cait.

Desmond's eyebrows rose. "Why not? I thought you didn't want anything to do with me."

"I never—" Cait cut herself off. It didn't matter what she'd never said. It's how things needed to be.

Trying and failing to scoot farther away in her seat, Cait rephrased her words. "Mrs. Davis paired us together because she and the rest of the school believe we're strangers," she reminded him. "And it'd be best that they continued to think that."

Desmond didn't respond, his quiet frustration stretching across the short distance between them. She wondered if anyone else on the bus could feel their tension. To her, it was as palpable as the vehicle around them.

Several seconds passed, confirming Desmond's silence. Cait turned to the window. They drove through Porthaven's downtown, past the church with its Gothic spires and arched stained glass windows. Businesses lined the streets with planters of greenery and hearty flowers on the sidewalks before them. Small groupings of people walked in and out of the colorful red, yellow, blue, and green buildings. Some tourists lingered from the end of the autumn rush. Most of the trees had already lost their leaves, and shortly, the streets and shops would be bare for the few weeks before the Fisher's Festival. Then, they'd brim with life once more—almost too many people to fit within their cottage-like confines.

"You're wrong."

Cait whipped around to stare at Desmond. He kept his gaze ahead, expression blank. The words were spoken so quietly that she questioned if she'd heard them at all. And considering how little emotion showed on his face, it made her even more unsure.

Then, Desmond turned, meeting her stare. His dark eyes bore heavy emotion within them. They impressed their weight onto her. But he said nothing as the bus rumbled into the library parking lot a moment later. When it rolled to a stop, Desmond broke eye contact, reaching for his backpack.

Cait blinked. She was wrong? About what? She thought back to her last words, stating that the "not-friends" they'd once been should remain a secret. He'd been the one to insist on that for the last ten years. Why would he change his mind about their public status now?

The students all left the confines of the bus, ambling awkwardly with their partners to the library. Like the church, it featured an antique façade comprised of rich red brick, turreted spires, and a large circular window at its peak. Naked-branched trees grew across the lawn, their fallen leaves covering the drying grass with a blanket of canary yellow, vermilion, and rusty orange.

The circulation desk welcomed the students into the library. Two women manned the desk—one middle-aged and demure, the other silver-haired and grizzled. Mrs. Davis greeted them, and the librarians assured the students that should they need help finding anything, they'd be happy to assist.

Several tall windows lined the walls, letting the sun reflect brightly off the cream-tiled floors. Despite the many renovations in Porthaven recently, the library seemed left to its aged devices. The wooden shelves were well-worn, the pendant lights hanging above their heads casting an unflattering yellow pallor. An open second story wound around the top of the building, thousands of heavily used books lying in wait on the shelves.

Rese was the reader in their family, but Cait remembered many fond trips to the library with her nan and sisters when she was little. The musty smell lingered in her memories, causing her muscles to instinctively relax as Penny guided them farther into the library. She gave them final instructions and then set them free.

Many students moved straight to the bookcases, seeking out their research. But Desmond drifted toward the study desks, picking the one farthest from the others in a shadowy alcove that really wasn't conducive to good research. He dropped his backpack in one of the four seats around the circular table.

Cait watched as he plopped down next to it. "You planning to join me, or what?" he asked.

Seeing no better option, Cait pulled the straps of her backpack free. "Shouldn't we go find the books we need before everyone else takes them?"

"I don't need them," Desmond said matter-of-factly. "I probably know more about Porthaven than anything those books will offer."

"But we have to use reference material," she argued. "That's what Mrs. Davis said. We need three sources for our—"

"Lewan," Desmond cut her off. "Sit down."

Caught between the urge to defy him and the instinct to do as instructed, Cait hesitated.

Desmond sighed. "We haven't even discussed what the focus of the essay is yet, Caity." He spoke quietly so that only she could hear the softness in his tone. "Please, sit down."

Reluctantly, she took the seat across from him.

"Thanks," he said.

She gave a singular, sharp nod. "What are your ideas?"

"About what?"

"The paper."

"Oh, that." He waved a hand through the air. "Don't worry about that. I'll write it tonight."

Cait furrowed her brow. "What?"

He shrugged. "It'll take two hours tops."

"That's . . ." Cait stared at him, baffled. "That's not right. I need to do my part."

"It's not necessary."

"Yes, it is!" Cait's voice sounded unusually high-pitched to her own ears. She took a deep breath, forcing herself to calm down. "Desmond, the assignment is for us to write this essay *together*. I need to have some part in it to earn whatever grade we receive."

Desmond eyed her, one arm draped lazily over the back of his seat. "You're going to make us work for this, aren't you?" He heaved a dramatic sigh. "Fine, fine. I was planning to focus on the Festival of 1896, which, incidentally, was canceled due to a horrible storm that killed nineteen residents, including my great-great-great uncle, Martin. He's the reason we Simons became the leaders here, so I feel it's a particularly potent homage to him. What are your thoughts?"

The bland smile Desmond gave her after his spiel made Cait roll her eyes. "You're the worst," she muttered, opening her notebook to jot down his idea.

"I know," Desmond replied. He sat forward in his seat. "Why are you *really* spending time with Hunter and his yuppies?"

Cait stopped mid-word to look up at him. She couldn't tell why he was asking. It couldn't be out of jealousy. He'd done nothing to try to win back her friendship—*not*-friendship, she amended.

She returned to her note-taking. "Why would it matter to you?" she asked.

"Because Hunter's a twerp," he grumbled.

"Actually," she kept writing, "he's very pleasant and kind. He invited Matt to join the basketball team on their trip this weekend just so that he could meet more people."

"What a saint." He leaned more heavily on the table, descending into her eyeline. "Cait, he's dangerous."

Her hand jerked, making the end of her E longer than it needed to be. "What?"

"Hunter's family is in direct opposition to mine," he said. "It's their goal to ruin us and take back the town. And they'll do underhanded things to accomplish that, trust me."

Cait narrowed her eyes. "Have you ever *tried* to be friends with Hunter? Have you even had one conversation with him where you didn't view him as your enemy?"

Desmond's face scrunched up with an incredulous look. "No."

"Maybe you should," she suggested, then went back to writing. When she'd finished the final sentence, she looked back up at him. "Where do we find more information about this canceled Festival?"

With a disgruntled look, Desmond tapped an erratic rhythm on the tabletop. "You don't really believe that they're your friends, do you?"

The question felt like a slap in the face.

Cait drew her shoulders back. "Is it so impossible that people could like me?"

"No." His eyes narrowed. "It's impossible that you'd *want* to be friends with someone like Hunter."

"And why's that?"

"Because you don't want attention, Caity," he said. "You don't want people staring at you. You want to hide from them. You want them to leave you alone so that you can live your life without worrying about what they think of you."

Cait's fingers gripped her pencil so tightly that it began to hurt.

"Same as me," Desmond concluded.

Tossing the pencil onto her notebook, Cait tried to ignore the truth of his accusation. She didn't like the way the students had stared at her the last few days. They'd done it before, but it was different now. With Hunter and Liz as friends, the other students had begun to survey Cait with a new glimmer in their eyes. A look that questioned if friendship with her was of great value, suggesting they might take a risk on the outsider.

It scared Cait. What if all those students started talking to her? What if they wanted to get to know her? Friendship with Matt had already disrupted her life so much. She'd lost Desmond to it. And while she knew that was necessary, she already questioned what else she'd have to give up to permit more people into her life.

"Why are you spending time with him?" Desmond pressed. "What do you get out of it?"

Unsure how he knew she was after something, Cait heard herself mutter, "Answers."

A pinch of some emotion—could it be hurt?—drew Desmond's eyebrows together. "Why didn't you come to me?"

"Why would I?" Cait demanded in a furious whisper. "After everything that happened . . . You haven't said a word to me all week, staring at me like I'm some sort of freak. You left me to question my sanity and, worse, to be afraid of myself."

Desmond's expression grew desperate as he set a hand to his chest. "Caity, I told you I'd explain."

"No, you didn't."

"Yes, I did!" he insisted. "Didn't you see my note?"

Cait froze. "What note?"

"The—the note," he stuttered. "I left it in your sketchbook."

Cait looked down at her backpack, resting on the floor beside her. She hadn't used the sketchbook all week since the beasts hadn't reappeared in her dreams. And her mind had been too cluttered and fearful to even consider sketching the new tree and the figures that haunted her now.

Reaching down, Cait retrieved the book. "Where?" she demanded, dropping it onto the table.

"By the picture of me," he told her. As she flipped to the page, he continued. "I left it open to be sure you saw it. That's why I never said anything. I thought . . ."

Cait found the sketch as he paused, and she pressed the book to lie flat. At the top of the page, a note with sloped handwriting promised, *"I'll explain everything - Des."* She looked up to meet Desmond's tight expression.

"Well, I thought if you hadn't asked for answers, then you didn't want them," he concluded.

A twin wash of shame and relief flooded Cait's whole body. Her muscles felt both relaxed and exhausted, like she'd been holding back a storm, and now she was free to let it fall. This whole time, it'd been her fault. She hadn't thought to look for a note from Desmond, and she'd assumed the worst.

"I'm sorry," Cait whispered.

Desmond shook his head, his expression turning adamant. "No—no, Cait, *I'm* sorry. I should have checked to be sure you were okay."

"Why? You thought I was ignoring you." Cait dropped her head into her hands, embarrassed. "I *was* ignoring you."

"Only because you thought I was an ass," he argued.

She looked up at him sharply, finding him grinning.

"Which I am," he added. "In case you weren't aware."

Cait gripped her pencil, ready to throw it at him. But then she remembered they were in public, so she just let herself smile. A real, full smile, knowing that Desmond hadn't abandoned her.

The thought made the expression drop, her gut twisting.

He needed to let her go. Just as she needed to let him go. It was the best course for them both, the surest way to sanity in the years to come.

"Cait," Desmond called under his breath. "I'll tell you whatever you want to know. I promise."

Answers. That's what he was promising her. And she'd told herself she would find them.

But he was the very person she *couldn't* get them from.

Desmond wasn't safe for her. Being around him meant putting herself in danger. Time with Desmond meant time for her to convince herself she didn't have to move on. And she couldn't risk that.

Looking over her shoulder, Cait surveyed the students dispersed through the library. Brady and Matt sat at a table on the other side of the room. Matt chattered, eyes on a thick book before him, while Brady leaned back in his chair, his gaze occasionally flickering toward their shadowy alcove. Hunter held a stack of books, his partner, Gabrielle, pulling another from the shelf. Sterling looked about ready to hurl his whole backpack at Garrett while the burly jock flicked through one of their books with an utterly bemused expression on his face.

Cait's dreams of the tree and Sterling filtered through her mind. The memory of the power she'd wielded tingled in her fingers. The figure that stood in the shadows taunted her. And the questions piled ever higher.

When she turned back to look at Desmond, the hum rumbled encouragingly. She stared into his dark eyes, wondering what it would hurt. She needed answers. He could give them to her. They could meet at the cove one last time, couldn't they? To talk it all through. He could help her understand just how she could protect herself and how she could protect her family.

Cait's heart stirred at Desmond's adamant expression. He *wanted* to help her.

But then she hardened her heart, knowing that even one more moment spent with him would break her even further.

"I appreciate the offer," Cait said, voice flat.

Desmond blinked at her, his face falling. "But you're not gonna take it?"

With a single shake of her head, Cait tightened her resolve.

Desmond's jaw clenched. He returned to tapping on the tabletop, his expression turning hard and his gaze shuttering. "Right."

Cait pushed back her chair, determined to find some space from him. "I'm going to look for some references," she stated. "You said 1876?"

"Ninety-six," he corrected but didn't move to get up with her.

Grateful, Cait nodded and left him sitting alone in the alcove.

# Desmond

The rest of the school day, Desmond had to check the scowl on his face.

She'd rejected him, outright rejected his offer to help, to give her the answers she sought. He'd promised to explain everything, and she shoved his honesty in his face. All because he was too much of a coward to have been the friend she'd needed years ago.

Desmond supposed he couldn't blame Cait. It wasn't exactly fair to her, constantly coming and going from her life. She had a right to be angry with him.

But Desmond was done with that. He didn't want to be the nonexistent friend—there one minute and gone the next. He didn't want to keep secrets from her anymore. He was ready to forgo the expectations of his family and his future. At last, he was ready to let all that go, if only to be with her.

Yet, all the while, she'd already decided to let *him* go.

And now, he'd lost her for good.

While the other guys went to basketball practice, Desmond headed for the town hall. His sour mood lasted him through the two hours of his internship. Most of his time was spent on data entry, inputting receipts and expenses for the upcoming Fisher's Festival. The rote task allowed his mind to drift, ruminating on everything he'd lost. Ten years of secret meetups, ten years of comfort and hidden friendship. Ten years of wishes and hopes. All of them dashed upon the cliffsides of the cove.

He'd known this was coming, of course. This was always how it would have ended, with heartbreak and disappointment. Even with all his research, with all his attempts to fix the situation, he'd known they never could become anything. He'd deluded himself into hoping that if he could remove the spirit-being from her, he could be with her. But that was just as much of a fantasy as the novels he read.

These melancholy thoughts followed Desmond home. His mom had a ladies' meeting at the church that night, so she'd left a note on the fridge for the Simon men to eat leftovers for dinner. He'd not seen his dad the entire day, which wasn't a surprise. The Fisher's Festival kept William busier than usual this time of year, and Desmond often went an entire day without interaction with his dad.

Desmond went to his room to divest himself of his backpack, jacket, and boots. Then, he darted downstairs to scrounge the fridge. He perused the stacks of glass containers, none of the previous week's meals catching his fancy.

He scrunched his nose at the broccoli-cheddar casserole just as a voice spoke behind him. "Are you looking for something in particular?"

Desmond jumped, whirling around to find William standing on the far side of the island. He muttered a low curse, his heart beating double-time. "Don't sneak up on a guy like that."

The faintest glimmer of a smile lifted the corner of William's mouth. He pointed to the fridge. "There's nothing in there," he said.

"I think Mom would disagree," Desmond said, tossing a foul grimace at the stacks of leftovers.

William shrugged. "I've already ordered pizza."

"You did?"

"It'll be here in . . ." William checked his watch. "About five minutes."

The refrigerator bell dinged at Desmond irritably. He let the door swing closed with a *thwump*. "Works for me," he said, moving to the cabinet for paper plates.

Due to his dad's pleasant demeanor and offering of pizza, Desmond knew to be skeptical. With only five minutes until delivery, that meant William had placed his order at least fifteen minutes ago. As Desmond hadn't heard the garage or any doors open or close, William had been at home all that time.

His dad was *never* home before him.

"So," Desmond said, dropping the plates on the island between them. "You left work early?"

William was turned away, opening a cabinet at the far end of the kitchen. He retrieved two glasses from the bottom shelf and then reached up to the top, pulling down a bottle of liquor. "I had some things to take care of," he explained.

Warily, Desmond watched as William set the glasses on the island. They clinked against the marble before the bottle of The Glenlivet Single Malt Scotch landed with a gentle *clonk*. He removed the cap. "Care to join me?"

Alarm bells whirred in Desmond's head. "You've never offered me a drink," he said.

William poured two fingers of the liquor into each of the tumblers. "That hasn't stopped you before," he noted. "Here."

Desmond hesitantly accepted the glass. Was this some sort of test? Or maybe it was a dream. Maybe he'd come home, sat on his bed to remove his boots, and passed out without realizing it.

Holding out his own tumbler, William offered a toast. "To pizza."

Keeping a keen eye on his dad, Desmond repeated the toast, tapping the rims of their glasses. He took a cautious sip. His dad was right—he'd snuck some of The Glenlivet plenty of times. He couldn't say he had a particular taste for scotch. He'd always found it a little too close to leather, in his personal opinion. Still, he liked drinking it because it made him feel more like a grown-up. And he figured if he could get used to the taste, then he'd eventually earn some respect from the men around him.

William set his glass on the counter, a relaxed smile on his face. He still wore his workwear: black slacks and a white button up, though the top two buttons were undone, and he'd removed his tie and jacket. The undone look didn't suit him. It was as unnatural as a fish on land.

Just as the silence between them grew particularly uncomfortable, the doorbell rang. While William went to retrieve the pizza, Desmond considered disappearing up to his room. His dad's suspicious behavior made him antsy. It was his one chance to slip away, and the loss of dinner was almost worth it.

But Desmond's unhealthy curiosity for answers and hunger for greasy pepperoni and gooey cheese kept him in place.

William returned and dropped two pizza boxes onto the counter. They both filled their paper plates until they overflowed.

"Well," Desmond said, raising his glass in a salute, "guess I'll eat in my room."

"Or," William cut in, "we could eat in here. Together."

Desmond felt his eye twitch. Just as he suspected. "I've got some homework."

"That you'll put off until you finish your meal anyway." He gestured to the small table at the back of the kitchen. "Take ten minutes and eat with me."

William didn't wait for a response but moved to the eat-in dining set. White lace curtains framed the large picture window at the outer edge. The wrought iron and glass table in front of it was more of a decoration than a practical piece of furnishing. They so rarely shared a meal at this table that Desmond often wondered as to the point of it.

"Did you have a good day?" William asked, already seated as Desmond approached.

Slowly taking the chair on the opposite side, Desmond bit back a sharp retort. Over the past month, his dad had made it clear that he wanted to repair the relationship between them. He'd said that he wanted them to work together. Was this another of his attempts to buddy up to him?

Swallowing his first bite of pizza, Desmond decided to play along. "Yeah, it was fine."

"What did you do?"

"I went to school," he replied, then realized he ought to check his snark if he wanted to suss out his dad's odd behavior. "Actually, we went on a trip to the library. Our history teacher has us doing this essay about the Fisher's Festival."

William tipped his chin up. "Yes, your mother mentioned signing a permission slip for that."

Without knowing what to add, Desmond took another bite of pizza. A glob of cheese and sauce dropped onto his plate.

After a sip of his scotch, William's expression shifted dramatically as though a thought struck him. "I had an interesting visit with Fish on Wednesday," he said.

Desmond's throat closed, and he nearly choked on the bite. He managed to get it down before coughing out, "Fish visited you?"

"He did."

Sure that he'd already blown his cover—not that there was much cover left if Fish had told William *anything*—Desmond did his best to rein in his emotions anyway. He composed himself with a sip of scotch that burned down into his chest. "Is everything all right with the Veil?" he asked.

"It's the same as before," William said, then paused. "More or less."

"That's good."

"It is."

Desmond picked at the crust of his pizza.

William swirled the scotch in his tumbler. "How long have you been seeing Caitriona Lewan?"

An instant tingle of panic curled across Desmond's scalp. His stomach twisted, all taste for pizza gone.

He couldn't believe it. He'd trusted Fish, and the lightkeeper had outed them.

But Desmond had been lying his entire life. He could talk his way out of this.

Raising his glass nonchalantly, Desmond schooled his expression thoughtfully. "She and her family moved here, what was it? Eleven—twelve years ago?" He lifted his shoulder in a shrug and took a sip. "Guess I've seen her around town and at school since then."

Something like pride lifted the corner of William's mouth. "You're a natural," he said. "I never taught you to lie like that, and yet, you picked it up all on your own."

"I'm not sure what you're talking about, Dad."

William didn't even pretend to believe him. "How long have you been involved with Cait Lewan?" he restated the question. "Romantically or otherwise."

Desmond fought the urge to clench his jaw. Instead, he adopted his wryest smirk. "I'm not involved with Lewan in any way. I'm smarter than that."

"Are you?" His dad cocked an eyebrow as though it was merely an intriguing conversation rather than an interrogation. "How interesting. Fischer was under the impression that you have quite the attachment to the girl. Seeing as how you've taken it upon yourself to . . . what, exactly? Save her from the spirit-being?"

Three thoughts flew through Desmond's head in rapid succession. First, he should walk away. His dad couldn't interrogate him if he wasn't in the room. Second, there was no point in lying about the situation anymore. Fish had ratted them out, and now his dad knew who carried the Wolf. Third, now his dad *knew* who carried the Wolf. This meant that Cait was in danger of losing everything because of Desmond.

Tossing back the remainder of his scotch, Desmond let it trickle down into his chest, burning in his veins. He set the tumbler in front of his dad. "If we're gonna have this conversation, I'm gonna need another of those."

William took the glass and set it to the side. "I'm afraid you'll have to remain reasonably sober for this."

"Some father-son bonding experience," Desmond muttered, then tossed a hand flippantly. "Yeah, fine. I've hung out with Cait a time or two. What of it?"

"How long have you known that she's the chosen Vessel?"

Desmond ran through the best options of how to answer. He could do what came naturally, deflecting and telling half-truths to mitigate as much damage as possible. But with his dad's newfound information, there seemed little reason for that anymore.

"For sure?" Desmond counted back the days. "About a week ago."

"And you chose not to tell me?" William looked almost hurt.

Desmond scoffed. "Of course I did."

"Mind explaining why that should be your expected response?"

"Oh, come on. I don't trust you any more than you trust me. Why would I tell you?"

"Because it is our job, yours and mine, to protect this town and the spirit world," William said, almost in accusation. "Caitriona Lewan and that creature attached to her are a part of *both* those things."

"And what about protecting Cait?" Desmond shot back. "Where does that factor into this all-important job of ours?"

William's shoulders drew back. "So," he muttered, "you are in love with her."

An embarrassed laugh worked its way out of Desmond. That was a truth he refused to admit even now. "I just happen to have a conscience that finds child imprisonment abhorrent."

William leaned against the glass tabletop. "You do understand that she's in danger, just being what she is, don't you? We keep Vessels contained for their own safety. Even their grandmother consented to their blocks and their living arrangements. Maeve knows this is for their best. Same as the Faulks."

"For their best?" Desmond scoffed. "Don't tell me you care about their best. You just care about keeping them tame."

"You don't know what you're talking about."

"What are you planning to do, huh?" Desmond demanded. "Now that you know about Cait, what do you plan to do about her?"

William hesitated, then said, "I'll follow protocol."

"Meaning you'll double down on the block, move her in with some Warden family for extra surveillance, and then marry her off to the first wacko who offers to sacrifice himself for the greater good."

A strange look of desperation came to William's gaze. "What else am I supposed to do, Desmond? This is part of the job, whether I like it or not. We have to ensure that she's safe and that the Wolf is controlled. That means securing the bloodline, one way or another."

"Then, choose the other way," Desmond insisted. "Let her have some say over what happens to her."

"It's not that simple."

"Isn't it?" Desmond's voice caught over the question. "She's a kid, Dad. Same as me. It isn't fair of you to force her to grow up before she's ready."

A flash of understanding warmed William's dark eyes. He sighed, sitting back in his chair, shoulders slumping.

Desmond had never seen his dad look so defeated. But then, to be fair, Desmond had never been this honest with his dad. The realization of what he'd just admitted hit him at that moment. Perhaps he'd said it about Cait, but he'd also revealed the truth behind his impetuous and selfish behavior.

He was a kid, and he wasn't ready to grow up.

He was too young, too inexperienced, and too scared to take on the responsibilities of his inheritance.

Same as Cait.

"You can't do this to her," Desmond heard himself whisper. "Cait's already terrified that she's becoming possessed by a demon. If you force this on her—if you turn her into a prisoner—she'll be even more convinced of it. And she'll be afraid of herself for the rest of her life."

William pinched the bridge of his nose. "Those damn rumors," he muttered. He shook his head, an angry glint in his eyes. "I told my father they were a bad idea, but he wouldn't listen. He said we needed the town to keep the family at arm's length and that it'd be dangerous for the girls to assimilate too quickly without properly fearing their past."

Desmond scowled at the thought.

William picked up his scotch. "I told him to shove it."

Looking up at his dad, Desmond's eyes went wide. "You did?"

He tipped the tumbler in acknowledgment. "We're not so different, you and I."

Though Desmond still questioned that assessment, he was beginning to see the validity of it.

"How long have you been seeing her, Desmond?"

The dark gazes of father and son locked.

The question felt less like a challenge and more like an invitation for Desmond to open up to him. William wanted to hear him out. He'd already admitted to wanting an improved relationship with him, unlike the one he'd had with his own father.

Running a finger along the rim of his paper plate, Desmond stared down at the congealing pizza slices. "Ten years, three months, and . . ." he did a quick calculation of the current date, "twenty-four days."

William stared at him, an eyebrow cocked in disbelief.

"Roughly," Desmond muttered.

"Ten years?"

The inflection of his dad's words made Desmond squirm. It was clear what he believed about that time between Cait and him. He felt obligated to correct the assumption. "It's never been—we've never been. . . ." The words crumbled before Desmond could finish them.

He sighed and tried again. "We're not dating."

William scanned him thoughtfully. "But you love her?"

Unable to find words, Desmond felt his chin dip in admittance.

William let out a heavy exhale that sounded more tired than disappointed. "You can't be with her," he warned. "You know that, right?"

Desmond nodded.

"Fish told me that she wielded the spirit world?"

"She did."

William hummed in thought. "That means her block is failing."

"That's what I thought," Desmond agreed.

"Which means it's only a matter of time," his dad said, his tone taking on a contemplative tilt. "The Wolf will emerge, and whether I want to or not, the Warden will have to secure her."

Desmond looked up, a mere fraction of hope left in him. "What if we can stop it?" he asked.

William gave him an apologetic look. "It's prophesied, Desmond. After Owen Lewan's death, the next Vessel was marked as our salvation or our demise."

"Yeah, at her great sacrifice," he challenged.

William frowned. "You read the whole thing?"

"No thanks to you."

His dad let out a dry chuckle. "Don't be too upset. I was going to show it to you after your eighteenth birthday. I do recognize the importance of youth, whether you think so or not."

Desmond didn't know how to respond, so he returned to his earlier statement. "If we let the Wolf truly take hold, that would mean turning Cait into a sacrifice," he said. "I won't let that happen."

"It's not a matter of *if* the Wolf will be freed, Desmond. It's simply a question of *when*."

"Not if we separate them," he argued.

An instant look of worry overcame William's expression. "That's impossible."

"Is it?" Desmond demanded. "We thought damaged Veils and beasts without a summoner were impossible, too, a month ago."

"Don't pin your hopes on the futile."

Desmond threw his hands in the air. "We don't know half of what's possible with the spirit world. How do we know that separating a Vessel from its spirit-being is any less possible than however Cait freaking manifested on the island out of nowhere?"

"Yes, Fish mentioned that anomaly as well."

"Exactly!" Desmond felt himself getting desperate. He had to convince his dad to give him time. If he could free Cait, then he could change everything. If he could free her, he could be with her. "I can't give up, Dad. I have to believe there's a way to save her."

Running a hand over his jaw, William stared at the tabletop. He was quiet for so long that Desmond thought he might not answer at all. Then, abruptly, he looked up.

"Tell me everything you know," William ordered. "About Caitriona Lewan, about her family, about her connection to the spirit world—all of it. Everything you've learned over the past ten years, I want to know."

An instant surge of worry passed through Desmond. It must have manifested on his face because William held up a placating hand. "I'm not asking you to break her confidence," his dad assured him. "I'm asking that you let me help you."

"Help me?" Desmond repeated.

William gave him a firm nod, and their dark eyes locked together. "You are my son," he said. "No matter what, I will do everything I can to protect you. And if you're going to risk your life to save this girl, then I'll be damned if I don't help you."

Desmond couldn't believe it. He'd been so sure that going to his dad for help was the last thing he should do. His entire life, the Warden had come before him. It was hard to believe that, suddenly, things had changed.

Whether Desmond trusted him or not, William now knew everything.

There was no chance of hiding from him anymore. And he had to admit that having the leader of the Warden at his disposal wasn't an altogether bad thing, even if his dad's end goal was suspect.

Holding his adamant stare, Desmond felt guilty for questioning him. Whatever William's hopes for his future, Desmond did not doubt the sincerity of his dad's offer of help. It was plain in his expression—he wanted to see his son safe and happy.

"All right," Desmond agreed. "I'll tell you."

Relief loosened the muscles of William's face. "Good," he said, then gestured to Desmond's plate. "Finish your pizza first. Then, we'll talk in my office."

Desmond readily bit into one of the now-cold slices, rising to pop the other two into the microwave.

William stood with him, waiting for his turn to reheat his food. "Another thing," he said, reaching into the pocket of his slacks. He pulled out a set of keys—Desmond's keys. "Your grounding is officially lifted."

Desmond grinned, taking them. "Seriously?"

"Seriously." William returned the smile. "I called your coach earlier to let him know you'll rejoin the team tomorrow. Needless to say, he was thrilled."

Desmond spun the keys around his finger. He didn't care about being back on the team, but he did care about regaining his freedom.

He smiled. "You know," he looked up at his dad as the microwave beeped, "you may not be so bad after all."

# Rese

The *whir* of the coffee grinder filled the air. Rese had to lean forward, straining to hear the teen's order across the counter. She hated working Saturday mornings. Monday through Friday consisted of the regular businessmen and women of town coming in for their usual morning pick-me-ups. But when school was out, the kids of Porthaven flocked to the dingy coffee shop.

Adults were so much easier to deal with than teenagers. Rese had always thought so—even when she was a teen herself.

Her internal critic reminded her that at nineteen, *she* was still a teen as well.

But Rese hadn't felt like a child since her parents died. At seven years old, she'd become the parent, even if Maeve was their legal guardian. Their nan was a wonderful caregiver, but she wasn't much of a leader. Her broken heart had seen to that. She'd raised her granddaughters with distant guidance, putting silly rules like "no dating until sixteen" in place as a means of reassuring herself that she was doing enough.

So, Rese had stepped up. She'd seen what her sisters needed and had determined to provide it for them.

Ringing up the teenager, Rese accepted his cash and set the cup on the order line. Her manager was the only worker on shift with her. Marcy Yates had opened the coffee shop thirty years ago, and it showed—on both the woman and the building. Gray streaked her mousy brown hair, the thick mane full of curlicues that stuck out like a poodle's fur. It matched the Pindler Curly fabric pillows that graced the rusty brown corduroy benches. Tiny gold-framed glasses perched on Marcy's nose, a pearl-studded eyeglass chain strung around her neck. That, too, matched the pearled vinyl tabletops.

The worst of Marcy's crimes against the modern world was the age-worn houndstooth blazer she insisted on wearing that matched the checkerboard flooring and inevitably clashed with whatever outfit she'd chosen for the day.

Despite Marcy's offenses, Rese had a strange fondness for the woman. She felt protective of her and her antiquated ways. Marcy was kind to everyone. She always spoke like she was whispering, the tiny rasp in her voice giving it character. She said things like "Isn't that nice?" and "Aren't you a dear?" She kept a chalkboard by the register to write out inspiring notes. Today, it read, *"Be the sunshine in someone's dreary day."*

Though Rese would jump at the opportunity to update the paneled walls and seashell pendant lights, she thought she'd keep that little chalkboard.

The minute Rese graduated from Porthaven High last spring, she'd gone to Marcy, begging her for a job. The middle-aged woman tapped a finger to her lips, surveyed her shop, then gave a sunbright smile to Rese and said, "Why, I think I could find a place for you, deary."

Rese had been thrilled. Coffee reminded her of her mum. Every morning, Sabine Lewan would make herself a *café au lait* and sit at the dining room table to read her Bible in the golden dawn light. Spending each day surrounded by the scent of coffee made Rese feel as though she were constantly in her mum's embrace.

The gentle chime of the coffee shop's bell drew Rese's gaze. Three more teens walked in. She had to suppress a scowl of recognition. They were Desmond Simon's friends. The big, blond lout, Garrett, led the way, talking loudly. His girlfriend, Whitney, followed, their fingers intertwined. Whitney stood out in Porthaven with her mahogany brown skin and lush natural curls. Rese had always wondered what she saw in the great lummox at her side. She'd seemed too smart for a boy like him.

Last to enter was perhaps Rese's second-least-favorite Porthavenian. Brady Lavigne nearly filled the doorway with his broad shoulders and muscled build. While Garrett kept talking, the reverend's son gave the busy shop a scan. He took in the crowded tables and chairs, face expressionless.

Maybe that was what Rese didn't like about Brady. He seemed incapable of emotion. He was taciturn and standoffish. And he was best friends with Desmond, which was the greatest sin Rese could think of.

In his scan, Brady's gaze fell on Rese at the register. His expression didn't alter, and she didn't bother to smile. The last time she'd been around the boy had been at Ryan and Liz's party. Their one interaction the whole night? Brady insulted her in front of Ryan.

Now, it seemed he held no more goodwill toward her than she did toward him.

Brady nudged Garrett's arm, then gestured to a small, open table wedged between two massive parties. While he headed for the table, Garrett and Whitney approached the register.

"Hiya," Whitney greeted with a polite smile.

Donning her professionalism, Rese beat the girl's grin. She could feel her whole face soften as she asked, "What can I getcha?"

Whitney pursed her lips, and her dark eyes drifted to the board. "What's 'The Great Pumpkin Latte'?" she asked.

Rese thought the answer was rather obvious. "It's a latte, hot or iced, with vanilla, cinnamon, and pumpkin," she explained.

"Whoa!" Garrett gasped, eyes going wide. "That sounds freakin' fantastic!"

Slowly, Whitney began to nod. "Yeah, I think I'll have one too."

"Okay, so two Great Pumpkins. Hot?" At their nods, she wrote the shorthand on two paper cups. "Anything else?"

Whitney looked up at Garrett, giving him the initiative. "Brade told me to get 'im whatever," he said with a shrug. "So, I guess, make that three Great Pumpkins."

"Cool." Rese added another to-go cup to the line, tendered the sale, and happily accepted the couple's departure.

While Marcy busily made drinks and delivered them to their tables, Rese kept at her job. More and more high school boys wound up in the coffee shop. She heard several of them talking about their basketball game later that day. The coach himself came in, ordering a drink and talking to Marcy. He informed her that he'd told the team to meet at the shop before they headed off for the mainland.

"I find," Coach Favreau said, "that the boys do better when they're buzzing on sugar and caffeine. Sure, it's a nuisance on the drive, but it gets them hyped for the game. And really, that's what I call a winning start."

The doorbell chimed again, and Rese found herself tensing once more. Desmond walked in, giving the room a quick scan before finding his comrades. He didn't even glance toward the register. He simply walked over and took the singular open seat in the building.

While Marcy and the coach continued their talk, Rese found herself glaring at the table. She'd thought about confronting Cait about Monday night. She'd fully intended on questioning her sister's sanity. Of all people, why Desmond Simon? But Rese couldn't figure out how to bring it up.

What was she supposed to say? *"Hey, Cait, so I saw that you got blackout drunk with Desmond on Monday night. You really shouldn't do stuff like that."*

Somehow, Rese didn't think that would go over well. So, she kept quiet, internally debating how she could protect her sister from the Simon boy's dangerous influence.

At another chime, Rese turned back to the door. Her expression softened, and she let her troubled thoughts drift away as Ryan approached the register. His straw blond hair looked darker than usual in the dim light of the shop. "Hey, Reese's Puff," he said teasingly.

Rese tipped her brow disapprovingly. "I told you not to call me that," she said.

He set his hands on the counter, leaning forward. "But it's so cute," he said, then winked. "Like you."

Rese couldn't help laughing at the absurd line. Ryan wasn't the cleverest of guys, but he was amusing and mostly sincere. "What are you doing here?" she asked.

"Maybe I came to see my girlfriend."

She gave him a playfully bored stare. "You don't drink coffee. And you haven't come to visit me once."

"Guilty." Ryan glanced over at the gathering of the basketball team. "Coach asked me to wish the guys well."

Rese frowned. "Why? You aren't actually friends with any of them, are you?"

"Nah, but I'm sort of a big deal, what with leading the Tridents to State three years in a row." He said it like she should be impressed.

As Rese didn't care about sports, she wasn't.

"Since it's the first game of the season," Ryan continued, "Coach thought my presence would be a morale boost."

"So, this is, like, a public service," she said dryly.

He grinned. "Something like that."

"How magnanimous of you."

Ryan looked as though he were processing what "magnanimous" meant. Then, he gave her a sly grin. "Well, Coach did tell me it'd be here," he said. "And since we haven't gotten to go out all week . . . knowing I'd see you may have swayed my decision."

Rese pressed her lips together around a smile. Her heart didn't stutter, nor did she get butterflies when Ryan was around, but she did enjoy his attention. What girl wouldn't? He was handsome, popular, and rich. Everything a social climber could want. And he matched every one of her requirements for a husband.

Leaning across the counter, Rese kissed his cheek. "That would be adorable," she teased, "if we didn't already have plans for tonight."

He grinned brightly. "I'm always adorable," he said.

She slapped his arm, seeing a teen waiting in his shadow. "Go rally the troops. I've got work to do."

Once Ryan headed toward the basketball crowd, Rese rang up the next kid. As Marcy was still off talking to some customers, Rese started making the drink herself. She took her time, carefully creating the design of a basketball in the foam. The rush appeared to have died down now. Or perhaps no one else wanted to enter a coffee shop filled with teen boys.

Rese set the boy's drink on the counter, calling out his name. Out of her peripheral vision, she saw someone step up to the register. "Excuse me," a voice murmured.

Rese turned to find Brady standing there, coffee cup in hand. Her chest flared with heat as she stared into his rich brown eyes. *"Try not to get plastered."* That was the last thing he'd said to her. *"Ryan's not known for his restraint."* Like she was some kind of lush. As though she were easy.

Bearing herself up, Rese scanned him with a bored glare. "Can I help you?" she asked placidly.

"Yeah, uh—" Brady brandished his cup. "Does this have cinnamon in it?"

With a glance at the cup, Rese pointed up to the board. "It's the seasonal special," she explained. "Your friend ordered it."

"So . . ." His thick eyebrows drew together. "It *does* have cinnamon?"

"Yes."

Brady nodded. "I thought so. Uh, sorry—could I get another drink?"

Rese surveyed him as he set the cup on the counter. "You got a problem with cinnamon?"

He held her stare. "I'm allergic to it."

Rese's expression must have shown her panic because he held up a hand. "Not, like, deathly allergic," he hurried to say. "Just, like, my throat starts to itch, and I break out in hives, kind of allergic."

"Oh."

"Yeah."

Rese took the cup, glancing over her shoulder to find Marcy had moved on to talk with some old friends at the back of the shop. "I'll, uh—" She turned back to Brady. "I'll make you something else. What would you like?"

"Just the drip is fine."

She raised an eyebrow, moving for a new cup. "I *do* have the skill to make something more complicated," she said.

Brady's ever-impassive face broke its impassivity as he gave her a sly grin. "I don't doubt your ability," he promised. "I just want drip coffee."

"Your friend paid for a specialty latte. Drip is, like, a buck."

He shrugged. "Maybe I'm just a cheap date."

Rese huffed, half in amusement and half in confusion. She turned away to pour his coffee, not entirely sure whether he was flirting with her or simply being weird.

When she glanced over her shoulder to ask if he wanted room for cream, he was staring at the pastry case with pointed fixation, making it clear that he was intentionally *not* watching her. He jumped when she asked her question, then replied, "Black is fine."

Returning to the counter with the piping hot coffee, she couldn't help herself. "So, you really don't doubt my ability. You're just a boring person in general?"

Brady hesitated, confusion etched into a crease on his brow. Rese could admit he was cute with his serious stare and chiseled jawline. Quite frankly, he was cuter than Ryan. Maybe it was because Ryan *knew* he was attractive. But Brady had that same masculine height and sports-trained muscle as Ryan, plus that dark hair that flopped lazily onto his forehead, making him sort of mysteriously handsome—and he didn't seem to notice any of it.

If he weren't so young and friends with Desmond, she might have considered him a candidate for her future. The Lavigne name was even more revered than the Greenes'. She knew that the Warden in Porthaven regarded his family as imperative to the safety of their people. Marriage to a Lavigne would mean far more than simply protection. It would mean she could hold a degree of power.

Unfortunately, no Lavigne men met her candidacy guidelines.

Brady's mouth turned up at the corner. "You know," he began, "you've got a way of making people feel decidedly inferior."

Rese grabbed a lid for the paper cup. "Only when they deserve it," she replied, then smiled at him. "Enjoy your coffee."

She slid the cup toward him.

He ignored it. "And I deserve it because . . . ?" he prompted.

Rese frowned, caught off guard. People never fought back against her cutting remarks. Not that she had to use them often. But she'd found that a clever insult now and then was a good way to get people to properly respect her.

Yet, here Brady stood, stoically waiting for her response.

Faced with the question, Rese couldn't really say why Brady deserved it. Because he was callous? Because he'd insulted her at the party? Because he was friends with Desmond?

The last one rang the most true. Yes, it was because of Desmond. It was because she related Brady to his friend, and Desmond was messing with her sister.

Rese raised her chin. "You deserve it because you and your friends don't care about anyone or anything but yourselves," she spat under her breath, thinking that was the end of it. But as she swung away, dismissing him from her presence, his response stopped her in her tracks.

"Says the girl dating Ryan Greene."

She whirled back and glared at him.

His stoic expression gave nothing away. "There's irony for you," he said, then added, "Thanks for the coffee."

Rese's hand shot out, landing heavily on the lid before he could take the cup away. She didn't know why, but the words leaped out of her. "Tell your friend to stay away from my sister," she hissed.

A flinch gave away Brady's surprise.

Rese released the cup, but hearing his scoff held her in place. "What?" she demanded.

Brady watched her coolly. "I'm gonna go out on a limb and guess that neither of them told you."

She just stared back at him.

"Right." He crossed his arms casually as though settling in for a conversation that Rese had no interest in joining. "First, you're smart enough to know I can't control anything Desmond does. Second, I happen to think they're good for each other."

Rese opened her mouth to protest, but he kept going. "Third, if either of you would take two minutes to drop your acts, you'd find that you and Desmond are actually pretty much the same person." He paused, scanned her, and shrugged. "Aside from the whole you being a girl and him being a guy thing."

Baffled, Rese found herself gaping at him. She snapped her jaw shut. "I am *nothing* like that prick."

"Really?" Brady grinned knowingly. "You graduated with a four-point-oh, right? So will Desmond. Yet, neither of you likes people to know how hard you work to get those grades. You dress fancy and wear tons of makeup to make people think you're shallower than you are. Obviously, Desmond's not quite the same there, but he wears expensive, brand-name stuff for the same reason. Also, you act indifferent and haughty because you don't want people to know how much you care or how much it scares you that you care. Once again, Desmond's the same."

Rese found her breath caught in her chest, at a complete loss as to how he knew these things about her. Or that he could ascribe them to Desmond as well.

Lifting the coffee cup, Brady saluted her with it. "Maybe if you spent your time with someone a little more discerning than Ryan Greene, you'd know that. Have a nice day."

And he walked away.

Rese felt frozen in place. None of his words made sense. There was no way that Brady Lavigne knew her that well. Or that his comparisons were correct either. She and Desmond were as opposite as two people could get. She wouldn't hate him so much otherwise.

And what was that nonsense about Cait and Desmond being good for one another?

If anyone had a way of making people feel inferior, it was Brady. Rese had never felt so insignificant in her life.

Before she could comprehend much more, Coach Favreau called his team together to get on the bus. The coffee shop roared with the sound of young men. She watched absentmindedly as Matt Davis walked out with Hunter, Scott, and Sterling. She hadn't even noticed the boy entering the building.

Desmond blew past the counter with his posse in tow. Brady didn't so much as glance her way.

Rese chewed on her bottom lip. He was wrong. She wasn't like Desmond. She wasn't afraid of people discovering how much she cared. Everything she did was to prove just how much she *did* care. She was dating Ryan because she cared about her sisters' futures. She dressed perfectly because she cared to make a good impression. She pretended to be shallow because she wanted people to underestimate her so they didn't get in the way of following through with her plan to keep the Warden from confining whichever of them had inherited the monster—which turned out to be Cait.

Everything she did was because she wanted to protect her sister.

Ryan appeared at the register once more. "You okay, Reese's Puff?"

Flinching out of her stupor, Rese forced her eyes away from the door. "Oh, yeah." She plastered a smile on her face and brushed the thought aside. "Just happy to see them go. Teen boys are obnoxious."

He smirked, then motioned to the door. "I've gotta get going too. Pick you up at seven?"

"Sounds good."

Ryan leaned across to give her a peck on the lips, then winked as he drew back. "Mm. I'm looking forward to it," he said suggestively.

Rese returned his smile, though she didn't feel it at all. She watched as the door shut behind him.

*"Maybe if you spent your time with someone more discerning than Ryan Greene, you'd know that."* Her mind stuck again on Brady's words.

She wasn't like Desmond. She wasn't afraid of caring. She was afraid of failing.

Rese grabbed a rag to wipe down the counter and decided on her new course. She'd thought marrying a son of the founding families would be enough. Now, she knew it wouldn't. It was her job to protect her sisters. It was her job to make sure they were safe. And if she didn't find some way to get Cait released from carrying the Wolf, she would fail.

First things first, she needed to figure out how to set her sister free.

# CHAPTER ELEVEN

# William

The Lewan house was quaint, though worn down. Its soft blue siding and dirty white trim could have been charming if the Warden had taken better care of it.

William always felt guilty for the state of the Lewan residence. There was only so much room in the town's budget for repairs and housing costs. They already supplemented so much of the Lewan ladies' lives. Maeve worked part-time doing bookkeeping, but she had three granddaughters and a house to care for. Her meager income couldn't cover the cost of a full exterior paint job. Or fixing the numerous issues of a century-old house.

Stepping out of his car, William moved to the back door. He glanced around the dingy yard. In the frigid Maine autumn, the maple had shed all its leaves, and what little landscaping there was had withered as well. The door to the shed hung off-kilter. The padlock hooked through the latch remained unlocked.

William stepped onto the closed-in back porch and knocked on the kitchen door. He'd been to the Lewan residence many times over the past dozen years. Yet, this time, it was as though he had new eyes.

This wasn't just the home of the Lewans. This was the home of Caitriona, the girl his son loved.

William swallowed down the discomfort of the thought. After his conversation with Fish, he'd concluded that if he'd meant what he said to Desmond all those weeks ago—if he wanted to fix their relationship, if he wanted to work alongside him for the whole of his career—then he couldn't alienate his son. He couldn't be the leader of the Warden. He needed to be Desmond's dad.

And that meant finding some way to help his son.

Now that he'd gotten Desmond to open up to him, William had a renewed sense of purpose. He was still focused on fixing the Veil on Aster Island. He was still searching for the second Veil hidden somewhere on the rest of the peninsula. But more importantly, he was seeking a way to save Caitriona Lewan from the prophecy of Corva. Whether that meant removing the spirit-being from her or not.

Maeve opened the kitchen door with a nervously pleasant smile. He'd called, letting her know that he intended to come by. She welcomed him in and offered him a seat at their rickety table, where tea and a smattering of store-bought baked goods waited.

"Sorry," Maeve said, her thick Irish accent filtering each word. "I didn't have time to make anything proper."

William waved off her apology. "I didn't give you much time to prepare."

She tipped her head in acceptance. "Yeh said yeh have questions?"

"I do." William settled into the narrow chair, unbuttoning his suit jacket. It stretched uncomfortably across his shoulders. He'd never liked wearing suits, but it was ingrained in him from his father's teaching. "We've had a situation arise with the Veil—nothing serious," he reassured her upon the worried expression that instantly crossed her face. "Just something we're looking into."

"I'm not sure how I can help with that."

"I was hoping you could tell me—" He held her gaze to gently emphasize the importance of the conversation. "Do you remember the Veil in Bushmills?"

Slowly, Maeve stirred a splash of cream into her tea. "No," she said softly. "I was not . . ."

She stopped, let the spoon rest along the side of her teacup, then looked out the window. Her red hair caught the low lamplight. In the overcast morning, she'd turned on the overhead light, though only one bulb seemed to be working. William made an internal note to purchase more light bulbs.

Maeve turned back to him with a sad smile. "Did yeh know that it came to Owen through my family?" she said. "The McCarthy bloodline is broken and twisted but dates back to the early settlement in Bushmills. We can track our family directly to Whalen, did yeh know that?"

William had known that. The Warden made sure to inform him and his father of the Lewan family's history when they'd moved the girls and their grandmother to the town. The McCarthys weren't of Caillín Whalen's direct bloodline, but that of his brother's. When the Warden had lost the Wolf's Vessel without an heir, the spirit-being went free for more than three hundred years—with devastating consequences. Which was another reason they followed such strict protocols in Porthaven.

William kept his knowledge to himself, allowing her to continue her story.

"There were generations of incompatibility," she said. "But even if there hadn't been, we knew to stay away from the Causeway. That's where the Veil was. None of us was willing to risk it. Not until Owen . . ."

Maeve sighed, her eyes glimmering with memories. "My son was impetuous as a boy," she said. "He was fearless. And he went searching when I told him not to."

"He became the first Vessel in centuries," William noted.

"He did."

"But you didn't learn what all that entailed?"

Maeve's shoulders straightened. "I didn't care to. The spirit world is dangerous, especially for my family. It got many of our ancestors killed. It got my son killed. Why should I want anything to do with it?"

William could understand her reaction, though he felt it was missing key information. "So, you wouldn't happen to know what form the Veil took in Bushmills?" he asked.

Her brow furrowed. "As I said, it was at the Giant's Causeway. I believe it was attached to the ocean, or perhaps the stones there."

"Mm."

"If yeh . . ." Maeve paused, running a finger along the rim of her teacup. "If yeh want to know more, I'd suggest yeh talk to the reverend there. Reverend Cunningham was a bit of a mentor to Owen, especially during those first few years. Though he would be quite old now, so he might have retired."

William nodded, the idea sinking in. Why hadn't he considered that himself? Just as Ben knew almost everything about the Warden in Porthaven, the reverend in Bushmills would likely have plenty of information regarding the Lewans' past as well as the spirit-being and the Veil connected to them.

"I think I'll do that," he said, preparing to rise. "Thank you for your help, Mrs. Lewan."

"Anytime," she said with a smile that didn't quite reach her eyes.

William hesitated. He'd hoped to see Caitriona while he was there, but he didn't want to ask to see her specifically. It might tip Maeve off to which of her granddaughters bore her son's affliction.

Looking for some excuse, William remembered that Maeve had once made the comment about Cait fixing things around the house. "I noticed that there was some damage to your shed," he said. "I wanted to take a closer look and make a list of repairs that need doing. I believe you said that one of your granddaughters is good at making fixes?"

"Cait," Maeve confirmed.

"Could I speak with her? I thought she might have more improvements to add to the list."

Maeve's lips formed an apologetic O. "She's not home at the moment," she said. "She took our dog on a walk, and she's bound to stay out for—"

As though summoned by their talk, a bark and the *whir* of a bike sounded from outside. They turned to the window, catching a glimpse of Cait and their terrier coming to a stop by the shed.

Maeve looked up at William, amused. "It's yer lucky day," she said. "She's normally gone for hours."

Wondering if these long walks of hers were the occasions that Cait and Desmond used to meet up, William thanked Maeve for her time, then stepped onto the back porch. He moved across the lawn just as Cait reemerged from storing her bike in the shed. She glanced up the driveway at his car before catching sight of him. Her eyes went wide, and her gait stuttered.

William adopted his most unassuming smile. "Good morning," he called, motioning to the house. "I was just talking with your grandmother."

Cait shuffled on the gravel drive, the terrier trotting on ahead of her to the porch. He slipped past the screen door just before it shut.

"Um—" Cait tucked some hair behind her ear. "That's. . . ." She didn't seem to know what it was.

Knowing he likely intimidated the poor girl, William eased his posture. "I was just about to leave, but I noticed that your shed could use some help."

Cait glanced at the door, which hung askew.

"And I was wondering if there are any other repairs to be made."

"Oh." Cait chewed on her bottom lip. "Yeah. There are."

William gestured to the shed once more. "Would you show me?"

"Most of the repairs are in the house," she said.

"That's all right. You can show me the shed and give me a list of the rest."

Nervously, Cait turned to lead him. William kept a healthy distance between them, not wanting to spook her any more than she already was. He eyed the girl's back. She kept her shoulders hunched, as though trying to make herself smaller. If anyone had asked him in the past, he wouldn't have thought it possible for his son to choose a girl so unassuming. But then, he supposed Cait Lewan's withdrawn nature might be due to fear.

He wondered who the true Caitriona was.

"Uh, like you saw, the shed's door is falling off the hinge," Cait said, pointing to the damage. "There's also a hole in the ceiling, but it's small, so I've got a bucket that catches the drip. But the window is broken, so . . ."

"It sounds like you just need a new shed," William said, surveying the building.

Cait let out a small scoff-laugh. "That'd be too expensive."

A surge of guilt cut through William. He remembered a conversation with Desmond weeks ago. *"We live in a newly renovated house while they pass down their clothes."* His son was right. They were hypocrites. And while William couldn't legally siphon more money from Porthaven's reserves, he could buy the Lewans a new shed out of his own funds.

"I'll see what I can do." William turned to look down at Cait. "Could you write up a list of the other repairs the house needs?"

Cait nodded but remained silent, clearly not believing that the task would amount to anything.

"When you finish it," William said, "you can give it to Desmond."

Cait froze, her expression blank.

William held her sharp gaze unflinchingly. "I wanted to tell you, Caitriona," he lowered his voice to be sure no one else would hear, "that I'm sorry."

She blinked.

"Twelve years ago, my father made some decisions that I didn't agree with," he told her. "But unfortunately . . . I wasn't brave enough to counter his orders. Not then, nor when I took office myself."

Cait shifted farther away from him.

William dipped his head penitently. "I'm sorry that I didn't have the courage to do what I knew was right. But I want to promise you something now." He didn't release her gaze, hoping his own revealed the truth within. "As the leader of the Warden, it's my job to protect the spirit world and follow certain protocols to ensure its safety."

A surge of frightened understanding passed through her gaze.

William's heart pinched for her. "As Desmond's father," he added, "it's my job to ignore all of that to ensure *his* safety. His happiness."

Her lips parted, and her breaths came out shallow. He'd frightened her, but he would set her at ease.

"No matter what," William continued, "I will protect my son. And now, that means protecting you too."

Cait's brows drew together. "Desmond and I aren't—"

"I know."

Desmond had already told him about Cait's decision to part ways with his son. And while William could see no future for Cait and Desmond, that didn't mean he wouldn't try to find one for them.

He took a step forward, pressing his point. "We will find a way. I promise you that."

A long silence drew out between them. Cait eyed him warily. She wrapped her fingers around the hem of her jacket, looking as though she was struggling to find words. But at last, she whispered, "I don't think you understand, Mayor Simon. Your son and I . . . We're strangers—no, not even strangers. We're nothing."

There was anger in her stare then, a long-suppressed thing that rumbled out of her like a growl. "And that's all we'll ever be."

Without giving him a chance to respond, Cait hurried past William, racing up the porch steps and into the house.

He stood on the gravel driveway for several seconds, the cold breeze nipping at his skin. He could feel the tension of the frown that creased his brow. There was no mistaking the source of her anger, her hurt. Ten years, three months, and twenty-four—now, twenty-five days.

Over ten years of "nothing" had grown into the most damaging "something." And just as Desmond was gaining the courage to do something about it, Cait had given them up.

William sighed and moved toward his car. He might have failed in his role of father for the first eighteen years of his son's life, but he wouldn't fail now. No matter the cost, William would find a way to fix this. He would find the answers to the damaged and second Veils, he would protect Cait's secret, and he would find a way—come hell or high water, William would find a way to save her life.

For Desmond's sake.

# CHAPTER TWELVE

# Cait

Cait wasn't sure what to make of the conversation with William Simon. He seemed to know more than he should, but she couldn't fathom that Desmond had actually spoken about them to his dad. He hated his dad. She'd always known that.

Yet, why would William ever think she and Desmond had formed any relationship at all? Why would he make such pointed promises? It didn't make any sense.

And it didn't change Cait's determination.

She'd gone to the cove that morning as a final farewell. It wasn't safe to return there, not as long as Desmond might take a chance and show up, hoping to see her. So, she'd risked it that morning, trusting that his grounding and their awkward experience at school would keep him away.

Cait sat by the log, and, for the first time that week, she sketched. She let her strange new dream come to life on the page. She drew the tree, first in its original form that night on the island and then as it appeared in her dream. Comparing the two images, she wondered at the split in its bark. What could have caused something like that?

Next, she moved on to the raven. She sketched its feathers with care, giving them the same silky quality they carried in her dreams. Something about the bird scared Cait. And she didn't think it had only to do with the fact that its appearance marked the start of all the recent trouble in her life. There was something more, something she couldn't identify that frightened her.

Finally, Cait drew the shadowed figure that hung back in the trees. Her mind lingered on the hidden person. Was it someone she knew? The redhead was a stranger, so maybe this figure would be too. But what about Sterling? Why was he in the dream?

Cait had no answers. And when she went to bed that night, she had the same dream again.

The following morning, the Lewan ladies prepared to attend church in their usual chaotic state. With only one bathroom, the endeavor was filled with lots of shouting and shoving between Rese and Genni, lots of Maeve fussing and pleading with them to get along, and lots of Cait holing up in her room to wait out the drama. She applied her makeup and tied back her hair before staring into her closet for several long seconds.

Their nan always required them to dress up for church. Nothing fancy—they couldn't afford anything but secondhand pieces at best—but something a little nicer than a t-shirt and threadbare jeans. For Cait, that often meant a hand-me-down blouse from Rese, her "nice" pair of jeans, and the one set of patent leather flats she owned.

However, after noticing the way Desmond responded to her appearance a handful of Sundays ago, Cait had begun to pay more attention to her clothing. She'd found herself choosing the prettier and more showy pieces Rese had offered her. Cait had even dug out a box of hand-me-downs that neither she nor Genni had chosen because they were too frilly, floral, or feminine for their tastes.

Cait stared at the collection of blush pink, lavender, and baby blue blouses at her disposal, wondering what had gotten into her. Why had she ever thought it was a good idea to try catching Desmond's attention that way? She knew better than to hope for anything with him. And yet, she'd allowed herself to change the way she dressed all to . . . all to what?

For the first time, Cait genuinely asked herself: What had she hoped to gain? What did she think dressing prettily for Desmond would do for her? Did she think he'd forget all the obstacles in their way, ignore all the warnings he'd given, and fall in love with her?

Shaking her head, Cait abandoned the loveliest tops to select one of her older blouses—a dull, sage green one that she'd always worried gave her pale skin a jaundiced tint. She threw on a gray cardigan to ward off the chilly autumnal air and looked in the mirror. *That* was the Cait Lewan she recognized. The wallflower no one would bother giving a second glance.

Feeling settled in her familiar fashion, Cait waited for the rest of her family to ready themselves. She sat on the couch, scratching Red's wiry fur as he snuggled against her side. A soft drizzle dampened the world outside the windows, casting a gray haze through the house. It reminded her of Ireland, where chilly rain often pattered the wooden shingled roof of their cottage.

The four Lewans piled into their rusty old sedan, setting out for downtown. Cait stared out the window, lost in her thoughts about their previous life. She wondered what their lives would be like today if their parents were still alive. She knew her da and mum would have explained whatever their nan and the Warden were hiding from them now. They would have told her and her sisters about the curse, explaining what it really meant and how it'd really come to pass.

Instead of Cait having to sneak around, desperate for information, she'd know the truth. She would understand what this demon wanted of their family.

These thoughts plagued Cait all through the morning, even as Matt tried to tell her about the basketball game. She managed to smile and nod as he talked about all the new students he'd gotten to meet and the game-winning shot made by Hunter.

"Coach Favreau even said I could join as a ball boy for the rest of the season," he said.

Distractedly, Cait congratulated him. She didn't care about basketball or the students of Porthaven High. She just wanted the answers that she knew the leadership of their town was hiding.

During the whole church service, Cait surveyed the large crowd. Seated at the back of the building, she had to look past the majority of the parishioners to see the founding families at the front. The dim light of the overcast day through the stained glass windows fought with the yellow glow of the sconces that lined the walls. The warm light caught on Liz's dirty blonde hair, making it appear bronzed. The Greene family sat next to the Varons, Hunter and Liz seated side by side. The extensive lineage of both families stretched out in the rows behind them on the right side of the church.

On the opposite side sat the Edgars, Lavigne, and Simon families. Cait intentionally kept herself from seeking out Desmond in the front row. She could hear the soft rumble of his presence, the hum tingling at the base of her skull. He and Brady always sat in front together, Brady taking notes while Desmond made snide remarks.

Once, Desmond told Cait that he sometimes felt guilty about his inability to focus during service. *"It's just so . . . boring,"* he'd lamented. *"How's anyone supposed to pay attention?"*

Cait hadn't bothered to tell him that his struggle with distraction was likely because he didn't *want* to pay attention. After ten years of revealing their secrets to one another, she'd learned that when Desmond set his mind to something, he never failed to accomplish it. And if he truly wanted to learn from the sermons, he'd find a way.

Instead of telling him the truth—that he feared the person being a responsible, dedicated Christian would force him to become and what he'd have to give up—she let him pretend that his guilt was about distraction. And she, too, pretended because if he became the man he was supposed to be, she would be one of the things he'd have to give up.

Now, Cait regretted her cowardice. She should have been honest with him years ago. They should have said goodbye and relinquished their damaging relationship. It would have been easier on them both.

A handful of rows ahead of the Lewans, Cait caught sight of the Faulk family. Timothy, light-haired and equally light-complexioned, contrasted heavily with his wife and son. Sahila and Sterling shared thick, dark hair and rich brown skin. It was just the three of them now that Sterling's grandfather had passed away.

Though Cait had no aunts or uncles, and therefore no cousins, on either side of her family, at least she had her sisters. She glanced sidelong at Rese, who sat on the other side of Genni. Yes, even on the days when she fought with one of them, she was thankful to have her sisters.

Cait wondered if Sterling ever felt lonely. Despite his friendship with Hunter, he still kept to himself. He was quiet and reserved—a lot like her. But did that mean that he felt alone too?

The service finally ended after the chapel's grand ceilings reverberated with the final prayer of the reverend and the churchgoers. Maeve and Penny began conversing, and Rese drifted off to find Ryan. Matt immediately began asking Cait about her Saturday, apologizing for leaving her alone. Genni piped up, saying, "Cait doesn't mind being alone. And besides, she hung out with me."

"Oh, good." Matt gave a little sigh of relief as though Cait was hopeless without someone to keep her company. "What did you guys do?"

Genni told him about the board game they'd played. Through it all, Cait remained distracted. The hum tugged at her senses, attempting to draw her attention to Desmond at the front. It surged from time to time, drawing her involuntary gaze, which she immediately redirected toward Sterling. Even if he hadn't taken to her joining his friend group quite yet, she still looked for every opportunity to talk with him.

But after the third glance, he wasn't there.

Cait blinked, then looked to the front, where Hunter stood with Liz, Scott, and Melissa.

Sterling was notably not with them either.

A strange sense of desperation shot through her as she scanned the church. His parents still stood by their pew, chatting with several of the townspeople around them, somber and conciliatory expressions on their faces. Their son had slipped away to who knew where.

Then, Cait saw him.

At the far side of Porthaven Chapel, Sterling slipped through the side door. Alone.

A sprig of hope burst to life in Cait's chest. "I, uh—" she began, interrupting Matt and Genni mid-conversation. "I'll be right back."

"Where're you going?" Genni asked, her nose wrinkled.

Cait sent her a disparaging look. "To the bathroom," she muttered the lie as though embarrassed to say it in front of Matt.

Appeased, Genni let her slip away.

Cait moved to follow Sterling out the side door, winding her way around the pews and people easily. She pushed through the heavy wooden door and into the misty midmorning. Wishing she'd brought her rain jacket, she tugged her cardigan closer around her, crossing her arms against the greeting of the cold wind.

Scanning the gray landscape around her, Cait caught sight of Sterling leaning against the graveyard fence. He wore his dark hair pulled back in a low knot, some strands hanging loose around his face. She watched as he pulled a hand from the pocket of his tan corduroy jacket. He attached his headphones to his cell, thumb brushing over the screen to select music.

Though Cait worried she might interrupt some private moment, she moved toward him before he could get the second headphone in. She called his name, hurrying to close the gap. Sterling looked up, a furrow on his brow. She couldn't tell whether he was confused or annoyed. She chose not to care.

"Hey," Cait greeted, coming to a stop next to him. "Do you have a second?"

Sterling's dark eyes narrowed. He draped the headphones around his neck with a sigh. "I suppose."

"I just have a quick question," Cait said, hoping she didn't sound as desperate as she felt. "If you don't mind."

Indifference ruled Sterling's face as he stared at her.

Realizing she wouldn't get a direct reply, Cait tucked a section of dampening hair behind her ear. Now that she was here, she didn't know how to approach the question. She couldn't blurt out what she really wanted to know; specifically, was his family like hers?

But what *did* she say? How did you begin that kind of conversation?

"Do you—" Cait stopped. She was holding her chin dipped under Sterling's direct stare, but then she realized that was the wrong approach. For her whole life in Porthaven, she'd cowered to avoid the ire of those around her. But with Sterling, she knew she couldn't maintain her shrinking manner.

Straightening up, Cait started again. "The other day, I heard you mention your dreams to Hunter."

Sterling's bushy eyebrows drew together.

"You said you'd had the same dream two nights in a row," she continued. "So had I. Except now it's been a week."

Sterling turned away from her. He stared at the chapel for a lingering second. "Your boyfriend put you up to this?" he asked.

Cait's face pinched with confusion. She knew that the kids at school gossiped. She'd heard many of them laughing about her and Matt's relationship. What she couldn't figure out was why Sterling would think Matt would care about their dreams.

"Matt and I aren't—"

"I'm not talking about Matt," Sterling interrupted.

His dark gaze locked with Cait's as her whole body stalled.

He gave her a humorless smirk. "Of all people, you know what it's like—being the outsider. We see what no one else can because they're too busy focusing on how people perceive *them*. You and me? We catch the little things they can't. Like the way Simon looks directly at you every chance he gets."

Cait blanched.

"Don't worry." Sterling crossed his arms, leaning heavily against the fence. "No one else knows. For now, at least."

Unsure if he was threatening her, Cait shook her head. "He's . . ." The words stuck in her throat, coming out unevenly. "He's not my boyfriend."

"Keep telling yourself that." Sterling tipped his chin up. "Here's the deal, Cait. You keep whatever you think you know about my dreams to yourself, and no one will have reason to suspect your screwed-up relationship with that prick. Got it?"

Cait gaped at him. He *was* threatening her. In fact, he glared at her with unrestrained contempt.

Well, he wasn't the only angry one.

Cait could feel heat rising in her chest and along her neck. She imagined her cheeks were blazing red despite the cold droplets of rain that speckled them. She was tired of being ignored and having her questions smothered. And she'd get her answers, one way or another.

"Why are you in my dream?" she demanded.

Sterling's expression pinched with confusion for only a second. Then, he scoffed and began to step away.

Cait stepped into his path.

He glared at her. "Ask your boyfriend."

"First of all," Cait stepped closer, her words a fierce hiss, "he is not my boyfriend. We aren't even friends. And whatever you *think* you see between us isn't real."

The corner of Sterling's mouth tipped up as though amused by her denial.

"Second," Cait pointed a finger at her chest, "maybe you should consider befriending the one person in this town who understands you."

"You don't know the first thing about me."

Cait raised her eyebrows. "We outsiders see things others can't," she said, using his words against him. "I know as much about you as you know about me."

"Which is, admittedly, very little."

"We're the same, Sterling," she spat. "Your dream about the tree?"

His eyes went wide.

Cait lifted a shoulder in a lazy shrug, the way Desmond might. "I'm having the same one."

"That's not possible," Sterling mumbled.

"Not unless you, like me, inherited your family's curse."

Sterling's expression tightened. "You don't know what you're talking about."

"Then, why are you scared?" she demanded. "Why do you listen to music constantly, isolating yourself from everyone? Why do you hide?"

His jaw flexed angrily, but he remained silent.

"What do you know about the curse, Sterling?"

"Nothing!" he insisted. "It's not a curse."

She could hear the lack of sincerity in his tone. "Why won't you help me?" she asked.

Sterling held up his hands, backing away. "I don't have anything more to say. And if you know what's good for you, you'll stop asking questions."

"Aren't you curious about what it all means?" Cait asked desperately. "Or why we're having the same dream?"

Sterling gritted his teeth, looking ready to run. The loose strands of his dark hair were now plastered to his bronzed cheeks and temples. He studied her hesitantly. "I—"

Suddenly, the side door opened, cutting him off. They both swung toward the sound. Timothy Faulk's head popped out. A flicker of nervousness passed across his face upon seeing them before a gentle smile masked the slipup. "Ready to head out, Sterling?" he asked.

Sterling let out a low huff. "Yeah. Be right there," he promised, then muttered to Cait, "Tomorrow. Four-thirty at the park."

Then, without giving her the chance to respond, Sterling turned and walked away. He and his father disappeared into the chapel together, Timothy resting a hand on his son's shoulder. She caught the way Sterling tensed at the touch.

Cait stood in place, confused. Had Sterling just agreed to meet with her? Had she convinced him? She could hardly believe it.

The cold mist turned into a drizzle, spurring Cait into action. She dashed for the chapel. The second her family and Matt found her, damp and shivering, they pestered her about her absence. But she didn't care. She easily shrugged off their concern and questions, saying that she'd simply seen a fox and tried—and failed—to get a picture before it ran off. They believed her, and she felt as though her time with Desmond had prepared her for the duplicity she needed to survive her life.

Cait smiled to herself. She'd done it. And for once, she truly felt the words she said. She didn't need Desmond anymore. She could get the answers herself.

# CHAPTER THIRTEEN

# Desmond

Desmond had never been so depressed in his life. Yeah, that was probably overdramatic, but all he could think about was the fact that Cait was moving on.

Desmond *refused* to move on. Nor was he about to be thrown off. He'd find a way to meet with Cait, he'd tell her everything, and he'd win back her trust. Then, they could return to what they'd been—no, better than they'd been! He'd actually be her friend this time, and he'd find a way to free her from the Wolf.

Even if that seemed like an increasingly impossible mission by the day.

After church, Brady came over to continue their work. They'd both read the laborious Warden books through the week, though Desmond still didn't think it'd do much good. But the biggest reason for Brady's visit was to get on the same page with William.

Brady had been just as shocked as Desmond by his dad's willingness to help. He'd also been indignant that Fish would out them like that. Then, he accepted it, saying, "If anyone can help us figure this out, it's Uncle Will."

So, they piled into William's home office, prepared to discuss their research and solve the problem of the Veil. The small room sat at the back of the main floor, next to the master bedroom. It had been renovated along with the rest of the house, adding a larger window to one wall and new finishes to the floor, baseboards, and fixtures. They'd put built-in bookcases in there, too, with filing cabinets and doors to store all the more sensitive paperwork.

"Where do we start?" Desmond asked, settling into one of the chairs they'd pulled in from the dining room. Unlike his office at the town hall, William didn't keep seats for visitors at home. Aside from a low wingback chair in the corner, reserved for when Robin decided to sit with him, the small office was decidedly devoid of excess furnishings.

William ran a hand along his jaw thoughtfully. "Why don't you two start by catching me up?" he said.

Desmond and Brady exchanged a look. Desmond had already brought his dad up to speed on everything leading to their fight on the island. He'd also explained the research he and Brady had done. Now, the boys shared the handful of findings they thought might pertain to Cait's predicament. William rejected them all, denouncing their research altogether.

When Desmond and Brady began to lament his constant negativity, he held up a hand to quiet them. "There are few Warden theologians who cared to speculate on the Vessels and their burdens," William said. "For one thing, too many believed that the spirit-beings were devils or some other evil incarnate. Like most religious individuals, they kept clear of studying anything that could be construed as occult or satanic."

Brady played with the leather binding of his book. "But . . . they're not demons, right? That's just outdated information rooted in fear?"

William tipped his head to the side. "From my understanding? Yes." He gave them both an apologetic look. "But if we're being frank, I haven't studied it much. Whatever these spirit-beings are, they're still not . . . safe. And the leadership of the Warden either knows very little about them or has chosen only to share what little bit I know."

"So, it's pointless to do this research?" Desmond asked, giving the edge of his book a flippant lift.

"Most likely," William confirmed. "However, there are other authors who might have more to say on the subject."

"Like who?"

His dark eyes went to the ceiling to recall the information. "Eugene Faulk and Ariane Valente, though neither of them was prolific, and their works are harder to procure. And then there was Yvan Rayne, but his works disappeared along with many of Faulk's in the late eighteen hundreds."

"Faulk, as in *Faulk* Faulk?" Brady asked.

William nodded. "Eugene is an ancestor of Timothy Faulk, yes."

"So, his writings would have the answers," Brady said excitedly.

"Probably," William admitted. "Except that no one can find them."

"And that's it?" Desmond asked, incredulous. "Only three people wrote about these creatures?"

William shrugged. "Well, in the last century, there *was* a Sheraton . . . what was his name?" He set a hand to his mouth, scanning the room as he dredged his memory. "Harrison? No—Harold. *Harold* Sheraton. He wrote about the spirit-beings, but many members of the Warden disregarded his theories because he was . . ."

Desmond stared at his dad as he trailed off. "He was what?" he pressed.

William shrugged, a slight flush coming to his temples. "He was discredited."

"Why?"

"Because," William drew out the word as though he didn't want to discuss the matter, "he was having an affair with one of the Vessels."

"Oh." Desmond shared a glance with Brady. That was not what he'd expected.

He turned back to his dad. "Shouldn't that make his information more reliable?"

"They were both married," William said as though that explained everything.

"So?"

"*So*," he impressed extra weight on the word, "that sort of transgression typically calls into question one's integrity. After Sheraton and the young lady were caught in their indiscretion, he claimed to be in love with her. That made his writings even more suspect."

"Why?"

"How could they be impartial?" William asked. "If he was willing to enter into an affair with this woman, why wouldn't he lie in his writings to prove that the spirit-being connected to her wasn't as dangerous as people have claimed for centuries?"

Desmond supposed he understood. After all, wasn't he willing to do whatever it took to save Cait?

But he also couldn't help feeling the injustice of labeling the man a fraud just because he'd committed one sin. Desmond might not have been as good a Christian as he was meant to be, but he knew the Bible stories like he knew the history of Porthaven. And it seemed to him that there were plenty of Biblical men and women who committed just as heinous of sins and were still highly revered.

"Do you think we could get copies of his books?" Desmond asked.

William hesitated. "We don't have any in Porthaven."

"Okay, but we could order them or something, right?"

"We could . . ." The way his dad's words trailed off gave Desmond the distinct impression that he didn't think it would be worth it.

Leaning forward in his seat, Desmond held William's stare. "Dad, if we want answers, we have to take *every* opportunity. Whether it's perfectly reliable or not."

Though William took several seconds to ponder his son's words, he eventually nodded.

Desmond returned the nod resolutely.

"Now, however," William said, steering the conversation in a new direction, "we need to discuss the problem of the Veil. Or Veils, if Timothy Faulk is correct."

Brady sat up straighter. "Are we sure the Faulks' Veil didn't just absorb Cait's?"

Desmond didn't like attributing the Veil to Cait, but he kept his discomfort to himself. "Tim didn't mention anything about that," he said. "But there is a chance. I mean, that's sort of what we always assumed happened."

William nodded, though his eyes were narrowed doubtfully. "I'd rather not assume when we can know."

"Can we know?" Brady asked.

"We can search," William said. "Which I have been and will continue to do. I don't like the idea that there's a second Veil out there, potentially with the same damage."

"Wouldn't we have heard if there was another Veil producing beasts somewhere on the peninsula?" Desmond asked. "Like, wouldn't there be sightings?"

"Maybe. But they're not aggressive." William stared into the corner of the room as he thought. "They could simply be hiding in the day, emerging in the shadows of the night. If the Veil is secluded, which it almost certainly is, then there may be no one around to discover the beasts."

Desmond frowned. Somehow, that didn't sound right. Even if the beasts on Aster Island weren't aggressive, they had spread across the forest. If another Veil existed and was letting beasts through, surely they'd spread too. And *someone* would have found them.

"Why would someone want to damage a Veil?" Brady asked. "What would be the point of it?"

William sighed, leaning back in his seat. "That's the question we've been asking from the beginning. Why? And who? What motivation could anyone have for damaging a Veil, allowing untethered beasts to slip through?"

Desmond picked at the binding of the book on his lap. "We thought it might be practice at first," he reminded him. "What if the damage was an accident?"

"And who do you imagine would be practicing?"

Thinking back to his theory from a week ago, Desmond shrugged. "What if it's Sterling? It's his family's Veil, and he is friends with Hunter. Maybe Hunt gave him too much information, and Sterling decided to test out the spirit world for himself. Maybe it wound up damaging the Veil somehow, even if Sterling doesn't know it."

"That's a lot of speculation," William said.

Desmond tossed his hands in the air. "All theories are speculation. Everything we're doing here is speculation. But what if I'm right?"

William frowned but didn't speak.

In the wingback chair, Brady shifted. "It isn't a bad theory," he said, though Desmond could hear the doubt in his tone. "But what if it's something more nefarious than that?"

"What do you mean?" Desmond asked.

Brady shrugged. "We have two Vessels in Porthaven. Something we know the Druids want—something they've killed for. Many times."

A labored sigh escaped William. "We've considered the Druids," he said. "But we haven't seen any evidence of their arrival."

"Would you?" Brady asked. "They're smart. Probably smarter than we give them credit. And they'd do everything they could to show up undetected, create a hidden army, and then capture both Vessels uncontested, right?"

Desmond pursed his lips. "You know, sometimes, you're kind of clever, Brade."

"Thanks," he said flatly. He continued to address William. "The Veil is damaged. That's something we didn't even know was possible. And it didn't just happen. So, the question is: What caused it?"

William's brow furrowed, his thick eyebrows low. "Druids? Coming for our Vessels?"

Brady shrugged.

Desmond frowned. "Coming for Cait," he murmured.

"Maybe," William said uncertainly. He shook his head. "They couldn't slip through completely unnoticed. We keep tabs on all travelers and residents for this very reason. Unless they found some way to camp in the outer reaches of the town, we would know that they're here."

"Well, what about that, then?" Brady asked. "What if they're pretending to be tourists?"

After several seconds of thought, William shook his head again. "None have stayed around long enough to fit the timeline."

"What is the timeline?" Desmond asked.

"Roughly a month," he said. "Possibly a week longer."

Desmond did the calculation. "At the start of September?"

"As best as we can tell."

An idea sparked in Desmond's mind, and he thought back, double-checking the dates. His brow rose. It fit.

He turned back to his dad. "What about the Davises?" he asked.

William and Brady both frowned.

"You mean . . ." Brady scrunched his nose. "Like, Mrs. Davis? And Mattie?"

Desmond nodded, a knowing grin on his lips.

Brady scoffed. "Seriously, man?"

"They moved here at the beginning of September," Desmond said. "Right when all of this started."

His friend gave him a bored look. "You're only saying that because you're jealous."

Desmond gaped at him indignantly. "I am not! The timeline matches, that's all."

"Hold on—" William held up his hand, stalling their bickering. "Are you suggesting that Penny Davis and her son are Druids?"

Desmond shrugged dramatically. "The math checks out, Dad. They moved to town, and the beasts started appearing."

William dipped his chin in thought. "She grew up here."

"Which means there's a better chance she knew about the Vessels all along."

An extended silence revealed William's serious consideration.

Brady heaved a sigh. "I can't believe you really think Matt could be a Druid."

"Dude, it would make sense," Desmond defended. "Why else has he been buddying up to Cait from the second he got to town?"

"*Dude*," Brady mocked. "I'm writing a paper with the guy. He's too lame to be a Druid."

Desmond rolled his eyes.

Brady pressed on. "He's also weirdly talkative. He'd try to befriend a brick wall. Beyond that, he, like most guys at school, has a huge crush on Cait. She's hot. Why wouldn't he give it a shot?"

Desmond glowered, slumping in his seat.

William raised a singular eyebrow at their exchange. His eyes flicked from one boy to the other. "You both have valid points," he said. "The fact is that it all remains speculation. I will continue to search for a secondary Veil, and I will keep my eyes out for any signs that there are Druids in Porthaven. In the meantime, we can only do our best to find ways to solve the problems in front of us. Namely, repairing the Veil and learning more about Caitriona's connection to the Wolf."

Desmond and Brady shared a curious look.

"I thought Cait already repaired the Veil," Desmond said.

William rested a hand on his jaw. "I haven't gotten to visit it yet," he said disappointedly. "But based on the description you and Fish have given me . . . I don't think she did."

"What do you mean?" Brady asked. "It's all sealed up with amber, thanks to her."

"Exactly," William said. "It's *sealed*. That doesn't mean the damage is reversed."

"Maybe it will be," Desmond suggested. "Maybe it's like a Band-Aid. It'll allow the Veil to heal now that it's not open to the elements."

"Or," William countered, "maybe it's like a stopper on a bottle. It won't reverse the damage; it'll just prevent anything from getting out."

Desmond opened his mouth to argue, but William held up a hand. "I will visit the Veil tomorrow afternoon," he said. "You can come with me if you'd like."

Though the idea of returning to the Veil sent a cold tingle racing along Desmond's spine, he nodded enthusiastically. He wanted to get a better look at the amber. Maybe they could figure out what was beneath it in the daylight.

"Has anyone asked," Brady began with obvious reluctance, "*how* Cait sealed the Veil?"

They both looked at him, confused.

Brady held out a hand. "She has a block. She shouldn't be able to wield at all, and yet, she controlled seven beasts like it was nothing and put a seal on the Veil—something even *Desmond* couldn't do."

Desmond swallowed hard. It was a question he'd refused to ask himself. He didn't want to think about what it meant, the way she'd wielded so easily through a block.

Slowly, William nodded. "It's unheard of," he confirmed. "Most of her power remains locked behind the block. What she managed to accomplish . . . It's likely the surface of her abilities."

"'Power like we've never seen.'" The line of the prophecy slipped out of Desmond before he even processed that he'd said it.

William dipped his chin. "It also brings into question: Is it a coincidence that on the night Cait grasped hold of her powers, George Faulk died?"

Desmond's gaze shot up to his dad's. "You think—she didn't kill him," he insisted.

"Of course not," William said in a placating tone. "But there may be a chance that his death is linked to the surge of power she used to seal the Veil, especially if he was the Vessel connected to it."

"What—what does that mean? Do you think she's . . ." Desmond blanched. "Dangerous?"

"I don't know."

"Cool."

William gave him a perturbed glare.

Desmond held up his hands. "I'm not trying to be a smart ass, okay? Old habits."

William sighed. "Regardless of the timing of George's death, Cait is stronger than she should be. Which suggests the prophecy is correct."

Brady watched them uncertainly. He knew about the prophecy, but only like the synopsis of a book. He had the general overview, but he didn't know the full weight behind it.

Desmond didn't bother keeping him in the dark anymore. "And it says that she'll have to die," he muttered.

William gave him a disappointed look. "It says she'll have to make a sacrifice."

"Yeah, and sacrifice typically means giving up your favorite teddy bear in prophecies."

William pinched the bridge of his nose. "Prophecies are always ambiguous. It's one of the reasons I've never trusted the Raven."

"Raven?"

"Corva."

"Right." Desmond thought about the rest of the letter and the spirit-being's prophecy. He tightened his jaw, heart clenching at the truth. "Dad, the Warden knew about Cait's parents."

Brady flinched, and William brushed a finger over the Varon ring, eyes downcast.

"They *knew*," Desmond said again. "And they chose to let them die."

"I know," William said weakly.

"That's wrong."

"I know."

"Then, why do you work for them?" Desmond demanded. "You're the mayor. Why don't you tell the others what kind of hypocrites they work for? Why don't we break off from the Warden and protect the Veil and the Vessels ourselves?"

Brady squirmed uncomfortably at his side.

William, however, held his glare steadily. "It isn't that simple."

"Yeah, it is," he insisted. "They're murderers."

"Are they?" William returned. "*All* of them?"

Desmond was about to say yes when his dad continued, "The Warden is made up of hundreds of thousands of individuals. And what a handful of people in a boardroom decided does not reflect the beliefs and opinions of every other member."

"But they're the ones making decisions," Desmond returned.

"For now."

Desmond sat up straighter, glancing at Brady by his side. "You planning a coup?" he asked.

William gave a humorless laugh. "Not exactly." He sighed then, leaning onto his desk. His dark gaze locked with Desmond's, impressing upon him a calm assurance. "But I have to believe that if enough of us stand up for what's right, we can choose better leaders. We can *be* better leaders."

Desmond dropped his chin, uncertain of the reality of his father's conviction coming to pass but accepting, nonetheless.

"And more than anything," William added, "I believe that the Warden, at its core, is our only hope to stop the Druids from taking control of the spirit world."

A long silence stretched through the room. Desmond didn't want to hear his dad's logic. He wanted to reject the Warden's tenants, regulations, and secrets. He wanted answers. He wanted freedom for Cait and himself.

Brady spoke up then, gently prodding. "If you don't believe in the Warden's rules . . ." He held William's stare as though there weren't three decades between them. "Why do you follow them? Why keep the Faulks and Lewans locked up like prisoners?"

A weighted sigh fell from William. "It's not *them* we're locking up."

"They didn't even get a choice," Desmond said with a sudden surge of anger.

"None of us is given the choice of our birth," William said. "Neither you nor I *chose* to be a Simon any more than Cait chose to be a Lewan. Yet, here we all are. And it's up to us to use the influence and power we've been given to make changes where we can."

Desmond ground his teeth. "Then, why don't you change it?" he demanded. "If you disagree with their protocols, why do you uphold them?"

"Because I don't know what else to do," William admitted.

Desmond didn't have a response to that. Brady didn't either, dipping his chin.

"Have you told her?" William asked in their prolonged silence. "About her parents' deaths."

Desmond looked down at his hands, clasped over the book in his lap. "No."

"Do you intend to?"

"No."

There was no response, so Desmond raised his eyes to see his dad's expression. William had dropped his head into a hand, massaging his temples. It was such a defeated posture, and it caused Desmond's gut to twist. He didn't like seeing his dad so unsure, so at a loss. It made him feel unmoored, adrift in the ocean of his own self-doubt.

Desperate for some guiding light, Desmond whispered, "Do you think I should tell her?"

"Truthfully?" William looked up at him, dark eyes sorrowful. "I don't know."

# CHAPTER FOURTEEN

# Desmond

Sitting through school the next day was a special kind of torture. All Desmond could think about was how useless it all felt. Since their talk with his dad, a tremor had worked into his muscles, leaving him shaky and unsettled. He was desperate for answers, restless for a fraction of information that would give them hope.

Instead, their research was fruitless. Their theories were baseless. Their hopes were empty.

Worse, what was the point of it all when Cait wouldn't even look at him?

All day, she ignored him. He couldn't even catch her eye. When she wasn't chatting with Matt, she'd begun to hang around Elizabeth and Melissa. It was an odd sight, though Desmond felt a small swell of pride that she'd finally worked up the gumption to connect with other students, even if he would prefer it not to be Hunter's crew.

It was just another reminder of how she'd given up on their friendship.

During lunch, Desmond watched as Cait talked and laughed with her new friends. His heart squeezed at every smile. Was she truly happy without him? Or was it all an act?

He raked a fork through his meal, suddenly unable to stomach anything. Why wouldn't she talk to him? Why had she so completely turned her back on him when he would do anything to save her?

Because she didn't know.

That's the only answer Desmond could come up with. Cait didn't know how hard he was working to save her. She didn't know that he was spending every spare second researching the spirit world, looking for ways to free her of her burden, seeking a way for them to be together. She couldn't know.

Because she wouldn't talk to him.

The thought twisted in his gut. He tightened his grip on the fork, glaring surreptitiously over at Cait. The sunlight streaming through the skylight caught on her silvery blonde hair, causing her to glow. It made his anger flare. She didn't know because she wouldn't listen. If he could just get her alone for two minutes . . . If he could *just* make her hear him out . . . All of this would be fixed.

An idea solidified in Desmond's mind then. One that he perfected through the rest of the school day. He even whispered it to Brady, getting his advice on the matter. And then, he waited.

When the final bell rang and the mass of students began pouring out of the classroom to go home, Desmond stepped into the hall. He hung back as Brady deftly herded Garrett to the door, per their plan. Desmond wanted witnesses, but not too many. The school was already gossiping about their project pairing. Desmond and that Lewan girl—how ridiculous. The derision of their peers would work in his favor.

Nonchalantly leaning against a row of lockers at the end of the hall, Desmond waited. He stared down at his phone, attempting to appear caught up in a text conversation as cluster after cluster of students and teachers ambled by. He kept an eye on the classroom door, alert to each individual who walked out. Hunter's original gang stepped into the hall, the boys parting from the girls to head to basketball practice.

Behind them all, Cait appeared with Matt at her side. His face was twisted up in some wildly animated expression as he spoke. Desmond tried not to scowl as he heard Cait laugh. She had a bright, airy laugh that seemed to bubble out of her. It was a contagious sort of laugh. The kind that could wiggle its way inside your chest and scoop out a laugh of your own.

After last night's revelation, he had a newfound dislike of Cait and Matt's relationship. It was so obvious now. The kid had attached himself to her like a leech from the start. Just as a Druid looking to buddy up to a Vessel would. Brady might have shunted off the idea, but Desmond still thought the odds were too coincidental.

Matt and his mom arrived, and beasts began to appear. Too convenient.

With a wave, Matt hurried off to follow Hunter, Sterling, and Scott toward the gym. Desmond kept his head down and turned away as the boy passed by. Then, he carefully peeled away from the lockers, following at a distance as Cait moved toward the front of the school.

She walked slowly while the rest of the students hurried around her. Genni met up with her along the way, a curly-headed brunette at her side. Desmond lingered behind several feet, unable to hear their conversation. Several students waved to him along the way, and he gave them each noncommittal nods, ensuring they wouldn't try to start a conversation.

The girls exited the school, letting in a flash of light before the door shut, cutting them off from Desmond's view. He forced himself to walk at a reasonable pace. It would take them time to unlock their bikes before pedaling home. His heart might be pounding with desperation, but no one else could see that.

When he stepped into the soft yellow light of the afternoon, Desmond didn't bother keeping his intention a secret any longer. He looked straight toward the bike rack, spotting the girls as the brunette split away from

Cait and Genni, and he headed in their direction. Only a smattering of students loitered around the paved entryway.

"Lewan," he called, intentionally gaining the stragglers' attention along with Cait and Genni's.

The duo looked up from their bikes, wide-eyed. Genni's expression showed blatant shock, while Cait's held a tinge of irritation.

Desmond forced his signature smirk onto his lips rather than the frown that wanted to come forth. What did *she* have to be irritated about? She'd said she wanted answers, and he'd promised to give them. Yet, she wasn't willing to give him a chance to prove himself. She'd rejected him, going to *Hunter* instead. If anyone had the right to be upset, it was he.

Striding up to the pair casually, Desmond could feel the eyes of the lingering students on them. He tipped his chin toward Genni in a flippant greeting. Then, he addressed Cait alone. "You avoiding me?" he asked.

From the corner of his eye, Desmond caught the way Genni's brow furrowed.

Cait's jaw tensed, but she'd adopted her usual stance around him: head dipped, shoulders drawn in, and eyes down. "No," she muttered.

"Sure seems like it," he replied, infusing his voice with lazy arrogance. "Which is weird since *you're* the one who wanted to work on this essay together when I could have had it done in a night."

Her blue-gray eyes flashed to his face, a slight pinch between her dark blonde eyebrows.

Desmond could practically feel the victorious glimmer in his eyes. He couldn't say outright why he wanted to meet with her. But if he demanded she work with him on their project, how could she say no? They were partners. They *had* to work together.

"So, what's it gonna be?" he asked, pressing on with his scheme. "My place or yours?"

Cait's lips parted in something between disbelief and horror.

Genni glared at him as though she wanted to give Desmond a piece of her mind.

Desmond leveled the girl with an unconcerned stare.

"I—I don't—" Cait began, then sighed. "Your parents won't mind?"

Desmond grinned flippantly. "Not at all. Mom will insist you stay for dinner. Tomorrow work?"

Blinking rapidly as though to settle her thoughts, Cait gave him a sharp nod. "Yeah," she mumbled.

"Great. I can give you a ride after school." Desmond turned to Genni for a fraction of a second. Then, he met Cait's gaze again, letting his disappointment surface for a single second. He saw her temples flush pink, and he knew she understood. Her avoidance hurt him. After everything they'd been through together, her rejection stung worse than lemon juice on a paper cut.

"See you tomorrow, Lewan," he said, inflection flat. And before she could respond, he turned on his heel and headed back for the school.

The second his back was to the pair, Desmond felt his face contort. He hated how he had to handle public meetings with Cait. He despised the way he had to carry himself with such arrogance and speak with such a caustic tone. It wasn't who he was. It wasn't who *they* were. But it was what everyone needed to see.

Desmond pushed down his shame as he walked into the school. The halls were empty now. He moved steadily toward the locker room to change before basketball practice. When he'd started at Porthaven High, his dad insisted he join all the sports teams. And while Desmond wasn't exactly a sports fan, he found himself enjoying the physical competition.

But now, things felt different. He no longer found the competition stimulating or the physicality pleasantly distracting. Instead, it felt like a waste of time. It took away from far more important things. Things like finding a way to save Cait.

Practice dragged by, and Coach Favreau even pulled Desmond aside, commenting that his time off during last summer break seemed to be affecting his skill. Having a distracted team captain wasn't good for morale. Desmond promised it was simply a fluke, and he'd be back to his usual self by their next practice on Wednesday.

Favreau eyed him warily but didn't challenge him on it.

Soon, Desmond changed into his street clothes, left the building, and headed for the town hall. Despite the end of his grounding, he still had his internship every afternoon. And with basketball practice, that cut into his evenings.

However, he found himself surprisingly hopeful as he pulled into the town hall's parking lot. His dad had promised they'd visit the Veil today. If he had to waste time doing "government" work, at least it could be in the service of Cait.

When Desmond entered the building, William stood at the receptionist's desk. "Ah, good," he said, motioning him over.

"Were you waiting for me?" Desmond asked.

William gave the receptionist a nod in farewell, then set a hand on Desmond's shoulder, guiding him toward the stairs. "I just finished a meeting about the Festival, and I knew you'd arrive soon," he said. He leveled him with a pointed stare. "I have news."

With a glance around the entry hall, Desmond lowered his voice. "You talked to the reverend?" he asked.

William had informed Desmond of his plans that morning. After his conversation with Maeve Lewan, he intended to call the reverend in Bushmills. He hoped to get information that would benefit them in their study today.

"I did," William said. "His name is Patrick O'Sullivan. He's only led the chapel in Bushmills for two years, but he's close with the previous reverend, who knew the Lewan family well."

Desmond felt his mouth drop open, inordinately curious to know more about Cait's family. "So, he knew Cait?" he asked.

William dipped his chin in confirmation, remaining silent as they passed Councilman Moyer. Once they were out of earshot, he said, "He did. O'Sullivan, however, did not. He moved to Bushmills to take the job after seminary at Watson University."

"He was in America?"

"It's where most of the Warden's reverends attend." They moved down the hall, nearing the mayor's office. "But the important thing is that he confirmed what we thought: During Owen Lewan's time as the Vessel, the town had a Veil. A year after the Lewan family's relocation, it disappeared."

Desmond screwed up his face in thought. "How does that work? I mean, did a tree just disappear and wind up over here?"

"It wasn't a tree," William began, but he was interrupted as he surveyed the waiting area outside his office. Lori, his receptionist, looked up at their approach, nervous expectation in her expression. Her eyes flickered tellingly toward the man sitting in a chair against the far wall.

Desmond and his dad followed her sight line to see the middle-aged Asian man rise. He buttoned his suit jacket tightly against his broad, muscular frame. He was dressed like an FBI agent: black suit, white button up, short, professional haircut, no facial hair, and a pair of aviator sunglasses tucked into the breast pocket of his jacket.

"Mayor Simon?" the man said, stepping forward with an outstretched hand. He moved with such confidence and intentionality that it felt as though they were coming to *his* office.

A flash of concern flickered through Desmond. He'd never seen the man before, and he didn't like how intimidated he felt by his presence. The guy was even shorter than him. He shouldn't be allowed to be so formidable.

William accepted the handshake. "How can I help you?" he asked.

"My name is Kevin Jun," the man said. "I'm a Municipality Analyst for Sheraton Corporation."

William went rigid, and Desmond's blood ran cold.

"Could I have a word with you?" Jun asked.

A long, tense pause lingered as William scanned the man. They knew Jun's purpose in Porthaven. Sheraton Corporation was a shell corp for the Warden, a working name that kept their true business hidden.

Last week, when Desmond, Brady, and Fish made their way to the Veil, they overheard a conversation between Brett Varon and Kenneth Greene. Brett had called Jeremiah Rhader, the head of the Warden's "Municipality Supervision Department." Essentially, Rhader and his people made sure that each Warden town's leader was doing their job. Calling their department was calling your leader into question.

Desmond heard Kenneth's incredulous words in his head again. *"That's like contacting internal affairs on a cop."*

William stepped aside, motioning to his office. "Of course, Mr. Jun." He opened the door. "Come right in."

Still in shock, Desmond didn't know whether to leave or to stay. He didn't exactly want to be present to see his dad get the news that he was under investigation. But he couldn't help feeling somewhat responsible.

As Jun moved past Desmond, he smiled blandly, then looked to William. "Your son?" he asked.

William made a quick introduction.

Jun turned his dark gaze back to Desmond. "In that case, Mr. Simon," he said, "you ought to join us."

Desmond blanched. "Why?"

His thick eyebrows rose. "I was under the impression that you are Mayor Simon's only child. Am I incorrect?"

"No."

"Then, you're his heir, yes?"

"Yes."

Jun nodded as though that solved everything. "Then, this pertains to you as well," he concluded and stepped into the waiting office.

Desmond exchanged a wary look with his dad and followed the Warden agent. Jun readily took a seat, unbuttoning his jacket once again. William shut the door and motioned for Desmond to sit before moving behind his cherry wood desk. He kept his desk clean and organized, with neat stacks of reports, requests, and documents for review. Framed photos of both Desmond and his mom sat by the computer monitor.

Once they were all settled, William calmly addressed the analyst. "How can I help you, Mr. Jun?" he asked.

"Please," Jun said, expression friendly despite the monotone of his voice, "call me Jun. And as I'm sure you're aware, in the MSD, we work to oversee our organization's townships and ensure that they're running in accordance with our policies and principles. We try to keep a loose grip, but sometimes, there are situations where firmer guidance is required."

William listened patiently, accepting the clear threat despite Jun's easy tone.

Desmond slouched as Jun concluded his speech. "As a Municipality Analyst, it is my job to conduct an inquiry when a town's compliance has been brought into question."

Somehow, William's expression remained placid while he calmly said, "And Porthaven's compliance has been questioned?"

"It has," Jun replied.

"I see," William said flatly. He rested his clasped hands on the desktop. "I will, of course, comply with whatever your investigation requires."

"We don't like to call them investigations," Jun corrected. "It's an inquiry."

Whatever they *liked* to call them, Desmond thought it made little difference. Investigation or inquiry, his dad's job was on the line. And that meant *his* future was on the line too.

William gave an acquiescent dip of his chin. "I understand. May I ask in what capacity our town is being questioned?"

"It isn't the town, Mayor Simon," Jun said. "It's your leadership."

Though no emotion showed on William's face, Desmond knew the degree of tension rising within his dad. After Jun left, there would be hell to pay at the Varon family's expense. Because there could never have been any doubt—even if Desmond hadn't overheard the conversation between Brett and Kenneth—the Varon and Simon feud had reached its climax.

"I understand," William repeated. "In that case, I will assent to whatever your inquiry requires of me. Is there anything else I should know?"

Jun sat upright in his seat, a professional lift to his head. "I'll be spending the next two weeks assessing the town and how your leadership has guided it," he said. "At which point, I will make a decision on your compliance with our ordinances and either approve your continued leadership or begin the process of instating your replacement."

Tingles raced along Desmond's skin. They only had two weeks to prove to this Warden analyst that their leadership was sound. They didn't have time for that kind of pressure. Not when they needed to fix the Veil, find the second one, and figure out how to save Cait.

"So, this is a probationary period?" William said.

"It is," Jun confirmed.

With a sharp intake of breath, William somehow maintained his composure. "Very well." He leaned back in his seat. "What can I do to facilitate your work?"

"During my inquiry, I'll spend most of my time working directly with you," Jun said. "Observing your day-to-day and the like. I'll also be interviewing the members of your council. And I need to visit the Veil. Does tomorrow morning work for you?"

"I'll have Lori rearrange my schedule," William said.

"Excellent." Jun gave an annoyingly companionable smile. Then, he turned to Desmond for the first time in the conversation. "I believe you're an honorary member of the Warden and its council, correct?"

Desmond confirmed through gritted teeth.

Jun's deep brown eyes peered knowingly into him. "In that case, I'll need to meet with you as well. Both regarding the inquiry and as an assessment."

"An assessment of what?" Desmond demanded, unable to restrain his irritation.

Jun didn't blink at his gruff tone. "Of the future, Mr. Simon," he explained. "While we don't recognize the authority of the reputed 'true' Varons, we understand that your family does. As such, we like to be aware of what we might expect for the future of our relationship with the Varon bloodline."

Desmond had difficulty holding back the sharp retort that came to mind. Instead, he gripped the arms of his chair tightly. "Sure thing, boss," he ground out.

Jun didn't appear to recognize the snark in his words. He gave him a grateful nod, turning back to the mayor. "Unless you have any questions, I'll leave you to your work and return in the morning," he said.

"My questions can wait until tomorrow," William said. "Have you found a place to stay?"

"Arrangements were made prior to my arrival."

"I hope you enjoy your time in Porthaven, then."

"I'm sure I will." Jun rose and shook hands with William again. He smiled blandly at Desmond. "Have a good afternoon, gentlemen."

And with that, the analyst left.

The instant the door shut behind the man, William sucked in a deep breath and turned a glare on Desmond.

"What?" he asked, knowing perfectly well "what."

William's dark eyes revealed the severity of their situation. "That man can have our jobs," he said coolly. "Any sign of disrespect, any hint of aggression, and you will confirm every lie he was brought here to investigate."

Unsure if they were truly lies, Desmond slumped. "It's an *inquiry*," he mocked.

William pinched the bridge of his nose in a long-suffering manner. "Do you understand what happens if he removes us from leadership?" he said, voice taut. "We not only lose our authority in this town, but we also lose all ability to protect Caitriona. *You* lose your opportunity to save her."

Desmond tried to mask the panic rising within him, voicing the question he'd always held back. "What if losing our authority is the only way I can be with her?"

William flinched. "You do understand what's at stake here, don't you? If they remove us from this office, it isn't just my leadership that they call into question. It's our family's character. They'd never let you marry the Vessel if they think you're a danger to their control over her."

Though the thought of marriage made Desmond uncomfortable, he knew that was his ultimate wish. He wanted to be with Cait. Forever. He'd just never admitted it to himself before because he knew what his dad was telling him now: Warden leader or not, he could never be with her.

The only thing left for him was to protect her, and they needed to maintain their role as leaders to do that.

After the long silence that stretched between them, William sighed. "You should get down to the clerk's office," he said.

"We were supposed to visit the Veil," Desmond said. "And you never finished telling me about your conversation with the reverend in Bushmills."

William ran a hand over his face. "Later," he said in a defeated tone. "I—I need to prepare. With Jun here. . . ."

His dad didn't need to finish the thought. With Jun in Porthaven, there was a far more pressing danger than Cait's eventual discovery. They could handle solving the problem of the spirit-being *later*. For now, William had to make sure the analyst couldn't find fault in his leadership of the town. He had to shore up control, ensuring their lies were properly hidden.

Desmond left, any hope that remained in his heart fizzling like sea-foam against the pebbles of the shoreline.

# CHAPTER FIFTEEN

# Cait

Cait's head buzzed with the memory of Desmond's voice, repeating over and over again, *"See you tomorrow, Lewan."*

*See you tomorrow.*

*Tomorrow.*

Her stomach sank. Tomorrow. She would be going to Desmond's house tomorrow.

No matter what he said, she knew the intention wasn't to study together. He was going to try to convince her to listen. He was going to attempt to refix himself as part of her life. And she couldn't take that.

Cait gritted her teeth, slumping on the bench. She sat at the wharf, watching the steel blue ocean churn against the rocky shoreline. Genni had gone to Alexis's house for the afternoon, and Matt had joined basketball practice as the new ball boy. Cait hadn't bothered biking home, knowing she'd only have to turn around minutes later to return for her meeting with Sterling. So, now she waited at the docks alone, her thoughts tormenting her.

The cold breeze stung the tips of her ears, its salty edge tickling her nose. Cait tried to sketch as she sat there. But she couldn't get Desmond out of her head. His words. His expression. His disappointment.

Inexplicably, Cait's heart pinched as she remembered the hurt that flashed across his face. But he didn't understand. He was hurting *her* with his very presence. If she was going to move on, if she was going to have a happy life, he couldn't be in it.

A sigh escaped her, drifting away on the wind like the seagulls swooping above the waves. She turned back to her sketchbook. The page held the rough lines of a drawing just begun. She'd intended to sketch the redhead. If she could get her on paper, perhaps she could ask Sterling if he knew her.

Cait returned to her work. Though Sterling's original instructions were vague, he'd managed to whisper to her in the hall that morning. "Meet me at the oceanfront park," he'd instructed. "There's a bench by the walking trail. It's got a Radiohead sticker on it."

So, after school, Cait biked to Haddock Park. She hardly considered it a real park. It was simply a collection of paved walking paths, small, grassy areas, and pavilions for picnicking. The tourists loved it, but she preferred the cove.

And while Cait didn't know what Radiohead was—she assumed it might be some music band if it was relevant to Sterling—she'd found the bench in question.

Now, she sat in the cold, tucking her jacket closer around her as she waited. Her fingers grew numb as she sketched. In the hour of waiting, she managed to get a good likeness of the redhead onto the page. She hadn't seen the young woman close up, so the features lacked detail. But she thought she'd captured the gentleness in her demeanor.

Cait shaded in the rough shape of the raven on the woman's shoulder just as Sterling walked into view. He wore the same ragged jacket as yesterday at church. His headphones trailed from his pocket to his ears, and he'd pulled back his hair in a sloppy knot.

He followed the curved sidewalk to the bench where she sat, keeping his eyes mostly averted. Then, he sat down on the far end. "Kinda surprised you showed," he said dully, tugging his headphones out.

Cait turned to face him even as he stared out at the water. "I want answers," she said. "And you're the only person who can give them to me."

"'Fraid you'll be disappointed."

"Then, why'd you invite me here?"

Sterling ground his teeth. "Look, I don't know much, okay? It's sort of the Faulk prerogative. Keep your head down, and no one will mess with you." He paused, hands fisting at his sides. "But I've overheard my parents sometimes, and . . . I've picked up a handful of things. None of it great."

Cait frowned, annoyed that he wouldn't look at her. "What do you mean?" she asked.

"Basically, our lives suck," he said flatly. "My family's and yours. We're hosts for these spirit-beings, and it's up to us to make sure they don't go free and terrorize the world. Unfortunately, our ancestors chose this for us, and now we don't get a say in it."

That caused Cait to pause. Spirit-beings. She'd never heard that term before. Was that what the demon was? A spirit-being?

"And these dreams . . ." Cait prompted. "They're normal?"

Sterling hesitated. "Not that I know of."

"Do you have any idea why we're having them, then?"

"Not a clue." He picked at the bench seat, adding, "So, are they, like, exactly the same? Yours and mine?"

Cait shrugged. "I'm not sure. My dreams used to be different," she admitted. "Until a week ago, they always started in my childhood home. And there was something on the other side of the door trying to get in." She decided it would be best to leave Desmond and the cove out of her explanation, so she focused on the biggest change in her dreams. "Now, I'm at the tree, but the door is still there."

For the first time, Sterling met her gaze. "The tree," he repeated in a whisper. "Yeah, that's . . . that's the dream I've been having this last week. I'm standing at the tree, and when I look behind me, there's a door. And I know—somehow, I know—there's something on the other side trying to get through. But it doesn't make sense because we're in the forest, and the door is just there. Whatever's on the other side should be able to walk around it."

Cait nodded, her chest tightening as her mind played the dream behind her eyes. "Is your door . . . is it cracked?"

His brow raised. "Yeah."

Cait sank farther down on the bench, arms draped over the pages of her sketchbook. Their dreams were the same. What did that mean . . . ?

Turning back to Sterling, Cait felt her desperation rise. "Have you seen the raven?" she asked.

Sterling twirled his earbuds around his fingers. "Yeah," he murmured. "Yeah, it shows up in the tree. I, uh—I've started seeing you there too."

Cait raised her chin.

"I looked for you," Sterling explained. "After you said you'd seen me in yours."

"Have you seen anyone else?"

"Uh, there's this redheaded chick on the other side of the tree," he said. "I've seen you look at her. But that's it."

"Do you know who she is?"

"No, I've never seen her before."

Cait frowned. "Is there anyone else? In the shadows."

Sterling paused, then shrugged. "I dunno. I haven't looked." He shifted in his seat, leaning closer. "Look, this is freaking me out, okay? I know what it means—I inherited my grandpa's burden when he died. Like you must have inherited your dad's when . . ." He flinched as though worried he'd said too much. Then, he changed tack. "What I don't understand is why this is happening. The Faulks have carried this . . . this being for generations. And this is not part of what I was told to expect."

"What were you told to expect?" Cait asked, unreasonable hope rising within her.

"Well . . ." He grimaced, turning back to the sea. "*If* the being came to me—which wasn't a guarantee, by the way—my dad said it shouldn't affect my life much. He said the Warden placed blocks over us, making it so we can't wield. You know about wielding, right?"

Cait nodded, though she didn't know much.

Sterling returned the nod as though glad to know someone who understood. "Because we can't wield," he continued, "the spirit-being can't access us. It keeps us safe, though it weakens us, which is why the Warden has to keep us here. It's why our lives are pretty much dictated to us."

It was why, Cait realized, she and Desmond couldn't be friends.

All along, he'd been telling her: She was too dangerous to be friends with. They couldn't be anything because their future was already set for them: she as a captive, he as her captor.

And yet, now he wouldn't let her go.

Cait picked at the corner of her sketchbook. "Is there anything else?"

"Aside from the fact that we're required to marry a Warden member and have one kid to ensure the bloodline continues?" Sterling said bitterly. "Nah, that's pretty much it."

Her heart caught on that last tidbit. She'd have to marry a Warden member. Who? Who would be willing to marry a cursed girl only to bring a child into the same twisted life?

Sterling cleared his throat during her silence. "The door that you see," he said. "Is yours . . . ? The split in mine is almost halfway down."

Dejectedly, Cait met his gaze. "Mine is too."

"What do you think it means?" he whispered.

"That the monster is breaking free."

Sterling tightened his jaw and turned away. "Well, that sucks," he said flatly. He seemed to gather his resolve, raising his chin and glaring at her. "What do we do about it?"

Cait blinked. "I'm not sure there's anything we *can* do."

"Then, what's the point of us meeting?" he demanded. "Why get answers if we can't do anything with them?"

"Because it can help us protect our families," she replied. "If these . . . spirit-beings break through, then we have to be sure they can't hurt the people we love. We have to learn to control them."

"*We* don't control it. That's the block's job."

"But the blocks are breaking."

Sterling drew back, confused.

Cait pressed a hand to her chest. "At least, *mine* is. You said the blocks keep us from wielding, but I wielded last Monday night. Somehow, I connected with seven beasts, sending them back into the tree."

"The tree?" Sterling flinched. "The tree is real?"

Cait nodded. "It's on the island."

He stared at Aster Island in the distance as though he could see the tree from where they sat. "It's the Veil," he whispered.

"The what?"

Sterling swallowed, seemingly lost in thought, as he continued to stare at the island. He shifted on the bench, running a hand over his mouth. "The tree is damaged," he murmured as though putting a puzzle together. "In the dreams, it has a crack. Like the door."

Cait tipped her head to the side, realizing he was right. The fissure in the real tree matched the fissure in the door. Almost exactly.

"And the creatures are getting free," Sterling said in a hush that Cait almost didn't hear.

Suddenly, he whirled back to her. "Can you take me to the tree?"

Scooting back, Cait shook her head. "I don't . . . I don't know where it is."

"You just said it was on the island."

"Yeah, but I'm not sure *where* on the island."

"You were there, weren't you?"

Cait sucked in a sharp breath, unsure how to explain. "Sort of . . ."

"What does that mean? Did you see the tree in real life, or didn't you?"

"I did, but—" Cait paused, turning to face him more fully. "Look, I don't know how it happened. I was dreaming, and then I just woke up on the island. I don't know how I got there."

"How'd you get off, then?"

That caused Cait to hesitate again. "I don't know that either." And while it was a partial lie, it wasn't entirely false. Cait *assumed* that Desmond had gotten her off the island. But she'd been unconscious. She didn't know what happened from the time she dropped to the time she woke in bed the next morning.

Sterling pressed his hands to his face, then heaved a sigh. "This is way too complicated."

Nodding, Cait didn't know what to say.

"All right." Sterling turned to her, holding out a hand. "Here's the deal: No one can know about this. Once the Warden discovers that we're the ones who inherited, they're gonna make our lives a living hell. You got it?"

Cait's heart sank under his adamant stare.

"So, we keep this quiet," he insisted. "And in the meantime, we try to find a way to fix the blocks."

"How?" Cait murmured.

Sterling grimaced. "I guess I could talk to Hunter. He knows about the dreams, and he's worried about what it means for me, too, so he'd definitely be willing to help."

The blood rushed from Cait's head. "I don't think that's a good idea," she said in a frightened tone.

Sterling's brows pinched together. "Why not?"

"He's a Varon," she reminded. "They're dedicated to the Warden. If they find out that it's us, they'll tell."

Sterling shook his head. "Hunter's my friend."

"And you trust him not to say anything?"

"Enough to tell him about my dreams."

"So, you'd tell him you inherited the spirit-being from your grandfather?" she demanded.

Sterling shrugged. "I think he already assumes that I have."

Cait set her jaw, determined. "Well, he doesn't know that *I* inherited it from my da. And I want to keep it that way."

Understanding softened Sterling's expression, and for the first time, she saw what she thought might be the truest version of him. "You're our friend now, too, Cait," he said quietly.

Despite the genuineness of his words, Cait shook her head. "It's been a week," she returned. "I'm sorry if I don't feel comfortable putting my life in Hunter's hands."

With a heavy sigh, Sterling sat back. "I get it," he said. "Well, how do you want to figure this out, then? We *need* help if we're going to learn how to fix this."

Cait chewed on the inside of her lip. She'd see Desmond tomorrow. He *had* offered to answer her questions. But she couldn't handle bringing him back into her life, even for this.

"I'm not sure," she whispered, playing with the zipper on her jacket. Her eyes lifted to the island, an idea forming. "Maybe . . ."

Sterling caught on, but his expression was dark. "You may not trust Hunter, but I *definitely* don't trust your 'not-boyfriend.'"

Cait brushed his worry away. "I'm not talking to him anymore, anyway," she said. "No, I—I have another idea."

"Yeah?"

"I could talk to Brady."

"Lavigne?" Sterling scoffed. "He's Desmond's right hand."

"I know, but . . ." Cait drew one knee onto the bench so she could face him fully. "Look, last week, something happened, and Brady was there. I think he already knows about me. So, I could talk to him. He *is* a Lavigne, which means he's allowed to wield. And that means he's more likely to have information than anyone else."

Sterling's reluctance eased. "And you'd keep me out of it?"

"Yeah," she promised.

He pressed his lips together. "I guess it's better than nothing."

"Then, do we agree? I'll talk with Brady, and we won't tell anyone else."

He nodded. "And maybe we should keep our meetings to a minimum," he suggested. "I'm pretty sure Liz thinks we should date, and you're not my type."

Cait felt her face scrunch. "Really? Why?"

"You're too quiet, and I like brunettes."

"No, I mean, why does she think we should date?"

"She's a high school girl," he said as though that explained everything. "She's obsessed with setting up her friends. That's why Scott and Mel got together in the first place. Now, she's trying it with us."

"Oh."

"Don't worry. I know I'm not your type either. Apparently, you like narcissistic pricks."

Cait pursed her lips. "Not anymore."

"Good for you." Sterling took a deep breath, pushing himself off the bench. "Well, I guess that's that, right? Let me know what you find out."

Cait rose with him. "Thanks," she said. "For meeting with me and for . . . everything else."

Sterling gave a slow nod. "For sure. Take care, Cait."

Slipping her sketchbook back into her backpack, Cait watched Sterling walk away. The conversation hadn't gone exactly to plan, but she knew more now than before. She had names.

Spirit-beings. The Veil.

Even if Cait didn't have answers, she was one step closer to getting them. With names, she could ask Brady specific questions. She could force him to give her answers.

Now, she just had to find a way to talk to him.

# CHAPTER SIXTEEN

# William

The midmorning sun glinted off the gray-blue waves, causing William to squint in its light. Seabirds circled the docks up the shoreline, making piercing squawks. He led the Warden's Municipality Analyst, Jun, across the rock bridge linking Porthaven to Aster Island. The craggy shoreline jutted from the sea, the white lighthouse soaring into the cloudless sky above them.

Under normal circumstances, William would have brought Desmond with them. But he thought it best to keep Jun's exposure to his son at a minimum.

Despite their improved relationship over the last few days, the past tension between William and Desmond haunted his thoughts. It'd been a part of their lives for so long that he feared saying or doing the wrong thing and sending them back to the start.

William had never been satisfied with the state of their relationship. It had always frightened him—the idea of being a father. His own father, Charles Simon, had been a hard man. Patriarchal in all the *wrong* ways.

Not fatherly or caring, but rigid and demanding. A result of their job, Charles excused himself. Being the leader of the town was difficult enough. It required absolute dedication and attention. Being a *Simon* leader made the job immeasurably harder.

As the great-grandson of the first Simon to inherit the Varon bloodline, William had witnessed not only the difficulties his father had faced but also the challenges endured by his grandfather. The careers of both men had been filled with constant questions and opposition. Neither of them could do a thing without a slew of angry remarks and pushback from the Varons, who felt *their* ancestors should have been granted the ring.

William understood why his father had to be an aggressive, harsh, and calculating leader. He understood that Charles treated every day as a battle one had to survive. He understood why the then-mayor Simon felt the need to garner respect through fear.

What he'd never understood—what he still didn't understand forty-seven years later—was why his father felt the need for his family to fear him as well.

William had always been afraid of his father. He feared his temper. He feared his wrath. He feared his fists. Up until the day Charles Simon died earlier that year, any time his father raised a hand, William flinched. The days of his youth weren't as cushy as children's now. A beating was an apt punishment—a just lesson. And Charles hit harder than most.

However, his father drew the line at hitting women. William's sister, Priscilla, never endured the lessons to "toughen up," "be a man," and "act like a leader." She wasn't the heir. She wouldn't carry the family name. She wasn't an eternal symbol of Simon authority.

Parenthood scared William ever since he could remember. What must it bring upon a man to raise a son for such a purpose, he'd wondered. How could he bear the weight of such a burden? How could he ever impress such importance on his son without becoming the monster that his father had been?

The fear bled through every moment of Robin's pregnancy. William prayed—he *literally* prayed—that it would be a girl. He and Robin struggled to conceive, and her pregnancy was fraught with difficulty. The doctor—Kenneth's grandfather—had urged them not to try for another. And when the birth nearly killed Robin, they'd taken his advice.

William wanted his only child to be a girl. He still wished they'd had a daughter. Then, she wouldn't have to carry this weight. She could have married outside the founding families, had she wanted to. She could have chosen not to take part in the Warden at all. She could have done anything and everything she ever wanted.

But they'd had a boy.

William could still remember how it felt to hold his son in his arms for the first time. The fear and disappointment wrung his gut, knowing the weight that tiny, soft-fleshed child was destined to bear. And yet, the deepest, tenderest love also welled in William's chest as he watched his son swing his tiny fists like mad, almost as though, even only moments out of the womb, Desmond knew the future he faced and fought against it.

William had whispered a promise to that wrinkled, little newborn. "We'll be different," he'd sworn. "You and me, we'll be different."

He'd intended to keep that promise. He wasn't quite sure when or how he'd failed. But he had failed, and his son viewed him with the same disdain William felt for Charles.

But perhaps that could change.

Glancing over at Jun as they reached the edge of the bridge, William worked to dampen his anger. He'd failed in more ways than with his son alone. And after only five generations of Simons, he was on the brink of losing their legacy.

Absentmindedly adjusting the Varon ring on his right ring finger—the sigil that marked them as Edmond Varon's true bloodline—William gestured to the island before them. "We'll make a brief stop at the lightkeeper's home," he explained to Jun. "He's the guardian of the Veil and its woods, so he'll lead us to our destination."

Short and stout, Jun had a similar build to William. But the similarities stopped there. The analyst carried a deeper, yellow undertone in his skin, and his eyebrows rested above his slanted eyes rather than on top of them. He let his dark gaze scan the island as they took the path to Fischer and Laurel's cottage.

"This is a beautiful place," Jun noted. "You said the Veil is located in the forest?"

"Yes," William said.

"Interesting."

William wondered if Jun knew about their situation in Porthaven. He was sure the man knew everything the Warden had on paper, which meant he had to be aware of the two Vessels they housed. That made William question if the analyst also knew they were potentially safeguarding two Veils as well.

When Timothy Faulk had mentioned the likelihood of a secondary Veil located in Porthaven, William had immediately begun scouring the peninsula. He'd taken long lunches, searching the least populated areas. He kept a map in his home office, marking any and all possibilities, then crossing them out once he'd searched them.

Despite it being their job to protect two of their hosts, William didn't know much about spirit-beings. The Warden didn't deem it necessary to share the details. The mayors of Porthaven were told what they needed to know to ensure the security of the Vessels, and that was all. As they'd safely held the Leviathan for well over two centuries, it had always seemed like enough.

When the Warden placed the Lewan girls under Porthaven's care, William had just assumed that the Veil of the Leviathan would also become the Veil of the Wolf. One Veil for two spirit-beings. He'd never had any reason to question his presumption until Timothy's assertion.

*"Whichever of the girls that thing attached itself to doesn't matter . . . It would have come here with them."*

But William hadn't been able to find it. Though Reverend O'Sullivan assured him that the Veil had left Bushmills, he was beginning to think that if it hadn't appeared after twelve years, then it never would. Or perhaps, he admitted to himself, he just wasn't looking in the right place.

Fish met them at the door. Introductions were made, and the three men headed for the tree line. Jun began to ask the lightkeeper questions about the forest and his history with the Warden. William maintained his silence.

The myriad of trees were mostly barren in the early fall. It didn't snow as heavily on the peninsula as the rest of the mainland, but that didn't stop winter from coming early in the form of chilled winds and sleepy nature.

Jun had dressed for the occasion, forgoing his suit and tie for jeans, hiking boots, and a more casual button up under his canvas jacket. Fish always looked like a rugged woodsman. His scraggly silver beard and fleece-lined, threadbare corduroy jacket guaranteed it. Even William had dressed down for their trek. To the uninformed onlooker, the trio would look like a normal group of men hiking through the woods.

But the way Fish kept glancing at William—his steely eyes knowing and cautious—made it clear that they were all aware of how serious this meeting was.

"Where's Desmond?" Fish asked.

William kept his voice easy as he replied, "At school."

Fish raised his chin as though having forgotten that school existed. He turned to Jun, practically towering over the man. "Don't let Desmond fool you," he said, deep voice gravelly. "The kid doesn't like people to know how much he cares, but he's got a better heart than most."

"That's good to know," Jun said flatly. "I'll take that into consideration when I talk with him."

The glimmer in Fish's eyes said the analyst had unknowingly answered his question.

William's lips turned up slightly. Fish was as slippery as his namesake and far too cunning for most of the townspeople. He'd brought up Desmond's whereabouts to suss out whether or not the Warden's analyst planned to interview him along with the rest of the Warden members. Fish was conducting his own investigation.

Coming up to the clearing where the Veil stood, Fish slowed his gait. The large sycamore sat dead center, the ground carpeted with its fallen leaves. The spotted trunk bore no signs of tampering on this side, giving a false sense of security to the scene.

As always, the atmosphere around the Veil grew increasingly peaceful. The closer they stepped, the more at ease they grew. A phenomenon that always made William anxious. Something that could alter your mood so readily gave him pause.

Though Jun had said nothing about the damage to the Veil, William had no doubt he knew about it. He continued to lead as they stepped into the clearing, leaving Fish standing within the tree line.

"I don't get close," the lightkeeper explained when Jun commented on it.

"For personal reasons?" Jun asked.

Fish cocked his head. "I suppose you could call it that."

When Jun waited for clarification, Fish continued, "I don't like how it makes me feel. The thing tugs at my connection to the spirit world. I've no interest in letting it use me."

"Veils are not sentient beings, Mr. Lavigne," Jun said. "They're merely a thinning of the planes."

"Doesn't mean I like the way it feels," Fish retorted.

Conceding the subject, Jun joined William once more. They crossed to the backside of the sycamore, coming within view of the large tear halfway down its trunk. The giant fissure peeled back the bark. It was hard to make out anything through the amber's rippled, orange-gold opacity.

William frowned. Desmond had described the amber and the growth of the tear, but he hadn't expected it to be this large.

Jun surveyed the tree. "That's different," he said dully.

William resisted the urge to roll his eyes. "We've studied all the information we have here in Porthaven," he said. "None of our records discuss any events or circumstances resembling this."

"Why didn't you call the archivists?" Jun asked.

The inquiry had begun.

William took it in stride. "I felt we should do whatever we could in-house before bothering the archivists," he said. "If we had the information here, I didn't want to waste the home office's time."

"And now that you've exhausted your sources of information?" Jun asked.

"I'm not sure that we have," he said. "I believe there are still answers to be found in Porthaven."

"What if you're wrong?"

William hesitated at the blunt question.

Jun pointed at the amber-encased tear. "*This* is not a waste of the home office's time," he said. "It's dangerous. The Veil is damaged. Whatever circumstances caused the split, it presents a threat to your town. And you're choosing to handle it without the help of the Warden's experts?"

"For the time being," William replied. "Despite the Veil's damage, it hasn't proven truly dangerous."

Dark, observant eyes watched him. "We were informed that the Veil was producing beasts on its own," he said. "Do you not find that dangerous?"

"What beasts *were* appearing were easily sent back to the spirit world," William said. "And with the amber now sealing it, no beasts have appeared since."

"Where did the amber come from?"

William tightened his jaw at the expected question. "My son," he lied.

Jun's eyes narrowed. "Your son sealed the Veil?"

"He did."

"How?"

With a casual shrug, William said, "He connected to the spirit world and created a seal with his will."

"How did he know how to do that?"

"He didn't."

Jun's brow rose. "You're telling me it was a fluke?"

"It was an act of desperation," William said. "Often, the best results are a meeting of desperate faith and determination. And Desmond is a particularly determined individual."

"Mm." Jun tucked his hands into his jacket pockets, turning back to the tree. "Now that the Veil is seemingly subdued, do you intend to keep your research limited to Porthaven?"

William wasn't deterred by this line of questioning. If there was one good thing his father taught him, it was that a leader needed to be strong. "Until such a time as I find our resources completely exhausted," he said, "we will handle it in-house."

With an indifferent nod, Jun took a step back. "I've seen what I need," he stated blandly. "If you have time, I'd like to hear more about the process you've followed, from learning of the Veil's damage to investigating who or what is causing it."

William led him back to Fish, and the men returned to Aster Island's coast. Whether or not the analyst approved of William's methods, he knew this "inquiry" had little chance of landing in his favor. The Varons were out for blood: his blood and his son's.

Control was William's only defense now. Control of the Veil, control of the Warden, control of the Vessels. He had to keep their lies covered. He had to protect his family and their lineage. And he had to find that second Veil.

# CHAPTER SEVENTEEN

# Cait

Cait's body thrummed with anticipation. Nervous energy caused her heart to tremble in her chest from the moment she opened her eyes. She'd stared into the bathroom mirror blankly for so long that Genni eventually rapped on the door, asking if she was okay.

Jolted out of her stupor, Cait forced herself to finish towel-drying her stick-straight hair from her morning shower. She slapped on a thin layer of moisturizer before rushing into her bedroom, apologizing to Genni on the way, only to lapse into another reverie as she peered into her closet.

Everything she owned was old: The hems of all her jeans were fraying, the fabric of her shirts was thinning, and the soles of her shoes were peeling. Cait stared at the Fair Isle cardigan, her newest and best-kept item, gifted to her by Rese for her last birthday. Her fingers brushed the soft knit. The cream flowers woven into the robin's egg blue stripes reminded her of the mountain avens that dotted the rocky valleys of Ireland.

She'd intentionally kept the cardigan for special occasions, wanting to keep it at its best. The blue complemented her complexion so well that she'd felt unashamedly pretty in it. Desmond had even remarked on how it brought out the blue in her eyes on the one day she'd allowed herself to wear it to the cove.

Now, she wondered if today was worthy of its use.

Cait shook the thought loose from her mind.

Today was no more special than any other. Her "study date" with Desmond meant nothing. She would go, work on the essay with him, and leave as quickly as possible. No matter what he wanted to say to her, she couldn't let go of her resolve. She couldn't let him work his way back into her life.

Intentionally selecting one of her older, worn-in pairs of jeans and her thrifted Chuck Taylors, she dressed to "un-impress." She slipped on a tank top, preparing to layer it under her oldest and baggiest gray sweater.

Then, her hand betrayed her.

Without knowing what drove her last-minute decision, Cait grabbed the cream and blue cardigan. She slipped it over her shoulders, fastened the wooden buttons, and told herself that it was only for her own confidence. After all, if she was going to shut down whatever requests Desmond tried to make, she needed to feel strong enough to do it.

Cait hurried through the rest of the morning, refusing to think any more about her evening. She'd already informed her nan that she was working on a school project that evening. Of course, she'd left out the fact that her project partner was the mayor's son. Or a boy at all.

When she and Genni brought their bikes to the edge of the driveway to wait for Matt, they heard a rumble from up the road where a brown truck puttered into sight.

"Surprise!" Matt called from inside the cab. His bright smile lit up his entire face. "Grandpa and I got her finished up last night. Hop in."

While Genni hurried to put her bike back in the shed, Cait asked for Matt's help putting hers in the bed of the truck. "I've got to work on the project with, uh—with Desmond tonight," she explained when Matt asked why they were taking her bike.

"Oh." He scratched his forehead, looking at the bike, then at the bed of his truck, and then at Cait. "I could pick you up after. You really shouldn't bike home in the cold."

"I do it all the time," Cait promised.

"Doesn't mean you have to anymore," he said with a bashful smile. "I don't mind."

Cait chewed on the inside of her lip. "I don't know how late I'll be," she warned.

"That's fine," he promised. "You can just text me when you're almost done. It's only, like, a ten-minute drive."

Though Cait wasn't entirely certain why, she didn't want to accept the ride. Having her bike would give her an easy escape should she need it. But how could she explain that to Matt without worrying him?

Accepting the kind offer, Cait returned her bike to the shed, then hurried back to the truck. Genni and Matt were already inside, and they scrunched together to make room for her on the bench seat.

"I still can't believe you have to work with Desmond Simon. Blech," Genni said, pretending to retch.

Hugging her backpack to her chest, Cait kept her eyes on the road. "It's fine," she said. "He already has most of the work done, I think, so it shouldn't take long."

"Still," Genni said. "He's such a jerk. I can't believe Mrs. Davis paired you together."

"I'm kind of surprised too," Matt said apologetically. "I mean, it's sort of known around the school, the kind of reputation he has."

Cait tightened her jaw, her skin warming. Yes, the school liked to talk about Desmond's "reputation" as a slacker, a show-off, and a player. He skipped class, was cocky, and dated around . . . allegedly. Cait happened to know that those behaviors were part of Desmond's façade.

His true self—the boy she spent time with at the cove—wasn't that way. He worked hard. He was considerate. And he only flirted, dated, and kissed girls to perpetuate the rumors he'd started for himself—to hide just how lonely he actually was.

Staring out the windshield, Cait's heart thudded in her chest. The barren trees passed by as they turned onto Lawrence Avenue. Gray clouds cluttered the sky, mirroring her somber mood.

Cait cleared her throat, responding to Matt at last. "Your mom's smart," she said. "She knows what everyone else does. No matter his *reputation*," the word came out bitterly, "you'd have to be an idiot to think he'd be interested in me."

Matt tapped his thumb on the steering wheel, lips pressed together. He seemed to be holding something in, or maybe he was just unsure what to say.

Genni rolled her eyes. "You clearly haven't heard the boys talking," she said. "*You're* their current obsession."

Confusion tugged Cait's lips into a frown. "What?"

Genni started braiding a random section of her hair with disinterest. "Jared told me there's a pool going to see who can get your attention first. Apparently, it's a big deal this year because you're a senior."

Utterly baffled, Cait turned away. She couldn't formulate a response to such a bizarre statement. No boys at the school had any sort of interest in her. Even if they did, how could they ever think she'd respond to any of them when they'd ignored her for the past twelve years?

Matt cleared his throat awkwardly. "It's true," he confirmed. "They tease me about it regularly."

Cait blanched, thankful for her sister sitting between them.

Oblivious to Cait's discomfort, Genni added, "It would be such a Desmond move to try and win."

"Can we talk about something else, please?" Cait said quickly, facing the window so neither of her companions saw the heat staining her cheeks.

"Uh, well, my grandpa told me he bought this truck in the fifties," Matt offered kindly. "That's pretty cool, right?"

"Whoa!" Genni surveyed the cab with what seemed to be renewed interest. "Does that make this, like, an antique or something?"

In the final few minutes of the car ride, Cait scrunched tightly against the door. Genni and Matt spoke casually, helping to diffuse the awkwardness, but she couldn't get the pit out of her stomach. She didn't know why, but she felt unsettled. It was as though knowing that the boys at school actually noticed her made her somehow vulnerable, at risk of exposure.

The fact that Genni assumed the worst about Desmond didn't bother Cait. She knew the truth—about him and his feelings for her. Bet or no bet, he'd never pursue her. Not while she carried her da's curse.

The discomfort stuck with Cait as they pulled into the parking lot. Most of the lot was full, but they found a spot near enough to the front that Hunter caught sight of them when they climbed out of the truck. He and Scott jogged over, in awe of Matt's new, old truck. Liz and Melissa hung back, disinterested.

Cait and Genni joined them. After a quick hello, Genni darted away to find Alexis and Jared, leaving Cait to smile shyly at the girls.

Liz tucked some of her dirty blonde hair behind her ear. "So," she said with a twinkle in her eyes, "what are you doing for your birthday?"

Distracted from her previous discomfort, Cait blanched. "How'd you know—?"

"Genni mentioned it," Liz explained. "She said she wants to pull together a party for you now that we're all hanging out. And I think she's completely right. It's your eighteenth birthday! We've got to do something big."

A swell of warmth filled Cait's heart. Even if Genni did live in her own world at times, she had the sincerest heart. But that didn't mean Cait wanted to celebrate.

"Oh, that's all right," she deflected. "I'm not much for parties."

"Nonsense!" Liz insisted while Melissa smiled along beside her. "We've got two weeks, right? What's your dream birthday?"

Cait was blindsided by the question. "Uh . . . I don't know. I've never really thought about it."

Although if Cait were being honest, she knew exactly what her dream birthday would involve: a day at the cove with the one person she *couldn't* spend time with anymore.

"Hm." Liz and Melissa exchanged knowing looks. "We'll have to come up with something then."

Thinking of the party that Liz and her brother had thrown only a week ago, Cait blanched. "Well, maybe something with just us," she suggested. "Like, a girls' night or something."

"Oh, yeah," Melissa said, her blonde ponytail bouncing as she nodded. "That would be so fun. It can just be us three and Genni."

"And maybe Rese too," Cait added.

Liz pursed her lips at Rese's name but didn't reject the idea. For the first time, Cait wondered what Liz thought of Rese dating her brother, but she didn't think it was the right time to ask.

"I like it," Liz said, approval in her tone. "We'll have it at my place. Okay. So, what are your favorites, Cait? Food. Color. Movie. Everything. I need details so I can plan."

The boys joined them—including Sterling, who had wandered over after his arrival at school—and they walked to class like a herd of sheep. The rest of the morning, Liz and Melissa pestered Cait about her likes and dislikes. And strangely, Cait didn't mind the millions of personal questions. She'd never had a girls' night aside from with her family, and that hardly counted. Sisters didn't invite you to sleep over, eat popcorn, and paint each other's nails. They pushed into your room with blankets and snacks, ready to snuggle up in your bed.

Sisters were a comfortable love, but it wasn't a choice.

Friends *chose* you. They went out of their way to make you a part of their life.

Both were wonderful, but for the first time in her life, Cait felt chosen. And she couldn't deny that it felt somehow more special.

The high from Liz and Melissa's company wore off the instant school ended.

Cait gathered her things, the tremble working its way back into her fingers. She fought with the zipper on her backpack as Matt chatted about the upcoming basketball game beside her. The hum trilled softly through her head, reminding her that Desmond waited. She had a whole evening of fighting to maintain her distance ahead of her. And she feared she wouldn't be strong enough.

Genni met them in the halls as they headed to the parking lot. Cait gripped the straps of her backpack, trying not to let her nervousness show. She, Matt, and Genni said their final farewells to their friends before continuing up the rows to the truck.

"Lewan." Desmond's voice rang out behind the trio. They all turned to see him walking up.

Cait's heart stalled. He looked especially good today in the cool blue tee he wore under his bomber jacket. That shade reminded her of the cerulean blue in her set of pastels, and she wondered if she could ever draw a portrait that did him justice.

Clenching her jaw, Cait worked to dampen the hum in her head. "Yes?" she said, her voice sounding taut to her own ears.

Desmond spared a single glance for Matt and Genni. Then, he held Cait's gaze. "Where are you going?" he asked.

Cait's brow furrowed. "To Matt's truck. I'll meet you—"

"No."

Cait blinked at Desmond's interruption. "What?"

The sea-chilled wind ruffled his unruly hair. "I told you yesterday," he said, "I'll drive you."

Cait blanched. "Oh, no, that's—that's not necessary. Matt's gonna—"

"Go out of his way to drop you off and pick you up?" Desmond said with a bored inflection. "That's cute but not necessary."

"I don't mind," Matt said.

Desmond leveled him with a flat stare. "Neither do I." Then, he turned back to Cait expectantly.

Holding her breath, Cait struggled to hold her anger with it. He was doing this on purpose. His logic was sound. Why should Matt drop her off when she was going to the same place as Desmond? Why make Matt wait for a text when Desmond could just return her home when they finished their paper?

He was trapping her. And she had no means of escape without looking irrational.

"Fine," Cait said weakly. "Thanks."

"No problem," Desmond said, his tone filled with indifference.

Matt tapped Cait's arm with an encouraging rap. "We'll see you later," he said, turning to continue to his truck.

Genni lingered long enough to meet Desmond's gaze and say, "Try anything, and I'll make sure you can't play basketball for the rest of the season." Then, she spun on her heel and followed Matt.

Desmond let out an amused snort. "Your sister's got spunk," he remarked. He tipped his head to the far side of the parking lot. "Come on, Lewan."

Heaving a sigh, Cait trailed behind Desmond, keeping enough space between them to make it clear she wasn't comfortable with this arrangement. Not only because that was the behavior people would expect of her, but because she actually was uncomfortable. A week ago, she would have leaped at the opportunity to ride in Desmond's car with him. But now, she feared what that sort of closeness might bring.

The parking lot was still full of students, many stopping to whisper to one another as Cait and Desmond walked by. She felt her shoulders slump, her chin dipping in tandem. Was this what it would be like to be Desmond's real friend? Would people watch them everywhere they went? How could he stand it?

They arrived at his black muscle car, its shiny paint and tinted windows reflecting Cait's image back at her. She thought she looked appropriately nervous in his presence.

Sinking into the passenger seat, Cait marveled at the butter-smooth leather. Desmond carelessly tossed his backpack into the backseat, but she set hers gently at her feet. She'd never been in a car this nice before. More remarkably, she'd never been in *Desmond's* car. The experience was extraordinarily disorienting.

With a rumble that mimicked the hum in her skull, the engine purred to life. Cait carefully drew the seat belt across her chest, doing all she could not to think about how the car smelled like leather, cedar, and musk—like Desmond.

She kept her eyes forward, keenly aware of his every movement, even as she tried to ignore him. Since the vehicle's dark windows dimmed the already dark interior, they were encapsulated, separated from the rest of the world. And Cait didn't like it.

Putting the car into gear, Desmond began to back it out of the parking space. "You're making this very weird," he said.

Cait played with the hem of her sweater, eyes locked on the black dashboard. "Sorry," she murmured.

She saw him shake his head in her peripheral vision. But he didn't say anything else.

The drive to the Simon house took less than five minutes. Yet, it felt like thirty as the silence stretched between them.

Cait gritted her teeth. Desmond was right. She *was* making this weird. But wasn't that better? It would help them focus on writing the paper and ending the night as soon as possible. It wouldn't allow any resurfacing of who they used to be.

They turned onto Osprey Street, the beautiful vintage homes welcoming them into the neighborhood. Each of the whitewashed houses sat on narrow but deep lots of lush green lawns. Picket fences enclosed each home, flowering bushes and sophisticated lawn furniture within their cozy embrace.

Desmond pulled into his family's driveway, its smooth pavement so different from the gravel of Cait's home. The driveway wrapped around to the back of the house, where a detached two-car garage waited. He parked next to it, the world settling into a jarring silence when the engine ceased its roar.

Suddenly, Cait felt her throat dry up as she stared at the garage.

Desmond had parked *next* to it, suggesting that his parents' cars took up the garage space.

Breathing was suddenly a whole lot harder. Were his parents home? Of course, she knew William. Both because of his yearly visits and from whatever that conversation was on Saturday. But she would hardly consider them so much as mere acquaintances.

And Desmond's mom? Cait hadn't even met her.

Oh, she'd seen her from a distance. Robin Simon was the epitome of an elegant woman. No matter the occasion, she dressed immaculately, and her soft brown hair draped over her shoulders with a perfect, sleek curl. She carried herself with a gentle confidence that Cait could only dream of having.

And Cait knew she'd never measure up—to the woman or what she desired for her son.

"You coming?" Desmond asked. He already stood outside the vehicle, peering at her through his open door.

Desperately wishing she could find some way to avoid entering the Simon home, Cait grabbed her backpack. "Yeah."

With reluctance, Cait followed him into the backyard through a low fence. The yard exuded pure charm. A white wicker swing rested between two rows of flowering bushes, their blooms hibernating for the season. The misty windows of a modest greenhouse hinted at burgeoning growth in its interior. Stone pavers led to the back door, and ivy climbed up a white lattice on the wall.

Desmond trotted across the well-groomed lawn and up the short steps to the door.

And Cait froze.

Her entire life in Porthaven, she'd wanted to see into the Simon house. Time after time, she'd imagined what it would be like inside its dignified walls. And she'd always resigned herself to never knowing.

Now, she was about to walk in as a welcome guest.

Cait frowned. Would she be welcome? Yes, Desmond had invited her, but would his parents be pleased to have her there? How could they be, even if she was Desmond's project partner?

Desmond stepped inside, casually hooking his keys on the rack next to the door. Then, he turned, waiting for her.

Forcing her foot onto the first step, Cait steeled herself for whatever she'd find inside.

They stepped straight into a kitchen as immaculate and lovely as Cait had envisioned. Even in the dim, overcast afternoon, the crisp white cabinets lining the walls and the sparkling countertops glowed from the undercabinet lighting. A single glass sat beside the sink, the only sign that the house wasn't a model.

Two arched entryways flanked the cabinetry on the far wall. Desmond gestured toward them as he moved into the kitchen. "We'll work up in my room," he said. "Do you want anything before—"

"That you, seabird?" a feminine voice called, interrupting him.

Desmond flinched, and Cait felt her eyebrows rise. "Seabird?" she wanted to ask, but she kept her mouth shut as Robin appeared.

"Oh." The woman paused at the sight of them. She flicked on the kitchen light. Her blue eyes shifted between her son and the girl he'd brought with him.

A slow smile tugged up the corner of Robin's mouth, and Cait got the impression the woman innately divined the relationship between them.

"Hello," Robin said, stepping forward. "I wasn't aware that Desmond was bringing a friend over." She shot a look at her son with the last words.

Desmond sighed and gestured to Cait. "Mom, this is . . ." He let the introduction hang as though he couldn't remember her name.

"Caitriona Lewan," Robin finished for him.

Cait was equally surprised that the woman knew her on sight *and* that she pronounced her name correctly. "Yes, ma'am," she confirmed.

Robin's smile softened as though she were genuinely happy to see her. "It's nice to meet you, Caitriona. Welcome to our home. Please, call me Robin."

Unsure what else to say, she sheepishly replied, "Thanks."

"We're partners on a history project," Desmond said, with exaggerated disinterest.

Robin eyed him for a lingering second before saying, "How fun."

"Yeah, tons." Desmond pointed past her toward the exit. "So, we're gonna. . . ."

Ignoring her son's attempted escape, Robin turned to Cait. "Will you be joining us for dinner?" she asked. "I'm making Desmond's favorite: chicken Alfredo."

A deep urge welled up within Cait to accept the offer. For years, she'd longed for this very moment—the chance to be welcomed into Desmond's life. Discovering that his mother was this kind made it all the more appealing.

But her sense of self-preservation forced her to say, "Oh, no. Thank you, but I can't stay that long."

A muscle spasmed in Desmond's jaw despite his otherwise placid expression.

Cait knew that reaction of his, and it made her hesitate. The familiar twitch was Desmond's tell before he shoved down whatever emotion he wanted to hide. She wondered if Robin caught it as well.

By the knowing lift of the woman's chin, Cait guessed she did.

Robin smirked at her son, then turned back to Cait. "You're sure? It's a special night—"

"Mom," Desmond said, his tone surprisingly sharp. "She said she can't stay."

A long stare passed between mother and son, the two exchanging some battle of wills that Cait couldn't fully understand. She'd lost her mum well before she could ever experience whatever kind of familial understanding the Simons shared. It made her feel as though she'd missed out on one of the most frustratingly wonderful experiences of life.

Eventually, Robin conceded. "Let me know if you change your mind."

"Thanks," Cait repeated.

"Right," Desmond said, moving toward the hall. "This way."

But as he tried to pass her, Robin set a hand on his chest, bringing them to a temporary halt. She locked eyes with her son. "Door open."

Cait felt her face heat while Desmond froze.

The serious expression on Robin's face eased, her hand falling back to her side.

Desmond scoffed, his signature grin lighting up his face. "Like I'm that stupid."

She winked at him. "A mother can't be too careful."

A pleased laugh escaped Desmond, surprising Cait. He began to walk around his mother, a finger held up as though scolding her. "That hurts," he said. "I thought you trusted me."

Awkwardly, Cait followed him out of the kitchen just as Robin replied, "Always, seabird."

Shaking his head, the grin stayed on Desmond's face. He led Cait through the hall into the large living space, which was just as perfectly luxurious as the kitchen but immeasurably cozier. Built-in shelves lined nearly every wall, filled with books, seaside knickknacks, and other decorative pieces like photos, candlesticks, and vases. Somehow, Robin Simon had managed to make the cliché of driftwood and conch shells elegant.

The colors were warm and inviting: creams, browns, and charcoals. A woven blanket was draped across one of the plush couches, with numerous pillows scattered across the front. Cait suddenly had the urge to dive onto the perfect landing pad those pillows created.

Instead, she followed Desmond up the large wooden staircase to the second floor.

Anticipation and dread swirled in her stomach. In spite of all the years she'd known him and all the secrets she'd uncovered that no one else had, being in Desmond's house caused a riotous effect in her body. She simultaneously yearned for and cowered at the prospect of seeing and being within his most private space.

The second floor was a winding passage of rooms, reminding her that despite the modern renovations, the home was still over two hundred years old. A window lit the dark wood floors and trim, the overcast sky keeping it soft and shadowed. They passed the first two closed doors on their way toward the back of the house.

A solitary door awaited them, an old, fading sign hanging on its cherry wood face. A hand-painted seabird flew above the lettering of Desmond's name. Cait couldn't help her small smile, knowing that Robin must have crafted the sign, and even as a high school senior, her son hadn't had the heart to remove the sentimental object.

Desmond opened the door, letting it swing wide before gesturing for her to enter.

For a heartbeat, Cait hesitated in the hall. Then, she stepped forward, knowing she had no escape.

Crossing the threshold felt like stepping over a line she couldn't come back from. Unlike the rest of the Simon house, Cait could honestly say she hadn't ever considered what Desmond's room might look like. She'd managed to keep her thoughts from drifting to such an intimate space. But seeing it before her, she realized it was exactly what she would have envisioned.

Dark, moss green walls shrouded the room in an earthy mantle. The same rich wood as the door trimmed the room and built-in bookcases, cluttered with the science fiction, horror, and fantasy novels he'd read at the cove through the years. The space was almost three times the size of her own room, housing a sofa in front of a mounted flat-screen TV, an ample-sized desk nestled under a large double-hung window, and a queen bed made up with the fluffiest comforter she had ever seen.

If she'd thought the couch downstairs was inviting her to leap into its comfy embrace, she had to say that the bed practically demanded it. She took an involuntary step in its direction as the hum grew louder in her mind than ever before. The cedar scent she'd come to attribute to Desmond overwhelmed her within the room, warping her sense of reason. Her brain betrayed her, imagining what it'd be like to climb under that charcoal gray comforter, smothering herself in his lingering scent.

Cait's stomach dropped.

To distract herself, she looked back at Desmond, who was just entering the room behind her. "So . . ." She pressed her lips together in a nervous smile. "Seabird?"

Desmond grimaced, though she could see the fondness he held for the endearment secreted away in his eyes. Leaving the door open as instructed, he walked over to the sofa, depositing his backpack on its cushions. "She's called me that my whole life," he admitted.

"Why?" she heard herself ask, immediately regretting the question. She shouldn't care—shouldn't try to learn more about him and his home life. That was too close to returning to who they'd once been.

He met her gaze, a question in the furrow of his brow. He understood the distance she'd been trying to place between them too. His answering shrug was half-hearted. "Who knows why parents choose weird nicknames?"

Cait could hear the lie in his response. He knew exactly why his mom called him "seabird." He simply didn't want to tell her.

Clearing his throat, Desmond gestured to the door cracked open to the right of the TV. "If you need it, the bathroom is there," he said, then motioned to a mini fridge by the entertainment center, "and there's some water and pop in the fridge."

Unsure what to think of his previous lie and the space in general, Cait chose the least offensive topic. "You have your own bathroom?"

"Yeah, uh—it used to be attached to the hall, but when we renovated a few years back, my parents decided to make it an . . ." He paused as though realizing how vastly different their lives were. He had a private bathroom, while she, her sisters, and her nan shared one. His whole house looked like it belonged in a magazine. Her house showcased peeling wallpaper, donated furnishings, and a broken dishwasher.

Desmond cleared his throat. "An en suite," he finished, the words quiet.

Suddenly, Cait couldn't help herself. She snorted, a laugh bubbling within her.

Desmond stared at her like she'd lost her mind.

She set a hand to her mouth, failing to hold in her laughter. "Sorry," she said around her amusement. "It's just so absurd."

A cautious smile lifted his lips. "What is?"

She waved her hand in the air, the gesture encompassing his whole room. "All of this," she said. "It's—it's like you live in a movie. Nothing's out of place. There's no clutter anywhere. No random stacks of paper or dirty dishes. No shoes kicked off by the door or crumbs on the counter. Does your family even live here?"

Something between humor and defensiveness drew his eyebrows together. "Of course we do."

"Do you have a maid or something?"

He tipped his head to the side. "We have a lady come in once a week. But she just takes care of the kitchen and bathrooms."

Cait gaped at him.

"You know my dad, Cait," he said. "Between his military-like need for control and my mom's urge to keep everything 'pretty' all the time, there isn't really room for a messy house."

"But you're *you*," Cait returned. "The guy who rebels for fun."

"What's your point?"

"Your bed is made."

Desmond blinked, confused. "Yeah?"

"Like, pillows fluffed and everything."

He frowned at her. "Don't you make your bed?"

"Sometimes."

He looked baffled. "Sometimes?"

"Wow. You are. . . ." She stopped herself from admitting her thoughts but couldn't hold back her smile.

"I'm what?" Desmond asked.

Cait shook her head, but she could read in his intense expression that he wouldn't let her get away with staying silent. So, she distilled her complicated feelings into one word. "Unreal."

She meant it in that he was too good to be true, too perfect and impossible. Too fantastic to be anything but a fairy tale. He and his whole life were charmed. He was a modern-day prince, and she was the peasant who could never be worthy of him.

But she could see by the tightness of Desmond's jaw that he took it to mean that he and his family were impractical and foolish in their overly beautiful life. He took offense at the suggestion that she thought they were living in an indulgently perfected daydream.

Cait decided not to correct his interpretation.

"Well, thanks," he said, tone notably curt. "You want to work on this essay? Or would you like me to give you a tour of my alphabetized video game collection?"

Further amused despite his harsh tone, Cait smirked. "Do you alphabetize your books too?"

"By author."

She nodded. "Cool."

Catching her barely contained laughter, Desmond finally relaxed. His next breath came out in a relieved scoff. He grabbed a small pillow from the sofa and hurled it at Cait.

A giggle slipped out of her as she narrowly dodged the projectile.

"You're freaking making fun of me," Desmond accused.

Cait raised her brow. "About time you figured it out."

His smile lit up his whole face. "I thought you didn't want to be here."

Cait's expression fell. She didn't need to say anything for Desmond to see his previous assumption confirmed.

He deflated. "So, why act like . . . ?"

"It's a habit," she admitted.

"One you're trying to break?"

"Yes."

Desmond's face twisted up in confusion. "Why?"

Cait stared back at him, the comfort of the previous moments shattered. How she'd let herself slip back into their old ways, she didn't know. But she couldn't bear to have this discussion now in his bedroom. She feared what honesty could do to them in an intimate setting like this.

She shifted her weight from foot to foot, fighting the urge within her to flee. "I already told you once. Let's just write the essay and . . . and then we can move on."

"What if I don't want to move on?"

His question made Cait's heart catch in her throat.

They stared at each other, the sofa a barrier between them.

"I do," she whispered.

He flinched but moved forward, kneeling on the sofa to lean closer. "Caity," his voice was low and adamant, "please, let me explain."

Taking a step back, Cait pulled in a tight breath.

Desmond kept speaking, seeing her hesitation. "What happened last week—on the island—I can explain all of that," he promised. "And I'll tell you whatever else you want to know as well. About anything. And if I don't know the answers, then we'll find them. Together."

"Stop," Cait heard herself murmur, the hum rumbling through her head.

"You said you were mad at me," he reminded her. "At the Greenes', you said that. And—and I told you I'd do what I could to fix it. So, let me fix it, Cait."

"Stop!" Cait spat the word, lifting her hands next to her ears. She wanted to cover them, to block out his voice and the emotion within it, to smother the hum and the way it urged her toward him.

Steeling herself, Cait met Desmond's pained stare. She refused to feel sorry for him. "I don't want your help," she said. "I don't want your answers. And I don't want you to fix it."

He opened his mouth, but she cut him off.

"I don't want *you*." The words hissed out of her, a broken half-truth. "So, please, just write this essay with me, and then leave me alone."

Hurt etched every inch of Desmond's face. Slowly, he donned a mask of detachment. He backed off the sofa, grabbed his backpack, and motioned to the newly freed space. "You can sit here," he stated blandly. "I'll work at the desk."

Cait considered thanking him for accepting her request and for thoughtfully giving them separate spaces to work in. Instead, she stayed silent, knowing he wouldn't appreciate the gesture.

They took their seats, each removing supplies from their backpacks. Cait noted that despite haphazardly tossing a notebook and a pencil case on the desktop, Desmond methodically put the rest of his things away. She wondered about his organization. She never would have expected it from him, and it made her wonder what else she'd missed.

Ignoring the hollowness in her chest at the thought, Cait opened her notebook. "Did you still want to write about the Festival of 1896?" she asked.

"Unless you had a better idea." He spoke in the same tone he used when they were in public together—flat and disinterested.

Cait shook her head. "No, I . . . I like your idea."

"Cool." He pointed to a stack of three books. "These are from my dad's personal library. I've already marked individual passages that should work for our sources."

"Oh, that's great." She stared at her page of notes rather than at him. "How do we want to go about this? Should we make an outline first?"

Desmond held out his now-open notebook between them. "Already did that."

Cait frowned. "I thought we were going to do equal—"

"Cait," he interrupted, "I'm making this easy for you. Read the outline, tell me if you want to make any adjustments, and we'll take an hour to write the thing. Then, you can go home."

Despite her need to do her part, Cait couldn't deny the offer's appeal. The less time spent in his presence and room, the better. Equal work be damned.

Cait grabbed the proffered notebook, internally scolding herself for the unspoken curse. She read the outline, annoyed by how clean and attractive Desmond's handwriting was. He'd done a good job, detailing just enough so she could understand the thesis and see its throughline.

"Do you think we can get five pages out of this?" Cait asked, daring to look up at him.

He still wore the same bored expression as his desk chair spun around to face her. "I could make it ten," he said, then pointed to the page. "Any thoughts?"

Cait looked back at the bulleted paragraphs. "I don't really know enough about it to make any suggestions yet. Maybe you could show me the sources you found?"

"Sure thing."

For the next fifteen minutes, Desmond walked her through his references and the plans he had for the essay. He regurgitated most of the information from memory. It impressed Cait how much he knew about Porthaven's history without help to recall the details. He could tell her the exact number of visitors who had traveled to the town to attend the Festival, the highlighted vendors and shows that were to be put on, as well as the wind speeds that the storm had swept up.

"Great-uncle Martin was a hero," Desmond explained. "The storm came in unexpectedly, one of the worst the town has ever seen. The lightning was what caused the old factory to catch on fire, but that's not really relevant to our paper. While people rushed for cover, Martin stayed out with the rest of the Varons and several other Warden members to help get people to safety."

"Just Warden members?" Cait asked.

"Yeah."

"Why?"

"Because that's our job," he replied as though it were obvious.

She gave a nod, and he continued, "The winds were so strong that the men struggled to keep their footing even as they ushered people inside. Some of the booths were even ripped apart. The wood splintered, and the wind carried the debris, impaling a dozen people. Three of them died.

"As they were trying to get the survivors into the buildings, Martin noticed a boat in the water near the docks. Some stupid kids had gone out in a rowboat without anyone's knowledge. When the storm started, they'd tried to row back to shore, but it came in so suddenly, they couldn't make it." Desmond shrugged as though the story wasn't horrific. "Martin ran to the docks, dove into the water, and hauled the boat close enough for the other men to pull the kids to safety."

"But he didn't make it?" Cait surmised.

Desmond shook his head. "He drowned."

"That's horrible," she whispered.

"Yeah," he agreed. "That's when good ol' Lyndon Simon became Christopher Varon's heir. He and Martin were best friends as well as brothers-in-law, so Christopher viewed him as a second son."

"And that was the start of the Varon-Simon feud, I take it?" she asked.

"Yep." He smirked. "But we'll leave that out of the essay."

From there, the first draft came together readily. Cait knew it was almost entirely thanks to Desmond, but she felt she'd added enough small adjustments or thoughts to make it a team effort. He typed it up on his laptop, and within another hour, they settled on a mutually agreed-upon revision.

"You take it home and read it through," Desmond said, handing her the printed pages. "Make whatever notes you like, and I'll make the changes when you return them."

Cait carefully tucked the essay into the pages of her notebook. "Okay. Is that it, then?"

Desmond gave a reluctant nod. "That's it."

"Then, I guess . . ." She pulled her backpack over one shoulder, letting the unspoken request hang.

"I'll take you home," he answered.

Cait gave one last look at Desmond's room as he grabbed his jacket. She'd never return here. This had been her one chance to be part of his life. And she had rejected it.

They went back downstairs, through the kitchen where Robin had begun preparing dinner. She made one last attempt to get Cait to stay for the meal, but Cait held firm to her decision. Desmond grabbed his keys from the hook, promising to be home in half an hour. Then, they were back in his car, speeding off Lawrence Avenue and onto the state road that connected the peninsula to the mainland.

Cait was proud of herself. She'd done what had felt impossible. And after Desmond dropped her off, they'd be over for good. She wouldn't have to protect herself from him. She wouldn't linger on wishful dreams or foolish memories. She would be free.

The hum gave a disgruntled pulse in the back of her head.

She wondered if she'd still feel it—that vibration that seemed to point her in his direction. When she truly and completely gave up on him, would it fade away? Could she exist in a room with Desmond Simon and not feel his presence in her soul?

The turn onto Lure Road came up on their left, leading to her neighborhood. The car slowed to make the turn. Another few minutes and it would be over. Cait couldn't help the relieved sigh that escaped her.

Then, Desmond's fingers tightened on the wheel. "Screw it," he said, and his foot hit the gas.

The engine let out a sudden roar as the car lurched forward, sending Cait back into her seat. "What are you doing?" she demanded as they zoomed past the turn.

"Making you listen to me."

# CHAPTER EIGHTEEN

# Desmond

Abduction was a new low for Desmond. And while he wasn't proud of his decision, he did feel a certain justice within it.

This was it, he told himself. He would plead his case, tell her the truth, and if she still wanted nothing to do with him afterward, he'd let her go.

"Turn around," Cait demanded as they careened down the highway.

The coastline faded to the purple and orange watercolor of sunset, the overcast sky only allowing a sliver of the sun to peek through on the horizon. Desmond let the darkness seep into his mood. "Like hell I will," he retorted.

"Desmond." Cait said his name like a curse. "Take. Me. Home." She punctuated each word with so much force that it almost sounded like she was growling.

He didn't care. She could bare her teeth all she wanted. His fear of losing her outweighed every instinct of safety. "Not until you listen to me," he returned.

Cait whirled away from him, arms crossing as she glared at the encroaching night. They both fell silent, their anger at one another charging the air.

Desmond's foot pressed harder on the gas, taking them at an unreasonable speed up the peninsula. The car carried them across the macadam, the world a frightening blur. He jerked the wheel to the left, sending them sailing into the ancient parking lot of the old factory. The brakes squealed as he slammed his foot down, the back tires skidding. Cait's hand grew white-knuckled on the door handle, her eyes wide.

Desmond threw the car into park and jerked to face her. "You gonna listen?" he asked.

Glaring at him, the blue of Cait's eyes had faded to the slimmest halos in the dark. "No."

"Glad you're so willing," Desmond sniped. He flipped off the headlights, making the car harder to spot in the factory's shadow. "Good news: You're stuck with me until I've had my say, so get comfortable."

Cait rolled her eyes and turned away to stare out the windshield. Perhaps he should have been wary of pushing her even farther away from him, but Desmond thrived on the disapproval and outrage of others.

Unlatching his seat belt, Desmond shifted to face her fully. "First," he began, "you need to understand that I'm not your enemy, okay? I'm the one person you *can* trust."

She huffed her disagreement.

"What do you want from me, Caity?" he demanded. "Huh? Do you want me to apologize for lying about the beasts in your dreams? I'm sorry. I thought I was protecting you, but it was a stupid mistake. Do you want me to tell you the truth? I'm more than happy to do that."

"Like I could believe anything you said," she muttered.

"But you can believe Hunter?" He scoffed. "Did the past ten years mean nothing to you?"

Her head whipped in his direction, fury in her open-mouthed expression. He'd never seen her so angry, and he found it strangely attractive. The quickly dimming sky washed through the windshield, casting her in a blend of bronze light and rusty shadow. It emphasized the elegant lines of her face, drawing attention to how her rosy lips lifted in a scowl.

"You're the one who lied that whole time," she accused.

"Yeah, I did," he readily admitted. "And I'm owning up to it. You know me, Caity. You know I lie about everything, not because I want to, but because I have to."

"You *never* have to lie, Desmond."

"Do you *want* me to tell the Warden that you inherited the Wolf?" he asked, acknowledging to her for the first time that he believed in the legacy she called a curse.

Cait's face fell with instant panic.

"Because if I do," he said, voice softening, "they'll chain you to some random Warden member, imprisoning you in this town forever."

Her eyes filled with tears, but none of them fell.

Desmond's heart twisted. "But if I don't," he went on, "if I *lie* to them, you'll remain hidden long enough for me to find a way to free you."

The sun dipped below the horizon, and the world was smothered under a growing blue-black blanket.

Cait's eyes darted back and forth between his, anger replaced by fear. Her pale skin grew wan beneath the bluish light of night. "Then, it's true?" she whispered. "It's me?"

Unable to voice a confirmation, he nodded.

Cait screwed up her face, turning away. Her silver-blonde hair slipped from behind her ear, hanging like a veil to obscure his view of her face. "How long have you known?"

He could hear the desperation in her question. She feared that he'd kept this secret from her all along.

"Since you told me about the beasts killing me in your dreams." He paused, then asked, "Am I . . . is that still happening? Am I still dying?"

With a slow breath in, Cait shook her head.

He didn't know whether to be relieved or not. "That's good, I guess," he murmured. He leaned against the back of his seat, trying to catch her gaze. "I don't really know how the dreams work, but they're pretty definitive proof. You dreamed about the bears and wolves on the nights when they appeared. Add that to the fact that you managed to wield through a block, and I don't see any way to refute it."

"The block," she whispered knowingly. Then, she closed her eyes, releasing a tired breath. "I appreciate you trying to be honest with me, Desmond, but I . . . I can't do this anymore."

Desmond's heart sank. "Do what?" he asked, though he already knew the answer.

"I need you to leave me alone, Desmond," Cait said, her words firm. "Whatever happens . . . whatever curse I carry, I will accept it. And I need you to stop trying to fix it."

"No." The word breathed out of Desmond.

"Don't do this," she pleaded.

Desmond leaned forward. "I'm not going to let you sacrifice yourself, Cait," he insisted, knowing she didn't understand the full truth behind his confession.

"It's too late," she said. "Whatever you try to do, this is who I am. How are you going to *fix* that?"

"I'm already looking for a way," he explained. "I have some theories. There are . . . the Warden has some legends surrounding the spirit-beings. I'm looking into them, and I'm going to find a way to remove it from you."

Cait set her head in her hands. "No," she whispered, then raised her voice. "No, it doesn't matter. There's no solution to this. And I need you to let it go."

"I won't."

"Please, Desmond," she begged, eyes glimmering with unshed tears in the glow of his car's dashboard lights. She looked so frightened, with her nose scrunched up and eyebrows pinched together. "Just leave it alone."

Once more, Desmond said, "No."

"Why not?" Cait demanded, voice breaking around the words.

Desmond held her tear-filled gaze, wanting to answer her as truthfully as possible. He wanted to say that he would do anything to save her. He wanted to tell her he'd never give up because she meant more to him than anyone else. He wanted to speak every cliché line that had welled inside him over the past ten years and reaffirm what he'd told her almost two weeks ago: Their relationship and the feelings between them *were* real, and he wouldn't stop until they could be together.

But the words stuck in his chest, never even reaching his mouth.

A pained sigh slipped from Cait, and she began to turn away.

Desmond's hand shot out, cupping her cheek and turning her back to him. Before either of them could process what he was doing, he kissed her.

Not one of those stupid, playful kisses he'd given her on her birthday the past four years. This was no longer a game he was content to lose. He wasn't willing to lie to her anymore.

So, when Desmond kissed her, it was a real kiss. A full, lingering, fervent kiss.

Her lips were cool under his, the tip of her nose tickling his cheek. He'd expected her to tense or pull away—to do *something*. But she simply sat there, still and unresponsive.

Certain he'd made the biggest mistake of his life, Desmond began to draw back, opening his eyes to discover whatever rejection he knew he'd read in her expression. But then, Cait's hands were pressed to his face, her lips finding his to continue the kiss.

Desmond's head spun, a chill funneling from his scalp to his chest. It felt as though all the blood had rushed straight to his heart, sending it into overdrive. He wondered if it would explode.

Then, he stopped wondering about anything at all.

Desmond found himself completely lost in kissing Cait. He'd wanted to do it for so long that he wasn't sure if the moment was reality or some strange waking dream. His hand found the latch on her seat belt, releasing her to draw her nearer. He tightened his hold on her, the pads of his fingers tingling where they touched her skin. Her hair tangled between them, confirming the truth: This was real.

*They* were real.

Somewhere along the way, ten years of secret friendship had morphed into an aching love neither of them had been willing to act upon. For Cait, he'd always assumed it was due to fear of his rejection. For Desmond, it was all because he was too weak and cowardly to forsake his family's expectations. Now, the barrier was broken, and none of those things mattered anymore.

Desmond found himself practically sitting on the center console to get closer to her. His long-repressed feelings for Cait flooded out of him with such force that he wasn't entirely aware of his actions. Somehow, one hand had found its way to her waist while the other slipped under her cardigan to press her against him. He could hear their breath growing ragged but didn't experience the shortness in his lungs. If ever there was an out-of-body experience, he was pretty sure this was it.

Suddenly, Cait jerked back. "I can't do this," she gasped.

Head drowning in the waves of emotion rolling through him, Desmond struggled to focus. He blinked wildly, taking in the sight of her as she scrambled back in her seat with something like panic in her eyes. Her words hit him, and his body turned cold.

"Why not?" he heard himself ask, though he wasn't entirely sure how he'd found the presence of mind to formulate a sentence.

Cait shook her head, cheeks flushing pink. "I—I'm not like you," she said softly. "I can't pretend that this doesn't mean anything to me."

Desmond found himself gaping at her. She thought that this—him kissing her—was only a distraction for him. She thought that he didn't mean it. And he couldn't blame her. For years, they'd both pretended. They'd hidden everything they felt for one another from the world. They'd attempted to hide it from each other too.

Holding her gaze, Desmond made sure she saw his sincerity as well as heard it when he said, "I'm done pretending."

Cait's lips parted as she sucked in a short breath.

Then, they crashed together again like a wave against the shore. With the truth finally spoken—the admission of their feelings made—everything felt different. The moment was electrically charged and stunningly free. A desperate push and pull of lips and hands and arms and tongues.

The once cold October evening turned to balmy heat in the car. Desmond shrugged out of his jacket before reaching for Cait's cardigan. He pushed it back, his fingers brushing over the thin strap of her tank top and the rose-petal-soft skin of her shoulder. He leaned farther in, sure that close could never be close enough.

Then, Desmond's foot slipped and depressed the gas pedal.

The engine revved with a ferocious roar, and they both startled, breaking the kiss.

"Sorry," he muttered, leaning in once more only to find Cait's hand on his chest, holding him back.

She smiled, breath stilted as she pulled away. "We should probably stop anyway," she said.

Desmond furrowed his brow. "Why?"

A soft laugh escaped her. "Des," her eyes wouldn't meet his as she straightened her cardigan, "we shouldn't do this—act like hormonal teenagers."

"We *are* hormonal teenagers," he reminded her.

Her blush rose to her temples, though her bashful grin said she found the humor in his reply. But Desmond knew she was right. There was a tension that came from withholding the affection you felt for someone. And when the band finally snapped, it could cause a violent backlash in the wake of its release.

If they weren't careful, things could readily get out of hand.

Pressing his lips together, Desmond forced himself to take a long inhale. "Okay," he said, sitting back. "You're right."

They settled into their separate seats, staring out into the night. Desmond placed his hands on the steering wheel to avoid reaching for her again. A dreadful silence descended between them. Where did they go from here? He hadn't thought that far. They couldn't deny their desire to be together now. Yet, nothing had changed.

Cait was still the Vessel, and Desmond was her ultimate captor. Unless, of course, the Warden decided to depose his dad. Then, what would Desmond become? He'd still be the true Varon, right? Or would Hunter's family force William to pass the inheritance on to one of them? If the Simons were no longer the leaders of the Warden in Porthaven, could they hold their claim to the role of true Varon?

And if he wasn't the true Varon, would that free him to be with Cait? He supposed that wouldn't be such a bad fate. Although he wasn't sure what he'd do about a career. His future had been dictated to him for so long that he'd had no reason to put much thought into becoming anything but the head of the Warden and Porthaven's mayor.

Cait shifted in her seat, the leather squeaking against her jeans. "So," she murmured.

Desmond swallowed the lump in his throat, worried about what conclusions she'd come to during their individual reveries.

She turned to meet his gaze, her chin dipped low. "Do you think we could do this again sometime?" she asked meekly.

It took Desmond a few seconds to process what she'd said.

A laugh puffed out of him. "How's tomorrow?" he suggested.

They shared a smile.

"Don't you have practice?" she asked.

Desmond sighed. "And my internship."

"Maybe Thursday?"

"Are you trying to schedule an illicit rendezvous with me, Lewan?"

"Do you have a problem with that?"

Desmond paused. "I like this version of you," he said. "You're snarkier."

She bit the corner of her bottom lip sheepishly, giving him a myriad of inappropriate ideas. "I learned from the best," she said.

Sucking in a taut breath, Desmond shoved away all thoughts of kissing her again right then. His eyes flashed to the clock on his dashboard. He'd well surpassed his promise of returning for dinner in half an hour.

"I'd better get you home," he said.

Cait nodded, though she looked no more pleased by the idea than he was.

They both relatched their seat belts, and Desmond turned the lights back on. Night had truly descended, stars dotting the indigo sky. The sea pulsed gently against the rocky cliffside as they drove back the way they'd come.

Desmond reached across to scoop Cait's hand from her lap. He linked their fingers, enjoying the chance to be in her presence once again. It'd been so long since they'd been able to meet, and he missed her— dreadfully.

No matter the difficulties facing them, Desmond found himself unreasonably hopeful. Even if Cait was the Vessel, even if his dad was under investigation, even if they lost everything else, *this* gave him hope that it would all work out. Because if he could be with Cait, then nothing else really mattered anyway.

Though he had to admit, things were strangely awkward after that kiss.

Neither of them spoke on the drive back to her house. It was as though they couldn't figure out what to say, even though they'd been best friends for a decade. He had to release her hand to turn off the highway, and he found it was a relief, as though holding her hand had clarified to him that he didn't know what they were doing. Did he even have the right to hold her hand? Sure, they'd just spent nearly an hour kissing in his car. But that didn't make him her boyfriend.

He wasn't even sure if he *could* be her boyfriend. After all, they couldn't really date, not like a real couple. It was enough of a struggle for them to meet up. How would they ever find the time to develop this part of their relationship? As much as he liked kissing her, he didn't want that to be all that their time together devolved into.

Pulling to the side of the road in front of the Lewan house, Desmond cleared his throat. "Thanks," he said, "for hearing me out."

Cait stared at the front door of her house, mouth quirked to the side. "I'm sorry it took me so long."

"Don't be." Desmond shifted to face her, incredulous that she would apologize. "Cait, you're the last person who should be sorry about any of this."

She shrugged.

With a quick check to be sure the coast was clear, Desmond crossed the distance to press one small kiss to her lips. She gasped nervously, but he pulled back fast enough to end the moment. Still, he held her gaze intently as he said, "I'm not going to let anything stop me. I *will* find a way to free you."

A shy smile spread across her face. "I should go," she whispered. "My family will notice if we sit here too long."

Desmond nodded. "Goodnight," he said, feeling that the night deserved a better ending but not knowing how to change it.

Cait picked up her backpack and opened the car door. She tossed him a smirk. "Happy birthday, Des."

Warmth spread through his chest. "You remembered?"

"When have I forgotten?"

"Never."

Cait smiled. "Goodnight."

She shut the door with a soft *thump*, then hurried up the gravel drive toward the back of the house. Desmond watched until she was out of sight. He reminded himself not to linger any longer. No matter the honesty they'd been able to establish between them, there were still appearances to keep up.

That was the problem. It didn't matter how much he wanted to stop pretending; he couldn't. Not until she was free.

Desmond turned his car around and headed back toward Lawrence Avenue.

He'd meant what he said. He *would* find a way to free Cait. He would find a way for them to be together. And since none of his current research was helping him to find that path, he decided it was time to change tactics.

He told his dad the other night that if they wanted answers, they had to take every opportunity available to them, whether it was perfectly reliable or not.

But there was one resource Desmond knew they'd left untapped.

And tomorrow, with or without his dad's permission, he'd visit Lilith Drake and learn what she knew of Veils and Vessels.

# Rese

Shutting her bedroom door cautiously behind her, Rese knew it was stupid. She didn't need to sneak into her own room. But she couldn't fight the need to be secretive. To keep her nan and Genni from peeking in on her.

Cait was off working on her school project, so after dinner and clearing the table, Rese excused herself. Now, she flipped the lock on her door and tiptoed to her bedside. She knelt, reaching out an arm to push aside the numerous shoeboxes and storage bins filled with trinkets and stuffed animals from her childhood stored beneath the bed frame. Her fingers caught on the etched ridges of the wooden box for which she searched.

She'd managed to talk herself out of this the last few days. She'd told herself that it wasn't that big of a deal. She remembered enough; she knew the truth. She didn't need to dredge up the past to confirm it.

But then Rese realized that to protect her sister, she needed more than confirmation. She needed a way to fix the problem.

Rese pulled the box from the bed's shadow, placing it on her lap. When she was nine, she'd found it at the souvenir shop downtown where her nan did accounting work. The signature of *T. Faulk* was etched on the inside of the lid; his pieces always sold for high prices to the tourists. Made of rich brown wood, it featured an inlay of lighter wood in a floral pattern and thin bands of ropelike trimming along the rim. The flowers were roses. A cliché choice, maybe, but Rese's mum had always called her "little rose" because she'd been born in June, and roses were the flower of June.

Rese had begged her nan to purchase it. As a child, she'd had no money of her own, so Rese had promised that it could be her birthday and Christmas present for the year. She just had to have it—she was desperate for the physical symbol of her mum's term of endearment.

Things were always important to Rese. So much so that when the Warden came to save her and her sisters and their house was burning down around them, she lingered behind to gather her most precious possessions rather than worrying about escaping with her life. And she'd never regretted it.

These prized items, Rese had squirreled away from her sisters, afraid that they'd ruin them, tainting the memories attached. Though she'd been seven at the time, she'd known it was wrong of her. They missed their parents and their life in Ireland just as much as she did. But she couldn't bear the idea of sharing her keepsakes. They were too sacred, too special, too important.

For the first several years, Rese kept them in shoeboxes like all her other special belongings. But when she'd seen the wooden box before her, she'd *needed* it. She'd *had* to have it to store her most treasured possessions.

Now, Rese carefully lifted the lid and drew out its contents one by one. Despite her love for the objects, she'd not opened the box in months, avoiding the emotions that came with them. But in the face of her sister's potential suffering, she needed answers only these tangible memories could provide.

Rising to sit on her bed, Rese sorted the items, laying them across her ticking stripe comforter. A stack of pictures, handmade birthday cards from her sisters, a dried flower crown, a crocheted stuffed animal from her mum, rocks and shells from the Bushmills coastline, and a small spiral-bound notebook. The rain-damp and emerald-grass scent of Ireland still lingered on the contents. The flower crown retained its floral musk. And if she lifted the notebook and closed her eyes, she could smell the faintest trace of malt and pipe tobacco.

Rese's eyes caught on the stack of photos. A candid shot of her parents, Owen and Sabine, sat on top. Her mum was midsentence, talking to someone out of frame, while her da gazed lovingly at his wife. Rese looked more like her mother, sharing her dark golden-blonde hair and fuller figure. Cait and Genni took after their da, slender and tall.

It was Rese's favorite photo, the edges more worn from her touch than the others. She'd kept it hidden under her pillow for a time, staring at it each night, whispering her secret fears and loneliness to her parents.

Then, she'd put it away with the rest of her things, exhausted by her sorrow.

Rese stared at her da's image for another lingering moment. His eyes resembled their nan's and Cait's, a bright, piercing blue-gray. His features were severe, but they softened every time he smiled or laughed. She could still feel the scruff of his rusty golden beard tickling her temple when he held her close and read to her each night.

Taking a steadying breath, Rese turned away from the picture. She picked up the spiral-bound notebook, its paper cover worn and hanging on by a mere five holes. Ever so gently, she opened it, turning the age-thinned pages.

Owen Lewan had been a storyteller. He was famous around their grandda's pub for his captivating tall tales. And while he'd never aspired to be an author, he'd written down his favorite stories for his daughters, fine-tuning and perfecting their craft to read to them each night.

Rese sucked in her bottom lip against the emotion burning in her throat. She wouldn't risk crying, splotching the faded ink of her da's handwriting. Not when this was the last piece of him that she had.

Finding the story she sought, Rese read, hearing her da's heavy, deep voice with each word. It wrapped around her memory as clearly as though he sat beside her. Owen Lewan's voice felt like a fire—warm, fierce, and smoky. His Irish accent had been cleaner than their nan's, an intentional effort on his part to make it easier for him to talk with tourists at the pub. Perhaps he also found it easier to tell his stories with a smoother lilt.

When he wrote down the tales, he catered them to his daughters, ensuring they were the perfect amount of cheerful and eerie to entertain them. While he read, his massive black wolfhound lay across the bed, head resting on his knee. The dog's russet brown eyes were so rich they almost glinted with the color of scarlet in the lamplight. He had a long snout with a black nose and large, pointed ears that were always alert. Conroy, their da had named the dog—keeper (or king, as Owen often proclaimed) of hounds.

Wherever Owen went, the dog followed like a shadow. And when their da snuggled up with his daughters to read them his stories, Conroy joined them. Despite the wolfhound's fierce appearance, his presence was comforting, and his demeanor was gentle. Rese had never been afraid of him, not until her sixth birthday, when she discovered the truth behind the story she sought now.

"The Boy and the Wolf" read the title, which was centered on the top line.

Rese tightened her jaw, then let the memory of her da's voice wash over her. *"For centuries, the Shepherd's Steps were haunted—dark and full of danger. For along the seaside, a great and vicious wolf ruled. This wolf was stronger, fiercer, and more powerful than any beast, and his hunger was insatiable.*

*"He ravaged the County Antrim, eating up all creatures, wee and grand. He roved the countryside, taking their sheep without regret, desperate to sate his hunger. The quaint village of* Muileann na Buaise

*suffered the worst of all. He attacked the townsfolk when they tried to catch him, leaving them marred by his great might. All trembled in fear of the wolf, knowing they could not subdue him."*

Rese paused there as her da always did, his face animated by the story. He had a serious bearing naturally, one that contradicted his jovial personality. But when he told stories, Owen's face lit up. The sharp lines of his features grew expressive, his strong brow moved with feeling, and his rigid jaw relaxed.

He always smiled after that pause, his deep voice alive with the story as he continued, *"But the wolf was misunderstood. He was a lone wolf, though not by choice. He was afraid, separated from his pack all those centuries ago. In his loneliness and fear, the wolf was driven to madness. It made him violent and cruel. He trusted none, for he had lost all. And he could not see hope in the darkness of his isolation."*

Owen's eyes would light up then. *"One day, a young boy journeyed to the sea. Unafraid, he was, of the tales about this wolf. So, he walked along the Shepherd's Steps in search of this wild monster the townsfolk feared. He wandered along the slick stones and steep paths until, finally, he stumbled upon the great king of beasts.*

*"Beholding the fantastic hound that stalked the county, the boy was in awe. This king was even grander than the stories told. He was more massive, more mighty, and more terrible. But the boy did not cower before him. The wolf's eyes glowed crimson with fury at finding a human boldly passing through his territory. He would kill the boy as a lesson to all who would underestimate his power.*

*"But the boy surprised the wolf. Fearlessly, he held out his hand in an offer of friendship and trust. Nearly rabid in his isolation, the wolf didn't recognize the gesture, and he lunged for the boy. But the lad was not without protection."*

Owen's smile always took on a wry quality at that point. *"The boy had a secret he'd carried to the seaside. And as the wolf pounced, ready to tear him apart, he suddenly froze. Through his madness, the wolf finally caught the boy's scent. This was the secret: The boy and the wolf were of the same pack. The boy shared a bloodline with the wolf.*

*"And finding himself face-to-face with his lost family, the wolf bowed to the boy, his mind restored. And from that day forward, the two were inseparable—boy and beast. The wolf no longer snarled and hunted out of fear or madness. He found his home with the boy and swore to protect his family for all eternity, never to be lonely again."*

Rese stared at the final line.

She remembered asking her da once why he'd ended it that way. *"Why eternity?"* she'd asked. *"Wolves don't live that long."*

*"This wolf does,"* he'd said.

Turning back to the first page, Rese searched the story again, looking for clues. She'd always thought her da had made up the story, like all his others. But it was on her sixth birthday that he told her the truth.

Owen was the boy, and Conroy was the Wolf.

From that moment on, Rese didn't like dogs anymore. She decided they were duplicitous and dangerous. If their da's pet could be an eternal wolf that had ravaged the countryside in his madness, then the animals were too unpredictable to be trusted.

Yet, the story of the boy and his wolf had turned from a fable into a biography. And now, Rese studied it for answers, for advice, for any means to separate her sister from the Wolf who plagued their family. No matter her da's assurance that the Wolf was good and trustworthy, Rese knew that was only true so long as the beast was sated. And she wouldn't let Cait be its prey.

Owen had prepared Rese for her role as the Wolf's Vessel. In only a few small conversations, to be fair, but enough for her to know it was *her* job. *She* was the one who was intended to inherit. And no matter how much she feared it, she'd spent her whole life expecting it. She could carry the burden. She could keep the Wolf tamed. She'd designed her life to ensure it.

So, Rese reread the story. She noted the way the boy had offered the wolf companionship, and she wondered, could she do that? If she offered herself to the Wolf, would it readily leave her sister? Why had it chosen Cait in the first place? Perhaps because she was the most submissive of the sisters. The Wolf saw her as easily subdued and chose to prey on her weakness.

Well, Rese would put an end to that. She'd show the Wolf that she was his true match. Her strength would provide him with a better companion. Her willingness to sacrifice would convince him of her value. And she would save her sister.

She just had to figure out how to reach him.

# CHAPTER TWENTY

# Cait

The darkness came and the presence along with it.

Cait's eyes fluttered open, and she startled. She stood in her childhood bedroom with the twin beds and bassinet, the dried flowers and wooden rafters, the handmade quilts and children's art. The moonlight glittered through the window at her back, casting her shadow across the door.

A tremor of fear worked its way across her skin in tiny pinpricks. The hum vibrated in her skull. Beneath the door, she could see the shadow pacing on the other side. But her focus was locked on the fissure that now splintered more than halfway across its face.

She was back. Why was she back?

Smoke seeped through the bottom and sides of the door. It swirled over the floor, and Cait took a step back. She knew what awaited her out there. She had a name for the monster, the spirit-being.

The Wolf.

Desmond had slipped up when he'd said that. He may have promised to explain everything to her, but he couldn't have meant to give away such a damning piece of information so early.

The pacing reverberated more clearly in her ears. The heavy padding of paws and the grinding scratch of claws echoed. A rumbling growl accompanied each snorting breath. Its hulking shadow reared and slammed its muscular form against the door, rattling it within its frame and tearing the fissure even more.

Cait took another step back.

The Wolf was breaking through.

Smoke coiled and curled, now reaching to her waist. The monster's growl deepened as it paced again.

Cait kept backing up. Her hand brushed the footboard of her childhood bed, solid and plagued with memories. She wished she could crawl under the blankets and hide from this nightmare. She wished her da would appear, placing his arms around her as he whispered, "It's just a dream, sweet pea. The wolf won't hurt yeh."

Instead, the raven flew into the room, appearing as if from the smoke itself.

The sapphire-and-onyx-colored wings tucked into the raven's sides as it landed on the dresser. Its talons clacked against the wood. "Caw," it cried.

Cait watched the raven with one eye and the door with the other. She didn't trust either creature. One was determined to break through and claim her. The other was an omen of frightful change.

The smoke twisted higher, and the raven called out again. It flew over Cait's head and into the night.

Fear lanced Cait's heart as she turned to see the cove awaiting her, rather than her childhood room. The hum spiked, loud and warning. Desmond stood on the shoreline, waves lapping at his feet. The beasts wouldn't come, would they? But the waves—they raged ever higher. A lightning strike pierced the sky. Storm clouds encroached on the midnight blue, twisting around the full moon.

Cait sprinted for Desmond. Whether the beasts came or the sea rose, she was desperate to save him. To stop him from crumbling to sand in her arms beneath the waves.

"Desmond," she called, barreling up to him.

He spun around at her voice. "Cait?" The waves enclosed his calves, swirling like a whirlpool. "What are you doing here?"

Cait struggled to keep her footing in the wet sand, and Desmond reached out to steady her. She grabbed his arms. "We have to get out of here," she insisted.

Though she tried to pull him out of the ocean's grip, Desmond didn't move. "What's going on, Caity?"

Tears sprang to Cait's eyes. Why was she here again? For the last week, she'd been free of these dreams. After last night, after she'd just gotten him, she couldn't bear to lose him.

"Please, Desmond," she begged, tugging harder on his arms. "We have to go. Please."

Another wave crashed into their knees, causing both of them to stumble. Desmond's arm slipped around her waist, and for the first time, Cait realized she knew that sensation outside of her dream. She'd truly felt Desmond's arm around her waist as he kissed her in his car.

"Cait?" He stared down at her, their faces inches apart once more.

Gripping tightly to his jacket, Cait felt the tears coursing down her cheeks. She couldn't let him die. "Please," she whispered through her tears.

Water rushed around them, sucking their feet deeper into the sand as it receded. Desmond held them steady, his arms tightening around her. His hand rose to cup her cheek. Her skin tingled at the touch. It was exactly how he'd touched her that night to draw her face to his.

The déjà vu caused Cait's mind to fumble, the hum in her head rising to a howl. Desmond's head dipped toward hers, but she didn't try to stop him. She didn't say a word. Because she knew what it was like now. She knew how his lips felt against hers. And she was desperate to experience it again, even if it was just in a dream.

"You're not real," Cait whispered, the words a soft reminder rather than an objection.

"I told you, Lewan," his eyes locked with hers, "it *is* real."

Cait didn't wait for him; she leaned in herself and kissed him, remembering every second of the reality that had been. She reveled in the sensation. The ocean rose to encircle their waists, but she paid it no heed, lost to the hum that pulsed in time with her heart. She allowed herself to be swept away in Desmond's embrace, and he held her so securely she knew he'd never let her go.

A wave slammed into them without warning, cascading over their heads. It pummeled them with its force. Cait gripped tightly to Desmond, panicked that she'd find only sand. But she was wrong.

Her fingers clung to him, solid and sure. She opened her eyes, the salt water stinging them. Desmond remained before her, his unruly hair drifting like seaweed in the water. They held on to one another, and her heart began to still.

She hadn't lost him.

Then, Desmond's dark eyes went wide. Air bubbles exploded from his mouth as he gasped. And suddenly, he was jerked back.

Cait tried to cling to him, their hands tightening desperately on one another. Frantically, her eyes searched through the water. There, on his arms, waist, and legs, thick tendrils of black clung to him. Shiny scales wrapped around their length. They glinted in the moonlight under the water, tugging with unnatural force.

Lungs burning, Cait struggled to hold on. The tendrilled monster only pulled harder. Panic shone in Desmond's eyes. He mouthed her name, more air escaping his lips.

With another powerful jerk, the monster ripped him free from her grasp.

Cait screamed Desmond's name as the monster swam away, its speed like the blink of an eye. She treaded water in desperation, attempting to follow as she watched Desmond's body shrink to a pinprick of shadow in the stormy sea.

Another wave crashed in, picking her up and throwing her out of its icy clutches. Cait coughed and spluttered to free her lungs of the salty water. Tremors racked her body as she rose onto her hands and knees. Desmond was gone.

Her fingers curled in the grass, the hum still rumbling in her head. Tears burned in her chest. They fell free with her sob, heating her face.

Desmond was gone.

Lightning flashed, thunder rumbling only seconds after. The frozen patter of rain worked through her sweater, which was dry despite her tumble in the sea. Cait rose to find herself face-to-face with the tree.

Anger lit her core as she glared at its tangled branches. Whatever this tree was—whatever it represented—she hated it. The raven fluttered between its branches. She hated the bird too. All that these dreams had brought her was fear and loss. And she'd had enough of those for a lifetime.

Rain pelted Cait, striking her cheeks as she glanced at the full moon. Three streaks of lightning arced above her. The raven cawed in the fork of the tree limbs and flew to the redhead's shoulder.

Cait looked to see Sterling standing off to the side. He met her gaze as though he were there in the dream with her. But this time, she didn't wait.

Walking straight to the other side of the tree, Cait was determined to see the fourth figure shrouded in darkness. She wanted answers. She *would* have them. And this shadowed individual would not stay secret any longer.

Suddenly, a bright amber light flashed. It exploded out of the tree in a spray of glittering shards. The hum grew to a nearly painful howl, ricocheting through her skull. Cait doubled over, hands to her ears, as she dropped to her knees. The hum grew and grew and grew, deafening her. Her eyes squeezed shut, not so much in pain as in concentration.

Pressure built at the base of her skull. Her skin prickled like an electric current was running across her body. Power filled her veins until they felt ready to burst. A wash of cool filled her mind—a calm, a presence.

Abruptly, the hum ceased, her mind stilled, the pressure settled, and a tension she hadn't known was in her chest released.

Cait pulled in what felt like her first clear breath in twelve years.

Then, she awoke.

~

Cait stared blankly across the classroom at Desmond's empty seat. He'd texted her that morning in his usual manner.

*"Skipping today. Got something to take care of."*

She tried not to read into it. But after her dream, watching him be wrenched away from her by that monster, she was overly paranoid. She couldn't help fearing that he regretted their kiss. She wouldn't blame him if he'd decided their relationship wasn't worth it. They might have admitted their feelings for one another, but that didn't make their situation any different. She and Desmond couldn't be together. So, she wouldn't hold him to the empty promises their moment of weakness proclaimed.

Even if that moment gave her heart a painful sense of hope every time she remembered his words: *"I'm done pretending."*

Blinking away the memory, Cait turned her gaze toward the front of the class, attempting to concentrate. Mrs. Toussaint, the English teacher, lectured on *Great Expectations* by Charles Dickens. Though she knew Desmond was enjoying the readings this quarter, she found it difficult to slog through the complex prose of the 1800s. She felt as though she needed a translation to understand the tale.

Beside her, Matt fidgeted in his seat. His pencil beat out an erratic *thump, thump, thump* on his notebook. His eyes kept flickering to the clock above the chalkboard.

Cait leaned toward him to whisper, "You okay?"

He gave her a bashful glance, his face coloring with a red flush. "Yeah, I—I just chugged that milkshake too fast," he muttered.

She nodded. The ice cream stand, Salty's Scoops, had come to the school offering free milkshakes for all the students and faculty. It was meant to drum up excitement for the Fisher's Festival, and nearly every teacher capitalized on the opportunity to preach about the Festival's importance to their town.

Matt had been too busy chatting at lunch and had to slurp his strawberry milkshake with desperate speed as they made their way to class. So, the second Mrs. Toussaint excused them, he was up and out of his seat, calling over his shoulder to Cait, "I'll meet you in study hall."

As he bolted out of the classroom, Cait gathered her things and joined the rest of their friends at the door. Hunter and Scott were already moving down the hall, Sterling ambling slowly after them. He had his headphones in, eyes down as he read something on his phone. Liz and Melissa waited for Cait to catch up before following the guys. They were already conversing about people Cait didn't know, so she simply listened as they walked. Sometimes, her friendship with them felt off. Not as though they didn't want her, but more like she didn't quite fit in.

Cait chewed on her bottom lip, remembering what Desmond had said last week in the library. Her friendship with Hunter and Liz *didn't* fit. She, like Sterling, drifted in the background, welcome but still separate. The two of them could never truly be like the others. Their family's curses made sure of it.

"Hey," Sterling whispered, causing Cait to jump at his unexpected presence. He'd drifted back, letting Liz and Melissa pass him so he could walk beside her. One of his headphones was now draped over his shoulder, a soft vibration of music emitting out of it. "You got a sec?"

Glancing ahead of them, Cait slowed her steps to match Sterling's pace. "Sure. What's up?"

"Did your, uh . . . did anything weird happen in your dream last night?"

Cait raised her eyebrows. "Yeah. You?"

"Yeah." He sighed and ran a hand through his thick hair. "Most everything was the same, but then the tree . . ."

"What happened to it?" Cait almost demanded, her words coming out in a rush.

Sterling eyed her. "What happened in *your* dream?"

Swallowing past her discomfort, Cait forced herself to remember. "I'm not sure," she said. "I wanted to see the other side, so I started walking that way."

"Yeah, I saw you."

Cait's steps faltered. "Wait, what?"

Sterling ducked his head, visibly uncomfortable. "We made eye contact, and then you took off for the other side of the tree."

Cait gaped at him for a second before nodding. "Then, there was the explosion . . . or whatever it was. I couldn't really see."

Sterling was nodding as well. "That's exactly what happened," he said, shrugging. "I thought for a second that you'd done something because you were going toward the tree, and then suddenly, this huge flash of light burst from the crack. Then, this sound . . . I don't know how to describe it. It was like a . . . a vibration or something."

"A hum?"

Sterling's brow furrowed. "Nah, more like—more like a resonance. It had an almost electric quality to it."

"That's not what I heard," Cait said uncertainly. "I saw the light of the explosion, but . . ." She hesitated to tell him about the hum. It only came with Desmond's presence and when she stood at the tree. And despite her need for answers, she didn't know if she trusted Sterling enough yet to share that information.

Deciding to keep the details to herself, Cait rephrased it. "I heard a sound, too, but it was more like a hum. Kind of like a . . ." She blinked, revelation dawning on her. "Like a howl."

Sterling frowned at the description, but Cait realized for the first time what the sound that reverberated through her body truly was. It wasn't a hum. It was a howl—it was *the Wolf's* howl.

Cait and Sterling slowed as they neared the entrance of the study hall. Students funneled past them, so they kept their voices low.

"I wouldn't call what I heard a howl," Sterling said.

"I think, um—" Cait pursed her lips, not wanting to admit her discovery. But that was foolish. Sterling deserved to know as much as she did. "I think that's because the sound has to do with the . . . the things that we carry."

"You mean the spirit-beings?"

Cait's breaths grew tight in her lungs, and she nodded, unable to speak.

Sterling's jaw tightened, his bushy eyebrows dipping low. He looked nearly angry as he muttered, "Did you feel anything? After the explosion happened."

"Yes." Cait stared at the aqua-blue and white linoleum tiles beneath their feet. "It felt like pressure building up inside my head. And then . . ."

"It stopped," he finished ominously. "The pressure eased, but it stayed, yet it felt right. And you could breathe."

Cait met his intense stare. "I've never felt freer than in that moment."

"Me either."

"And it was gone when I woke."

Sterling's dark brows tipped up. "Same."

Cait wrung the hem of her jacket. "What do you think it means?"

"No clue. But I'll tell you this," he straightened his shoulders, voice dipping into a determined monotone, "I'm gonna find out."

Cait pulled in a labored breath but nodded in agreement.

He tipped his chin toward the study hall. "So, I think we should have a chat with Hunter."

Cait blanched. "I don't know—"

"Cait, he's the only person we can trust."

That was the exact opposite of what Desmond had told her last night.

"You've been friends with him for years," she said. "If he was willing to tell you about this stuff, wouldn't he have done it by now?"

"I didn't know to ask about this," he countered. "Every time I've gone to Hunter for anything, he's been completely honest with me. We can trust him. He'll help us."

Scratching her temple, Cait didn't know who to believe. Desmond did hold a bias against Hunter. But that didn't mean he was necessarily blind because of it. Yet, Sterling had confided in Hunter about his changing dreams. Hunter already believed Sterling had inherited the spirit-being. If he hadn't betrayed him by now, why would he upon learning about Cait?

"I just—" Cait heaved a sigh. "I've never talked to anyone about this before." Though it was a partial lie, somehow, she felt that her conversations with Desmond didn't count. He would never expose her to the Warden. She'd always known that. Talking to him wasn't a risk.

Talking to Hunter was.

"Well, I have," Sterling said. Adamance filled his stare. "If you don't trust him, then trust me. My family has been captive in this town for over two hundred years. My life isn't something I get to choose. Every step will be dictated to me."

"But they don't know you've inherited," she said. "And they won't, right? Not unless you tell them."

"That doesn't matter," he said. "I'm in the bloodline. That means I have to be controlled just like everyone else. Same as my dad and his dad and his dad and . . . on and on. Vessels don't have choices in Porthaven. We carry on the bloodline and behave like good little pets."

Cait bristled at his words but focused on that new term. Vessels. "What about my sisters?" she asked. "They're not . . . Vessels."

"Yeah, they are," he said. "Just unfilled ones."

Cait frowned. "So, they'll be—"

"They'll be treated the same. Like you said, the Warden won't know who the Vessel is unless *you* tell them. So, they'll have to treat all three of you with equal fear. You'll each get to have one kid—and *only* one kid—and they'll monitor them the same way they monitor you."

"And you want to out ourselves to Hunter?" she asked incredulously.

"I don't *want* to," he said. "I *have* to. Because he's the only person in this town who gives a damn about us."

A hollow fear filled Cait's lungs as she sucked in a shaky breath. Could she risk this? What if they revealed themselves only for Hunter to turn around and tell the Warden? What would they do? Desmond had said something about chaining her to a random member. Did that mean she'd have to marry that man, producing a child to carry on the line as Sterling just suggested? Could she stand that?

Another, more frightening thought came into Cait's mind: What if she told the Warden that she carried the Wolf? Would they allow her sisters to live free lives, knowing that only her bloodline would matter? Could she sacrifice her life and happiness for her sisters' freedom?

Cait sighed. What did it really matter? She'd always known that her happiness was unobtainable. The life she wanted—a life with Desmond— was impossible. So, why not risk talking with Hunter? In the best outcome, she and Sterling wound up with answers. And in the worst, she met her inevitable future sooner than expected.

"All right," she murmured. "Just . . . talk with Hunter and find a time for us to—"

"Hey," Matt said, popping up beside them.

Cait and Sterling jumped at his sudden arrival, then glanced at each other. She wondered if she wore the same anxious expression as he did, eyes wide and mouth tense.

Matt's brown stare flicked from one to the other. "What're you guys doing out here?"

"Uh—" Cait looked up at Sterling, who'd finally settled his expression back into his typical stoic indifference. She tried to offer Matt a smile. "Nothing. Sterling was just telling me about . . ." She floundered for a lie, then caught the subtle drift of music still coming from his headphones. "About a band he thought I'd like. The, uh . . ."

Sterling caught on and offered, "The Strokes."

Matt's brow furrowed. "The Strokes?"

"Yeah."

He turned to Cait. "Do you like alt-rock?"

Cait blinked. Did she like alt-rock? "Yeah."

"Huh." Matt eyed Sterling again, then shrugged. "Cool. I'm more of a classics guy. Ya know, the Eagles and the Allman Brothers and stuff."

Sterling nodded, a glimmer of humor in the lift of his lips. "I coulda guessed that."

Pulling in a tight breath, Cait tried to appear nonchalant as she pointed to the classroom. "Should we head in?" she asked.

Without waiting, Sterling turned and walked into the room. Matt followed at Cait's side, though his eyes kept flickering toward Sterling, who had taken a seat at Hunter's side. Cait and Matt found seats across from one another and sat down to work.

Fingers trembling, Cait dug her homework out of her backpack, along with her phone. The dreams were getting too intense, too damning. The door was breaking. Desmond had been ripped from her arms. And the tree had exploded in amber light.

Yes, she'd talk with Hunter. But first, she wanted to speak with the person she trusted most.

Cait snuck her phone under the table and quickly typed out a text: *"We need to talk."*

# Desmond

Thick gray rain clouds drifted in, covering the bright blue sky of the morning. Desmond gave the ominous weather a dismissive glance as he stepped out of his car. He shut the door behind him, intentionally avoiding looking at the passenger seat where Cait had sat last night.

He kept playing their kisses on a loop in his head. The moment had been as magical as he'd anticipated. If only he hadn't been clumsy enough to hit the gas. Stupid.

Shaking off those thoughts, Desmond walked across the small lawn toward the house ahead of him. The breeze that carried the storm clouds closer stirred up the wind chimes hanging from the roof. Small patches of wood siding peeked through the plant life that twisted its way up the walls. His second visit to Lilith Drake's home felt no less menacing than the first.

Desmond had barely stepped onto the porch when the door opened. He paused on its edge, wide-eyed as Lilith pushed open the screen door, a knowing look on her face.

"I wondered when you'd show up," she said, her rich and raspy voice as foreboding as her landscaping.

A trickle of anxiety coursed through Desmond. How had she known he was at her house? And why would she be expecting him?

Then, Desmond took hold of his sense of reason. He pointed back over his shoulder. "It was my car, wasn't it?" he asked.

Lilith simply grinned.

"You're not psychic; you're just observant," he concluded.

"And you have a very loud vehicle." Lilith moved out of the way and offered entry to her house. "I take it you have questions."

Desmond bolstered his courage and entered the ex-Druid's lair once again. "The Warden isn't very good at sharing information," he said, stepping into her living room. The terrarium sat against the far wall, her large pet snake coiled under a heat lamp. He repressed the shiver that ran down his spine. "But you seemed willing when I was here before."

Lilith walked past him toward the kitchen. "Do you like tea, Mr. Simon?" she asked.

Desmond followed. "I guess."

"Excellent. I'll make you some."

As the woman filled a teakettle, Desmond moved to sit at the island.

"Don't bother," Lilith said, halting him. She hadn't even looked over her shoulder. "We'll sit in the living room. I prefer to entertain guests in a more comfortable atmosphere."

"We didn't do that before."

"That's because your father was here." She set the kettle on the stovetop. "He likes to keep his visits formal."

There was a quiet grace to Lilith's mannerisms. Every movement had a near-ethereal quality, making Desmond wonder offhandedly if she were a phantom. Of course, that was ridiculous. Phantoms never changed in appearance, and he distinctly remembered her wearing a lacy black blouse the first time he'd visited. Today, she wore a navy blue silk tunic top that caused her dusty-blue eyes to stand out with striking definition.

"Please," Lilith said, motioning toward the couches. "Have a seat."

They sat across from one another, Desmond taking closer stock of the room. An overcast light left the corners of the room hazed in shadow. Rich wood shelves covered most of the walls. Books filled many of them, but there were also jars of herbs, potted plants, all sizes of crystals and rocks, decorative chests, and flickering candles. The whole house smelled of earth, musk, and flowers. It would be inviting if it weren't so creepy.

Desmond ran his hands along the velveteen fabric of the couch cushion. "Since you were expecting me," he began, "I assume that means you know what I want to talk to you about?"

She smoothed out the pant leg of her trousers. "I don't *know* what you want to discuss, but thanks to your open expression when I mentioned Vessels and their connection to the Veils, I presume that's the topic you're most interested in."

Desmond scoffed. "I'm still not convinced you can't read minds."

"Not even Vessels can accomplish that," she remarked.

"You know a lot about Vessels?" Desmond asked, hoping he didn't sound *too* interested.

Lilith lifted a shoulder. "More than the Warden."

Desmond shook his head. When Lilith had moved to Porthaven, she'd offered her knowledge to the Warden. And they'd turned her down. It was idiotic. Not only could they have learned more about the Druids and their plans, but they might not be in their current predicament with the Veil.

"What can you tell me about them?" he asked.

A breathy chuckle escaped Lilith. "Where would you like me to begin? Perhaps with their origin? I could tell you the tale of the first connection. Would that do? Or would you like more practical knowledge? Perhaps I can tell you of their skills and the way their ties work?"

Desmond stared blankly at her. In her sarcastic offering alone, she'd revealed how little he and the Warden within Porthaven knew. And now, he felt he hadn't come prepared for all he'd need to learn.

"I don't know anything about them," he admitted. "Everything I thought I knew . . . it's all half-truths. I want to know what's really true."

Lilith waited.

Desmond leaned forward. "I want you to teach me everything you know about the Vessels and the spirit-beings attached to them."

A furious, high-pitched squeal cut through the air, causing Desmond to jump in his seat.

Lilith calmly rose from hers, moving toward the kitchen.

Running a hand down his face, Desmond realized it was just the kettle boiling. He turned around to watch as Lilith poured the water into a glass teapot. The liquid turned a soft brown as it filtered through the infuser.

"The subject of Vessels is wide enough on its own," she said, setting the now full teapot on a tray alongside two colored-glass mugs. "However, it is clear to me by your use of the term 'spirit-being' that you don't understand the creatures they house."

She met his gaze from across the room. "And *that* knowledge is imperative to understanding anything I would teach you about Vessels."

Desmond frowned as she lifted the tray, rejoining him in the living room. "Do you mean that the Warden doesn't understand Vessels or their burdens?" he asked.

Lilith laughed, startling him. She sat, setting the tray on the coffee table between them. "My boy, Vessels don't carry burdens," she said. "They host divine power."

Desmond was sure his face showed his shock because Lilith's smile turned wry as she added, "Anyone who perceives the life of a Vessel to be a 'burden' doesn't understand the gift they've been given."

That statement went against everything Desmond had ever heard. The Warden viewed the spirit-beings as dangerous because they'd witnessed the destruction that could be wrought at the hands of their Vessels. He didn't know the specifics of those events—another secret held closely by their leadership. But he knew that until the Warden had obtained control over a handful of Vessels, damage and death followed the Wielders whose souls were tied to the spirit-beings.

He knew this because Gabriel Varon—the "first Varon"—was the man who led that charge. And, like all Varons, Desmond had inherited the responsibility of finding and controlling the Vessels for the sake of the world, just as it was their job to protect the spirit world from the Druids.

The room darkened as the storm clouds' promised rain began to pelt the windows. "The Druids regard Vessels highly, then?" Desmond asked.

The left corner of Lilith's lips lifted. "Like demigods amongst mortals," she said, raising her thin blonde eyebrows. "That's what they were, you know? 'Demigod' is just an antiquated, misinformed term for Vessel. And 'spirit-beings' is a misinformed term for their kindred."

Desmond sucked in a tight breath. "Kindred? That's what they're called?"

"It's an epithet," she corrected. "Or a term of endearment."

Sitting on the edge of his seat, Desmond leaned in. "What's their real name, then?"

Lilith glanced at the dainty gold watchband on her wrist. Reaching forward, she lifted the teapot, gracefully pouring the brew into the two colored-glass mugs. "Cream or sugar?" she asked.

"Neither, thanks," Desmond ground out.

Lilith ignored his irritation. She offered him the semi-translucent charcoal-gray mug before taking the jade-green one for herself. A curl of steam swirled from the mug, bringing forth a heady scent of earth and the barest tang of citrus.

Lifting her chin, Lilith finally met his gaze again. "Are you sure you want to know?" she asked.

"I wouldn't have asked if I didn't."

"That's not entirely true," she said. "Many times, we ask for answers before we understand the consequences those answers might bring with them. To know the true name of the kindred is to bear a sacred burden."

"I thought you said they weren't burdens," he said.

She smiled. "They're not. But the knowledge of them, of who they truly are and what they can do . . ." Her dusty-blue eyes drifted toward the terrarium in thought. "Not everyone can bear up under such provocative understanding."

Desmond felt his face twist. She spoke in such secretive ways that he found himself baffled. Who said things like "provocative understanding" anyway?

Taking a moment to clear his head, Desmond sipped the tea. And immediately choked as the smooth yet bitter flavor stung his tongue. "That's . . ." He glanced down into the cup, unsure how to describe the taste. It wasn't bad. He actually kind of liked it. But he'd been expecting a typical English breakfast or Earl Grey. This wasn't nearly as floral or soft as those. This was . . .

"Intense," he concluded.

A dry twinkle lit Lilith's eyes. "It's Assam," she said. "I like to match the tea to my visitor."

Desmond pursed his lips. "That's my defining trait, huh?"

Her shoulder lifted in a small shrug. "Assam requires a delicate hand. Brew it too long or at the wrong temperature, and it will turn incredibly bitter and unsalvageable. However," her eyebrow rose, "treat it with care, and you'll draw out the notes of caramelized mandarin zest, turning it into a soothing delight."

His nose wrinkled. "Which am I?"

"Well, that's the thing," she said. "You're both."

Desmond didn't have a snarky retort for that. Somehow, Lilith had managed to define him all with tea. Bitter and unsalvageable? Yes, he identified with that. A soothing delight? Maybe the wording was weird, but he thought he understood her point. Given his good days, he *could* make people happy, he supposed.

Cait's smile flashed across his mind, all the memories of their days at the cove coming with it.

"You're rather like them," Lilith said, breaking through his reverie.

He met her stare.

"The kindred," she clarified.

Desmond raised his chin. "How so?"

"They are a dichotomy in themselves," she said. "Both good and evil. Light and dark."

Ready for the truth, Desmond sat forward, arms on his thighs. "What are they?"

Lilith eyed him, determining if he could truly handle her knowledge. Whatever she found in his expression, she must have deemed him worthy because she said, "They're the Spectrals."

The room seemed to darken into a new shade of gray. A shiver ran down Desmond's spine. It felt the same as when they repeated the prayer to see the unseen at church. The sensation pulled at him, nudging him to feel its importance.

Lilith's expression softened nearly into awe as she spoke. "They are the fathers and mothers of the spirit world. The greatest source of power anyone could ever channel. They bind themselves to the bloodline of their Vessel, granting them their power for eternity."

Desmond's lips parted, breath catching in his lungs.

"And the Warden calls them a burden," Lilith sneered.

*That* was what was tied to Cait? A creature of power immense enough to spawn the spirit world.

A line from the prophecy whispered in his head: *"The bond of spirit and child will bring forth power like we've never seen."*

Forcing himself to ignore the way Lilith clearly still held to some of the beliefs of her childhood, Desmond sought more understanding. "These . . . Spectrals—" The word tingled on his lips. "What do they want?"

"The same thing we all want," Lilith replied. "To live. To see their desires come to fruition."

"And what are those desires?"

"It varies from Spectral to Spectral," she said. "But now that you know *what* the Vessels truly carry, do you care to learn more about the Vessels themselves?"

Though Desmond thought there was far more to learn about the creature bound to Cait, he nodded in favor of learning about what *she* was.

"You requested everything I know," Lilith mused. "It's a wide subject. As I said, the Druids highly regard them. From my understanding, the Vessels are the highest possible class of Wielder. However, unlike every other class, you cannot train into it. You are either born a Vessel, or you're not. I assume you're aware of the other classes?"

"Herald, Advocate, Cleric, Sage," Desmond rattled off, thanks to his earliest training. He didn't mention Archsages because there was no proof they actually existed.

"Precisely," she said. "Spectrals can only attach to the bloodline of a Vessel. However, not all Vessels will carry a Spectral. In fact, even as rare as they are, most won't."

"Why not?"

"Because there aren't enough Spectrals for that."

"Do you know how many there are?"

Lilith gave him a challenging frown. "Surely you know the answer to that yourself."

"I definitely don't," he returned.

"You're an heir of the Varon line," she said incredulously. At his surprised expression, she added, "Yes, even the Druids understand and envy the strength you Varons carry. And we also know that you teach your children the progeny of the spirit world from the start."

"The prog—" Desmond interrupted himself, her words clicking into place. "Do you mean the beasts?"

The slightest dip of her chin confirmed it.

"What do the beasts have to do with . . . ?" Again, he tapered off, finding the answers within himself. "You said that the Spectrals are the fathers and mothers. And the beasts are . . . their kids?"

A gust of wind threw a sheet of rain, splattering against the windows. The sky was covered in dark gray clouds, sending the room into greater darkness. Lilith reached over to flip on a side table light. Its golden orange glow lit up the side of her face.

"Only in the most symbolic of meanings," she said. "They're more like diminutive replications of the Spectrals themselves."

Desmond realized at that moment that he did know how many Spectrals were in existence. "Twelve beasts," he said, "twelve Spectrals."

Her steady expression gave him confirmation enough.

"Okay . . ." Desmond considered the revelation for a moment before moving on. "And the Vessels, they don't get a choice in taking on one of these Spectrals?"

Lilith's expression grew thoughtful once more. "Choice is . . . a difficult term to define. While at first glance it may seem that the Spectral tethers to the Vessel without permission, we later find that they chose the Vessel because the Vessel would have chosen them."

"What if that's not the case?" Desmond asked. "What if the Vessel was never given a choice, and they want to get rid of the Spectral?"

"These are very specific questions," Lilith remarked.

"I'm just curious."

She narrowed her eyes but continued without further inquiry. "No," she said. "There are rumors that a Vessel can part with their Spectral, but that's all they are: rumors. Once the connection is established, there is no breaking it."

Desmond couldn't accept that. "Rumors start somewhere."

"Like the one that says you're irresponsible, flippant, and arrogant?" Lilith looked to the ceiling in sarcastic contemplation. "I wonder where that rumor started."

It was with him. Years ago, when Desmond found himself too overwhelmed by the weight of the responsibility in his life and overcome by the fear that he'd never be good enough, he donned his rebellious persona to keep people from discovering how sincerely and desperately he wanted to be good. He began numerous rumors about himself, all without a shred of truth. He'd planted them amongst his classmates and nurtured them at his internship. And no one questioned him.

Could Lilith be right? Were the rumors about freeing a Vessel from its Spectral just as baseless?

"What else can you tell me about the Vessels?" he asked, attempting to deflect her from discovering how much he needed that rumor to prove valid. "Are they . . . dangerous?"

"Are humans dangerous?" Lilith countered, the lamp beside her flickering.

"I see your point." He sighed, running a hand over his face. "So, what? What's the big deal with these Vessels? Why do the Druids and the Warden want control of them so badly?"

"Don't you know that people crave power, Mr. Simon?"

Desmond rolled his eyes. "That's not a good enough reason to go to war—" He paused, noting the still flickering lamp. Then, he looked to the shadow-shrouded corner of Lilith's living room.

An unnatural, inky black had settled over the edge of the bookcase, growing almost imperceptibly wider moment by moment. He'd noticed it before but excused it as the result of the storm. Now, he thought it had a decidedly sinister appearance.

Lilith caught his stare and turned to look over her shoulder. Instantly, she gasped, beginning to rise. But she wasn't fast enough.

Out of the shadow, a silky-skinned wing protruded just before beady neon eyes winked to life. Spindly onyx talons tipped the highest arc of the wing, a second limb forming in the blink of an eye. A thickly muscled body and a squat head followed, fearsome black fangs bared in its mouth.

A nyct.

Desmond scrambled out of his seat in awed panic. They were nowhere near the Veil, and this beast was the blackest shade of night. The beasts on the island all bore the color of graphite, a smoky gray that felt far less threatening than what was before him. Though Hades had black fur, it also had a distinct blue tinge to its fluffy depths.

This beast wasn't a result of the Veil's damage. Nor was it untethered.

This was the work of a Druid. A beast summoned to kill.

The thought had no sooner crossed his mind than the nyct took flight. Desmond instinctively raised his hand, sending a deep blue arc at it. It struck, the creature emitting an earsplitting shriek.

Unfortunately, he'd been so focused on it that he'd failed to realize that the nyct wasn't alone.

Another beast crashed into his back, knocking him into the coffee table. Unlike in the movies, the furnishing didn't split in half. Desmond's ribcage burst with fire as it struck the wooden table, the second nyct wrestling him down to the floor.

He heard Lilith cry out in alarm, but he was too busy grappling with the nyct to see what she was doing. The beast let out a vicious hiss, spittle sprinkling over his face. Its talons sliced at his throat. He managed to hold the limb at bay, its soft flesh wrinkling under his grip, but a single talon struck the edge of his chin.

For a moment, Desmond didn't feel the cut. Then, it seared, causing him to flinch. The momentary weakening of his muscles allowed the nyct to slip its clawed wing down, striking his chest with blinding pain.

His head spun, and his vision went blurry. Something hot and wet slid down his neck, and he tasted iron. He could feel the talons in his chest grinding against his ribs.

Then, they were gone, the beast above him evaporating into smoke.

Desmond gasped, sputtering for air. None came. Instead, he felt a sharp stab of pain. Every time he tried to take a breath, it felt like the nyct was inserting its talon over and over again.

He stared at the cream-colored ceiling, his throat clogged with what he was sure was his own blood.

He was dying, he realized. Slain by beasts because he wasn't paying enough attention. His dad would have a field day of lessons with that.

Suddenly, Lilith was there, one hand pressed to his chest and another to his face. Her white-blonde hair was disheveled, a streak of blood marring her cheek. She muttered under her breath in what sounded like Latin. Or maybe it was Spanish. He was pretty sure he heard some choice curse words mixed in.

But he couldn't focus on her words because his vision was beginning to go black. Desmond was desperate for a clear breath, his lungs spasming and aching. His body felt like it was stuffed with bricks, immovable and unwieldy. Was this how dying felt? If so, it sucked.

"Hang on, Desmond," Lilith said, both hands gripping his chest. Was she going to try CPR?

Desmond realized that was stupid. If his spinning head was any indication, he was bleeding out. Maybe she was trying to staunch the bleeding? If so, then why was she closing her eyes?

A burst of darkness flashed, and suddenly, Desmond could breathe.

He gulped in a huge breath of air, and then his lungs kicked into overdrive, greedily clamoring for more. He was pretty sure he was about to hyperventilate when Lilith grabbed his face, her hands warm with slick blood as they pressed into his skin. "Slowly," she ordered, her eyes locked on his. "Deep breaths. In. Out. Again. In. Hold it. Out."

Desmond heaved a sigh as his body regained control.

Lilith released him and sat back. She ran a hand through her hair, staining the short, light strands with the drying burgundy of his blood. She looked panicked, her eyes glassy with what he assumed were tears.

Finding his way up to a seated position on the floor, Desmond looked around the room. The couches sat askew, with the coffee table pressed against the far one. Their overturned teacups puddled Assam on the rug. A rip pierced the velveteen cushion he'd sat on just minutes ago. The corners no longer bore inky shadows but normal overcast light.

"I—" Desmond stopped, his throat feeling full and scratchy. He coughed, tasting the remains of his blood.

Dejectedly, Lilith handed him a tissue.

He wiped his mouth, grimacing at the stain when he drew it away. "So . . ." He looked up at Lilith. "I think we should call my dad."

259

# CHAPTER TWENTY-TWO

# Desmond

Lilith allowed Desmond the use of her bathroom to clean up. He'd looked worse than he expected. Though she'd healed him enough to save his life, Lilith hadn't had the skill to repair his more superficial wounds.

Healing wasn't exactly common amongst Wielders, but even a skilled Cleric could handle it occasionally. It wasn't that hard. Desmond had once healed a scraped knee he'd earned while goofing off with Brady on the rocky beachside. Of course, he hadn't let Brady know what he'd done.

After washing off the blood, Desmond didn't think it made much of an improvement to his appearance. He applied butterfly bandages to the cut along his jaw, swearing under his breath a couple of times at the pain as fresh blood attempted to seep through. Since he'd wiped his neck clean, the collar of his gray tee now held a ring of dampness, as well as drying splatters of his blood.

He'd have to get rid of this shirt before his mom saw it. She'd never let him leave the house again.

Jagged holes marred the tee right below his heart, a jarring reminder of the brutality of the nyct's talons. Lilith had closed those wounds on his chest, but as he wiped the blood away, he could still see five puckering white marks on his skin. He wondered if they'd leave a scar. Then, he wondered if Cait would mind. She'd probably be angry that he'd put his life in danger and call him stupid.

Despite the shakiness that remained after his near death experience, he smiled at the thought and glanced at his phone, finding a text from her. *"We need to talk."* His throat tightened, worried that she regretted their kiss last night. Was that what she wanted to talk about? He hoped not.

Desmond sent a quick reply, telling her he might have trouble meeting that afternoon but would be back at school tomorrow. He left the bathroom to find his dad and Kevin Jun in the kitchen, listening to Lilith's recounting of the event.

"And you don't have any idea why someone would send beasts after you?" Jun was asking as Desmond walked into the room.

Lilith rolled her eyes, though her hands shook around her teacup. "No," she said. "I haven't had any contact with the Druids in over fifteen years. I didn't even think they knew where I was. Unless one of your people has gone rogue, William, I have no idea who would have wanted to kill me."

"Maybe it wasn't you they wanted to kill," Jun suggested casually.

Desmond felt his stomach twist, but he played it cool, leaning against the doorframe. "Why would anyone attack me?" he asked.

William's jaw was tight as he turned to Jun, waiting for the agent's answer.

Jun showed no sign of concern at the idea. "Makes about as much sense as an attack on Ms. Drake." He turned back to Lilith. "Thank you for your cooperation, ma'am. We'll let you get back to your day." And with that, he abruptly turned to leave.

"They sent four nyct into my home," Lilith said caustically. "We barely made it out with our lives. And you want to leave me here alone?"

Jun turned to William, watching to see what his choice would be as Porthaven's leader.

William maintained his composure as he spoke to Lilith. "As Mr. Jun suggested, we aren't even sure you were the intended target," he said. "However, if it would make you feel better, we can send someone to watch your house for the time being."

Though that didn't seem to please Lilith, she accepted the guard.

Desmond questioned the validity of that choice. Though the patrol at the Veil had been canceled thanks to "Desmond's assistance," the Warden members were still recovering. He wasn't sure that Uncle Rick would have the manpower or cooperation to take on such a task.

Once Lilith shut the door behind the three men, William turned to Jun. "If it's all right with you, I'd like to ride back with my son," he said.

The constantly bland expression on Jun's face never wavered. "Of course," he said. "I'd feel the same if it were my son."

William passed Jun his keys, allowing the man to drive his sedan back to town. Then, he and Desmond moved toward the black muscle car. It was a strange sight, watching his dad hunch to slide into the low-riding vehicle. Desmond felt the urge to drive more recklessly than usual, but it faded quickly.

After nearly dying, Desmond couldn't find it in him to be quite so flippant.

Carefully backing out of Lilith's driveway, Desmond drove at a reasonable speed down the road.

"Are you okay?" William asked, well-controlled concern lacing his voice.

Desmond swallowed through the lingering fear from his experience. "Sort of."

"Lilith said . . ." His dad paused, the control slipping as his voice thickened. "Did you really almost die?"

Hearing his parental worry—feeling the terrified affection it held—Desmond considered saying that Lilith had blown the situation out of proportion. But he was tired of lying.

Keeping his eyes on the road, Desmond replied with a simple, "Yeah."

A heavy silence filled the car. He knew his honesty was causing his dad distress, just like everything else he ever did. And for the first time in a long time, he regretted every second of it.

"I'm sorry, Dad," he muttered.

William looked at him but didn't speak.

He tightened his grip on the steering wheel, holding his silence too. What else could he say? There was no need to specify when he was sorry for everything.

Clearing his throat, William sat back. When he spoke, Desmond could hear his return to professionalism. He wasn't a dad anymore; he was the mayor. "I'm going to need to know what you were doing there," he said.

Desmond took comfort in the detachment of his dad's tone. He allowed himself to take on his own persona as well. "Getting the information you weren't willing to get," he replied, letting a hint of snark slip into his tone.

He saw William frown in his peripheral vision. "We can't trust her."

"She saved my life, Dad," he countered. "What else does she have to do?"

William ignored the question. "We have to have a better story than that," he said. "I'll tell them that you went there on my behalf. I've been busy with my mayoral responsibilities as well as concluding the investigation of the Veil. Since you're of age now and you were with me at my previous meeting with her, I sent you to ask Lilith if she had any more thoughts on how someone might damage a Veil."

Desmond drew his eyebrows together. "Do you think they'll believe that? I mean, what did Lilith tell Jun about why I was there?"

"She was intentionally vague," he said. "Said you had questions about the spirit world and her experience with it."

"I guess that'll work." Desmond caught sight of Jun driving his dad's car in the rearview mirror. "Why'd you bring Mr. It's-Not-An-Investigation with you?"

"I didn't have much choice," he said. "He had me running through the past ten years' books with him when you called."

Desmond grimaced. "Sorry."

"He would have found out one way or another." William pulled in an agitated breath. "I need to make some calls. Head to the town hall, will you?"

~

Within an hour, all the members of the town council had filed into the meeting room. It was still working hours, so they all had to remain nonchalant about their arrival. They couldn't let the unenlightened government workers know they were calling an emergency meeting about the spirit world.

Sixteen of the seventeen council members sat around the table. While his cousin Dustin—Uncle Rick's eldest son—was off at the police academy in Vassalboro, Desmond was now an official member, thanks to his birthday yesterday. He scanned the other members: Greene, Varon, Lavigne, and Edgars, all present in addition to himself and his dad. And then there was Jun, standing at the back of the room, despite the seat offered to him.

William had just finished bringing the men up to speed on the day's events. Desmond couldn't tell which of them bought their lies. He could tell by the glint in some of their eyes that they were suspicious, but Jun's expression remained impassive.

"What does this mean?" Gary Lavigne asked. The retired reverend furrowed his wrinkled brow. "Are there Druids in Porthaven?"

"That is how it seems," William admitted. "However, we don't have conclusive proof."

"Don't we?" Ryan Greene asked sharply. "Seems to me like the damaged Veil is perfect proof of that."

Desmond couldn't help glaring at the young man. Ryan was one of the few who made his doubt of Desmond's involvement evident, his green eyes sharp. He thought Ryan Greene and Therese Lewan were a perfect couple. Not because they were so complementary but because they used the same egotistical feint. Ryan wasn't nearly the stupid jock he portrayed himself to be, and Therese wasn't the preppy airhead she mimicked. They were a cunning, self-serving match made in hell.

Though to be fair, Desmond wouldn't have had any inkling of Therese's intelligence if Brady hadn't been keen enough to point it out. He didn't know if that meant she was a better actress or if she was riding the line more closely.

William dismissed Ryan's suggestion with a slow shake of his head. "We can't assume something that important," he said. "While both events certainly suggest there could be Druids, we have to pursue every avenue before coming to conclusions."

"Didn't we run into a dead end on the investigation of who damaged the Veil?" Raymond Edgars asked. "If there are Druids lurking in town, that might explain why we haven't found a viable suspect."

"And who do you think those Druids would be, Raymond?" Fish jumped in. "The last tourists left last week. We don't expect any more until the Festival. Who does that leave as suspects?"

No one around the table wanted to admit the truth.

"Exactly," Fish said. "Our friends and neighbors. Maybe even some of our own family."

Desmond tugged on the collar of his freshly changed shirt but kept his personal suspicions to himself.

"*If* there are Druids," William interjected, "then, yes, Fish, you're correct. But that's why we can't operate from that place of fear."

"We already suspected those folks, William," Fish countered. "Knowing they're Druids just makes their crime more heinous."

The whole table was silent, taking in the back-and-forth.

Ben Lavigne looked to Desmond. "You said you didn't notice any arcs of the spirit world, correct?"

"No," Desmond confirmed. "Granted, I was bleeding out, so I could've missed something. But she admitted to us a couple of weeks ago that she's a Cleric."

"And she saved your life?"

Desmond pointed to the cut on his jaw, now properly bandaged, thanks to his dad's help and the town hall first aid kit. "This is the equivalent of a cat scratch compared to what that nyct did to my chest."

Ben's expression grew haunted, and Desmond knew he was nearly as distraught about the idea as William had been.

"She got injured as well," Desmond added, feeling newly supportive of the ex-Druid. "I think it's pretty safe to assume that Lilith isn't our enemy. If anything, she wants to help us."

Though no one ratified his opinion, a handful of the men gave considering nods.

"Why attack her in the first place?" Ryan's dad, Kenneth Greene, asked. "Whoever it was—Druid or not."

"Maybe she can identify them," Uncle Rick suggested. "If they *are* Druids—which makes the most sense to me, by the way—maybe she'd recognize them."

"Or maybe she has information they don't want her giving us," Fish added.

Jun finally spoke up from the back of the room. "We're not entirely sure that it was Ms. Drake they were after."

Desmond bristled.

However, William nodded. "It is a rather notable coincidence that my son was there during the attack. If they wanted to kill Lilith, why do it when she had a visitor?"

Desmond could hear the unspoken addition to his dad's words: Why do it when the power-filled Varon heir was present?

"Perhaps someone sent them, and it just happened to be bad timing," Troy Lavigne, Fish's youngest son, suggested.

"They manifested in the room," Desmond said. "If someone had sent them, they wouldn't have bled out of the shadows like that."

"How would you know?" Ryan asked. "You summon beasts regularly?"

Ignoring the fact that he actually did summon one beast on a daily basis, Desmond used the facts provided to him by all the research his dad forced on him as a child. "According to Henry Lawrence's essay 'The Daemons of the Druids and Their Distinctions,' beasts can appear in two ways: either by shadow, morphing into a space, like our experience at Lilith's, or in a flash, appearing suddenly before you. The latter is only possible near a Veil, by the way, as it's effectively pulling it back to allow the spirit world entrance into the physical. Should a beast have been sent, it wouldn't have manifested in such a way. It was summoned, which means the Wielder who summoned it was nearby."

In the wake of his metaphorical mic drop, the council members shifted uncomfortably in their seats. Ryan's jaw ticked with irritation. Desmond smirked at him.

Fish snorted, always supportive of Desmond's antics. "The question is," he raised his bushy eyebrows, "how did our attackers know you'd be there at that time?"

The lightkeeper had a point. If someone had sent the beasts after Desmond, they would have found him, one way or another. But as the person had summoned them at the time of the attack, they either knew in advance he'd be at Lilith's house or had followed him there.

While that realization sank in, Desmond looked toward his dad at the head of the table. Was someone following him? If so, had they followed him last night? Did they know about him and Cait?

A thread of panic wove around his spine.

"What *were* you doing there?" Ryan demanded.

Fear and irritation melding, Desmond's body tensed at the not-so-subtle accusation. "I'm pretty sure my dad already explained that," he ground out. Then, he held up a placating hand. "Oh, sorry. I forget how vacuous you can be."

Ryan glared at him.

"Vacuous means empty-headed, by the way."

"I heard the mayor's explanation," Ryan replied, words clipped. "It just seems to me that you've been showing up in places you shouldn't be an awful lot these days. First, you seal the Veil, and now, you're caught visiting the witch and wielding as well?"

"First," Desmond mimicked, "you're welcome. And yeah, I was wielding. My life was in danger. I did what I had to do to protect myself."

"But why were you *there*?" Ryan pressed.

Kenneth set a hand on his son's arm. "That's enough," he chastised.

Ryan snarled but sat back.

From the corner, Jun watched with a perceptive eye.

Desmond let his chin dip. He didn't want to appear guilty in front of the Warden agent, but he could feel the man's observation of him, and he equally feared earning his disapproval as well as his insight. For the first time in his life, he realized just how much his behavior affected his dad. If he hoped to help his dad maintain the leadership of Porthaven, he couldn't appear to be some irreverent ass. He had to earn Jun's respect. And he didn't foresee the man approving of a snide brat.

Somehow, William managed to corral the meeting back into order. The final subject of discussion was "What do we do now?" The Veil might be sealed, keeping the town safe from untethered beasts, but now they were faced with the threat of unknown enemies in their midst— Druid or otherwise.

"I have a few leads that I want to check up on," William concluded, and Desmond knew he meant Sterling Faulk and Matt Davis. He felt a sudden chill, realizing both young men were getting rather close to Cait these days. "I'll report back as soon as I have something more concrete."

"No offense," Brett Varon spoke up, sounding very much like he meant offense, "but your secret 'leads' haven't been very effective these last few weeks. Care to share so that we can all do our part?"

What he meant, Desmond knew, was that they needed to know what was going on in case William screwed up.

"I wondered why you'd been so quiet," William replied, a threatening, hushed quality in his tone. "You team up with Ken's boy to make my son and me appear inept, Brett?"

The man sat straighter, his silence a confirmation.

Desmond wanted to scoff but kept his cool, letting his dad take charge.

"No," William said sharply. "I don't care to share with you. Partly because the more people involved, the messier this gets. But mostly because I'm not convinced you aren't playing a role in all this."

Desmond's eyes went wide while several men around the table gasped.

Brett Varon's expression went rigid. "How dare you?" he spat. "My family has—"

"Your family is my family, Brett," William said. "And yes, we've been a part of the Warden for centuries. Now, if you'd stop focusing on ways to undermine me, then maybe I *could* trust you with the intricate facets of this investigation. Until then, I'd ask that you prove your dedication to our organization by sharing what knowledge you have and letting us handle the details, all right?"

Surprised and pleasantly impressed with his dad's gumption, Desmond tamped down his proud smirk and checked on Jun's reaction. While he approved, he worried about what the Warden agent might think of this assertion of authority.

At first, he thought he saw censure in Jun's narrowed gaze. But then he caught the barest fraction of a smile, his lips curving up in thought.

Relief flooded Desmond.

Jun was intrigued by William's commanding response.

Maybe they wouldn't lose their position of leadership after all.

"If that's it," William said, pushing back his chair, "we can draw this meeting to a close. Rick, Ben—I'd like to discuss my plans with you. The rest of you are dismissed."

Knowing that he was included, Desmond rose to leave. The day had gotten away from him, and he had to get to the school in time for basketball practice. He may have skipped classes, but that didn't mean he could pass up his captain's duties.

Ryan bumped his shoulder on the way out. "Don't take it personally, kid. Times are changing, and I want to be on the right side of it, okay?"

Perhaps it was the blood loss, but Desmond couldn't find a quick quip. His feet stuttered to a stop as Ryan's long strides carried him easily across the town hall's atrium. Had he really just admitted to being involved in a coup?

Desmond scanned the rest of the Warden men as they headed for the exit. How many of them were involved? The Varons, obviously. What about Kenneth? He'd clearly been upset with Brett for calling Jun in, yet he could still be part of the team. And what about the rest? Surely, the Edgarses and Lavignes wouldn't take up against his dad. The Edgarses were family. The Lavignes were their friends. They could trust them, couldn't they?

Before he had time to come to any conclusions, Jun stepped up to his side. "I'm glad to catch you, Mr. Simon," the analyst said. "I wanted to ask: Would you have time for that meeting of ours this Saturday?"

Desmond scratched his forehead, his brain clouded from the fear of death, the weight of responsibility, and the threat of betrayal. "Uh, yeah . . . yeah, I think so."

"Great." Jun didn't look as enthusiastic as he sounded. "Shall we meet at nine at the coffee shop? Sea Beans, was it?" The ridiculous name sounded even more ridiculous in the man's monotone.

"Right, sure." Desmond pointed to the door. "I've gotta go."

"Of course. Have a good afternoon." Jun gave him a thin smile and turned, reentering the council room.

Desmond gaped as men and women milled about, going through their workday. His jaw hurt, and his head spun. He needed to shake off this miserable day. And yet, the one thing he wanted to do—go to the cove and talk to Cait—he couldn't.

Heaving a sigh he felt all the way to his toes, Desmond trudged out of the town hall. One day into being eighteen, and he was already tired of being a responsible adult.

# Cait

Cait couldn't stop herself from drumming her fingers against her desktop. She hadn't wanted to be the first to initiate a text between herself and Desmond, but she hadn't had much choice. She would have thought their kiss would make everything easier. Instead, she found herself reading into every silence and every word.

Yesterday, Desmond responded to her text with a simple and noncommittal, *"Okay. Hung up with internship and practice tonight. Be at school tomorrow."*

Per their unspoken texting agreement, she'd replied with an equally casual, *"See you then."*

For the remaining sixteen hours, there'd been no contact.

Last night, Sterling had texted her with the details about their meeting with Hunter. After school today, they'd return to Haddock Park to get his insight. And though she agreed to join, Cait still felt anxious about revealing herself to Hunter. All morning, she kept second-guessing the decision, sure she was making a big mistake.

Now, Cait sat in history class doing her absolute best not to stare at Desmond's still-empty seat. She kept reminding herself that he always showed up to class only seconds before it started. But she couldn't help fearing that he was avoiding her.

And she couldn't blame him. The very idea of dealing with their strange relationship made her want to curl up under her desk, throw the hood of her canvas jacket over her head, and pretend she didn't exist.

To make matters worse, Matt was acting weird again. It was clear he didn't believe the story Cait and Sterling told him. And now, he was distant, his scant conversation guarded and more awkward than usual. Genni even pointed it out on the car ride to school.

"Did you wake up on the wrong side of the bed or something?" she'd asked.

"No," Matt grumbled. "I'm just tired."

The lie was blatantly obvious, but Cait directed Genni's attention elsewhere to ensure her sister wouldn't push the subject.

Cait felt guilty about the situation with Matt. He was always trying so hard to be a good friend, and she was always making it harder on him. She wished she could be honest. In the few weeks he'd been in Porthaven, he'd proven to be a loyal friend, supportive to a fault. She owed him truthfulness, didn't she? But opening up about the spirit world wasn't exactly cafeteria lunch material. And she wasn't even sure she *could* tell him. Were there Warden regulations about such things?

Another thing to discuss with Desmond.

A tingle spread at the base of Cait's skull just before the hum sprang to life behind it. Desmond, Brady, and Garrett stepped into the classroom. It appeared that Garrett and Whitney were on the outs again as she turned away from his longing stare with a "humph." Brady corralled their big friend to their seats, blocking Cait's view of Desmond.

When his friends were finally out of the way, she saw that Desmond was seated, facing the front of the class. However, his phone was in his hands. And a matter of seconds later, her phone lit up on the desktop beside her.

She didn't pick it up but glanced at the notification.

*"When?"* the text read.

Despite Matt's awkward silence, Cait knew she wasn't safe to respond. He'd notice her texting. So, Cait waited until the class ended, excusing herself to go to the bathroom.

*"Can you disappear?"* she replied.

Desmond's text didn't come until lunch. *"You trying to get me alone?"*

Cait's face heated. Was he flirting with her?

Another message came in before she could reply. *"Yeah, probably. Now?"*

Checking the location of her friends in line, Cait quickly typed out her response. She'd already worked out her plan to sneak away without rousing suspicion. *"After lunch."*

He sent a thumbs-up emoji in reply.

Thankful to have so many people at their table to carry the conversation for her, Cait ate her meal in relative silence. She did her best not to act strange, but her brain kept reverting to Desmond. In just a short thirty minutes, they'd be alone again. Albeit on the rooftop of their school and only for a short time. But still.

After Tuesday night, being alone with Desmond felt like a dare.

Liz noticed Cait's unusual mood, remarking on it as they left the cafeteria. "Are you okay?" she asked.

Shrugging it off, Cait tried to appear casual. "Oh, yeah, I—" She intentionally kept her expression uneasy as she dropped her voice, giving it an embarrassed inflection. "I just don't feel great."

Liz's dark green eyes widened a fraction before she gave a knowing nod. "Ah." She lowered her voice too. "That time of the month, huh? I've got whatever you need in my bag. Even ibuprofen."

Thankful that her lie had worked, Cait gave a nervous smile. "Actually," she pressed a hand to her stomach, "that stuff doesn't really work for me."

Liz grimaced. "Bad cramps?"

"The worst."

"I get it." Liz came to a stop. "Why don't you go see the nurse? I bet she'd have something that can help."

"Thanks," Cait said genuinely. "I think I will."

Though part of her felt guilty for lying, she couldn't fight down the sense of accomplishment of having her plan work. While they all headed for English, she went to the school nurse's office. She added another lie to her tally, telling the nurse that she was allergic to all her medicines, earning her a pass to go home for the rest of the day.

The farce had taken her longer than she'd hoped, but now she had an excuse to be away from classes the rest of the afternoon. Which meant her meeting with Desmond didn't have a time limit.

After ensuring the halls were emptied, Cait walked to the back staircase. She raced up the steps, her heart pounding from the exertion and anticipation. Her fingers brushed the bottom of the fire extinguisher, and she found the key missing.

Desmond was already there and waiting for her.

She paused. Memories of the last time they'd been together—of their kiss—resurfaced. Her cheeks heated, and her stomach rolled. Suddenly, she didn't feel like she'd lied about feeling sick after all.

Cait pushed through the door and up the final flight of stairs to the rooftop. Fluffy white clouds filled the sky, sunbeams breaking through like beacons of light. Boats puttered around the harbor and out across the sloping waves. A gentle breeze ruffled her hair, keeping the afternoon temperately cool.

And the hum of Desmond's presence filled her head.

Cait turned, finding him perched on the lip of the cafeteria skylight. His black bomber jacket hung open over a deep crimson tee. He had his arms and ankles crossed in a casual cockiness that she shouldn't find attractive but did.

Their eyes met across the distance, and he tipped up his chin in greeting. "Hey," he said, his tone unusually warm.

Cait tried not to read into it.

She dropped her backpack next to his by the door and walked over, keeping a distance between them. She struggled to meet his gaze as she wrung the hem of her jacket. "Hi," she replied thinly.

A low chuckle came from Desmond. He stood, closing the space between them. "You scared of me or somethin', Lewan?" he teased.

"No," she breathed, though her mouth was drier than Genni's attempt at soda bread last week.

With everything so unknown between them, Cait feared she might say the wrong thing or read into his words the wrong way. What she wanted from their relationship might not be what he wanted. And she feared expecting more from him than he could—or would want—to give.

The wind cut through again, dragging some of Cait's hair across her cheek. She reached up to brush it away, only to find Desmond already tucking it behind her ear. His fingers brushed her cheek, sending shivers across her skin.

Finally, she met his gaze.

He was studying her face intently, his eyes dropping to her mouth. Her heart constricted. Then, she noticed the thin, red line on his jaw.

Cait's lips parted, realizing he'd been hurt. The cut was far too long and deep to have been a simple shaving mishap. So, what *had* happened?

Tapping her own jaw, Cait asked, "Where'd you get that?"

Desmond grimaced. "It's a long story," he said, then quirked a brow. "By the way, how do you feel about scars?"

Scrunching her nose, Cait took a step back. "I've never thought about it."

"It's not really something you think about," he said. "You either find them attractive, or you don't."

A nervous laugh slipped out of her. "Do you find them attractive?"

He paused. "Hm." He pursed his lips, eyebrows rising in consideration. "Yeah, I guess I do."

Cait wondered if she should tell him that her singular scar was from a vegetable-chopping incident, and the tiny white line on her left index finger could only be seen under the most intense scrutiny.

"So?" Desmond prompted.

"What?"

"Do you?"

"Do I what?"

"Find scars attractive?"

Cait's mouth formed an O before she said, "No."

He looked disappointed. "You don't?"

She shook her head. "No, but I don't find them *un*attractive either. They're just kind of there."

Desmond's mouth turned down in thought. "Huh. Never considered that as an option."

"Why are we talking about this?" she asked.

"Right." He snapped his fingers, then pointed to her. "You needed to talk, and we've gotta get back."

"I don't," she corrected.

He blinked. "You don't?"

"I got a pass from the nurse."

"How?"

She felt her cheeks redden. "I told her I wasn't feeling well."

"You lied?" Desmond looked impressed. He smirked. "I'm rubbing off on you."

Cait gave his arm a playful shove. "It's not a good thing."

"Agree to disagree." He grabbed her hands then, drawing her back toward the HVAC unit. "Well, *you* may not have to get back, but *I* do. So, what's up?"

Distracted by the tingle that spread up her arms from his grip on her hands, Cait wasn't sure she'd manage to say anything. "Uh—" Her mind felt empty as he pulled her closer. They stood toe to toe before he moved to pull her down under the unit with him.

Cait detached her hands from his. "I . . . I need a minute," she mumbled.

Surprise, then understanding crossed Desmond's expression. He scratched the back of his neck, sheepish in a way she'd never seen before. "Right, yeah, sure," he stuttered. "What, uh—whatever you need."

Rubbing her hands down her sides, Cait put distance between them. Her mind cleared, the hum softening. "So, I just—" She stopped, refocused, and started over. "Two things. First, I—my dreams changed again."

Desmond frowned, leaning back against the HVAC.

"Ever since the night on the island—at the Veil—"

His eyes went wide at that.

"I've been dreaming about it . . . about the tree," she clarified. "I wasn't in my room or at the cove, and you weren't in them anymore. It was just me, the tree, Sterling, this redheaded woman, and . . . someone else. I don't know who."

Desmond's eyes narrowed in thought. "Is that it?"

"No."

He gestured for her to keep explaining, so she told him about the rest: the door with its growing fissure, the tree and its strange tear, the raven and the redhead, and the shadow.

"But two nights ago," she continued, "it changed again. I'm back in my room, back at the cove, and . . . and you're there too."

Desmond frowned. "Two nights ago?"

Cait nodded, knowing his thoughts. He wasn't in her dreams, and then two nights ago, after their kiss, he'd returned.

Cait believed in coincidences, but somehow, this didn't feel like one. "Did I—?"

Cait cut him off, not needing the whole question. "No, you didn't die, but . . ." She hesitated, fidgeting with the zipper on her jacket. "We were in the water, and a wave crashed over us, and . . . We went underwater, and a monster took you."

"Took me?"

She nodded.

"Huh." Desmond rubbed the back of his neck. "That's weird."

"There's more," she said, then told him about her being washed ashore, back on the island with the tree. She told him about the amber explosion and the pressure at the back of her skull. "I think it means the Wolf is breaking free."

Desmond tightened his jaw. "Sounds plausible," he muttered tensely. Then, he cleared his throat. "Can I ask a couple of questions?"

"Sure."

"Sterling? He's in your dreams now?"

"Yeah," she whispered, knowing he wouldn't like her telling him this.

Desmond raised his brow knowingly. "He inherited his family's spirit-being?"

"We think so."

"We?"

Cait shrugged. "We're kind of talking about it in secret."

"Hm." Desmond stared past her in thought. "Is he the one who told you about the Veil?"

"Yes."

"What does he know about it?"

Cait shrugged. "Not much that I know of. He didn't even know it was on the island until I told him."

Desmond considered that for several seconds. It seemed like he was trying to puzzle something out, as though she were giving him answers rather than the other way around. Then, he met her gaze. "I'll be honest," he said, "this isn't great news."

Cait chewed on the inside of her lip. "I didn't think it would be."

"But . . ." He sighed. "It's kind of helpful. I'll talk to my dad about finding a way to strengthen your block. It might not work, but maybe . . . Maybe it'll give us more time."

Cait hesitated, remembering her conversation with William last Saturday. "You're working with your dad now?" she asked.

A dry grin lifted Desmond's lips. "Shocking, isn't it? But surprisingly, he's not so bad once you get to know him."

Cait wasn't sure how to take that. During the entirety of their friendship, Desmond had lamented how controlling and demanding his dad was. They'd been perpetually against one another. Yet now, the mayor was suddenly on Desmond's side.

"Did you tell him?" Cait asked nervously.

Desmond didn't need clarification. His expression softened apologetically. "He already knew."

Cait slumped. "How?"

"Fish told him."

Cait grimaced and turned away, but Desmond reached out. He grabbed her hand, pulling her closer. "It's okay, Caity," he promised. "Dad's on our side. He's not gonna tell anyone."

"How do you know?" Cait demanded. "Des, you spent the last twelve years fighting against him. Why would he help you now?"

"Because he's my dad," Desmond insisted. "And yeah, he was kind of a jerk at times, but he's trying to make up for it. He actually does care."

Cait pressed her lips together, wanting to believe him. But her better judgment said she couldn't.

Desmond held her gaze with a determined expression. "He's going to help me fix this."

Pulling away from him, Cait dropped her face into her hands. The truth was still so new, so raw. She was a Vessel for a spirit-being—the Wolf. She'd inherited her da's curse, and she was destined to be caged because of it. Her life would be dictated to her, just as Sterling had said.

And Desmond thought he could fix that.

With a sigh, Cait dropped her hands. She looked back at him. "One more thing," she said weakly. "I need to run something by you."

"Of course." He looked so adamant and anxious, with his eyes intent and jaw clamped shut, that Cait couldn't help the small smile that came to her lips.

"All right," she began, then told him everything she and Sterling had discovered about their shared dreams, convincing them *he* was the Faulk family's new Vessel.

"He told you that term?" Desmond asked when she mentioned it.

"Vessel? Yeah," she confirmed. "I think he said it by accident, but from what I understand, Vessels carry these spirit-beings. Though Sterling doesn't know any more about those beings than we do."

A muscle twitched in Desmond's jaw, but he nodded for her to go on.

"Now that our dreams have changed," she said, "he wants to talk with Hunter. We're supposed to meet after school today, but . . . I don't know if it's such a good idea. What if he tells the Warden?"

Desmond screwed up his face. "Are you asking me if I think you should tell Hunter that you're the Vessel?"

Cait shrugged. "Yeah."

"Hell, no!" he exclaimed. "You can't trust Hunter as far as you can throw him. Which, due to your adorably dainty size, I'm assuming is about two inches."

Cait found herself laughing and blushing at the same time. "You're sure that isn't your feud-addled brain speaking?"

He gave her a knowing smirk. "Caity, he's a sanctimonious know-it-all. If you tell him you're the Vessel, he'll run home to his daddy and spill his guts."

"Sterling doesn't think so."

"What does Sterling know?"

Cait could hear the sourness in his tone and knew he wasn't giving the situation fair consideration. "Hunter's his best friend," she countered.

"Scott is Hunter's best friend," Desmond corrected.

"You can have more than one best friend. You have two of them yourself."

He opened his mouth to argue, then reconsidered. "Dang it, you're right."

"Obviously," she teased. "Brady and Garrett will always be your best friends."

Desmond snorted in amusement. "Garrett's not my best friend. He's a *good* friend and my cousin, but he's nowhere near the closest to me."

"Then, who is? Brady and . . . ?"

His smirk softened. "You."

The warmth of joy snuggled up in Cait's chest. "Really?"

"Don't act like it's such an honor," he replied, that affectionate look still on his face. "I'm a shitty friend to have."

She ignored his blatant attempt to make her frown at his language. "No, you're not," she assured him, setting a hand on his arm.

A long moment hung between them as their gazes locked. She could have sworn he began to lean in. But then he simply shifted his weight, leaning back against the HVAC once more.

"Don't listen to my advice, Caity," he said. "I can't see things clearly as far as Hunter is concerned. If you feel like you can trust him . . . well, I wouldn't suggest it, but you can give it a shot."

"It isn't that I trust him," she said. "I just don't know who else to talk to."

"What about me?"

She frowned, and he waved a hand through the air, brushing away the idea. "I know, I know," he said. "Sterling would never talk to me."

Cait wasn't sure if that was completely true, but she thought it would take far more coaxing than any of them had time for.

"I don't feel like I have a choice in this, Des," she said. "We need answers, and I think Hunter can give them to us."

Reluctantly, he nodded. "I think so too. Even if he doesn't know much . . . it might give us a chance to learn what he *does* know. And while I can tell you what I know, it isn't enough. I'm sort of in the dark these days."

He paused then, brow furrowing. "And now that I think about it—" he raised a finger in thought, "this might actually work in our favor."

"What do you mean?"

"The Varons are up to something," he said, gaze distant and considering. "I don't know if Hunter's involved, but that's the problem. I don't know who's involved, and I need to. So, maybe . . ." He paused for a moment. "Maybe by talking to him, you can find out what they're up to."

"You want me to try to get information out of Hunter?"

"Kind of." He brushed a hand through the air as though brushing away his uncertainty. "Look, it's not a big deal if you can't. It's just . . . his dad is trying to take my dad's job. But if you *happen* to hear him say anything that might suggest what they're planning, it could really help. Because if his dad gets leadership of the Warden . . . Well, all our plans are gonna go sideways really fast."

Drawing in a heavy breath, Cait felt the weight of that charge. William was helping them. His words from Saturday returned to her. *"As Desmond's father, it's my job to ignore all of that to ensure his safety. His happiness . . . No matter what, I will protect my son. And now, that means protecting you too."*

Cait decided it was her job to protect them as well. "All right," she said. "I'll see what I can learn."

"Be careful, though," Desmond warned. "I don't want you to put yourself in danger."

"I won't," she said, though she knew if it meant taking care of Desmond, she would.

A long silence hung between them, neither wanting to leave but neither with anything more to say.

Desmond gestured toward the stairwell. "I should probably get back," he muttered.

She nodded, stepping out of his way. They moved toward their backpacks, a static tension pulsing in the air between their hands.

Desmond ruffled his hair. "Hey, so," he said. "I'm gonna be kind of unavailable the next few days."

Cait furrowed her brow, looking up at him.

"Like I was yesterday, I mean," he clarified. "We still need to have that conversation about everything that has been happening, and . . . well, I just don't want you to think I'm ignoring you."

"Oh, uh—" Cait brushed the thought away. "Yeah, no, I—I wasn't expecting that you'd be around all the time or anything."

He opened his mouth to reply when Cait cut him off, realizing how her words sounded. "Not that we're—it isn't that I think—I mean, we're not—"

"Caity," he interrupted, a strange smile on his lips. "We *are*."

Cait found herself stepping back into the brick wall of the stairwell. "We are?" she asked.

A slow smile spread over Desmond's face. He closed the distance between them, his fingers brushing hers. "If you want to be," he said.

Her body buzzed with the hum, her head spinning. She tried to gain some semblance of logic as he ducked his head toward hers. She closed her eyes as his words tickled her skin. "Do you want to be?" he asked.

Light danced behind her lids as she squeezed her eyes tighter. She felt frozen with anticipation as his fingers grazed her waist, slipping through a belt loop of her jeans. Her breathing sounded impossibly loud in her head, the hum's rumble overcoming her senses.

"Caity," he whispered.

"Hm?"

"Do you want to be?" he repeated.

The question rolled through Cait, lying to her. It promised things it could never deliver. Did she want to be with Desmond? Did she want to be his girlfriend? Did she want to be his future?

The truth slipped out of her before she could take it back.

"Yes."

Desmond blew out a sharp breath that carried a gentle relief. "Me too," he said.

The admission drew Cait to open her eyes, locking immediately with his. She was sure that her expression matched the one on his face, open-mouthed and filled with awe that they'd finally said it. She found her fingers curling around the hem of his shirt. His free hand came to rest on her lower back, pressing her closer to him.

Thinking that he was taking far too long to kiss her, Cait decided she didn't want to wait anymore. She tipped her head up, capturing his mouth with hers. The same wild instinct from the other night flashed through her mind. She lost her sense of reason, letting him carry them away in the kiss. She didn't know if he had a better imagination or simply more experience, but she was certain that while she'd started this kiss, he was leading it like a dance.

As they kissed, Desmond took hold of her wrists, guiding them to rest on his shoulders. His hands returned to her waist as her fingers found their way into his hair. It was thicker than she'd realized, the waves curling around her touch. Despite how much she thought she knew about Desmond, it seemed there was so much more to discover. Like how gentle his touch could be or how sure his embrace was. She'd never known how far a handful of inches of a height difference could feel, her head resting against the brick as he leaned down to her.

"You've," she started, words caught between each new kiss, "been gone . . . too long."

"Mm-hm," he murmured.

His thumb slipped under her shirt to graze the skin just above her jeans, eliciting a small gasp-turned-laugh from her.

"I can't," he kissed her again, "kiss you," and again, "when you," and again, "smile."

"You just did," she returned through another kiss.

He grunted his annoyed acceptance before deepening the press of his lips onto hers. It sent a thrill of desire through her sternum and down into her gut. She felt desperate to have more of him. After years of being so close with no hope of anything more, this release—this realization of a once-unattainable dream—sent her spiraling out of control.

Cait slid her hands from his hair to his face, wanting to keep him as close as possible.

Suddenly, Desmond jerked back with a sharp inhale. He grabbed her wrist, pulling her hand away from his jaw. She was about to ask what was wrong when she saw his grimace.

"Oh, Desmond, I'm sorry!" She clasped her hands to her mouth.

He gently prodded the cut along his jaw as though checking for blood. It looked redder than it had before, but it hadn't reopened.

Seeing his hand come away clean, Desmond let out a "humph." Then, he smirked at her. "It's probably for the best," he said. "This is . . ." He motioned between them. "Dangerous."

Cait felt her face heat, and she dropped her eyes to the rooftop. Their feet alternated with each other—his, hers, his, hers—keeping them close.

He affectionately brushed the hair off her forehead. "I've *really* been gone too long," he said.

Fighting against every urge within her to kiss him again, Cait snuck out of his touch and away from the wall. She snatched up her backpack, holding it as a barrier against her chest. When she looked back at Desmond, he watched her with an amused grin.

Cait blushed again. "You said we needed to find a time to talk, right?"

"Right." He grabbed his bag, hooking it over his shoulders. "I need to explain stuff. I could probably meet you tonight after practice."

"I'm meeting Hunter and Sterling tonight," she reminded, then added, "if you still think I should."

He considered it, sighing after a moment. "Yeah, you should. Well, we have a game tomorrow, so that's out too."

"What about Saturday morning?" she suggested. "We could meet at the cove."

Desmond frowned. "I have a meeting."

He said the words with such irritation that Cait ignored her curiosity about what meeting he could possibly have.

"What about the afternoon?" he asked. "We could say we're finishing up the essay."

"I have plans with Liz and Mel."

His expression showed his shock.

Cait shrugged. "They want to throw a birthday party for me, and we're supposed to have a planning committee."

"Your birthday's not for another two weeks."

"Liz is a planner."

He snorted. "All right. How about Sunday afternoon? Surely your social calendar hasn't changed *that* much."

Cait smiled at his clear jealousy over her time. "I'm free Sunday."

"Thank God!" He reached over and kissed her cheek before heading for the door. "Tell your nan you've got another study date, and we'll sneak off to the cove."

"I don't like lying, Desmond."

"It isn't a lie." He opened the door. "It's a misdirection."

She frowned.

"If it makes you feel better, we can actually work on the paper," he offered.

Though she didn't want to encourage his roguish behavior, Cait acquiesced. "Fine. I'll see you Sunday, then."

Desmond stood in the doorway, lips pursed. He let out a disgruntled growl. "Waiting's the worst," he grumbled, then disappeared.

# CHAPTER TWENTY-FOUR

# Cait

With several hours until her meeting with Sterling and Hunter, Cait decided she should do as the school nurse suggested and head home. She considered calling her nan to have her pick her up, but she didn't want to lie anymore. So, she walked down the road, zipping up her jacket against the chill in the breeze.

The leaves were on the ground now, the trees having shed their autumnal colors. Amber, burgundy, and mustard faded to drying brown leaves that skittered across the pavement, crunching under her sneakers on the road's shoulder. The air carried their crisp, earthy scent.

Cait smiled to herself, hands tucked into her jacket pockets. She couldn't remember the last time she'd been this happy. Unbidden, her feet did a giddy little jig.

Joy welled up within her until she couldn't contain it anymore. She broke into a sprint, laughing as she darted into the trees, shortening her distance home.

She felt brave for the first time in her life. She wasn't hiding in the shadows, waiting for answers to come to her. She was seeking them out for herself. She had friends, ones she'd chosen and who'd chosen her back.

And she had Desmond.

Truly and completely, he was finally hers.

Cait kicked up a cluster of leaves. That was possibly the most unbelievable of it all: Desmond and she were a couple. A secret one, but everything about them had been a secret for years. Why should this be any different?

But it couldn't stay that way forever, could it?

The joy receded. Cait's pace slowed.

Who were they kidding? Nothing had changed. They couldn't be a couple. Desires aside, it didn't matter. She was still cursed, and he was still destined to lead.

Their relationship was a secret because it couldn't be real. No matter how much Desmond assured her that it was. She wanted to be with Desmond, to be his girlfriend, to be his future.

But that was impossible.

The woods lost their feeling of fantasy. The fallen leaves lost their allure. And Cait walked the rest of the way home in silent dejection.

What a child she'd been, believing the fairy tale their kisses told. How foolish she'd been thinking it mattered what they felt. She might love Desmond, but that didn't change who they were. It didn't change the fact that they could never be together.

It didn't remove the Wolf she carried inside of her.

When Cait finally made it home, she found the house empty. Genni was still at school, Rese was at work, and Maeve had left a note saying she had work to do in town. Only Red awaited her, his tail wagging happily.

Cait scratched the dog's ears before heading to her room to deposit her schoolwork. Then, she set about distracting herself until the meeting.

The hours trickled by as she sketched. Beasts no longer plagued her nights, so she had none to add to her collection. Now, her sketches were dedicated to the redhead with the raven, the shadowed figure, and the massive tree.

Cait's sketches focused on the tree, bringing the tear in its trunk to life. Thus far, she'd never been able to get a good look at it, the darkness always shrouding it except when the lightning struck. Yet, its thick trunk seemed to have grown, something protruding from the rip in its bark.

She closed her eyes, trying to imagine the flash of its visage. Carefully, she shaped the bulging form, twisted and mottled, rising to tangle in the branches around it.

Staring at the completed drawing, Cait frowned. It looked like . . . trees. Two trees growing out of the gap, warping with the sycamore.

Sighing, Cait closed the sketchbook and glanced at her phone. School would let out soon. She tossed the sketchbook on her bed, grabbed her jacket, and prepared to leave. She darted down the stairs to find Rese walking in the back door.

"What are you doing home?" her sister asked in surprise.

"Oh, uh . . ." Cait grabbed Red's leash from the peg on the wall. "I wasn't feeling well, so the nurse sent me home early."

"How'd you get back?"

"I walked."

Rese's gaze dropped to the leash. "You're going back out?"

"I thought a walk might help my headache."

A long, weighted pause passed between them. The lift of her sister's brow said she knew Cait was lying. Rese opened her mouth as if to say something, then shook her head. "Just . . . be back in time for dinner, I guess," she said, moving farther into the house.

Cait promised she would (though not entirely meaning it), then affixed the leash to Red's collar and headed to the shed for her bike. She pedaled down the road toward downtown. Red trotted at her side, his claws clicking against the macadam. She couldn't pedal as fast with him by her side, but she'd known it would be less suspicious if she took him on a walk.

Though Red's terrier legs were short, he still had enough enthusiasm in his aged body to make up for it.

They'd grown up with a dog in their life. In Bushmills, their da had his Irish wolfhound, Conroy. The massive, wiry-haired dog never left his side. He'd been a tender, protective companion.

Cait could remember Conroy lying before the hearth of their living room fireplace. She'd loved curling up next to him, resting her head on his stomach as she petted his black fur. Conroy would lean back every so often to lick her fingers or nuzzle her face. She remembered him standing guard while she and Rese played in the yard or coming to herd them back to their parents if they strayed too far.

After her parents' deaths, Conroy disappeared. Their nan never told them what happened to the dog, which confirmed for Cait that he'd died trying to protect her da. The wolfhound would never abandon him.

When they came to Porthaven, it took two years for Cait and Genni to finally convince Maeve to get them another dog. She'd talked with William, and a few months later, the mayor came to visit them with a laundry basket covered in blankets, a tiny terrier puppy nestled inside.

Ten years later, Red still loved their walks, despite his slowing stride.

They were on the verge of being late for the meeting when they finally made it downtown. Cait rode down Lawrence Avenue, straight for the docks. Then, she biked up to the small grassy area, three public pavilions at its edge. Hunter and Sterling already sat on one of the picnic tables, watching for her.

"Sorry, I'm late," she said, guiding her bike to lean against the pavilion's column.

"You're not," Hunter replied. "We just got done early." He looked between her and Sterling. "So, what's this about?" he asked, though Cait could tell by his tone that he already suspected.

She let Sterling take the lead.

"We need answers, Hunter," he said. "And I mean complete, total, no bullshit answers."

Hunter scoffed. "I knew you were in a mood."

"I'm not in a mood."

"You're *always* in a mood."

Sterling crossed his arms. "You gonna tell us the truth or not?"

Hunter sighed and stared at his hands, which were clasped between his knees. The *whir* of a biker passed the pavilion. Red tugged on the leash to bark, drawing Cait to glance over her shoulder as the rider disappeared behind the copse of trees nearby.

Finally, Hunter looked at Cait, who still stood by her bike. "You may as well sit down," he said. "This is gonna take a while."

Since both boys were seated at the far table, Cait perched on the bench of the one nearest to her. Red plopped down at her feet. "You don't know our questions," she noted.

He lifted his brow in a Varon-like fashion, reminding her of Desmond. "I'm sitting here with the two Vessels," he said, voice pitched low. "I'm smart enough to figure it out."

Cait whirled to look at Sterling. "You told him?"

Sterling began to shake his head, but Hunter jumped in before he could reply.

"He didn't need to." Leaning forward, arms on his thighs, Hunter met Cait's stare. "I'm assuming Sterling told you everything that I've already told him in the past?"

She looked at Sterling, who confirmed, "Pretty much."

"Cool," Hunter grumbled. "Okay, so here's the deal: I'm not supposed to know, like, any of this. I'm still a minor until December, so I'm not technically a Warden member yet. But my family—we don't believe in refusing responsibility to children. Or anyone else, for that matter. I've known about the spirit world and wielding since I can remember."

"So have I," Cait said. "I knew about the Warden, about my da and mum being members. And they taught us about the spirit world. But . . . they never explained any of *this*."

Hunter pressed his lips together in thought. "That's probably because they wanted to protect you—to let you have a childhood before you had to face the very real possibility of your impending . . ."

"Doom?" she suggested.

Sterling gave a dry smirk. "Sounds about right to me."

"It isn't *doom*," Hunter argued. "You guys aren't cursed. You know that, right? Being a Vessel isn't some horrific inheritance. It's an honor."

"I'd like to see *you* inherit a monster and then call it an honor," Sterling retorted, just as a branch in the copse of trees snapped.

Red hopped up with an urgent bark. Cait glanced over, expecting to find a woodland creature scuttling through the branches. Instead, she saw the flash of pale skin and a vibrant yellow shirt.

Spotted, the lurker turned to run. But Cait wasn't the only one who'd seen him.

Sterling was already halfway to the trees when the eavesdropper attempted to flee. Cait worried he would lose him in the chase, but the spy hadn't run five feet before tripping over a root and tumbling forward.

An "oof" rang out, and then Sterling was upon him, hauling the sneak by the collar of his zip-up hoodie.

And that was when Cait recognized him.

"Matt?" she gasped as Red tugged on the leash, his tail wagging in welcome.

Shamefaced, Matt walked with Sterling back to the pavilion. Not that he had much choice with Sterling's firm grip on his jacket. Under the hoodie, his yellow tee had dirt streaked across the front. He kept his eyes down as he grumbled to Sterling, "I'm not gonna run."

"You already tried once," Sterling growled in return, grip still firm on his arm and collar. "Sorry if I don't trust that you won't try again."

"Let him go, Sterling," Hunter instructed.

"What if he tells someone?"

"Who's gonna believe him?" he said. "Outside the Warden, the rest of the town will think he's making stuff up."

"I don't even know what you guys are talking about," Matt defended. "I barely heard anything."

But as his eyes darted frantically between each member of the group, his shoulders hunched, Cait knew he'd heard enough. He seemed utterly bewildered and flinched under Sterling's hostile glare.

"See?" Hunter gestured to Matt. "He wouldn't even know what to say."

Begrudgingly, Sterling released him, and Matt stumbled to the side, straightening his clothes. He cast a chagrined look at Cait.

She frowned, understanding dawning on her. "You followed me," she accused.

Matt's face flushed red. "Yeah. I, uh—I heard you weren't feeling well, so I skipped basketball practice to come home and make you some muffins. It's what my mom always does when I'm sick, so I thought . . . Anyway, when I was making my way over, I saw you riding back toward town, so I . . . I decided to follow."

"Why?"

He shrugged. "You've been acting weird, and I . . . I just wanted to make sure you were okay, ya know?"

Cait heard what he didn't say. He hadn't followed her because he was concerned. He'd followed because he was jealous.

"No, I don't know," she said, crossing her arms. "You followed me because you thought I was meeting up with Sterling alone, didn't you?"

Matt pressed his lips together, the red now coating his ears.

Hunter broke out laughing while Sterling screwed up his face, confused. "Why would that matter?" he asked.

"He thinks you're after his girl, dude," Hunter said, and Matt's flush betrayed the truth. "I can't blame him, really. Liz and Mel have been talking now that you're starting to hang out."

Cait and Sterling shared nearly disgusted looks of horror.

Ignoring the quip about her being "Matt's girl," Cait decided to redirect the conversation. "Go home, Matt," she ordered.

That got him to meet her gaze at last. "No," he said, almost desperately. "No, I want to help. Whatever's going on . . . this has to do with your family's curse, right? The whole demon and witch-thing? Isn't that what Hunter said?"

"It's not a curse," Hunter reiterated. "And it's not a demon, either."

Cait didn't budge. "You can't help," she said crossly. "Forget whatever you heard here and go home."

But as she turned her back on him, Hunter pursed his lips. "I don't know if you're right about that, Cait," he argued.

"What?"

He shrugged. "He might be able to help."

"How?" Sterling demanded, clearly as baffled as Cait.

Matt simply looked eager to have an advocate.

"Look . . ." Hunter held out his hands, "he may be completely clueless as to what has been going on with this whole thing, but sometimes that's what you need."

Catching on, Matt began to nod. "An outside perspective," he offered.

"Exactly," Hunter said.

"You're seriously okay with this?" Sterling said.

Cait screwed up her face in matching disbelief. "I thought the policy was to keep this all a secret."

"Varons don't really care about 'policy,'" Hunter said with a flippancy that reminded her of Desmond. "Like you said, Cait: We've all been a part of this our whole lives. I can tell you what I know about your family's inheritances, but honestly? It's not that much. I've got the basics. And then a few details that might help you out. But I'm betting that neither of you is content to merely know of your inheritance's existence."

He met first Sterling's and then Cait's stare. "I think you want to do something about it," Hunter concluded.

"I want to get rid of it," Sterling said.

Realizing that this was what Desmond was offering to do for her, Cait chewed on her lip. She'd already considered this option. Being free of the

Wolf might mean she could be with Desmond, but it would also mean that one of her sisters had to take it on themselves. Cait would escape the cage only to lock one of them in it instead.

"That's not what I want," she said.

All three boys stared at her.

Cait sighed, taking her seat once more. "This is my responsibility. Whether I chose it or not, it chose me. In order to be free, I'd have to imprison someone else. I won't do that."

A silent moment passed. Matt hung his head, looking admittedly baffled, while Sterling stared off at the sea. But Cait didn't look away from Hunter's appraising stare. He scanned her, as though testing her resolve.

"All right." He gave her an encouraging smile. "Tell me what you want to know."

Cait turned to Sterling, content to let him take the lead. He and Matt sat on opposite benches as Red trotted to the edge of the pavilion to find a stick.

"Well," Sterling began, "you know those dreams I've been having?"

"Yeah."

"Cait's having them too."

"A version of them," Cait corrected.

"What do you mean?" Hunter asked.

Matt's hand shot up. "Um . . . I know I'm not really a part of this, but what dreams are you guys talking about?"

Cait and Sterling explained their dreams, relaying only the necessary details.

"Weird," Matt muttered, not seeming to fully comprehend anything they'd said.

"Very," Hunter agreed.

"Yeah, so what's up with them?" Sterling asked. "I've never heard about anyone in my family having dreams like this. Why's it happening now?"

Hunter hesitated, staring at his hands in thought. "I don't know, but . . . it doesn't bode well."

"What do you mean?" Cait asked.

"I mean, this shouldn't be happening," he replied. "There's a reason none of Sterling's ancestors had dreams like this. The Warden placed a block on their spirits, denying them access to the spirit world. It's a sucky way to live, but necessary for Vessels."

"Why?"

"Because it's the only way to ensure the spirit-beings can't get free."

Matt piped up, an apologetic grimace on his face. "What's a Vessel, again?"

Hunter hardly glanced at him. "It's a person who bears a connection to a spirit-being."

"And a spirit-being is . . . ?"

"A being of immense but unknown power."

Matt's nose scrunched. "How do you know it's immense if you don't know what it is?"

Hunter lifted his eyes to the pavilion's roof. "We know just enough of their powers to know they're dangerous. So, we keep them locked away."

"And is that all it means—to be a Vessel?" Cait asked. "It's just having this thing locked inside of you. Being locked away yourself."

"In the Warden?" Hunter shrugged. "Pretty much."

Cait frowned at that. "What about outside of the Warden?"

Hunter raised his brow. "Look, if you're a Vessel, you're either in the Warden or a Druid. And trust me, you don't want to be a Druid."

"Why not?" Matt asked curiously. His eyes were wide, and Cait wondered how much of the conversation he was actually grasping.

"Because they're evil. All they want to do is to destroy the world we know by taking the power of the spirit world for themselves and unleashing it."

Matt pursed his lips but didn't reply.

"Is that why the Druids want Vessels?" Cait pressed. "For their connection to the spirit-beings and their power?"

Hunter met her gaze, a reluctance in his blue stare. "They believe the Vessels are the key to controlling the spirit world."

Cait wasn't entirely certain how to feel about that. All of this was so new to her. She'd always known about the spirit world, but these beings and their power, the Druids and their dogma . . . That information she hadn't known.

"Are they right?" Cait found herself asking.

Hunter tugged at the hem of his shirt. "I don't know."

Cait stared past Hunter and Sterling to the gently churning sea. A soft fog drifted on the horizon as the sun slowly descended behind the clouds. Several fishing boats puttered around the docks and out amongst the haze. She wondered if Porthaven had always been like this: clouded and muddled by secrets.

Turning back to Hunter with a renewed sense of determination, Cait asked, "What does this mean for us? If the Druids need the Vessels to enact their plan, does that mean they'll come for us?"

"If they can find you," Hunter confirmed, though he didn't sound concerned by the idea. "But at this point, no one even knows we have Vessels. That's why Porthaven is so respected by the Warden as a whole. We've housed the Faulk family and their spirit-being for over two hundred years. That's unheard of."

"And now," Cait realized, "you have my family's spirit-being too."

"Yeah. A lot of our people didn't want to take your family on. They said it would be too big a risk. We've been successful with one, but hiding two Vessels . . . They didn't think it could be done. But here we are, twelve years later, and no Druid's the wiser."

Matt scratched his brow at Cait's side as she played with Red's leash. "So, we're safe here?" she asked.

"As safe as you can be, yeah," Hunter promised.

"And all it takes is our continued imprisonment," Sterling said sourly.

"You aren't imprisoned," Hunter argued. "You're being protected."

Sterling leveled him with a flat glare. "When your future's determined and you've got your marriage arranged for you, then you can tell me I'm not in prison."

"Hang on," Matt interjected. "You have an arranged marriage?"

"Not necessarily," Hunter said before Sterling could reply. "Only if he can't find a spouse here in town. Which he isn't doing a very good job of, by the way."

Sterling ignored him.

Matt surveyed Cait as though wondering if the same requirement applied to her.

Changing the subject, Cait said, "And what about the Veil?"

"What about it?" Hunter asked.

"It's damaged, right?"

His expression pinched. "How'd you know?"

Careful not to reveal her relationship with Desmond, Cait deflected. "It's the damaged tree in our dreams."

That seemed to appease him. "Right. Yeah, we don't know how that happened. No one's ever heard of something like that occurring before."

Cait frowned. "Do you think that's affecting our dreams?"

Hunter considered it. "Maybe. Yeah, that would make sense."

"I've overheard my dad when he thought my music was too loud," Sterling chimed in. "He's said that the Veils are tied to each of the spirits. That could mean that the damage is *causing* our dreams."

While Cait knew that couldn't be the case for her—after all, she'd been having her dreams since her parents died—the change in her dreams hadn't happened until recently. And maybe the Veil *had* affected that.

"What do you think that means?" she asked.

"I'm not sure," Hunter said. "But if the Veil's damage *is* causing problems with your dreams . . . then I think we have a bigger problem on our hands than we thought."

"Why's that?"

"Because if your dreams are any indication, the blocks on your spirits are breaking down. And that means the spirit-beings are breaking out."

Cait and Sterling shared a look, having already come to that conclusion themselves.

"How do we stop that from happening?" Sterling demanded.

Hunter tapped the table underneath him. "First, I think we have to figure out what's causing the damage. My dad said that Desmond somehow sealed the Veil," he said the words with annoyance, and Cait worked not to show her surprise, "so we have a little time on our hands. But I'm not sure how long what he did will hold."

"Um . . ." Matt lifted his hand again like he was in class. "I'm a little confused. There are two of these Veil-things, right?"

Hunter frowned. "Why would you think that?"

"Well, 'cause Sterling said his dad said they're each tied to the—the spirit-things. And you guys are each connected to a separate spirit, aren't you?"

They both nodded.

"So, wouldn't that mean there are two Veils?"

The three of them exchanged panicked looks.

"I've never heard of a second Veil in Porthaven," Hunter said resolutely.

"What if it's hidden?" Sterling asked.

Matt scrunched his nose. "How could something like that remain hidden for . . . however many years it's been here?"

"Twelve," Cait said. "If the Veils are connected to the spirits, then the Veil attached to mine would have arrived when I did. It would have been here for twelve years."

"There's no way," Hunter insisted. "We would have noticed if there were two Veils in Porthaven."

"So, what does that mean?"

Hunter shook his head, turning to Sterling. "Your dad's gotta be mistaken. The Veils are a link to the spirit world. Surely the spirit-beings' connections to them are simply like a chain. You detach it from one location and move it to the other."

Sterling didn't look convinced. "You sure?"

"We would *know* if there were two."

"All right, so what now?" Sterling asked with a huff. "If our blocks are breaking down because the Veil is damaged, how do we fix it? I don't want to be possessed by some freaky nightmare spirit."

Hunter dropped his eyes to his feet. "I'm not sure," he muttered. "But I want to find out. I'll do some digging and see if I can find some info in my dad's stuff. And if *he* doesn't have anything helpful, I'll find someone who does. In the meantime," he met Cait's and Sterling's gaze, "let me know if anything changes in your dreams or if you come up with any information on your own. Maybe your dreams will give you some insight."

"And we, what?" Sterling said tersely. "Meet back up in a couple of days?"

Hunter nodded. "I think that's the best we can do."

It didn't feel like enough. But it was all they had.

"You got any other thoughts for us, Matt?" Hunter asked.

"Huh?" Matt looked up, wide-eyed. "Oh, not really. I think I need some more, ya know, explanation and stuff."

Cait sighed. "You can ask me your questions while we bike home."

Slowly, they all stood, preparing to go their separate ways. Matt hurried to get his bike, still hidden behind the trees, while Hunter headed for his car. Cait had stepped over to Red to take away the stick he'd been chewing on when Sterling crouched down next to her.

"Hey," he whispered.

Cait looked at him in surprise.

His dark stare flickered behind him to be sure the others weren't watching. "Your *friend*," he said. "The one you were gonna talk to?"

Cait was confused for only a moment before she remembered: She had intended to talk to Brady. After everything with Desmond, she'd forgotten.

"Don't tell Hunter about it," Sterling advised.

Raising her chin, Cait understood. If Hunter caught wind of Brady's involvement, he'd naturally assume Desmond was involved too. And that wouldn't go over well.

Cait gave him a nod. "Thanks for keeping him out of it," she whispered.

Sterling returned the nod, rising just as Matt came around the bend. He waved at the boy and began walking toward the parking lot.

Matt met Cait by her bike, his head ducked low. "I'm really sorry, Cait," he said as she attached Red's leash to the bike handles. "It was stupid of me to follow you."

"Yeah, it was," she replied flatly. "But I don't hold it against you. You were right; I've been secretive these last few weeks. And now, you know why."

Matt hesitated, scratching his temple. "To be honest, I'm still really confused about all this. Still," he mumbled. "It wasn't really my place . . ."

Guiding her bike to the sidewalk, Cait warred with herself. She was annoyed with Matt, but she also felt guilty. He'd been such a good friend to her for the last month. It wasn't fair of her to keep secrets from him.

Yet, it wasn't fair of *him* to expect things from her either.

Cait met his gaze. "No, it wasn't your place," she admitted. "And this part of my life is . . . complicated. Which is why I didn't tell you about it."

He dipped his chin.

"But . . ." Cait sighed. "I'm glad you know about it now."

He looked up at her with wide, hopeful eyes.

"And I'm thankful that you want to help," she promised, then grinned. "Just don't secretly follow me around anymore."

Matt practically beamed at her. "Deal!" he said, then hopped on his bike.

They pushed off, heading for home.

"And I know you're not sick now, but," Matt glanced over at her bashfully, "I did already make those muffins. So, maybe when we get back, we could sit on the porch and eat them while you explain some of these things to me."

Cait found herself laughing. "It's a deal."

# CHAPTER TWENTY-FIVE

# William

This was it: the last spot marked on William's map where the second Veil could be hidden.

Though he supposed that wasn't entirely true. There was a chance that searching Porthaven's most secluded areas was unnecessary. The Veil could be hiding in plain sight. But he doubted it. Like Fish had said, being around a Veil tugged at a Wielder's connection to the spirit world. You *wanted* to access it. As no Warden members had mentioned feeling a particular tug on their will in an unexpected location, he had to assume the Veil was well hidden.

Which meant *this* was the last place it could be.

William had searched the rest of the peninsula and the tiny islands off its coastline with Fish and Ben's help. He'd scoured every tree-studded inch, every rocky shore, and every open field. If this final search failed, he'd have to take to the sea.

Veils made little sense to his level of understanding. They didn't line up with the spirit-beings or their animal-like penchants. The Leviathan's

Veil wasn't in the watery depths as one might expect but nestled inside a sycamore tree. Why that was, he had no idea. It just seemed that the thinning between their world and the spirit world chose a random natural occurrence and clung to it without obvious rhyme or reason.

Thus, William wasn't looking for a den where a wolf might hide. He wasn't looking for anything specific at all. He simply gazed around as he walked through the thick forest, the daylight filtering through the pines and birches around him.

The entire week, Jun had been looking over his shoulder at the town hall. William's probation was irritating. He felt like he couldn't complete a single day's work, having to stop to explain his every action to the analyst. But this afternoon, Jun was meeting with several Warden members, so William had the rest of the day to himself.

William paused, scanning the barren trees surrounding him and the drying leaves at his feet. He stood still, listening. If there was one good thing his father had taught him, it was the ability to hear the spirit world around him. While William hadn't wielded since he was an impetuous teen, he *had* tapped into the spirit world's essence. He knew how it felt and how to find it.

So, he listened, waiting for the sound beyond sound, the gentle whisper of the spirit.

He was tired of fighting, of striving to find the Wolf's Veil. His mind was exhausted, and his body was depleted. He'd been working so hard over the last month and a half. With the Fisher's Festival approaching, the Leviathan's Veil producing beasts, and the effort of trying to fix his relationship with Desmond, he felt worn at all edges.

He needed rest for his soul. So, he determined that today he would rest, allowing his spirit to guide him to the second Veil.

Closing his eyes, William steadied his breathing. He cleared his mind and stopped striving. He pushed out all external pressures and the fears that had built within him since Jun's arrival. And he simply listened.

The soft rustle of the breeze filled the forest. Late in the season, with the cold weather encroaching, few animals remained active, only the occasional scurry echoing off the trees. The world was going still just as he was, preparing for its wintertime rest.

As he waited, the faintest tingle rose along William's skin, a gentle tug pulling at his core. The softest whisper filled his mind, alerting him to the spirit world's presence. That was how it always felt, the subtle awareness when he turned his focus inward. A tangible but fragile perception. He could grab onto it if he wanted, accessing the spirit world and wielding its power. Or he could let it filter away, drifting on the breeze like a falling leaf.

Within the focus of his solitude, William heard the reverberation of a voice accompanied by footsteps. He opened his eyes. Someone was coming. He wasn't sure he wanted to be caught by whoever was hiking out in these woods.

The voice drew nearer, its words beginning to clarify in his ears. ". . . should be easy," a feminine voice grumbled. "Instead, we have to traipse across the peninsula like heathens."

William furrowed his brow, the voice finding its owner in his mind. Lilith.

Carefully, he moved forward, keeping to the shadows and trees to catch a glimpse of the woman. She came into view, dressed in a decidedly un-Lilith-like fashion: jeans and an oversized sweater under a canvas jacket. Her white-blonde hair barely peeked out beneath a knitted cap. Her shoulders were hunched, revealing her distaste for the chill that crept through the forest.

"God, I miss California," Lilith complained. "Why is it so damn cold here all the time?"

William searched the trees around the ex-Druid, but she was clearly alone. He couldn't help grinning. He hadn't known she talked to herself, but he couldn't exactly judge her for it. Robin often did the same, narrating the day to herself.

"Fifteen years," she continued. "One would think you'd get used to it."

"One would think," William said, stepping into view.

Lilith gasped, jumping at his sudden appearance. "William." She said his name like it was a curse. "What are you doing out here?"

"I could ask you the same thing," he remarked. "I thought you were under my people's protective custody."

Lilith rolled her eyes. "I happened to need some solitude to think through my problems," she replied flatly. "Turns out, an attempt on your life makes you stir-crazy."

"Mm." William scanned the forest around them. "This is a bit of a far walk from your house, though. There are easier places to find solitude."

Lilith crossed her arms, huddling against the cold breeze. "I like the view here."

William understood. He'd left this location as the last of his search upon Desmond's advice. It led to an inlet, a small circular cove where the sea met the pebble-studded shore. When he'd shown his son the map of his search, Desmond had instantly pointed to the little cove.

*"Don't worry about searching here,"* he'd said.

*"Why not?"* William asked.

*"I, uh—"* Desmond's jaw twitched guiltily. *"I've spent some time there, and I can promise, there's no Veil."*

It didn't take a genius to realize this was his son's special meeting place with Cait. So, William left it to be the last stop on the search grid. He'd already been to the water's edge, combing the beachfront, hoping to find something his son had missed. But he'd sensed nothing and was beginning his final trek through the woods toward the old factory when he and Lilith crossed paths.

It surprised him that Lilith knew about this place, though. The cove was particularly secluded. Unless you were looking for it, you'd be hard-pressed to stumble across it.

"I didn't realize you were a fan of nature," William said with a pointed glance down at Lilith's running shoes. They weren't exactly made for hikes through the woods, even on the well-worn path he'd found from the factory to the cove.

Lilith sniffled in the cold. "I was a Druid, William. Nature is our solace."

William nodded. He should have remembered that core tenet of Druidic belief. It was easy to forget Lilith's past; she'd been in Porthaven for so long. And though he'd never considered her a friend exactly, he'd come to know her reasonably well over the years.

During his first few visits with her when she originally sought refuge in Porthaven, William was surprised by Lilith's quick wit and candor. Shortly thereafter, he found that he liked the woman. He didn't trust her, but he appreciated what she'd been through and found her company amusing.

However, he'd always been careful to keep an appropriate distance between them, both due to his position in the Warden and for the sake of his marriage. It wouldn't do to have the leader of their town fraternizing with an attractive ex-Druid. Even if nothing between them was untoward, he wasn't foolish enough to think that others would believe that there hadn't been an affair or, worse, that he wasn't under the influence of the Druids.

Though he doubted Robin would ever believe it, even if he was accused of an affair. William and his wife were just as in love after twenty years of marriage as on the first day. While he wasn't prone to public displays of affection, their private life could never leave her in doubt of his devotion.

However, if the Varons found out, they would happily use it to their advantage.

A danger that Desmond hadn't seemed aware of when he visited Lilith alone.

"May I ask you a question?" William said, stepping closer to where she stood on the trail.

Lilith raised her sharp brows.

"Why do you think the Druids attacked you?"

Her expression turned downward. "I already told you. I don't know."

"You told Jun that," he corrected. "But I have to wonder if you kept your real thoughts hidden."

"And I would reveal them to you because . . . ?"

William tipped his head to the side. "I should hope that I've proven myself to you. I'm not your enemy, and you're not mine."

Her dusty-blue eyes caught the sunlight, glinting skeptically. "You don't trust me, William. And I don't trust you."

"I wouldn't expect you to," he said.

"Yet, you *do* expect me to open up to you."

"I don't expect it," he countered. "I'd simply appreciate it if you would."

Lilith shook her head, but her lips turned up in a dry grin. "You're changing," she noted. "You're becoming more like your old self, relaxed and sarcastic. What's gotten into you?"

William shrugged. "I'm trying to be a better father."

She snorted in humor. "And you find sarcasm is the only way to connect with your son? Knowing Desmond, that makes sense." Lilith sighed, then tossed a hand through the air. "Very well," she said. "I was honest with your . . . whoever that man is. I don't *know* why they attacked. But I can *assume* their possible reasons."

"Which are?" he prompted.

Lilith stared up at the trees with a thoughtful expression. "Perhaps they fear my knowledge. If they've found me, they may have decided to remove me before I can reveal their secrets. There's also a chance they want something I took from them, though I'm not telling you what that is. And beyond that . . ."

She paused, meeting his gaze once more. "If you're correct, William, and the Veil really has suffered damage, there's a chance they did it. The Druids may have come for the Vessel. And they may have attempted my murder to ensure that I can't identify them, putting an end to their scheme."

William considered those equally likely possibilities, all of them frightening. He hadn't known she'd stolen something from the Druids, and he didn't like that she'd chosen to keep the item of her theft secret, but he couldn't blame her either. Yet, it was the final possibility that worried him most. If the Druids had come for either of the Vessels, he'd failed. If the Druids knew of the Vessels' locations, somehow the news had leaked, and that would be his fault.

Worse, it left open the question: Did they know about both Vessels? Or just one?

One final query came to William's mind. "What about Jun's theory?" he asked. "Do you think it's possible they were after Desmond?"

Lilith drew in a long breath. Her expression turned sympathetic as she said, "Yes."

William felt his heart squeeze.

"As possible as it is that they attacked me, it's just as likely that your son was the target," she said. "He's your heir, your *only* heir. And the Varon bloodline is well known throughout the Druids. If they want to cause upheaval in your ranks, why not take out one of the strongest and most important members?"

"He's only a boy," William said, muscles tensing. He had the urge to call Desmond, to hear his voice and make sure he was safe.

Lilith eyed him. "The Druids don't delineate age from power. If someone is a threat, they're a threat. Child or not."

William gritted his teeth in disgust. That was why the Druids should be eradicated. If their people weren't willing to renounce their evil religion, they shouldn't be allowed to live. Not when they saw children as expendable. Not when they'd nearly killed his son.

"There is another alternative," Lilith said softly.

He lifted his eyes to her piercing gaze, confused.

Lilith held her head dipped low as though cautious of what she was about to suggest. "You assume that it's the Druids because they summoned beasts," she said. "But there are others who are capable of such deeds."

William drew back his shoulders, instantly on the defensive. "You're suggesting a Warden member is behind this?"

"I'm merely saying that Druids aren't the only Wielders in the world," she said. "The affinity of the Wielder or Wielders who attacked us is completely unknown. They may not side with either Druid or Warden."

He frowned. "You think there's a third organization—?"

"That's not what I'm suggesting," Lilith insisted, interrupting him. "I'm simply saying that there is always the option that someone is out for personal gain rather than being driven by some specific organization or religion."

"And you think whoever attacked you is the same Wielder who damaged the Veil?"

She shrugged. "Regardless of their affiliation, yes. That would seem most logical."

"Hm." William's phone vibrated in his pocket. He slipped it out, seeing a calendar notification reminding him of Desmond's basketball game that evening on the screen. He didn't always attend the games, but in the interest of being a better father, he thought the least he could do was make an effort. But if he was going to be there on time, he needed to head home now.

Tucking the phone into his pocket, William gave Lilith an appreciative nod. "Thank you for your thoughts," he said. "I will consider them as I continue my investigation."

"William," she called as he began to walk away.

He turned back.

Lilith's mouth quirked up in amusement. "You never said what *you* were doing out here."

He smiled. "That was intentional. Have a nice day, Lilith," he said, then walked through the forest to his awaiting car.

# CHAPTER TWENTY-SIX

# Rese

"We're adults, Ryan," she lamented. "I don't want to spend my Friday night at a diner with high schoolers."

Ryan put his shiny black Ford truck into park, its new engine an obnoxious rumble. He rested an arm on the steering wheel, turning to her with a lopsided grin. "Coach asked me to make an appearance," he said. "It'll be five minutes tops."

"We just spent almost three hours watching their game," Rese said. "That wasn't enough?"

Amused, he reached across to run a finger along her jaw. "I'll make it up to you," he said suggestively.

Rese raised an eyebrow. The flirtatious offer wasn't nearly as appealing to her as it was to him, but she could turn it to her advantage. Coyly wrapping her fingers around his hand, she leaned forward. "You mean, if I let you parade me in front of a bunch of postpubescent boys, you'll give me something in return?" she said.

His sharp green eyes narrowed in confusion. "I meant that we'd make out, but sure, if you want, I'll buy you, like, a milkshake or whatever."

Though Rese wanted to tell him that turning her into an exhibition for his male pride was more costly than a milkshake, she batted her lashes demurely. "What if I want something a little less . . . tangible?" she asked.

"Like what?"

Rese knew he wasn't as stupid as most people thought. Ryan was actually somewhat clever. But he was also aloof and tended to have a one-track mind.

"I've been curious," she said, keeping her tone lighthearted. "After all these years in Porthaven, I've heard the rumors about my family's past. And since you're a member of the Warden . . ." She slid her hand up his arm. "I thought you could tell me some things."

Ryan smirked at her. "Yeah, I'm not doing that."

Rese frowned. "Why not?"

"There's a reason no one has told you or your sisters anything, Rese," he said. "You're not supposed to know."

Pulling her hand away, Rese sat up straight. "Fine," she said, staring ahead into the diner's window. "Then, I'm not coming in."

"Don't be stupid."

She crossed her arms petulantly. "If you don't want to make a deal, I'm staying here."

"Rese—" He reached over to brush her arm, but she scooted away from his touch. He huffed. "You're being a brat."

Though Rese had to admit that he was right, it was the role expected of her. So, she continued playing it. "When you get back, you can take me home," she said. "I'm not feeling so well."

"Come on," he protested with obvious annoyance. "You don't have to go inside, but don't do that to me. We were gonna hang out."

She snorted derisively. The last thing Ryan wanted to do was "hang out." She knew perfectly well he planned to take her to his parents' house, where they'd make out in his room. She'd allowed it a handful of times in the past, finding the experience enjoyable but rather monotonous after the first few minutes. Kissing was fun, of course, and Ryan was good at it. Plus, he was attractive enough that she didn't object to the activity. But kissing Ryan was more of a chore than a pleasure. She thought it was probably because she didn't feel anything for him. She didn't even like him all that much. He just checked all the boxes that needed filling.

She held her silence, and Ryan sighed. "Seriously?"

She glared out the window, watching the high schoolers mill around the diner.

"Fine," he said sharply. "Whatever. Come with me, and I'll answer one question."

Rese tossed him a side-eyed glance. "Do you want to 'hang out' after?"

He gritted his teeth. "Yes."

"That'll cost you three questions, minimum."

"So, what? Like, four total?"

"Look at you," she quipped. "You *can* do math."

Ryan glowered at her. "Three total," he countered.

"I'm worth more than that."

"Not when you won't have sex with me."

Rese shot him a fierce glare. "Do I look cheap to you?"

He sat back, a provocative glint in his eyes. "No," he said slyly. "You look like the most expensive woman I've ever had the privilege to date. And I'm betting that when you finally do give in, it'll be damn well worth it."

"If that's your idea of a compliment," Rese said, leaning in as though for a kiss, "you might want to find a more gullible girl next time." She pulled back sharply before he could reach for her. "Four questions, or you take me home now."

Ryan cursed under his breath, then turned off the truck. "Go out with the Lewan girl, they said," he mocked. "It'll be fun, they said. She's easy, they said."

Rese's head snapped up. "Who said that?" she demanded.

He smirked at her, opening the door. "Everyone."

Clamping her jaw shut, Rese shoved down her anger. It shouldn't upset her. She'd intentionally worked to develop this reputation. Therese Lewan was the pretty, airheaded girl all the boys wanted because she was fun and flirty, and they could have a good time. Not *that* good of a time, but she'd kissed her fair share of frogs to catch her prince.

Even if that prince was a washed-up basketball star who still lived with his parents at twenty-one.

Drawing in a preparatory breath, Rese followed Ryan out of the truck and up to the diner. He held out his hand, and she accepted it, weaving their fingers together. Though his hand was warm and his touch gentle, she always had the distinctive urge to jerk away. But if she wanted her answers, she'd have to play her part.

Holding her chin high, Rese let Ryan lead her into the diner. She'd paired her skintight pleather leggings with a peplum blouse that hugged her torso before flaring at the waist, knowing Ryan would appreciate the way it emphasized her womanly figure. Why he liked to show her off in front of the local teens, she didn't know, but she supposed it had something to do with his ego.

Several students called out excitedly upon their arrival. The basketball coach greeted him immediately, and Ryan had to let go of Rese's hand to shake Favreau's. She scanned the diner as he talked with the coach and students. A waitress dropped plate after plate piled high with burgers and fries before the boys and girls. The grill sizzled in the back, and the jukebox played music too modern for its ancient build. Nearly the entire student body was present, including the basketball players with their dates and friends.

She saw Cait's friend, Mattie, sitting with Hunter Varon and his posse. She wondered why Cait hadn't joined them. They were all friends now. Shouldn't she be more sociable for once?

Irritated, Rese wished her sister would understand the importance of earning the town's approval. Popularity wasn't a luxury. It was a weapon. If people knew you, whether because they liked and respected you or simply because they wanted to *be* or *have* you, then they gave you power. And you could protect yourself with that level of control.

As Ryan continued to parade her around the room, Rese stayed aloof and coquettish, except for the moment they passed Mattie. Then, she smiled at the boy and said a proper hello, hoping her friendliness would encourage his interest in Cait.

Unfortunately, their procession led them past Desmond and his troop as well. Knowing that Ryan didn't care for the Simon boy any more than she did, Rese hoped they'd move on quickly.

However, Ryan slid an arm around her waist and came to a stop. "That was a sloppy play for you tonight, Simon," he remarked snidely. "You feeling all right?"

Desmond leaned back in his seat with lazy ease. A scabbed-over scratch ran along his jaw, and Rese wondered how he'd gotten it. Brady sat at his side, his eyes meeting Rese's before he took a sip of water.

"We all have our off days," Desmond replied, then furrowed his brow. "I seem to remember a game where you had six turnovers in a row. Though I think you were drunk, so that might've had something to do with it."

Ryan chuckled but didn't respond. Instead, he turned to Brady. Ryan's hand slid up Rese's side, pulling her against him. "You should teach your boy some manners," he said.

"Funny," Brady held his gaze disinterestedly, "I could say the same to your girlfriend."

Rese found herself fighting an amused grin. She set her hand on Ryan's, stopping it from creeping lower on her hip. "Five minutes have long passed," she said, dropping her voice to a whisper. "My price is going up."

Ryan didn't appear to hear her. He narrowed his eyes on Brady. "You got a problem, Lavigne?" he asked.

Turning back, Rese caught Brady's gaze as it shifted upward, as though he'd been staring at their hands clasped together on her waist. He shrugged casually. "Just curious as to why you seem so clingy all of a sudden," he said.

"What's that supposed to mean?" Ryan replied dumbly.

Brady gestured toward the rest of the diner. "The whole time you've been here, you've been so busy chatting it up that you practically ignored Rese. Then, you get to our table, and you can't keep your hands off her. You feeling possessive, Ry?"

Rese frowned as Ryan voiced her thoughts. "Were you watching us this whole time?" He laughed. "I knew you were jealous, but I didn't realize it was this bad."

Brady scoffed, turning to Desmond. "If I'm ever jealous of Ryan, tell Garrett to punch me to set my mind straight."

Desmond turned to Garrett, who sat across from him. "You heard that, right?"

"Yep!" Garrett said happily.

Desmond smirked at Brady and gave him a nod.

But as Brady's gaze flickered over Rese once more, she straightened her posture in Ryan's arms. She couldn't believe it. Ryan was right. The kid *did* have a crush on her.

Baffled, Rese didn't bother trying to understand Brady's motivation in insulting her, only to discover that he *liked* her.

"Well, this display of testosterone is underwhelmingly boring," she said, then looked up at Ryan. "Can we please go?"

Though Ryan's smug gaze lingered on Brady several seconds longer, he said, "Sure, babe."

Before he could make a bigger scene, Rese slipped out from under his arm. She sent Brady a pointed glare as she took Ryan's hand, dragging him toward the door.

Once they were back in his truck, Rese didn't waste time. It wasn't that far a drive to his parents' house, and she wanted answers before he could attempt to avoid her questions. "Why are the Lavignes the only Wielders in Porthaven?" she asked as the engine turned over.

Ryan looked at her, eyebrows pinched together. "Is this an official question? Or are you just curious 'cause Preacher Boy in there is obsessed with you?"

Rese tucked some hair behind her ear, sending him a smirk. "Are you jealous of a seventeen-year-old, Ryan?"

"No," he said tautly. "He's annoying, that's all. And I don't like the way he looks at you."

Scrunching her nose, Rese didn't bother saying that Brady looked at her more respectfully than Ryan ever had. "It was an official question," she said.

"Right." Ryan pulled out of the parking lot, the truck's headlights glinting off the windows of the surrounding businesses. "Well, it's pretty simple. The Lavignes are the religious authority in town, which, theoretically, makes them the least likely to abuse their powers."

Though Rese wanted to ask if that meant the Warden didn't trust the leadership of the Simons, she knew she had to be careful. Ryan would count each question, whether it was meant for clarification or otherwise. He would already use the excuse of their deal to touch her more freely than she cared for. She wasn't prepared to give him any further ground to push her physical boundaries.

Instead, she chose a more pertinent question. "Is that why Reverend Lavigne comes to visit my sisters and me every year to . . . do whatever it is that he does when he 'prays' over us?"

Ryan gripped the steering wheel tightly. "You're getting close to things I can't tell you, Rese."

"Oh. Well, then, I guess I can't come home with you tonight."

He heaved a sigh. "Yeah, that's why the reverend visits."

"And what is he doing when he sets his hand on our heads, mutters a prayer, and turns to the mayor to nod as though confirming the job's done?"

Ryan pressed his lips together. "There's a reason you're not supposed to know this stuff."

"So, what? You're protecting me?" Rese said with a scoff. "You're not exactly a white knight, Ryan."

"You don't want a good guy, Rese," he returned. "He would let you whore yourself out for answers."

Sucking in a sharp breath, Rese ignored the shame pressing against her chest. She was doing this to protect her sisters, even if it did make her feel sick inside. "If he were a good guy," she retorted, "he wouldn't make me."

"Ben's checking on your blocks," Ryan admitted, ignoring her quip. "Making sure they're still strong."

They pulled off Lawrence Avenue and were merely a minute away from his house. Rese only had one question left. She should be precise and careful with it. But she couldn't help blurting, "What's a block?"

"It's what it sounds like," he said. "It's a barrier keeping you from accessing the spirit world."

Though that opened up a whole other list of questions, Ryan pulled down the long driveway, the gravel crunching under the tires. He glanced at her. "I'll let you ask another one," he said. "For a trade."

"No, thanks," Rese muttered.

"Don't act like you're preserving your virtue here." He put the truck in park. "We both know there's not much of that left."

Rese stared at the large house. It was beautiful—grand without being garish, like the Greenes themselves. The whole family was beautiful, and they were nice too. She actually liked Kenneth and Kari, though she'd had a hard time getting on Elizabeth's good side. She suspected it had to do with her reputation around the school.

And Ryan . . . He was handsome and funny, athletic and charming. But most of all, he was entitled. He'd lived his entire life without having to work for anything. His idea of great loss was losing to a rival team. His future was set up for him; all he had to do was take it. Yet, he was too lazy to do anything about it.

Rese didn't like Ryan; she'd come to that conclusion quickly. He was fun, but he wasn't nice. He was safe, but he wasn't good. And she was starting to wonder if she could live with that choice.

Drawing her shoulders back, Rese turned to the man beside her. He *was* attractive. His masculine jawline, paired with his steady brow, gave him an almost rugged appearance. However, his clean haircut and crisp green eyes kept his overall look classic. He might not be a man she could love or respect, but she didn't think a cushy life as his wife would be the worst thing she'd experienced.

And if it would protect Cait and Genni, she'd happily make that sacrifice.

Reaching across the truck, Rese grabbed the collar of Ryan's jacket. She pulled him forward as she leaned in, their mouths meeting in the middle. It wasn't a particularly affectionate kiss, but when he rested his hand on her neck, his thumb rubbing her jaw, she felt tingles all the way to her toes.

When she drew back, Rese held his sharp stare. "Are you gonna invite me in or what?"

# Desmond

"This isn't exactly the best place for a clandestine meeting," Desmond said, taking his seat across from Jun.

As on each Saturday, the coffee shop bustled with activity. Half a dozen students had already waved their hellos to him. He wondered what gossip would spread related to why he was meeting with a stranger. Probably some nonsense about college recruitment.

Desmond hoped his unsettled mood didn't show on his face.

"I wouldn't call our meeting clandestine," Jun replied, his professionally bland persona in place. "I'd just like to get to know you better and ask some questions regarding my inquiry."

Desmond worked not to clench his jaw. "Sure. What would you like to know?"

"How long have you been working with your father?"

Knowing they couldn't be completely open in the presence of so many others, Desmond caught the rest of the question: How long had his dad allowed him to be part of the Warden?

"Officially? I began my internship at sixteen. But it hasn't been until this last month that we've started to work closely together."

"But you became an honorary member at thirteen, is that correct?"

"Yes, but that only involved sitting in on some meetings. I wasn't actually *doing* anything until a couple of years ago."

"I'd imagine those meetings gave you a good glimpse at the sort of work in your future." Jun's tone remained flat, but Desmond couldn't help hearing a trace of judgment in it. "How do you feel about the direction the town is going in?"

Desmond worked to control his frown. He took a sip of his coffee to give himself extra time to formulate a response. "I'm not sure I know what you mean."

"Is there anything you would change regarding the town's leadership?"

"You mean my dad's leadership?"

"Not necessarily. Your father doesn't have the ultimate say. There's also the council and the other government officials who work with him to consider."

"We're not talking about the government, though, are we?"

"Why wouldn't we be? That is part of your father's job."

Desmond decided not to play Jun's game. "Yeah, of course, there are things that I'd change. But that comes down to simple priorities."

"Such as what?"

"I don't understand."

"What would you change?"

Desmond's stomach clenched. He didn't know how honest to be. And yet, he felt certain that Jun would know if he lied.

"The way some people are treated," Desmond said with forced calmness. "I know there are reasons for everything, but I feel we could act more justly toward the people under our protection."

Jun's dark eyes glimmered with understanding.

"Other than that . . ." Desmond lightened his tone as he continued,

"I'd probably cut back on spending. I feel we're a little too frivolous with things like milkshake day at the school."

"I don't know," Jun replied, the hint of a grin on his lips. "I'd think milkshake day would prove to bolster town morale."

"I bet you're a vanilla guy, aren't you?"

Jun did smile then. "I like the classics."

For the first time, Desmond thought he might like Jun if his job wasn't to potentially ruin his dad's life.

"I'm curious," Jun continued, dropping his voice so only Desmond could hear it under the hum of the coffee shop. "What gave you the idea for that seal on the Veil?"

Desmond swallowed roughly. "It wasn't exactly an idea that I had," he said. "More of a hunch. I went to the island because I knew I could fix it. I didn't have a plan as to how; I just felt I could."

"And when you tried, you created the seal?"

"Yeah."

"What made you believe you could accomplish that?"

Desmond balked. He couldn't tell him that it was because he had wielded on a regular basis for years. He knew that not all Warden towns had such an ordinance against wielding, but nowhere was it deemed acceptable to summon beasts. Even if they were as tame as Hades.

"I guess you could say it's in my blood," he said instead. "Being the Varon heir and all."

"Right." Jun gave him an almost sarcastic nod. "What do you think of all that? Being the Varon heir? Inheriting leadership rather than earning it?"

Desmond felt a swell of indignation. "I wouldn't say we don't earn our position. There's a great deal of pressure in being the heir. My dad has prepared me for this role since I was a child. I know everything there is to know about the . . ." He stopped before completing his sentence and naming the spirit world in front of the whole town.

Clearing his throat, he started again. "Whatever knowledge

Porthaven has, I know it. And I've worked hard to ensure that when it's my time, I'll be the best leader I can be."

"That's good to hear," Jun said. "My interviews have produced some less-than-flattering statements about your dedication to your future role. But I'm glad that you feel so strongly about it."

Desmond restrained himself from asking who'd done the bad-mouthing. "Thanks," he muttered instead.

"However," Jun went on, "you didn't really answer my question. What do you think of the role of true Varon and the leadership that comes with it?"

Desmond felt his brow pull together in confusion. "I'm not sure I understand."

"I'll be more frank." Jun leaned forward, hands clasped on the tabletop. His dark eyes bore into Desmond accusingly. "There are some who believe that the role of true Varon is a farcical notion. The idea that you're automatically given a role of leadership simply because you're granted great power doesn't sit well with some. Would you say that you agree? Or do you believe that the Varon bloodline has the right to leadership simply because of their inherited power?"

Suddenly feeling attacked, Desmond drew back in his seat. "What does this have to do with your inquiry?"

"I told you when I arrived," Jun said flatly. "I'm here to assess both your father's leadership and your potential future."

The word "potential" struck Desmond like a heavy blow to the gut.

"You mean you're going to make decisions based on what I *might* do in the future?" he demanded.

"Not at all," Jun clarified. "I'm going to let this conversation guide my suggestion to my superiors for the future. As for my decision about your father's position, that will be made in isolation."

Agitated by the analyst's condescending tone, Desmond glared back at him. "No," he said, answering the man's earlier question. "I don't agree with those people. The role of true Varon isn't some arbitrary or natural inheritance like money or a house. It's an honor bestowed upon a worthy individual. It doesn't simply fall to someone because they happen to be the only choice."

"Though you are your father's only son," Jun interjected.

"And my great-great-grandfather lost his only son," Desmond retorted. "Which is the only reason that you're even talking to me. Christopher Varon didn't choose Lyndon Simon because he was the only option. He could have given it to his brother if it were about bloodline. But he didn't. Because he believed that Lyndon was a better choice than Thomas."

"So, if your father decided to choose, say, your cousin over you," Jun tilted his head, dark eyes glinting as he studied Desmond, "you'd accept it?"

Though Desmond bristled at the thought, he said, "I would."

"But he wouldn't do that, would he?" Jun returned. "He's molded you for your whole life, isn't that what you said? He's groomed you to take on the role of true Varon. So, when you went to the island, you didn't do it as a mere member—you did it under the authority of the power you stand to inherit."

Desmond's stomach roiled. He didn't know why Jun was so decidedly against him, but he determined that he didn't care anymore. An irritated smirk pulled up the corner of Desmond's mouth. "You've got it all wrong," he said, knowing his tone was too snide—too arrogant and irreverent. "I did it with the authority of the power I already have. Whatever comes with my inheritance is just a bonus."

Jun only had a moment to blink before Desmond asked, "Are we done here?"

"One last question," the analyst said sharply. "The attack at Ms. Drake's: Do you believe she was the target?"

Desmond had wondered about that same question for the past three days. The nyct had come at both of them. But he wasn't sure if that was due to their orders or simply because it was necessary to complete the job.

"I don't know," he said.

"Do you trust her?" Jun asked.

Desmond grabbed his still half-full cup, rising from the table. "You said one more question, Mr. Jun. I'm afraid your time is up."

Without giving the man a chance to reply, Desmond turned on his heel and marched toward the door, chucking the cup into the garbage. His hands fisted at his sides, his brain fuzzy with the anger raging inside of him. He lengthened his strides, desperate to put distance between himself and Jun. But when he reached for the door, it was already opening.

The bell tinkled, and Desmond almost barreled straight into the girl walking into the coffee shop.

Desmond's breath caught.

"Oh," Cait gasped, stumbling back.

They gaped at each other on either side of the threshold. Desmond's first instinct was relief. In his fury, all he wanted was to cling to her and find distraction in her arms. Then, reality kicked back in.

Behind Cait stood Liz and Melissa, both watching the exchange.

"Sorry," Cait muttered. Her shoulders drew in, intentionally making herself small in his presence.

Desmond forced himself to resume his smug demeanor. He tightened his grip on the door, pulling it out of her way. "Careful, Lewan," he said. "You could've busted my nose, and then where would we be?"

Liz sauntered in next to Cait, her green eyes twinkling. "Oh, I don't know, Desmond," she teased. "It might've been an improvement."

Desmond dipped his head in a mock bow. "Always a pleasure, Lizzie," he said, then exited without another look their way.

A fire burned in Desmond's chest, tingling along his arms as he walked across the street. His anger churned up his thoughts. How dare the Warden send that man to their town? He wasn't after a fair trial. This was simply a witch hunt.

Desmond stomped his way home, got into his car, and headed up the coast. He'd come to a conclusion over the last month. After reading the prophecy and learning of their wicked deeds—knowing that they'd let Cait's parents die intending to sacrifice her too—this was too much.

Some people didn't believe in the true Varons's claim to power, huh? Perhaps they should test them then and see just how powerful they were.

~

Desmond drove around for an hour before realizing he'd looped back to Lilith's house. Her car wasn't in the driveway, and neither was a Warden member on patrol. She was likely at work, running the tea shop. He glanced at his phone's clock, knowing she'd probably be back in another hour or so.

Desmond got out of the car and went to sit on the stoop.

He wasn't really sure why he'd stopped at her house. After meeting with Jun, he felt out of control and aimless. And he didn't know where else to turn.

Finally, Lilith pulled into the driveway. She parked alongside his Dodge. Desmond remained seated, watching as she took her time getting out and walking over to him.

"Are you allowed to be here?" she asked, making no move to get around him to the front door.

Ignoring her question, Desmond looked up at her. "Why did you come here?"

She raised a thin eyebrow. "This *is* my house."

"To Porthaven," he clarified.

Lilith pulled in a deep breath, either stalling or considering. "I do believe it's public knowledge amongst your people. I needed to get away from my home."

"Yeah, but why here? Why come to a Warden town? Why not just disappear somewhere with no affiliation to the spirit world?"

The rumble of tires on pavement fell on their ears, and Lilith sighed. "Let's go inside," she said. "I'd rather not have this conversation in front of one of your father's lackeys."

The Warden member on patrol pulled to a stop at the edge of Lilith's driveway just as they stepped over the threshold. Looking over his shoulder, Desmond recognized the driver as his Uncle Rick. He waved, earning a curious wave back.

Once inside the house, Lilith went straight into the kitchen, setting a kettle to boil on the stovetop before turning back to him. "The answer is twofold," she said. "First, my family is rather . . . notable within the Druids' ranks. At least amongst our faction. And if I hadn't gone somewhere they wouldn't dare to follow, then I couldn't guarantee the success of my escape."

"They would have come for you?"

She swallowed tightly, then nodded.

"Do you think that's what the attack was about? Have they finally decided to risk coming after you?"

"I don't know," she said. "Possibly. It's been fifteen years, but . . . the second reason for my choice might be reason enough for their change of heart."

"And that is . . . ?"

Awkwardly, Lilith adjusted her stance, and Desmond realized this was the first time he'd seen her truly uncomfortable.

"I stole something from them," she admitted.

Desmond's eyes widened. "What was it?"

"A book," she said. "It was intended to be my token of goodwill to the Warden. Turns out, it may have been my undoing, thanks to your family's unwillingness to cooperate."

Desmond scoffed, bemused. "Why would the Druids be so desperate for this book?"

"It's one of only five copies," she said. "And it details every prophecy and oral tradition passed down over the last millennium. It's called the Codex."

Desmond gaped at her. "Excuse me? You're saying that you have a literal copy of all the Druids' plans here in your house?"

"It isn't exactly their plans, but it would give you the information needed to understand them and potentially extrapolate enough to discover them on your own."

"And my dad said he didn't want it?" Desmond asked, incredulous.

"He doesn't know I have it."

Desmond frowned. "Grandpa kept it from him?"

"I didn't tell your grandfather either," she said. "He made it perfectly clear that he didn't want the information I had to offer, so I kept it to myself."

Understanding, Desmond lifted his chin. Neither his grandpa nor his dad had been willing to trust Lilith. So, she'd refused to trust them.

"Would you show it to me?" he dared to ask.

Her expression softened. "If you'd like. I will warn you: It isn't the easiest thing to understand. Most of the texts are written in archaic English. I have a hard enough time working them out."

"Mm."

Lilith eyed him. "Why did you come here? Surely, it wasn't simply to get my backstory."

Picking at the corner of her island's countertop, Desmond shrugged. "I don't know why I came here, actually. I . . . this Warden representative is in town—he's tasked with checking up on my dad."

"Why?"

"Apparently, the Varons are tired of submitting to the Simons' authority."

Lilith's gaze sharpened. "They're trying to depose William?"

"Looks that way."

From her reaction, Desmond couldn't tell if she was upset or confused by his confirmation.

"Anyway," he continued. "This rep—it seems he's biased. And . . . to be honest? I'm starting to question the Warden as a whole these days."

Lilith's demeanor shifted, her shoulders drawing back. "How so?" she asked gently.

"I've just learned some things about their procedures that I can't approve of," he admitted.

"Every organization has its faults."

"You sound like my dad," he said with a humorless chuckle. "He says the Warden might have its questionable members, but as a whole, it's on the right side of this. And if we don't stay in the organization, there won't be anyone to make the changes necessary."

Lilith eyed him. "Do you disagree?"

"I'm just not convinced that it's worth it anymore. I mean . . . are the Druids even out there? Aside from you, I've never even met one. Can they be that big of a problem?"

At the kettle's whistle, Lilith removed it from the stove. "Take it from someone who ran for her life," she said. "They *can* be."

Desmond sighed.

"But . . ."

At her hesitation, Desmond looked up. She poured the steaming water with her eyes on the pot. "What?"

"Your father is correct, Desmond," she said. "The individuals with questionable intentions do not represent the whole. In the Warden *or* amongst the Druids."

Desmond frowned. "You're saying . . . not all Druids are bad?"

Her lips lifted in a dry grin. "Would you consider me to be 'bad'?"

"No," he replied. "But you're an *ex*-Druid."

"I am an *escaped* Druid," she corrected. "My faction was of ill intentions. I refused to partake in their schemes, and thus, I left."

"And you chose to come to a Warden town for safety. If there are really good Druids out there, why wouldn't you go to them?"

"Would you consider Porthaven to be one of the 'good' Warden towns?" she returned.

Desmond had to think about that for several seconds. "Yeah. We may have our problems, but . . . all in all? My dad and I are working to change those things."

"I would agree," she said. "And yet, this Warden representative—he's able to come here and keep you and your father from doing that work if he so deems, correct?"

"Yeah," Desmond ground out.

Lilith gave him a slow nod. "Such as it is in the Druid factions that I would deem good. Should I have gone to them, one of my old faction members could have come in and taken me back by force. So, I ran as far as I could to the one organization I know my people fear."

Desmond thought about the irony in that statement. Lilith was saying that the Druids feared the Warden, but in his experience, the Warden feared the Druids. So, which one really held the power?

"Would you go back?" Desmond asked. "If you could. To one of those good factions?"

"I would," Lilith admitted.

Desmond's lips parted in shock as understanding hit. "So, you're still a Druid?"

"I am."

Desmond wondered at that revelation. His whole life, he'd been taught to fear and hate Druids. The Warden preached that they were all evil. And yet, here was Lilith—good, helpful, and kind. She'd saved his life, for goodness' sake. She'd offered them help. She'd come to them for protection. How could he proclaim her evil simply because of her beliefs?

"I don't trust them anymore," he said, the words quiet and unbidden.

Lilith didn't need clarification. She handed him a freshly poured cup of tea. "What do you plan to do about it?" she asked.

Desmond stared down into the teacup in his hands, the liquid an amber the color of Cait's powers. Could he be open with Lilith about her? Would she know something that would save her? Lilith had expressly told him there was no way to break the connection between Vessel and Spectral, so why confide his plan in her when she'd just tell him what everyone and every other resource told him: There was no hope of saving Cait.

With a sigh, Desmond looked back up at Lilith. "I haven't decided yet," he admitted.

Lilith dipped her chin down but remained silent.

Desmond took a sip of the tea, which had a lighter flavor than last time. He didn't bother asking what it was or why she hadn't matched it to her company. His mind was too muddled, torn between asking to see the Codex and wondering if it'd even prove to be worth the effort. Was all his research pointless? Could he truly not save Cait?

"May I ask *you* a question now?" Lilith said suddenly.

Desmond nodded, waiting.

She ran her fingers over the decorative ridges of her glass teacup. "You're a Varon, ancestrally," she prompted, then raised an eyebrow. "Yet, you may be the first to question the Warden's cause. Why? What's brought you to this place of doubt?"

Desmond allowed the hot tea to press its warmth into his palms. He had the strangest urge to tell her, to clear his chest of all the secrets he'd been carrying. The death of Cait's parents. The sacrifice she'd have to make. His fear of losing her. Yet, he couldn't quite bring himself to speak of those things.

Instead, he said, "Maybe I'm just tired of being told what to do."

Lilith's gaze narrowed knowingly. She hadn't been fooled by his words; she knew it was something deeper. But she didn't press him.

Desmond rose from his seat by the island. "Thanks for the tea," he said with a lightness he didn't feel.

"Anytime, Desmond," she said, and he heard what she really meant.

Anytime he needed to talk, she'd listen, she'd advise, and she'd help in whatever way she could.

With a grateful smile, Desmond gave his thanks, then turned to walk past the snake's terrarium and leave the Druid's house.

# CHAPTER TWENTY-EIGHT

# Cait

"So, when are we meeting again?" Matt asked. His chin dipped, and his voice was low as though he were a spy discussing a rendezvous with an informant. "Ya know," he added, "with Hunter and Sterling."

Cait pressed her lips together to keep from snapping at him. She scanned the chapel. The service had ended five minutes ago, and the congregants milled about as they greeted one another. Maeve and Penny were busy chatting with the couple in front of them, and Genni knelt backward on the pew, talking to Alexis right behind her. Rese had gone off to see Ryan, who sat near the front with his family, drawing Cait and Matt's attention to Liz and Hunter and prompting his ill-timed question.

"We shouldn't talk about that now," she whispered, hoping the seriousness of her tone impressed the importance of their discretion on Matt.

"Why not?" he asked. "We're friends with them. If anyone asks what we're talking about, we can easily say it's a hangout we're planning."

After his initial shock, Matt quickly accepted Cait's explanation of the spirit world on Thursday evening. She'd given him the most basic version on their bike ride home, then they sat on his grandpa's porch, eating muffins as she gave more details. But still, he'd taken every opportunity at school on Friday and through texting on Saturday to ask her any and every additional question he came up with.

It didn't surprise her that he was so accepting of such a bizarre reality. This was *Matt*. The guy was overenthusiastic about everything, and he'd readily latched on, saying that her family's "curse" made sense now. If there was some kind of strange spirit world out there, what else might be possible?

Cait frowned. "I don't want to lie." Not that she hadn't been lying plenty. But they were in a church. It made her recent sins seem all the worse.

His thin eyebrows pinched together, and he returned to his previous question. "So . . . ?"

"What?"

"When are we meeting them?"

Cait sighed. "Tomorrow after school."

"But we have practice," he said.

Though Cait didn't think he could consider it practice when he was simply there to gather the basketballs for the players, she said, "I mean, after that."

"What are you gonna do in the meantime?"

"Go home, I guess."

Matt frowned. "Only to turn around, like, an hour later? Why not just hang around town?"

"I'll have Genni with me," she whispered.

"Right." Matt grimaced. "What if you convinced her to hang out with Alexis and Jared?"

"Jared's on the team," Cait reminded him. "And I don't know about Alexis, but Genni will get suspicious if I *suggest* she spend time with her."

Matt tugged on the hem of his dress shirt. "You could just tell her that we, uh—we want to hang out just the two of us."

Cait frowned at the suggestion. Was he implying that they led Genni to think they were going on a date?

Not wanting to deal with that particular problem, Cait ignored the awkward insinuation. "It's fine," she said. "We'll just bring our bikes and head home after school, and I'll say I'm going on a walk when we get back."

"I thought you didn't want to lie," Matt said.

"It isn't a lie," Cait replied. "I will go on a walk. Just not in the woods."

Matt pursed his lips but let it go. Then, he scanned the church. "How many people know about it?" he asked, dropping his voice even lower to murmur, "The spirit world, I mean."

Cait opened her mouth to reply when Genni popped her head between theirs. "You told him?" she hissed.

They both gaped at her.

"Oh my gosh, Cait, I can't believe you!" Genni whisper-shouted. "We're not supposed to talk about it."

"I didn't—" Cait stopped herself from adding another lie to her tally.

Matt jumped in to help out. "It was my fault," he promised. "She didn't want to, but once I overheard her conversation with Hunter and Sterling—"

"Matt!" Cait exclaimed in a hush, but it was already too late.

Genni's jaw dropped. "Hunter and . . . *Sterling*?"

Cait closed her eyes and took a deep breath. "Yes."

"Why—when—how—I don't even know what to ask!" Genni gripped Cait's arm, stepping closer. Her adamant blue gaze locked with Cait's as she whispered, "Are you dating Sterling?"

"What? No!"

Genni sighed. "Thank God. I nearly had a conniption when Melissa told him to ask you out at lunch on Friday. He said no, but I worried it might be one of those 'the gentleman doth protest too much' situations."

Before Cait or Matt could get a response in—however one even responded to something like that—Genni went on, "So, what? You guys are getting together to talk about the . . ." She looked around, then mouthed, "Spirit world?"

"Kind of," Cait murmured.

"Why?" Genni looked genuinely puzzled for all of one second before worry creased her brow. "Do you—do they know something? About Da's. . . ." She let the words trail off.

Cait found her tongue tied around yet another lie. She was getting so tired of concealing the truth. But she couldn't tell Genni . . . could she?

"Yes," she heard herself whisper.

Genni's eyes grew to twice their normal size. Hope and grief fought for control over her expression. "They do?"

Cait nodded.

"Will you tell me—?"

"Lewan." Desmond's call startled them all.

Cait whirled around to see him standing at the end of the pew. Her heart stuttered under his fierce stare. He'd dressed up for church as usual. Why did he have to look so good in slacks?

She wanted to bolt to him and wrap her arms around his waist, burying her head in his neck. Just the idea of hugging him made her toes tingle.

Tamping down the self-destructive thought, Cait's shoulders slumped. "Yes?"

Everyone in the aisle was looking between Cait and Desmond now. Maeve eyed him with a confused glimmer while Penny gave him a teacherly smile.

Desmond tipped his chin up in greeting before turning back to Cait. "You comin' or what?" he asked blandly.

"Coming where?" Maeve asked, her Irish accent thick with hesitation.

Cait's mouth opened, but no words came out.

"We're studying," Desmond answered.

At Maeve's growing confusion, Penny explained, "Desmond is Cait's partner for the essay project I assigned recently."

Maeve raised her coppery eyebrows, looking at Cait with disapproval. "Is that so?"

"Yes," Cait muttered.

Her nan turned back to Desmond. "She'll meet yeh outside in a few moments," she said with such finality that Cait's shoulders shrank another inch.

Desmond glanced at Cait with something akin to shock. But he quickly covered it up with a grin. "Sure thing," he said. "Have a nice day . . . everyone."

Once he was out of earshot, Maeve turned to Cait.

Genni and Matt took an instant step away.

Cait sent them a scowl at their betrayal.

"Yeh never said that yer partner was a boy," Maeve said, the statement an accusation.

"I didn't think it mattered," Cait lied. "It's a school project, not a date."

"That's not the point, *a leanbh*." Her nan sounded more worried than upset now. "I wouldn't have even minded if it were a date, provided it wasn't with the *Simon* boy."

Penny's brow furrowed. "I'm sorry," she stepped up to Maeve's side, "is there something I should know? If there's some reason I shouldn't have paired Cait and Desmond together—well, it's a little late, but I can change it."

"No," Cait said, surprising herself and everyone else. Instantly, she softened her tone, addressing her teacher and her nan. "It's not necessary. Desmond's been fine to work with, and—and our paper is going well."

Penny didn't look convinced. "Maeve?" she asked.

Maeve crossed her arms, considering Cait for another moment before turning to Penny. "I don't trust the boy, that's all," she said. "He's known to be a rebel and a flirt, and I don't want Cait getting hurt because of it."

Cait knew it was more than that. Their nan didn't want her to be around Desmond because of his tie to the Warden. But she couldn't share that fact with Penny.

"He's not—" Cait paused, trying not to sound defensive. "I promise, Nan, he hasn't done or said anything wrong. We're just working on our project. That's all."

Maeve didn't look convinced.

"If it helps," Matt piped up, "he doesn't seem all that interested in her. Like, even as a friend or . . . or otherwise."

With a sigh, Maeve reached over to tuck some of Cait's hair behind her ear. "Jest tell me if there's anything I should know," she said.

Realizing that her nan trusted her more than she should, Cait's guilt rose overwhelmingly in her chest. "I will," she lied.

After muttering her goodbyes, Cait slipped out of the aisle, head dipped. She pushed through the line of people slowly making their way into the narthex. Their voices rose into the high vaulted ceiling, echoing loudly to reverberate in her head. The hum took their place the second she stepped outside.

Leaning against the wall, Desmond looked up at her arrival. He glanced around them before giving her a penitent frown. "I'm sorry," he said quickly. "I didn't realize your nan would freak out like that."

She ignored his apology, the embarrassment still too fresh to let go of yet. "I thought we were planning to meet after church," she reminded him. "Why did you do that?"

Desmond wrung his hands. "Would you believe me if I simply said I was an idiot?"

"I already knew that," she said, finding her mouth turning up at the corner. "What's the real reason?"

His lips turned up, too, giving her a bashful smile.

Cait's heart skipped a beat. He'd never looked so cute.

"Maybe I wanted to see Mattie's jealous reaction. Or . . ." He gave her one of his more flirtatious looks. "Maybe I just missed you, and it got the best of my good sense."

She couldn't help her smirk. "You never had any sense, to begin with."

The door opened behind Cait, forcing them both to take a step away from each other. The family—relatives of Desmond's—waved to him. He returned the greeting as they moved into the parking lot.

Desmond motioned toward his car, two rows back. "You ready?"

"My backpack is in Matt's truck."

He frowned. "Does that mean you need to get him?"

"He left it unlocked," she said.

"Way to live on the edge, Mattie."

Cait laughed, then led him to the brown truck. The salty breeze swept up her hair and tickled the hem of her skirt against her knees.

"That's a cute dress," Desmond said, a step behind her.

Cait's cheeks warmed, and she ran a hand across the ivory and blush floral. "Thanks. It was Rese's."

"It looks better on you."

She glanced over her shoulder at him. "You remember what it looked like on her?"

"Not a chance," he said, his dark gaze holding hers. "But it wouldn't matter—everything looks better on you."

The blush spread all the way down Cait's chest, and she fumbled to grip the door handle on Matt's truck. She turned to grab her backpack from the floor, giving it a yank onto the seat before slipping an arm through the strap.

When she turned around, Desmond stood directly in front of her, their faces inches apart. Her breath caught, his hand finding her waist. He dipped his head toward hers, and she leaned back in alarm. "Someone could see us," she whispered.

"I already checked," he replied, then he kissed her. It was quick but deep, causing the hum to pulsate down her spine.

Desmond pulled away, putting a respectful distance between them. But his gaze said how much he'd wanted to stay close. "I *really* missed you, Caity."

Cait bit the inside of her lip, unable to tame her smile any other way. She shut the truck's door behind her, stepping around Desmond to head for his car. "That's odd," she teased. "I didn't miss you at all."

~

They held hands the entire drive to the factory. Cait questioned him about the basketball game. She'd never gone to one, but she heard so many stories around the school that she wished she could see him in action.

"It was boring," he said. "Machias has a terrible team. We led by twenty the whole game."

Cait didn't know much about basketball, but twenty sounded like a serious difference. Somehow, she found the courage to ask, "Do you think you'll continue to play in college?"

Desmond glanced at her as though aware of her fishing. "No," was his only response.

Frustrated that he'd escaped her real question, she tried again. "Because you don't like it enough?"

His thumb brushed the back of her hand. "Because I'll be too busy with classes," he said.

Irrationally, her heart sank. There was no college—community or university—in Porthaven, so Desmond would have to leave.

"Where will you go?" she asked.

"Wherever my dad sends me," he said. "Probably his alma mater."

"Which is?"

"Watson University. It isn't technically run by the Warden, but a lot of members work there."

"I've never heard of it."

"Really? It's as close as you can get to Ivy League without actually *being* Ivy League."

"Is it in Maine?"

Desmond hesitated. "No. It's in Virginia."

"Oh." Cait's disappointment radiated through her whole body. Suddenly, she didn't feel like holding his hand anymore.

If he went to college in Maine, at least he'd be able to visit regularly. Even Portland was only a day trip. But Virginia was probably a thousand miles away. She'd be lucky to see him on holidays and summer breaks over the next four years.

"That's why I'll be so busy," he said, as though reading her mind.

She looked at him, confused.

He gave her a glance, a knowing smile on his lips. "I've worked it out," he said. "With my current credits from the AP and CLEP exams I've taken, if I take fifteen credit hours per semester, I can be out of there in three years. Less if I take summer courses, which I could probably do online."

Cait stared at him.

He squeezed her hand. "I'm not gonna leave you, Caity. Not forever."

They pulled into the uneven parking lot of the old factory. Desmond parked at the side of the building, out of view. He turned to her under the shadow cast by the large structure.

"Now, I'd love to stay here and make out with you for the next five hours," he said, sending the heat rushing back into her face. "But I think it'd be better if we actually made it to the cove."

He paused after hearing his words aloud. "Not because I want to make out with you at the cove," he corrected. "I mean, I do. But explaining things is more important. And *then* maybe we can make out."

Cait couldn't help her embarrassed laughter. "Maybe we should just go to the cove," she suggested.

"Yeah, probably," he said, staring at her mouth.

Before he could get any ideas, Cait opened the door and stepped out. She pulled her cardigan tighter under the shade of the trees. Desmond rushed to catch up with her. He flicked his wrist as they walked, Hades appearing from a blip of deep blue light. Her flats and his dress shoes looked out of place on the dirt path. They'd both brought changes of clothing, not wanting to wear their Sunday best to sit on the sandy shore. The thing they hadn't discussed was where they'd change.

Once they reached the cove, Cait stopped at the edge of the trees. "Should we take turns?" she asked, knowing he wouldn't need clarification.

Desmond wore one of his more cunning smirks. "Why?"

She didn't deign to respond but crossed her arms and raised her chin.

He leaned against an aspen.

"You want to change in front of each other?" she asked. The very idea made her nervous.

"I won't tell if you won't."

Having planned for this eventuality, Cait decided not to fight him. "Fine."

Desmond's face went blank as she dropped her backpack. "What?" he blurted.

Kicking off her shoes, Cait shrugged. "I said, fine."

"You're gonna—" He stood up straight as she took off her cardigan. "Yeah, okay."

Cait couldn't help smiling as she pulled out her jeans. Distracted, Desmond fumbled with the buttons on his shirt while she shook out the pants. She slid one leg in at a time.

Desmond froze as Cait skillfully and modestly slipped the jeans under the skirt of her dress. She turned around to button them before facing him with a mocking grin. Then, she reached behind to unzip the dress, pushed the sleeves off her shoulders, and shimmied out of it, revealing the tank she'd worn below.

"You cheated," he said.

Cait pulled the long-sleeved thermal tee she'd brought over her head. "I just know better than to argue with you," she replied.

"But—I—" He heaved a disgruntled sigh as she pulled on socks and her trainers. "You're a tease."

She threw one of her flats at him. "And you have a depraved mind," she shot back. "Did you really think I'd undress in front of you?"

"Well . . ." He held her shoe to his chest and stared out over the cove dejectedly. "Yeah, kind of."

Cait rolled her eyes, picked up her bag, and stepped over to him. "I'm not you," she said. Then, she kissed his nose. "Come join me when you're done."

With that, she plucked her flat from his hand and started down the hill. She reached into the hollow of the log, pulling out their stashed supplies. She laid out the blanket before reaching into her bag again. They'd agreed to each bring food for a shared meal, so she set out three plastic baggies of chips, veggies, and dried fruit.

A few minutes later, Desmond plopped down next to her, now in a dark green tee under his black jacket and jeans. "A tomato-free sandwich for the lady," he said, proffering a name-brand baggie of his own. "And extra pickles for me."

To Cait's relief, Desmond broached the conversation as they started eating. "So," he began, "what's your first question?"

Cait settled her open sketchbook onto her lap. She'd scribbled down all the questions she could think of over the last several days, developing a smaller list than she'd expected, and now she started at the top. "How did I get on the island?"

Desmond grimaced. "Sure, start with an easy one," he mumbled with a sigh. "Honestly, I don't know. I've never seen or *heard* of anything like that before."

"Really?"

"Really."

Cait didn't like that. She moved on. "Why were *you* on the island?"

He swallowed a bite of his sandwich. "Because I needed to inspect the tree."

"Why?"

"It has—well, it *had* some damage to it, and . . ." He trailed off, squirming. "Listen, Caity, there are some things . . . some Warden things that I'm not supposed to talk about."

"You said you'd tell me everything."

"And I will," he promised. "It just—it might not make total sense at first, okay? So, just hear me out before you ask more questions."

She nodded.

"The tree isn't just a tree," he said. "It's a link to the spirit world called a Veil."

"Sterling told me," she replied.

"Right, you said that." He paused, frowning. "He's—well, neither of you are supposed to know about it."

"Why not?"

"The more you know about the spirit world, the more likely you are to try to access it. Since that would lead you to connect with the spirit-being, it's something the Warden wants to try to prevent."

Cait leaned against the log, picking at her sandwich. "Makes sense. Go on."

"All right, so you know about Veils, more or less. Really, all that matters is that you understand it's a point where the space between our world and the spirit world is thinnest, making it easier to access the spirit world."

She nodded to confirm her understanding.

"Anyway, like I said, the Veil was damaged, and beasts were showing up on the island willy-nilly, which isn't supposed to be possible. You know how I have to summon Hades for him to be present? Well, these beasts weren't being summoned; they were just appearing out of the Veil."

He paused as though ashamed. "Once I found out that you were the Vessel and the beasts in your dreams were the same beasts appearing . . . I thought it was you, summoning them. Subconsciously, of course. I knew you weren't intentionally doing it. But it seemed to be the only scenario that made sense. However, Brady convinced me that wasn't possible."

"Brady did?" she asked, surprised.

"Yeah, we were talking over everything that happened with Fish the next day, and Brady realized it couldn't have been you. You've been having the dreams for years, and the beasts have only been appearing for the last month or so."

Cait was first relieved, then confused. "So, how were they showing up?"

"I don't know that either," he admitted. "No one seems to have a clue. But when I went to the island, I was still under the impression that you were involved. I wanted to inspect the tree to see if I could figure out what had caused the damage. And more importantly, I wanted to try to fix it. Turns out that you did that yourself."

"I fixed it?"

He plucked a pickle chip off his sandwich and popped it into his mouth. "Well, you sealed the Veil. And the beasts stopped coming out. So, it's as fixed as it needs to be, I guess."

Though she struggled to comprehend all his explanations, Cait went on to the next question. "That other man—Fish? You said he told your dad about me."

"Yeah, but," Desmond sat forward, impressing his next words on her, "he won't tell anyone else, Cait. I promise."

She tore off the crust of her bread. "What about Brady?"

"Brady's my best friend. He'd do anything I asked, and . . . he knows how I feel about you."

That prompted Cait to ask, "Does he know about . . . us?"

"Uh, well . . ." He turned away bashfully, giving her answer enough.

"You called the spirit-being attached to me the Wolf," she said, moving on. "Is it—it's not really a wolf, right?"

Desmond met her gaze again. "No, it's more like—" He paused, then set down his sandwich on the blanket. "Could I see your sketchbook?"

Cait handed it to him.

He flipped through the pages until he found the wolf-like beasts from her dreams several weeks ago. "These are called hellhounds," he explained. "Apparently—and this is something I just learned—the Wolf is the father of hellhounds. So, they're, like, a shade of him."

"Him?"

He nodded.

"He's a beast, then?"

"No, the spirit-beings are separate entities from beasts."

"What do they do?"

Desmond set the sketchbook down. "That, I'm not entirely sure of yet. It seems as though they're just really intense creatures of power. And they need to connect to a person in order to take form in our world."

Cait furrowed her brow. "Why do they want to be in our world?"

"That's one of the things I don't know."

Cautiously, Cait asked, "But he's not a demon?"

"No," he promised. "He's not a demon."

Cait sighed, staring at the sketchbook between them. "Could you tell me about them?" she asked, nudging it closer to him.

"Sure." Desmond picked the book back up, pointing to the page next to the hellhound. He gave a notable shudder before continuing, "This is a nyct. They're bat-like beasts and super deadly."

Slowly, he walked through each page of her notebook, explaining the names of the monsters she now knew so well. The death-bears were called artio, and the demon-horses were aughisky. Hades was the cat-like beast—a sith. Then, there were the valravn, bird-like beasts; the arachnid beasts, arachne; the lizard-like drakes; the snake-like hydra; the rodent-like ratatoskr; and the deer-like wendigo.

Finally, he pointed out the tentacled beasts, their bulbous frames octopod-like. "And these are scylla," he said. "They're, uh—they're connected to Sterling's spirit-being."

Cait considered all the monsters before his words clicked into place. "Wait—" She looked up from the sketchbook. "If the Wolf is the father of the hellhounds, and Sterling's spirit is connected to the scylla . . . Does that mean there are ten other spirit-beings out there?"

"Yes."

An unexpected anticipation rose within Cait. She couldn't call the feeling excitement but something closer to curiosity. "Where are they? Who are their Vessels? Can I talk to them?"

Taking her rapid-fire question in stride, Desmond grinned fondly. "I don't know the answer to the first two, but no, you can't. Vessels are a huge secret, Cait, even amongst most of the Warden. I have no idea how many of the Vessels are actually within the Warden's control, and the rest are probably working with the Druids."

Cait frowned. "Why would they work with the Druids?"

"It's probably different for each of them," he surmised. "But I'd guess it's because they don't want to be put in a cage for the rest of their lives."

Cait remembered the words he'd said to her the other day: *They'll chain you to some random Warden member, imprisoning you in this town forever.*

"Sterling said—" She caught the words before they were out of her mouth, but Desmond stared at her with a look that told her he'd question her until she answered.

Cait sighed. "Sterling said something about his future being determined, and . . . that he'd have his marriage arranged for him."

Desmond's chin lifted.

"Will that be the case for me too?"

He took his time to consider his reply. "If I don't figure out a way to free you first? Probably."

Cait's gaze dropped to her hands.

Desmond reached over, slipping his hand between hers. "I'm not gonna let that happen."

She stared at their fingers, laced together. "How do you intend to stop it?"

"By finding a way to release you from the Wolf."

She looked up at him. "Is that even possible?"

A muscle in his jaw twitched, but his gaze remained steady as he said, "I refuse to believe otherwise."

Cait realized the reason behind his blind belief. "Because you can't be with me if it's not?" she said.

He hesitated, then gave her a reluctant smirk. "What, you think just because you're the only girl I've ever dated, I wanna be with you or something?"

She rolled her eyes. "You've dated other girls."

"I've taken other girls on dates," he corrected. "It's completely different from—what do the old people call it? Going steady?"

Cait couldn't help laughing. "Is that what we're doing?"

His thumb rubbed against hers. "I thought we already had this conversation."

Her smile fell. "It can't last, Des," she whispered. "Whatever time we have together—we've always known it couldn't last."

His expression was adamant. "I'm gonna change that."

She wanted to ask him why. Why would he care enough to risk so much for her? Why would he want to be with *her* in the first place? What could she offer him? She was the cursed wallflower, and he was the beloved rogue. In what world did they end up together?

But Cait knew it wouldn't matter. Whatever Desmond *thought* he wanted from her, she knew it could never be serious. He might say that he never wanted their time together to end, but she knew it eventually would because a boy like Desmond Simon would never marry a girl like Cait Lewan.

So, she pulled her hand free and changed the subject. "Sterling said that he'd heard the spirit-beings are connected to the Veils," she said. "If the Veil is damaged, does that mean the spirit-beings are too?"

"I don't think so," he said. "It seems to me that the damage is simply to your blocks."

That made sense to Cait. Then, she remembered the rest of their meeting and grimaced. "There's something you should know."

Desmond waited.

"So, apparently, Matt was worried, and . . ."

Desmond's expression pinched.

"He followed me."

"To the meeting?"

"Yeah."

His dark eyes narrowed. "And you sent him home, right?"

"I tried to, but—" she grimaced, "he'd already been listening in before we discovered him."

"He *what*?"

"So, now he knows what's going on, and he wants to help."

"No!"

"Desmond—"

"No," he insisted. "He's not a member of the Warden. He doesn't get to help."

"He already has," she said.

"How?" He asked the question like the idea that Matt could offer anything useful was an impossibility.

"Well, when we were talking about the spirit-beings and their connection to the Veils, he brought up a really valid point: If there are two spirit-beings in Porthaven, wouldn't that mean there are two Veils?"

Desmond hesitated. "He came up with that on his own, huh?"

Unsure why he seemed so bothered by the suggestion, Cait shrugged. "Yeah. And honestly, I'm glad he knows now. I didn't like lying to him."

Desmond clenched his jaw, staring out at the ocean.

"Why does this bug you so much?"

"Because," he said flatly.

"Desmond," she pressed.

He fidgeted, scratching the side of his nose. "He's just . . ." He seemed to be fighting himself, working to figure out what to say. "He's such a Boy Scout," he grumbled.

Cait raised her brow. "He *was* a Boy Scout."

"Well, that explains it," Desmond said grumpily.

Cait couldn't help laughing. "Why do you dislike him so much?"

"Because," he repeated.

"That's not an answer."

Desmond threw his hands in the air, annoyed. "Because he's got a crush on you, Cait."

Cait froze, the truth of his statement shifting into place to solve the puzzle of Matt's changing moods and jealousies. Everyone joked, but she'd never had the suggestion confirmed. Until now.

Cait lifted her chin, meeting Desmond's waiting stare. "Why does that matter?" she asked.

He shrugged and turned away. "It doesn't," he muttered.

"So, why bring it up?"

Desmond wet his lips, shifting awkwardly on the blanket. "I don't want him hurting you."

"He can't," she promised. "Not like that."

His eyes met hers, a knowing look contained within his gentle smile.

Cait scooted closer, pressing against his side. "He's my friend," she whispered, "and that's all he'll ever be."

"I still don't think it's a good idea," he murmured, face now inches from hers.

Cait pulled in a slow breath, fighting to keep from kissing him. "Well, it's a little too late for him not to join the team," she said. "He's already planning to come with me when I meet with Hunter and Sterling again."

Desmond's brows pulled together. "Why are you meeting with them again?"

"Because Hunter said he'd spend the weekend checking out some books and seeing if he could get better answers for us," she explained. "I told you: He's Sterling's best friend. He wants to help, and he's not going to tell on us."

"Mm," Desmond hummed, the sound conveying that he remained unconvinced.

"Do you have any information that might be useful for me to bring to the meeting?" Cait asked.

Desmond picked at the blanket between them but sighed. "Yeah, probably. Here—" He dug his phone out of his pocket, then pulled up a photo. "I took a picture of the Veil's damage. I thought it would be helpful in our research."

Cait stared at the image of the tree. A large rip tore apart the bark, revealing two bulging stripes of wood beneath. But instead of the distinctive sycamore wood, each stripe was an entirely different type of tree. Her mind flashed to her sketch from the dream.

"I'm pretty sure this one is birch," he said, pointing to the white bark with soot-like streaks. "But I have no clue what this other one is."

Studying the dark, ridged bark, Cait chewed on her bottom lip. She had an idea, but she knew Desmond wouldn't like it.

"I, uh—" She looked up at him apologetically. "I know someone who could tell us."

"Who?"

"Matt."

Desmond snorted. "Are you serious?"

She shrugged. "Like I told you, he was a Boy Scout. He knows stuff like that."

Desmond sighed.

Cait tugged at her fingernail before she quietly suggested, "You could come to the meeting tomorrow. To show everyone."

With a caustic laugh, Desmond smirked at her. "I'm sorry. It sounded like you just suggested I meet with Hunter, Sterling, and Scouty McGee."

"And Genni."

"Excuse me?"

Cait lifted her shoulder in a shrug. "Genni wants to help too."

"You're not serious."

"She overheard Matt talking to me about it this morning, and I didn't have the heart to tell her no. This affects her as well."

"It absolutely does not!" he insisted. "She's not the Vessel."

"But she could have been. And apparently, if I die without having a kid, she could still inherit it."

Desmond scowled. "I don't see why I couldn't just text the photo to you."

Cait sighed. "Because I'm tired of running around behind people's backs, Desmond. And it doesn't make sense for me to talk to you only to relay the information to them—likely incorrectly. If *you* met with us, you and Hunter could share all your knowledge at once. Then, maybe we could make some sense out of all of this."

Desmond was silent for a long time. He watched the water, lips drawn into a tight line. The wind tugged at his dark hair, and Cait's fingers tingled with the urge to play with those thick waves. But she held still, letting him think things through.

Eventually, Desmond reached over, wrapping his arms around her waist to pull her to him. She was practically sitting in his lap as he captured her gaze. "They can't know about us, Caity," he whispered.

Setting her hands on his shoulders, Cait gave him a sad smile. "They won't."

"If I show up," he said tightly, "they will."

She shook her head. "All they'll know is that we're friends. We'll be careful, and they'll never have a reason to suspect anything else."

Except that Cait knew Sterling already suspected them. But he'd promised not to say anything, so why should he change his mind now?

Cait rubbed her thumb across the back of Desmond's neck, marveling at how natural such affection between them felt. "Please," she whispered.

His dark eyes held the faintest glimmer of humor in their depths. "How'd you learn that?" he asked.

She tipped her head, confused. "What?"

"How to manipulate a guy so easily." He gave her a bitter grin. "Fine. I'll come."

"Really?" she asked, her voice rising with excitement.

"Sure." He tightened his grip on her teasingly. "But you'll owe me."

Cait narrowed her eyes. "What could you possibly want that you don't already have, Mr. En Suite Bathroom?"

He leaned in, mouth precariously close to hers. "I'm sure I'll think of something."

# CHAPTER TWENTY-NINE

# Cait

Hunter had reserved the study room at the library. They'd decided it was the most inconspicuous and the safest place to speak freely. The library closed at five, but as one of the librarians was Hunter's aunt, she'd loaned him the key.

Cait and Genni walked into the library at 4:39 p.m. The girls had wandered the downtown shops for the whole afternoon, waiting for the boys to finish basketball practice. When they made their way to the library, only six cars sat in the lot, including Matt's truck, Sterling's sedan, and Hunter's SUV.

Knowing that the boys had already arrived, Cait and Genni moved toward the back of the building. A sign hung on the study room's door, marking it occupied. Cait took the lead, opening the door. Like the library itself, the walls were painted a bland beige, the yellow pendant light casting an unflattering glow over the space. A large brown table sat in the middle of the room, a whiteboard on the far wall. Three tall windows let in the scant light of evening.

Hunter, who seemed incapable of sitting like a normal person, perched on the edge of the table, a stack of books at his side. Sterling flipped through one of them, slouching in his seat, while Matt perused another across from him. They all looked up at the girls' entry.

"Sup?" Hunter said.

Sterling's brow furrowed. "You brought your baby sister?"

Genni crossed her arms. "I may be younger than you. But I'm pretty sure my three-point-nine can hold its own against your two-point-eight."

He gaped at her. "How do you know my GPA?"

"I know a lot of things," she said, sitting next to Matt. She clasped her hands on the tabletop and gave Sterling a superior grin.

Sterling eyed Genni with a clearly baffled look on his face.

"Genni wants to help," Cait explained, moving to the seat beside her. "Being a possible Vessel, I felt she had the right to be here too."

Hunter shrugged. "Fair enough. What about Rese?"

Cait exchanged a look with her sister, who rolled her eyes. "She wouldn't have any interest," Genni said.

"Can't say I blame her." He hopped off the table. "Should we get start—"

The door opened again, cutting him off. The hum prickled in Cait's ears, rolling through her skull. Desmond entered with Brady just behind him.

"Hey, Hunt," Desmond greeted. "How's it going, man?"

The room filled with palpable tension. Cait chewed on her lip. She hadn't realized he'd bring Brady, but it made sense. Matt and Sterling sat up straighter, and Genni frowned in annoyance.

Hunter merely glared across the room. "We're studying. What do you want?" he demanded.

Desmond scanned the table. "Studying with a sophomore now, huh?" He raised his brow. "Her schoolwork's a little over your head, don't you think?"

"Why are you here?" Hunter demanded.

Desmond dropped into a chair at the end of the table, dramatically spreading out his arms. "We're here for the meeting. What else?"

"Desmond," Cait chided.

That one word sent a charge of confusion rippling through the air. Brady casually took a seat beside Desmond while all her friends whirled to stare at her.

Cait took a deep breath. "I asked him to join us," she explained.

Immediately, Sterling scoffed.

Hunter frowned, first at his friend, then at her. "And why is that?"

"'Cause I know things," Desmond responded before she could speak. He propped his feet on the table. "And because Caity and I are friends."

Matt's eyes grew wide.

Hunter's brow furrowed.

Genni gasped, "Ew!"

Brady snickered.

"What's so funny, sidekick?" Genni snarled.

"Oh, I just enjoy seeing all your reactions," Brady said. "I can't say mine was any less surprised, but it *was* more supportive."

Desmond waved a dismissive hand. "I just have better friends."

"Stop showing off," Cait said, then turned to Hunter. "Desmond and I have been friends for years. We never told anyone for obvious reasons."

Hunter kept looking between them as though trying to deduce if it was something more.

But Cait and Desmond maintained the indifferent expressions they'd agreed to. If they didn't appear overly connected or affectionate, there was a higher chance that no one would question them too much.

With a heavy sigh, Hunter let it go. "Fine." He flipped his chair around and sat backward in it. "We're all here for the same reason: We want to help Cait and Sterling. Having more people on the team is . . . great."

"I'm not joining your team," Desmond returned sharply. "I'm here to provide information until it's no longer needed. Then, we'll part ways, our mutual dislike firmly intact."

"What if we don't want your information?" Matt asked quietly.

Cait heard the resentment in his tone. She decided to let Desmond handle it.

Dropping his feet off the table, Desmond leaned forward to spear Matt with his glare. "Cait asked me to be here, Mattie-boy. I don't care what you want."

"Because you only care about her," Sterling said, sending him a bored stare. "Is that it?"

Hearing the insinuation of his words, Cait opened her mouth in rebuttal, but Desmond beat her to it. "Compared to all you jokers? Hell, yeah."

"Why?" Genni asked suspiciously. "Why would Porthaven's most notoriously egotistical narcissist care about my sister?"

Desmond smirked, likely preparing to say something cutting, but Brady cleared his throat. He gave a subtle shake of his head, and Desmond took a deep, calming breath in response.

Cait took pity on him. "Because it's an act," she said.

Everyone looked at her dubiously.

Brady tapped out an amused rhythm on the table. "Oh, he's a narcissist," he quipped. "But she's right. Despite himself, he actually gives a crap about people."

"Thanks," Desmond grumbled.

"And . . ." Brady pointed at his friend before shifting his indication to Cait. "She brings out the best in him. So, I've got a dog in this race too. I'd like to keep my narcissist sane."

Realizing that Brady wasn't helping to maintain the platonic illusion of their relationship, Cait spoke up. "Point being, Desmond has some information to offer. Plus, as important members of the Warden, he *and* Brady can help shed light on anything confusing that we might discover."

"You don't have to convince us, Cait," Hunter said, though he seemed as bothered by their presence as everyone else. "If you trust him . . . we'll hear him out."

"How magnanimous of you, Hunt," Desmond retorted.

Cait sent him a dirty look.

He sighed. "Sorry. Force of habit."

Hunter tightened his jaw but let it go. "All right, I guess I'll start by telling you guys what I found. There are some old Varon journals my dad has in his study that were passed down through the generations. He let me read them when I was old enough, so I checked them out again."

Desmond tapped the table with clear irritation.

"I remembered that one talked about Veils in particular detail," Hunter continued, picking up a small leather-bound book from the table. "So, I went back and found it. Turns out, one of our ancestors did some serious study on Veils, even exchanging letters with a woman named Elizabeth Allard, who sounds as if she must be a Vessel as well."

"Elizabeth?" Desmond asked with a peculiar note in his voice.

"Yeah. You recognize the name?"

Desmond was quiet for a moment, and Cait could tell he was considering something. Finally, he pursed his lips and replied, "Aside from your girlfriend? Nah."

"Des," she prompted, knowing he was hiding something that might prove beneficial.

He lifted his eyes to the ceiling but caved. "I found a letter to Lyndon Simon in my dad's things from a woman named Elizabeth. She was . . ." He flashed a self-mocking grin. "She was writing to congratulate him on becoming the true Varon of Edmond's bloodline. Apparently, she was a good friend of our family."

Hunter looked almost angered by this news. "The journal I'm referring to was written by Martin Varon."

Desmond scratched the bridge of his nose but remained silent.

Matt frowned. "What do the two have to do with anything?"

Remembering the information from their essay, Cait explained.

"Martin Varon and Lyndon Simon were best friends. Lyndon married Martin's sister, and when Martin died, his father named Lyndon his heir."

"And Martin's uncle felt he should have been named the heir," Brady added. "Thus, the Simon-Varon feud began."

"That's stupid," Genni said.

"Yep," Desmond agreed. "What information did Martin's journal give you?"

Hunter gritted his teeth. "Matt, your theory was correct," he said. "Where a Vessel goes, a Veil follows. There should be two in town."

"Great!" Matt exclaimed. "Then, we just have to find it and see if it's damaged as well."

"Not so fast, Scout," Desmond said in a sharp tone. "We've already been looking, and we haven't found it."

Matt tipped his head to the side. "How did you know to look?"

"Sterling's dad suggested it."

Sterling frowned. "He did?"

"He knows more than he's telling you." Desmond turned back to Hunter. "If there's another Veil, my dad and I will find it. But it's like looking for a pine needle in a forest, so we need something else to focus on. What else you got?"

Hunter thumbed the journal's cover. "Martin didn't say anything about damage to Veils. As far as I can tell, it's never happened before. Have you . . ." He gave Desmond a hopeful glance. "You fixed it, right?"

Desmond hesitated, glancing at Cait.

"Actually," she replied nervously, "that was me."

Hunter raised his chin in surprise.

"Desmond took the credit to protect me."

Hunter looked up the length of the table toward Desmond with something like awe, as though realizing that maybe he wasn't so bad after all. "But you've seen the Veil? You've seen the damage?"

"I have," Desmond confirmed.

"Could you describe it?" Hunter asked. "Maybe that will help us figure out what caused the damage?"

"I'll do you one better." Desmond pulled out his phone and slid it across the table.

Hunter, Matt, Sterling, and Genni stood together and leaned over the table to get a look.

"Is that—" Hunter began.

"It's two new trees," Matt confirmed. He glanced up at Desmond. "They're growing out of the one?"

"That's what it looks like," Desmond said, eyeing the boy intently.

Cait jumped at the opportunity to ask, "Can you identify the types of trees, Matt?"

"Uh . . ." He scratched his brow, considering. Then, he picked up the phone to get a better look. "Yeah, I think so."

Desmond gestured to the device. "We already know the one is birch, but we aren't sure—"

"No, it's not," Matt interrupted.

"What?" Desmond gaped at him.

Matt pointed to the photo. "That's not a birch."

"What are you talking about?"

"Look at the leaves—" Matt held the phone so Desmond could see. "They're heart-shaped. Birch trees have oval leaves with pointed tips. This is an aspen."

Desmond blinked.

Matt shrugged. "It's a common mistake."

Cait pressed her lips together to keep from smiling.

Desmond noticed, sending her a glare. "Someone got their badge in treeology," he grumbled.

"Plant Science," Matt corrected distractedly. He zoomed in on the other tree. "This one . . . I'm pretty sure it's an ash tree."

He held the phone so that Cait could see it. "See those vertical furrows? That's indicative of ash. And those light spots on the gray? That makes me think it's a white ash."

Desmond muttered something to Brady, but Cait smiled at Matt. "That's really impressive," she said.

"Thanks," he said, pink creeping onto the corners of his ears.

He handed the phone back to Desmond. "The main tree is a sycamore, by the way."

"Yeah, I already knew that one," Desmond said sourly. "What does it mean, though? Two different types of trees growing through another."

"Oh," Matt shrugged, "I dunno. I've never heard of that before. I'll have to do some research to see if I can find anything."

"Would that even help?" Genni asked. "If it has to do with the spirit world, will science be able to explain it?"

"This doesn't seem supernatural," Hunter said. "I mean, it's just two trees growing through another one. It must be some strange phenomenon."

"But how did it get there?" Brady asked.

"And if it's natural," Desmond added, "how was it letting beasts out?"

"It's affecting our blocks too," Sterling noted.

"Maybe someone planted them," Hunter suggested, then frowned. "Supernaturally?"

"Okay, but who?" Sterling asked.

Cait looked at Desmond, finding him watching Matt intently.

He turned back to Hunter. "Any other info you care to offer?"

"Not really," Hunter admitted. "I couldn't find that much."

"Story of our lives." Desmond scanned the table. "Here's the deal: We don't know who caused the damage to the Veil, but we do know that if it's not reversed, Cait and Sterling are in danger of losing their blocks. If that happens, the spirit-beings break free, and the Warden finds out. And that will put both of them in positions we'd all rather save them from.

"So, if you want to help protect them, you keep all of this information between the seven of us," he ordered. "Are we agreed?"

One by one, everyone at the table nodded.

"Good." Desmond met Cait's gaze for a second before continuing, "I suggest we keep researching to see if we can find *anything* that's helpful. Mattie, you study up on your trees. See if there's anything to explain this phenomenon. Hunt, keep reading Martin's journals. And maybe hand over a couple so that Brady and I can help out."

"There's only one more," Hunter replied apologetically. "He died in his twenties, remember?"

"Right." Desmond sighed. "Well, then Brade and I will keep studying his dad's stuff. Maybe we'll finally find something useful in there."

"What can I do?" Genni asked.

Desmond eyed her. "You're good at getting information out of people, aren't you?"

"Oh, yeah! I love asking questions, and no one ever suspects that I'm anything but completely sincere." She smiled at Sterling. *"That's* how I found out your GPA."

"You asked?" Sterling looked baffled. "Who?"

Her eyes twinkled merrily. "The records clerk, Gloria, likes to talk to me. She says I'm an incorrigible delight."

"Perfect," Desmond said, ignoring their exchange. "Talk to your nan. See if she'll let something slip about your family's experience in Bushmills."

"Which just leaves us," Cait said, looking at Sterling.

"You two can't do anything," Desmond said immediately. "You can't look suspicious."

Sterling pressed his lips together but accepted the truth alongside Cait. If anyone in the Warden caught wind of their research, they'd know they were the Vessels in an instant.

In the resulting pause, Matt asked, "When do we meet again?"

"Whenever we find something more to discuss," Desmond said.

They all agreed. Then, slowly, they moved back through the now-dark library and out into the night.

"Sterling and I were gonna get some dinner at the diner," Hunter said, glancing nervously at Desmond and Brady before turning back to the rest of them. "You're all welcome to join."

Matt waited for Cait and Genni's approval before agreeing.

"I know it'll break your hearts," Desmond said casually. "But my reputation can't take a hit that big."

Brady held out a hand to Hunter. "Appreciate the offer," he said. "And the teamwork."

After considering the outstretched hand, Hunter finally accepted it. "Any time."

Cait watched as a look of regret passed over Desmond's face before he regained his smirk. "I'll hold you to it, Hunt."

"I still don't like you," Hunter replied.

"I'd be worried if you did."

Sterling and Hunter headed to their cars, Genni and Matt moving to follow. Cait smiled at Desmond and Brady. "Thanks for coming," she said, then began to turn to join the others.

Desmond caught her arm, pulling her to a stop.

"I'll, uh—" Brady motioned to the parking lot. "I'm gonna get going."

Matt turned back, realizing Cait wasn't with them. When he saw Desmond's grip on her arm, his eyes narrowed. "You okay, Cait?"

"Yeah, I—"

"Give us a second," Desmond said.

Matt drew his shoulders back, a look of suspicion on his face.

"Don't get defensive, kid," Desmond quipped. "I just want a word with her."

"I don't trust you," Matt said, his voice unusually tense. Genni watched warily beside him.

Desmond rolled his eyes, releasing his hold on Cait. "What do you think I'm gonna do, huh? She's my friend, same as yours."

"Except that you're never there for her, are you?" Matt accused.

"You let her be alone every single day. You let the other kids at school treat her like she was invisible. So, you weren't ever really her friend, were you?"

Desmond's jaw tightened, and Cait set a hand on his arm to stop him from replying. She turned to Matt. "I'll be there in a minute," she told him.

"Cait—"

"Matt." Her stare dared him to test her.

Taking a step back, Matt glared at Desmond. "Just a word, friend to friend, right?"

"Scout's honor," Desmond mocked.

Matt scowled but left them alone. Genni lingered a moment longer, staring at Cait.

With an encouraging smile, Cait nodded to her sister. Genni sighed but turned to follow Matt to the truck.

Desmond looked down at Cait. "He's literally the worst."

"Not if you're his friend," she said. "What did you need?"

Lowering his voice, Desmond whispered, "You."

Cait shook her head, fighting off a smile. "That's incredibly sappy. You know that, right?"

"But you liked it, didn't you?"

She crossed her arms, failing to hold in her joy. "Kind of."

He grinned, then adjusted the collar of her jacket. "I just wanted to tell you that you were right," he said. "This was a good idea. Even if I hated every minute of it."

She held his gaze, making sure to keep distance between them even as she wished to step closer. "You know, if you gave it even the smallest amount of effort, you could be the nicest person in the world."

"That sounds really boring," he teased, but she could see his gaze soften.

Cait let her smile take over her face. "I meant it before," she said. "Thank you for coming."

"Always, Lewan."

She reached over to pat his arm, her whole body fighting the urge to hug him. "I'll see you at school."

He caught her hand before she could pull away. "Meet me on the roof tomorrow? After lunch."

"I'll try."

"I'm busy the rest of the week."

Hearing what he meant, Cait nodded. If they couldn't sneak away to the roof, they wouldn't see each other for days.

She took a regretful step back. "I'll try," she promised again, infusing her sincerity into the words.

He nodded, letting her go.

She left him standing on the steps, denying herself the desire to look over her shoulder. When she reached the truck, Genni scooted closer to the middle to give her room. A thick silence filled the vehicle as Matt began to pull out of the lot. They hadn't even reached the entrance when Genni's silence broke.

"Seriously?" she exclaimed. "You're friends with Desmond Simon? Gross. He's like the worst human to ever exist."

"You don't know him," Cait said flatly.

"But apparently, you do."

Cait heaved a sigh, knowing that no matter what she said, neither Genni nor Matt would understand.

"Why did you hide it?" Matt asked, his voice unnaturally hushed. "Your friendship, I mean."

"I knew what you meant," Cait replied. "We couldn't tell anyone because no one would understand. He's the popular kid, and I'm the outcast. People would ask questions."

"So? If he's such a great guy, why wouldn't he use his popularity to show people how cool you are?"

"Because I don't want that," Cait snapped.

Sitting at the stop sign before turning onto Lawrence Avenue, they both stared at her.

Cait glared out the windshield. "It was never confirmed, but I always knew—*we* always knew that I was the one who inherited the curse. And if Desmond had brought me into his life . . . the Warden would have taken notice of me. They would have been paying attention to me. And they would have known the truth too."

Matt frowned at the steering wheel while Genni pursed her lips.

"He was protecting me," she told them sharply. "No matter what anyone else wants to think of him, he *is* a great guy. And he's never given me any reason to doubt him."

After idling for several seconds, Matt finally sighed and set the car back in motion. He didn't say anything, but Cait could tell he'd accepted her answer even if he didn't like it.

Genni, however, crossed her arms. "I still think he sucks."

# CHAPTER THIRTY

# Rese

Porthaven Chapel's bell tower loomed in the night sky, its outline spangled with stars. The crescent moon shone with the merest shimmer of silver. It cast the brick building into shadows, the arched doorways and stained glass windows darker than Rese had ever seen.

She stood in the line of trees by the empty parking lot, keeping out of sight. The dimmest yellow light lit the front left window of the church. She knew that the reverend kept the building unlocked for anyone who wished to pray within the chapel walls. Tonight was her first opportunity to exploit the lapse in security.

After pumping Ryan for answers, Rese had spent the rest of the weekend trying to determine what to do next. She knew the Lavignes were involved in whatever was keeping the Wolf contained within Cait's mind. But by the sketches in her notebook, it was clear that "block"— which she could now call by name—was breaking down.

Rese finally concluded that if she wanted to find a way to speak to the Wolf and convince him to accept *her* as his new Vessel, the answers would lie with the Lavignes. As she wasn't exactly on friendly terms with the family, her best opportunity for answers came through the reverend's private office in the chapel.

So, Rese waited in the shadows of the parking lot for ten minutes to ensure its vacancy before venturing inside.

The vaulted ceilings and Gothic columns lent a sense of grandeur to the building as she slipped through the unlocked door. Rese always felt like she was stepping into a Brontë sister's novel each service. Many times, she'd imagined scurrying down the center aisle in a full skirt and knitted shawl to entreat the reverend for sanctuary from the ghosts that haunted her. Or she'd imagined running away from the altar after discovering that her betrothed kept a wife locked in the upper room of his imposing house.

Rese grinned self-derisively as she walked from the narthex into the nave. She'd always had a flair for the dramatic. As a child, she loved fairy and ghost stories. As she grew, that love had passed to gothic romances and fantasy novels. There'd been a time when she hoped to become an actress, taking her love of stories to the stage.

Now, Rese just dreamed of a life where she didn't have to worry. Drama was entertaining but overrated. She'd had enough crises in her life. She didn't need to add "starving artist" to the list.

Rese passed through the sanctuary to the back right-hand side of the building. Though she didn't know the layout of the rest of the chapel, she'd seen Reverend Lavigne disappear behind these doors at the end of services. Thus, she entered the shadowy hall, intent on finding his office.

She didn't have to search long. There were only a handful of doors in the hall, two leading to bathrooms, one opening to a supply closet, and the last revealing the reverend's office.

Knowing the office couldn't be seen from the road or parking lot, Rese boldly turned on the light, flooding the room with a bright golden wash. Though the building was centuries old, the town had retrofitted modern lighting into the interior. A large stained glass pendant light hung from the arched ceiling. The decor suited the Victorian feel. A massive desk and several bookcases filled the room, all in dark wood. Papers littered the desktop, and a computer sat on the far corner.

Glancing over her shoulder, Rese slipped into the room, leaving the door ajar behind her. She needed to move quickly. Though it was a Tuesday night, there was no guarantee the reverend wouldn't come by.

Rese scanned the bookcases, ignoring the newer volumes to seek out anything that might touch on the spirit world or the Warden. She doubted they'd be easy to find. Her da had taught her that the organization liked to keep things quiet. The spirit world wasn't something to play with. And the average individual would find its presence thoroughly frightening.

The shelf nearest the desk proved her best bet. It held rows of leather-bound books, all giving the distinct impression of being older than the church. Exactly what she expected regarding books about the spirit world. There were a couple of holes where two books were missing, but otherwise, the numerous tomes gave her ample options.

The problem was that none of the spines were marked with titles.

Rese scowled at the shelf. She picked a book at random, flipping open its cover. She couldn't even read the title; its language was English too old to understand.

Shoving it back in place, Rese blew out a puff of air. This search was going to take forever.

One by one, Rese started at the top shelf and worked her way down. She found a few she'd like to read but knew that while one book might not be missed, a handful would. So, she put them back, wishing she could find a way to read them in the future.

When she found the book entitled *Theories of the Spirit: How We Wield* by Edwin Watson, she thought she might be on the right track. She checked the back for an index. When there wasn't one, she flipped through the pages, skimming to find the word "block." A few passages caught her eye, drawing her lingering study. She chewed on her thumbnail as she read.

Then, someone spoke behind her. "What are you doing here?"

Rese yelped, nearly dropping the book. She crushed it to her chest, whirling to find Brady Lavigne in the doorway, a pair of books in his arms.

Somehow, with her heart pumping and panic filling her head, she found the gumption to demand, "What are *you* doing here?"

Brady glanced at the bookcase beside her. Then, he hefted the two books he held. "Returning these."

"I didn't realize this was a library," Rese retorted.

Brady's eyes dropped to the book pressed against her chest. Pointedly, they rose to meet hers.

Pursing her lips, Rese slid the tome back on its shelf. "I was just looking," she lied.

"Mm-hm." Brady smirked, clearly not believing her. He crossed the room, coming to stand by her side. "Do you mind?" he asked.

Realizing she was standing in his way, Rese scooted aside.

Calmly, as though she weren't there, Brady reshelved his books before searching for another. "You didn't answer my question," he remarked, eyes on the spines.

"I didn't feel like it," she answered defensively.

He gave her a side-eyed glance, then pulled out a book, straightening fully to look down at her once it was in his hand. "What were you looking for?" he asked.

Taking a step back so she didn't have to crane her neck to see him, Rese realized just how tall he was. "Nothing," she lied again.

Brady eyed her, humor glinting in the darkness of his irises. "You said you were looking when I got here," he reminded her.

Face heating, Rese crossed her arms. "I was flustered," she said.

"You still seem flustered," he replied.

"That's because you aren't supposed to be here."

"You do realize this is my dad's office, right? What's your excuse?"

Rese shrugged, attempting to appear confident. "I don't need one."

"No?"

She raised her brow. "Are *you* gonna turn me in?"

Brady drew his shoulders back, mouth set in a hard line. "If you're referring to Ryan's assumptions about me and my . . . awareness of you," he said flatly, "he's wrong."

"Is he?" Her tone implied that she knew he wasn't telling the full truth.

"I don't bother with girls who feel the need to validate themselves by dating douchebags."

Rese blanched.

Brady held her glare steadily. "Do you need help finding something?" he asked.

Thrown off by the offer, Rese gaped at him. "You're—" She pointed to the shelf. "You'll let me take something?"

He held up the book in his hand. "I'm taking something."

"I'm not the pastor's kid."

"He's a reverend."

"What's the difference?" she asked, then realized she genuinely didn't know.

Brady sighed but ignored the question. "Do you want a book or not?"

Rese eyed him skeptically. "Why are you helping me?"

"Maybe it's because I've got a crush on you," he replied coolly, then smirked. "Or maybe it's just because I'm a nice guy."

"Nice guys aren't friends with Desmond Simon," Rese said.

"Then, it must be the first one."

"You said Ryan was wrong."

"Then, I guess it has to be the second."

Rese found herself baffled by his emotionless delivery. "You're very weird," she accused.

Brady shrugged. "I'm the pastor's kid. It comes with the territory."

A sudden, amused snort slipped out of Rese, and to her shock, he smiled. It was a surprisingly endearing look that brightened his usually serious face. She could admit she found it attractive. But she wasn't interested in stroking a teen boy's ego.

Rese composed herself, eyeing him cynically. "What do you want in return?" she asked.

Brady's brow furrowed. "Nothing."

"Come on, you've got to want something."

"I can't just want to help?"

Rese rolled her eyes, annoyed at his reluctance to admit he wanted something from her. "What, are you just too shy to ask for a kiss?"

"No," he spat out, anger flaring across his expression. "That's not—"

"I'm not some bashful church girl, Brady," she interrupted, then shrugged dismissively. "I'll kiss you if that's what you want."

"Do you think every guy's a total dick?" he retorted. "I'm not Ryan. Now, do you want a book or not?"

Rese stared up at him, doubtful of his goodness but surprised by his rejection of her offer.

Brady took a deep breath, then shook his head. He eyed her for a moment before gesturing to the shelf. "I'm assuming you're looking for answers about yours and your sisters' . . . situation." He slid out one of the books he'd replaced. "I just finished this one. It's not—well, it's probably not exactly what you're looking for, but it's a start."

Cautiously, Rese accepted the book.

"Once you're done," he continued casually, "let me know, and I'll give you another. Hopefully, I'll have a better idea of what's helpful by then."

Holding the book to her chest, Rese scanned him. "I don't believe you."

Brady didn't ask what she meant. It was clear to them both. She didn't believe him when he said that Ryan was wrong, nor when he said he didn't want something from her.

But instead of refuting either claim, Brady simply said, "I don't care."

Somehow, that declaration disappointed Rese. She couldn't

understand this boy. Every other guy in her life had been blatant about what they wanted from her. It wasn't hard to guess. They were teens, figuring out the balance of childhood and adulthood with raging hormones distorting their every thought.

Brady should be like them. He should be obvious. Yet, for all his bluntness, he was obnoxiously difficult to pin down.

"We should go," Brady said, the words a directive, not a request.

Still trying to work out his endgame with her, Rese let him lead her out of the office. They walked back through the sanctuary, a healthy distance between them. He didn't look at her once, the moon casting stained glass patterns on his pale skin.

Rese narrowed her eyes, still skeptical. He was either a good actor or Ryan truly had been wrong. "How exactly am I supposed to let you know when I'm done with the book?" she asked, keeping her voice low in the chapel. "We're not friends, and I'm not giving you my phone number."

Brady glanced at her blandly. "I didn't ask for it, did I?"

She shrugged.

He reached to open the front door for her, finally meeting her gaze. "I'll be around," he said. "You're smart enough to figure out the rest."

Rese stepped out into the cold night. She pursed her lips, surveying him. "And you say *I* make people feel inferior," she replied.

His brow rose. "I didn't realize you were paying that much attention to what I said." The church door shut behind him, and his eyes fell on the parking lot, empty of all vehicles but his. "Where's your car?"

"I left it at the café."

He sighed. "I'll drive you there."

"For someone supposedly not interested in me, you're finding a lot of ways to keep me around," she said with a sly grin.

"Rese—" He said her name flatly like she'd outworn his good nature. "You can either walk to your car alone in the cold, or I can be a gentleman and drive you there. Pick whichever you want. But I'll tell you as many times as it takes for you to understand: I'm not Ryan."

"Meaning what exactly?" she said sharply, finding herself unduly upset by his niceness. "That you don't want me? Or that you're too 'Christian' to admit you do?"

Brady's expression pinched, almost as though he was sad. But not for himself. For her.

Rese bristled, realizing that he pitied her.

Before he could respond, she began to walk down the steps. "Thanks for the book. I'll walk by myself."

She half expected him to come after her. Even as she heard his car door shut, she anticipated he'd drive over and insist she get in. But he didn't.

Brady drove past her and turned out of the church lot, his white sedan disappearing into the darkness of the night.

Rese pulled her coat tighter around herself, the wind from the sea cutting. She hugged the book to her chest as she made the trek through downtown and to her car. And all the while, she couldn't shake the irrational disappointment that he, like every other man, left her to face the world alone.

# CHAPTER THIRTY-ONE

# Cait

Their next meeting was far smaller.

Wednesday morning, Matt told them he had some news. But Hunter already had plans with Liz's family, Desmond didn't think he should risk meeting with them again, and Genni and Alexis were hanging out. So, after numerous convoluted texts, the plans were finally set.

After school, Cait and Matt met Sterling and Brady at the diner. The two boys sat in one of the back booths, away from the few other patrons, completely silent. Brady stared at his phone while Sterling kept his headphones in. As Cait and Matt approached the booth, there was an awkward moment when Matt floundered, trying to decide whom to sit by—Sterling or Brady—but Cait solved the problem for him.

She slid onto the bench next to the reverend's son. "Did you guys order anything?"

"Just a coffee and some fries," Brady said, then gestured across the table. "He splurged and got a water."

Unimpressed, Sterling slowly removed his earbuds. "I'm surprised you're even here," he said. "Weren't you afraid to be seen with us like your friend?"

Brady smirked in a fashion that reminded Cait an awful lot of Desmond. "Nah, it's easy to explain. Matt and I are partners on our history assignment, and we've already met here to work on that a couple of times. Obviously, Cait and he hang out all the time, so she decided to tag along. And if anyone asks—" he shrugged, "I'm tutoring you."

"In what? Religious studies?"

"Hey, I'm not the one flunking English."

Cait held up her hands. "Could we dispense with the snark? We're here for a reason."

"Speaking of—" Matt pulled a notebook out of his backpack. "I spent the last two days studying as much as I could about sycamores, aspens, and ash trees, as well as trees and their growth patterns in general. Here's what I've found."

He turned to a page and began reading his notes. "So, there's nothing out there that explains what's happening."

The waitress appeared then, bringing the water, coffee, and fries. She took the newcomers' orders—water for Cait and a strawberry milkshake for Matt—before heading back to the kitchen.

Alone again, the three of them stared at Matt in expectation, expressions blank.

Matt tapped the page. "That's it."

"That's it?" Brady asked. "That's the big news you brought us all together to announce. You found nothing?"

"Well, yeah," Matt said as though that should be good enough.

Cait dropped her head into her hand.

"But," Matt hurried to add, "that's the point, ya know? I couldn't find anything. I mean, there's this thing called inosculation where two trees fuse and continue to grow together. But that doesn't include two trees growing *out* of another. Let alone trees of different varieties. From my research, something like that isn't even possible."

"Then, how is it happening?" Sterling asked.

"I don't know," Matt said. "There's nothing in science to explain it. Isn't that great?"

"How could that be great?" Brady asked.

Understanding dawned in Cait's mind. "Because if it's impossible naturally, that means it can only be happening supernaturally."

Matt pointed to her. "Exactly. Whatever's causing the damage to this tree isn't natural."

"We already assumed that to be the case," Brady said.

"But now we know it," Sterling said. He angled in his seat to better address them all. "So, someone or something is supernaturally causing these trees to grow inside the sycamore. How?"

"I think the better question is: Why?"

Cait turned to Brady. "Don't we already know that?" she asked.

His brows dipped low. "Do we?"

The *whir* of the milkshake machine buzzed through the diner, giving her the confidence to speak without fear of being overheard. "Because of what we are. We determined that the Veil's damage is what's causing our blocks to fail, right? Wouldn't that be what this person is after?"

Brady held her stare, a thread of fear appearing in the depths of his dark eyes. "They're trying to release the spirit-beings."

Cait shrugged as Sterling muttered obscenities under his breath.

"Why would they want that?" Matt asked.

Brady glanced at him, his jaw tight.

"It's the Druids, isn't it?" Sterling said. "You all thought you were so clever, keeping us hidden, but now they've found us, and they're trying to get these monsters to take over so that we have no choice but to go with them."

"We don't know that," Brady said.

Sterling opened his mouth in rebuttal, but the waitress walked up, stalling any response. "Here we are," she said in a bubbly tone. "One water and one milkshake. Anything else I can get you guys?"

"No, thank you," Brady said.

When she was finally out of earshot, Sterling leaned forward, prepared to release his sharp reply, but Cait was ready. "It's not worth fighting about," she cut in. "Maybe it's the Druids, but maybe it's not."

"Who else would want this to happen?" Sterling demanded.

Cait's shoulders practically brushed her ears. "It could be anyone. Desmond said there are some people who want to take his dad's job away from him. Maybe they're doing this to make him look bad. Maybe they think that if our blocks fail and the spirit-beings get out, the Warden will fire him."

Brady grimaced, and Cait wondered if she'd said the wrong thing. If Desmond was right and Hunter's dad was leading the coup, would Sterling take the Varons' side? But if her theory proved correct, then Sterling certainly wouldn't support the release of his spirit-being.

"I still can't believe that you trust these two," Sterling said, tossing a hand in Brady's direction. "Their families are the very people imprisoning us here, Cait. If it weren't for them—"

"If it weren't for us," Brady interrupted, his voice taut, "you'd both be locked up somewhere else. And in case you haven't noticed, Desmond and I are trying to help you. Neither of us approves of the way your families have been treated. We're doing what we can to change it."

Sterling looked out the diner window, unable to argue Brady's point.

"Where does this leave us?" Matt asked.

Brady sighed. "We know the Veil's damage is supernatural, which means it was done by a Wielder. Our two suspects at the moment are the Druids and . . . the Varon coup."

Sterling's brow furrowed, but he didn't speak.

"Both have solid motives," Brady continued. "The Druids would want to collect you two and use your spirit-beings' powers."

"And the Varons want the town back," Sterling said thoughtfully. His face screwed up in something like an expression of hurt. "Do you really think they'd do this? Just so they can take control back from the Simons?"

Brady hesitated. "If you'd asked me a week ago? I would've said no, but. . . ."

Cait twisted the hem of her shirt. "It makes the most sense," she said. "The Veil was releasing beasts because the damage opened the doorway, right?"

"Yes," he said with something like regret in his tone. "And we never could figure out why a Druid would be summoning beasts without giving them any sort of directive. They seemed to have no purpose other than to exist."

"But I thought they weren't summoned," Sterling argued. "That the Veil was just creating them randomly."

"That's how it seemed, but . . ." Brady paused, considering his next words. "Well, who's to say they didn't know that is what would happen? If Hunter's dad has all those journals he hasn't shared with Uncle Will, then maybe he knows something that the rest of the Warden doesn't. Maybe he decided to damage the Veil supernaturally, aware or not of the consequences, simply to bring William under suspicion."

"Is Hunter's dad really that maniacal?" Matt asked, mouth gaping.

"No," Sterling insisted. "He's—he's a great guy. He's always been incredibly nice and welcoming to me."

"Could be a front," Brady stated.

Sterling glared at him. "It isn't."

"How can you be sure?" Cait asked.

He deflated at that. "I can't."

None of them spoke for a moment, considering the idea.

"You're right, Cait," Brady said. "It makes the most sense for this to be part of the Varons' plans. We've been wondering who would want to put Porthaven in danger, but the fact is, it's not been in danger this whole time. In all this time, no one has gotten hurt—except for when we were on the island. But they couldn't have known that we'd be there."

Sterling hung his head. "But the town's safety wouldn't matter if our spirit-beings broke free." He sighed reluctantly. "You're right. It's gotta be them."

Cait thought about everything that had happened in the last month. It all fit, pointing to the Varons' grudge against the Simons' leadership. Their ploy wouldn't hurt anyone but would get them everything they wanted. It would even reveal who carried the spirit-being in her family's line.

Which made Cait think . . .

"The beasts have stopped appearing," she said. "That's what Desmond told me. I sealed the Veil, and no more beasts have come out since then."

Brady nodded. "Yeah, the Warden stopped patrolling the island because there's no point anymore."

"Wouldn't that mean our blocks are safe now too?"

They all considered it.

Cait continued. "If I repaired the Veil—if I stopped the tear from growing—then wouldn't that mean we don't have to worry about the spirit-beings breaking free anymore?"

"That would make sense," Brady mused. "But I'm not sure it changes anything for the Varons either way. If they wanted to bring William's leadership into question, their plan would have already been successful. Seeing your spirit-beings released would only be a final nail in the coffin."

"So, they've already won," Matt surmised. "They don't care one way or another if your identities are revealed because what they really want, they've already got."

"Seems that way," Brady muttered.

Sterling shook his head but didn't say anything.

She understood his hesitation to believe the Varons were the enemy. If anyone told her that Matt and his family were at the center of some grand scheme, she'd question them as well. And she thought that Brady must feel the same about the Simons.

"There's just . . ." Brady rubbed a hand along his jaw.

"What is it?" Cait asked.

His dark eyes flickered over to Matt, and he shook his head. "Never mind. Desmond just had a theory. But it's not relevant anymore."

"What was it?" Matt asked.

Brady pressed his lips together and shrugged. "He, uh—he thought that maybe the ex-Druid had something to do with it."

"Lilith?" Cait gasped in surprise.

"The tea shop owner?" Matt said. "She was a Druid?"

Cait frowned. "He never said anything about that theory to me."

Brady sent her a hard stare as though trying to impress something on her. However, his calm tone belied the intensity of his expression. "He probably didn't want to scare you."

"Oh." Cait held Brady's gaze, trying to deduce what he was telling her. Whatever the case, she thought it best not to press. At least not here. "Yeah, you're probably right."

She could almost feel Brady's relief as he relaxed into his seat. He picked at his cooling fries.

"What do we do now?" Matt asked.

As Brady and Sterling seemed lost in their own thoughts, Cait took the lead. "I guess we talk to Desmond and Hunter and tell them—"

"No," Brady interrupted. "We can't tell Hunter. We can't include him in this anymore."

Sterling bristled. "He's trying to help us."

"He's a Varon," Brady shot back. "His dad is leading the charge against William. Brett is our number one suspect. Hunter's probably telling him everything that we know as it is."

"He's my friend," Sterling said, his hands fisting on the table. "I trust him."

"And do you trust his dad?"

Sterling hesitated.

Brady's expression shifted imperiously. "I didn't think so. Do you really want to let the test of your buddy's loyalty be handing him the key to your own cage?"

At that, Sterling clenched his jaw and dropped his gaze. "Let me out," he grumbled.

"Huh?" Matt's eyes grew wide in surprise.

"Let me out!" Sterling demanded with more force than necessary.

Matt leaped from his seat, and Sterling barreled out of the booth. He didn't say a word or look at any of them as he shoved his hands in the pockets of his corduroy jacket and bolted out of the diner.

Brady ran a hand through his hair. "That's not gonna end well," he mumbled. Then, he turned to Cait. "Listen, I'll get Desmond up to speed. You know he's busy the rest of the week, right?"

"He told me," she said.

"Good." Brady leaned on the table, his expression sincere as he continued, "We're on your side—both of us."

As the realization dawned that she had a friend she'd not known about until this moment, Cait smiled at him. "He thinks of you like a brother. You know that, right?" she said. "He probably never says it. He's not good at being honest. But it's true."

Brady grinned. "He sucks at being honest," he agreed. "But yeah, I know. Why do you think I'm here?"

He tapped her shoulder. "Let me out, will ya? I'm gonna get going."

Once he stood at the end of the table, he fished out his wallet. He gave a quick glance at Matt, tossing down some cash. "That should take care of it all," he said. "Feel free to eat the fries."

"Thanks," Matt replied.

"Mm." Brady turned back to Cait, a knowing smirk on his face. "I approve, by the way. Not that it matters."

Face heating, Cait worked to keep her expression indifferent. "It does."

He emitted a faint hum of appreciation. "See you around," he said, then headed out the door.

Running her fingers along the condensation of her water glass, Cait watched him as he walked to his car. She wondered at his approval of her.

They'd never talked before the night on the island. She knew about him from Desmond, of course, and she knew he was a good friend with a devoted heart. But that understanding of him informed her that he would be highly protective of Desmond. Brady wouldn't accept just anyone as his best friend's girl.

So, how was it that Brady Lavigne felt he knew her well enough to approve of her relationship with his best friend?

"I'll admit," Matt spoke up, his tone somewhat reluctant. "He's not as bad as I originally thought."

Brought back to the diner, Cait looked up at him with surprise.

"Like, he's actually pulled his weight and had some great insights on our history paper," he went on. "And with this whole . . . situation, he's been kind of nice."

"I think so too," she agreed.

Matt tapped his thumb along the edge of the table, taking a sip of his milkshake. His brow furrowed as he drank. "Why'd he say he approved?" he asked. "What does he approve of?"

Swirling the straw in her ice water, Cait considered her next words carefully. "I believe he was referring to my friendship with Desmond," she said. "Brady's kind of protective, from what I gather."

"Oh. Yeah, I get that." He sighed, and Cait smiled because she knew he did.

His expression turned serious, thin eyebrows low over his puppy-dog eyes. "I don't approve," he declared. "Not that I get a say, but . . . I still think he's a jerk."

Cait couldn't help laughing. "Matt, one day—" She held his adamant stare with confidence, thankful she had a friend who cared, even if it was irrationally. "One day, you'll change your mind about him. It'll probably be a long time from now, but . . . He has this tenacious way of caring about people that makes it impossible not to like him. And while he's darn good at hiding it, eventually he slips up."

She smiled as thoughts of Desmond rose—the boy that only she truly knew. The one who liked to hide his goodness behind rebellious and flippant behavior because he was too scared to fail the ones he loved.

"You two might not get along right now," she continued. "But trust me: One day, he'll slip up with you, too, and you'll find yourself wondering how you never saw his goodness before."

Matt frowned, considering her assertion. He was silent for a long time before he heaved a huge sigh. "The first day of school," he mumbled.

"What?"

Matt scrunched up his nose in disappointment. "The first day of school," he repeated. "In the hall, he stopped Sydney from bullying you."

Cait nodded.

He scrubbed a hand over his face. "Does he do that often?" he asked.

"No," she said. "But he protects me in other ways."

"Like what?"

"Like letting me hide. Giving me a place to run when I need to disappear. Helping me stay invisible."

Matt's brows pulled together. "Why do you want to be invisible?"

"Because I'm dangerous, Matt," she said, voicing for the first time what she'd always known to be true. "I carry a monster inside of me. If it gets out, there's no telling what damage I could cause."

"That would be the monster," he corrected. "Not you."

"It can only do it *through* me," she reminded him. "Before you, I didn't have friends because I didn't want them. I was afraid of them. I choose to be invisible because I don't want anyone to know just how flawed I am."

Matt reached across the table, taking her hand. "You aren't flawed," he insisted.

Slowly, Cait slipped out of his grip, Desmond's words at the cove drifting through her head. *"He's got a crush on you, Cait."*

For the first time, Cait wondered if that was the real reason behind Matt's friendship. Did he stick around her because he wanted to date her? Was his loyalty nothing more than infatuation?

Hands tucked safely in her lap, Cait held Matt's caring stare. She couldn't help the smile that came to her lips. Whatever feelings he might have, she knew he was too genuine to be that fickle. His dedication was real. And he'd be her friend no matter if she returned his feelings or not.

With a sigh, Cait finally answered his kind words. "Maybe not," she said quietly. "But I am cursed. And there's nothing that can change that."

# Desmond

"So, I kinda need to tell you something," Brady said.

They sat in Desmond's room, the TV pulsing with an electric glow as they played a first-person shooter video game. Brady had come over after the meeting at the diner to catch him up, and he'd been the one to suggest the game. The two of them had always had their most serious conversations that way. There was something about the distraction of shooting random strangers online that made it all easier.

Brady told him about their conclusion that the Varons were at the heart of all their problems. He'd immediately questioned the theory, citing the attack on Lilith as a sign that Druids were still the most likely candidates. "I even tried to gauge Matt's reaction to it all," he'd said. "But the kid gave me nothing."

"Think I should say something to him?" Desmond asked.

"Like what? 'Hey, I know this might sound weird, but are you a Druid?'" Brady scoffed. "Pretty sure he'll tell you no."

"So, what? I just wait it out?"

"Until you find other evidence, yeah."

Reluctantly admitting that Brady had a point, Desmond let it go.

Then, Brady had walked him through Rese's weird appearance at the chapel the previous night. He was suspicious of Cait's older sister, and Desmond agreed. Neither of them could quite figure out why Rese would want to sneak into the reverend's office or what she'd be looking for in those books. Either way, it worried them both.

After all that, Desmond wasn't sure what else there was to say. Yet, Brady "kinda needed to tell him something" more?

Desmond got a double kill before being taken out himself. "You just spent an hour telling me things, Brade," he remarked as he waited to respawn. "What else could you possibly say?"

Brady hesitated. "I've sort of been keeping something from you."

Desmond gave Brady the side-eye. "'Kinda ... Sort of,'" he repeated. "Must be bad."

"Depends on your definition, I guess." Brady sniped Desmond in the game.

"You screen-peeked," he accused.

"Swear I didn't."

Desmond tapped his thumb on the controller handle. "What's such a big deal that you've been keeping it from me?"

"I wouldn't call it a big deal."

"What would you call it?"

Brady shrugged.

Desmond snuck up behind and assassinated Brady's character.

"*You* screen-peeked!" Brady glowered at him.

"Yep."

With a heavy sigh, he returned to the game. "So, you remember last Friday after the game?"

Desmond huffed. "Obviously."

"And you know how Ryan was a douche?"

"Always."

"And we laughed off everything he said because it was definitely all crap."

Desmond glanced at him. "Yes . . . ?"

Brady swallowed audibly. "It wasn't."

"What wasn't?"

"It wasn't all crap."

Desmond frowned. "Which part?"

Brady shot him in the game again. "The part about me having a thing for Rese."

Blankly, Desmond stared at the TV screen even after he respawned. A random online player killed off his stagnant character, but he didn't notice as he lowered the controller and turned to face his friend. "Excuse me?"

Brady kept playing, his jaw tight.

"Rese?" Desmond repeated. "As in, Therese Lewan? Cait's sister?"

"Yeah."

Desmond turned back to the TV. He stared blankly as his character died again. He pressed pause.

Then, he whirled on Brady. "Why?" he demanded. "Who in their right mind—like, I know she's hot, but come on, man. She's the shallowest, most self-centered, airheaded—"

"You don't know shit about her," Brady shot back, a fire in his glare that Desmond had never seen.

Immediately, Desmond fell silent. He took caution any time Brady deigned to cuss. But that glare—that was something almost frightening.

Brady tossed his controller onto the coffee table. "Look—" He ran a hand over his face. "She's not—I know this sounds weird, but I've watched her since, like, fifth grade. She acts shallow, yeah, but she's not. She's really smart. Did you know she got the best grades in her entire year?"

"How do you know that?"

"My aunt's the principal," he reminded. "She mentioned it at one of our family things last graduation."

"Oh." Desmond frowned. "Weird."

"Yeah." Brady picked at his fingernails. "Anyway, she would have been the valedictorian, but she expressly asked my aunt *not* to give her the title."

"Why not?"

"Because she's like you." He said it almost like an accusation.

Desmond jerked back like he'd been hit. "First of all, how dare you?" he declared. "And second, what's that supposed to mean?"

Brady tossed his hands in the air. "You're both idiots. Neither one of you trusts anyone enough to be yourselves. You're both insanely smart, yet you hide it by skipping school or pretending to be vapid. You both go out of your way to appear as though you don't care how people perceive you, yet you're always showing off. And you both pretend to be aloof and unattached when, in reality, you'd do anything to protect the people you love."

Desmond stared at him, disconcerted by these claims.

Slumping, Brady leaned into the couch, avoiding Desmond's glare. "Cait's your exception," he said. "Her—you do trust."

His manner was dejected as he concluded—a jealous honesty that revealed itself.

Desmond slapped the back of Brady's head.

"What the hell?"

"You think I don't trust you?" Desmond scoffed. "Dude, who's the one person I told about Cait and me?"

He deflated. "Yeah, well, that could have simply been you bragging."

"Oh, like, you didn't make out with Miranda at prom last year."

"That doesn't count," Brady objected. "She was on the rebound."

"Whatever." Desmond shifted to face him fully. "You should know better."

He mumbled something that sounded a lot like "I do" through a sigh. "Anyway," he tossed a hand through the air, "I just felt the need to come clean. That's all."

"For what reason?"

"What do you mean?"

"Why come clean?" Desmond said. "It's just a crush, right?"

Brady stared at his hands.

"Right?" he pressed.

"Kind of."

Desmond whacked the back of his head again.

Brady swore again, swatting him away. "Fine! No, it's not. It's an interest. Like a serious, I've-been-thinking-about-how-I'd-like-to-marry-her-for-the-past-six-years kind of thing."

There was only one response Desmond could formulate. "*Why?*"

His shoulders lifted in a half-assed shrug. "Because I think she deserves someone who sees her for who she truly is."

Desmond stared at his best friend, wondering how he'd never discovered this secret he'd held for so long. But he realized he'd been so caught up in his own secret love for a Lewan girl that there were probably dozens of other things he'd missed in Brady's life.

"You know, forget I said anything." Brady slouched into the cushions. "It isn't like it'll ever happen anyway."

"She's Cait's sister," he heard himself reply. He didn't know if the statement was positive or negative.

"I know."

Desmond considered the situation. His brow lifted as understanding dawned. A sly grin came to his lips. "You want me to get Cait to convince her to give you a shot."

"No." Brady crossed his arms. "I'm not stupid, okay? It isn't like she's gonna throw over Ryan for me."

Desmond shrugged. "I dunno. In the grand scheme of Porthaven social climbers, you're technically a bigger prize than a Greene, even if he does become a doctor by some miracle."

Brady pummeled him with a throw pillow. "Shut up. I didn't tell you so that you could make fun of me."

"No, you told me because you want to use my girlfriend to your advantage."

"That's not it either," Brady protested, a strange edge to his tone.

Suddenly, Desmond realized that Brady was serious. He'd orchestrated everything to make this confession easier. He'd been the one to suggest *Call of Duty*. He'd even brought over their traditional snacks of cool ranch Doritos and Dr. Pepper.

Everything was perfectly set up for a night of confession.

Grabbing Brady's controller, Desmond handed it back to him without a word. They both knew the truth would emerge more easily if they didn't have to face one another.

Once they entered another game and scored a couple of kills each, Brady spoke again. "I don't remember a day when you weren't my best friend," he said, the edge from before taking on clarity, turning definitively hard. "And yet, you waited ten years to tell me that someone else mattered more to you than I did."

Desmond's stomach twisted with guilt. "That's—she's—"

"She *should* matter more to you, Desmond." Brady shot two online gamers in succession. "I'm not upset that you found someone. I just hate that you felt like you couldn't tell me. But last night, when Rese showed up, I realized . . . I felt like I couldn't tell you the truth either. And I decided I didn't want it to be like that anymore."

Mute, they sat there for a long time after that confession, fighting strangers and considering how their lives had changed in only a few weeks. And through it all, Desmond found his guilt spreading, worming its way up his sternum and into his throat. He couldn't identify precisely where that guilt originated. He asked himself why he felt guilty at all. He hadn't exactly done anything shameful.

But the feeling grew, and Desmond stared at the TV with sightless eyes.

Was this what he'd become? All his rebellion and playacting—had it led him here, becoming a person even his best friend couldn't trust? And what about his future? If he kept down this path of lying and covering up to avoid personal disappointment, could he ever earn the respect of the people he hoped to lead? Or had he lost that privilege already?

"I think I screwed up, Brade," he muttered.

"What do you mean?"

He blinked, hands frozen on the controller. "My meeting with Jun—I think I might've ruined my dad's chances."

Brady paused the game to look over at him. "Why would you think that?"

"I lost my temper," he admitted, the shame vining through his ribcage. "And you know me. I'm at my finest when I get angry."

"So, you acted like a dick?"

"Yep."

Brady sighed. "Well, that's not ideal. But, I mean, the guy can't base his inquiry solely on you, can he? He's investigating your dad, not you."

Desmond ran a hand through his hair, flopping back against the couch. "Even if you're right—even if my dad keeps his job—it won't fix the damage I've done. It won't change the fact that everyone in this town thinks I'm an arrogant prick. It won't change that no one trusts me." He scoffed, staring at his hands still locked on the controller. "Not even my best friend."

"Don't be melodramatic," Brady said lightly.

Desmond looked over, surprised to find his friend smirking.

"I wouldn't have told you all this if I didn't trust you." He shrugged. "Fact is, you have blackmail on me now."

Hearing the encouragement in his words, Desmond took hope in them. "I've always had blackmail on you." He nudged Brady's arm. "Now, shut up. We've got some gamers to kill."

They returned to their game, suddenly back to their usual quips and light chatter. And the air between them eased. Perhaps Desmond had a lot of making up to do, but with Brady and Cait at his side, he thought he had all the strength and support he'd need to do it.

~

"Desmond," Julia, one of the clerk's office workers, waved her phone in the air, "your dad's on the line."

He rose from his desk to cross the floor to the woman's cubicle. Since he did simple filing and data entry, he hadn't been given a work phone, which was fine with him. He didn't want to field random questions or pass messages anyway. He had seven months remaining of his high school career, during which he'd have to continue his internship. Then, he'd be free from government work.

At least until he was done with college.

Taking the phone from Julia with a polite "thanks," Desmond held it up to his ear. "Dad?"

"Jun's called a meeting," William said, tension in his voice.

Though Desmond was growing used to that tone, it caused him to tense as well. "What, just randomly? He say why?"

"He's completed his inquiry."

Cold dread tingled over his scalp and down his back. "I thought we had until tomorrow," he said.

William's voice came out flat and emotionless as he replied, "Jun said he didn't see a reason to wait."

Desmond glanced at Julia, hoping she couldn't read his discomfort. "Okay. How soon?"

"Immediately."

That caused his heart to stutter.

"All right," he said, working to keep his voice even and steady. "I'll be there."

He returned the phone to Julia and clocked out before heading out the door. The hall to the meeting room was short, a quick left turn and a minute's jaunt, and he was there. When he opened the double doors, he found nearly all the other Warden members cluttering the room.

The men milled about, some of them grumbling while others chatted languidly. Jun stood conspicuously by William's empty seat. He watched Desmond as he entered, the analyst's expression blank.

Desmond moved into the room, joining Fish and Ben. They all muttered greetings, but Desmond couldn't find it in him to keep up small talk. Not when his future was about to be decided.

As Fish and Ben spoke together casually, Desmond scanned the room. While Brett Varon and his brother, Kyle, were jovially chatting away, Kenneth Greene stroked a hand along his jaw. He didn't look particularly happy to be there, some unreadable emotion drawing his light eyebrows together. At the doctor's side, Ryan stared at his phone, tapping away at the screen.

The Lavignes each bore differing levels of interest and nervousness. While Fish was attentive yet calm, none of his sons appeared concerned by this impromptu meeting. Ben drifted over to take a seat by his father, Gary, the two speaking in hushed voices. Gary kept running a hand over his brow. Desmond's uncles, Rick and Raymond, laughed as they snacked on some doughnuts from the center of the table.

The doors opened one final time, announcing William's entrance. He stepped into the room with a fierce, commanding presence, his shoulders back and square jawline firm. His black suit emphasized his broad frame. The entirety of his demeanor sent a firm message: William Simon would not be bullied into submission.

His dark eyes met Desmond's before he addressed the group. "Afternoon, gentlemen." He strode to his chair. "I appreciate your flexibility."

"It isn't like *you* called this meeting, William," Brett said.

That implacable expression met Brett's inspection like a cliff meeting a wave. "You're right," the mayor replied, deep voice undaunted. "I didn't."

With that, William looked over the rest of the men. "Shall we sit?"

Impressed by his dad's courage, Desmond took a seat between his uncles, trying to calm his fear. His lungs filled with tension, making it hard to breathe. He tried to tell himself that it would be okay. Whatever Jun threw at them, it wouldn't matter. If his inquiry deemed William unfit for leadership, it wouldn't change that the Simons were the true Varons. They would still bear the most power, the most authority. And they could still save Cait.

But that didn't make breathing any easier.

William turned the meeting over to Jun. The Warden agent remained standing as though conducting a seminar. He held his hands clasped in front of him, as cool and collected as ever. "This morning, while reviewing my notes, I found that I have all the information I need to conclude my inquiry," he began in his characteristically flat tone. "After observing Mayor Simon at work, seeing his dedication to the job and his people, and watching as he went about his days without attempting to impress me . . . I questioned the reason for my assignment here at all. The situation with the Veil was resolved by Mayor Simon and his son before I even arrived. The death of George Faulk appears to be of no significance beyond old age and the physical wear of a block. Any allegations of questionable activity proved quite baseless."

Eyes flashing to his dad, Desmond felt hope spread through his heart.

"Furthermore," Jun continued, "I met with Mr. Desmond Simon to assess the claims against him. I'd been told he was impulsive, arrogant, and negligent."

Desmond flinched.

"I wanted to test the young man for myself," Jun admitted. "I directly insulted him to see if I could bait the narcissist I'd been warned of. He rose to my challenge with a cutting remark and an unflinching dedication to his family. As we'd expect of any member of the Varon bloodline."

Light chuckles passed across the table, but Desmond was locked on Jun's words. "Yes, there appears to be some maturing for Mr. Simon to do and some faith he needs to earn from his peers and elders," the agent remarked. "But coming away from that meeting, I concluded that this Varon heir has the strength and fortitude to do that work.

"Essentially," Jun concluded, "I was impressed by both father and son. And as I reviewed my notes, I was assured that they'd make some of the most devoted leaders in the Warden at large."

A sudden well broke apart in Desmond's chest. He white-knuckled the arms of his chair to keep the relief from filling his eyes with tears. He hadn't damaged his dad's chances. By some miracle, he'd earned the Warden agent's respect.

"However—"

That singular conditional word made Desmond's heart stutter.

"Shortly after my decision was made, I received a phone call," Jun said, his ever-stoic expression in place. "Mr. Varon, I'll give you the floor."

Brett stood, a steady smile on his face, and Desmond's heart stopped altogether in cold dread.

"Thank you, Mr. Jun," Brett said, then faced the rest of the Warden men. "I'll keep this brief." He wore a look of righteous indignation on his face as he met Desmond's glare. "Mr. Simon has been lying to us."

For a moment, Desmond felt as though the world paused. A tremor worked through his muscles, and he could feel every regret from the past decade of his life as though experiencing them for the first time.

It was over.

"What are you talking about, Brett?" Fish demanded.

"Oh, you're involved in this, too, Fischer," Brett said, umbrage hardening his tone. "Contrary to what you reported, Desmond didn't seal the Veil when you acted as his escort. He and William lied about that. *You* lied about that."

Fish leaned back in his seat, thoroughly rebuked.

The Warden council sat in silence, waiting for the truth to unfold.

Brett relished his captive audience. "While I don't have all the details, this is evidently not the only lie they fed us. Did you know that William is searching for a second Veil?"

A discontented rumble swept across the room.

"I didn't." Brett motioned to William. "He didn't care to warn us that we might have a second breach within our borders. Like his son, he took it upon himself to try to 'save' us. All the while, these two have been breaking our rules, wielding when we've all agreed that that responsibility lay solely in the hands of the Lavignes."

Rick rested an elbow on the table, pointing accusingly at Brett. "You'd better have proof to back this up."

"You think I'd bring this before the council without adequate evidence?"

Pressure built behind Desmond's eyes, heat climbing up his back and burning into his skull. Several grumbles rose in the room, but his head was beginning to spin as he tried to figure out how Brett had discovered their fabrications.

"Over the last couple of weeks," Brett continued, "my son has developed a friendship with Caitriona Lewan."

Desmond's body went numb.

"And she admitted to him that *she* is the one who sealed the Veil."

His pulse thumped wildly in his ears.

"What's more, she admitted to being the Vessel."

The room was filled with a whirl of sound, nearly drowning out Brett's voice, and Desmond realized it was the pounding of his own heart.

"She's dreaming of beasts and the Veil. Her block is failing."

Somehow, Desmond gained enough control to meet his dad's defeated stare.

"And this whole time, both William and Desmond knew."

At that, the meeting devolved into outrage. Desmond was fairly certain he saw Fish drop his head into his hands. He couldn't really be sure. White noise blurred his senses as fury burned in his chest.

He'd kill Hunter.

Questions flew around the room like seagulls attacking crumbs. They droned around Desmond. He couldn't process a word they said. He just sat there, stone-faced and devoid of any feeling but anger.

William held Desmond's deadened, hazy glare. He could feel the apology in his dad's heavy brow and turned-down lips. The hopelessness he found in his expression haunted him.

The deep monotone of Jun's voice drew Desmond back to the present. He looked toward the man, surprised to find regret etched in the slant of his eyes. The only emotion he'd displayed thus far.

"Due to the information Mr. Varon brought to my attention," Jun was saying, "I cannot in good conscience recommend that Mayor Simon keep his position as the head of the Warden. On behalf of Sheraton Corporation, Mayor Simon, your title as Municipality Supervisor is hereby revoked. I will stay in Porthaven for the next three months to facilitate the transfer of leadership to another member of the Corporation's choosing."

Jun kept talking, giving directives, and speaking of logistics, and Desmond checked out again. Blankly, he looked around the table. Men he'd known his whole life stared at him with anger, disgust, and, worst of all, pity. As though he were a child who'd lost his way. A prodigal who needed reformation. A degenerate who'd ruined his dad's good standing.

"Mr. Simon," Jun called.

Desmond blinked, realizing it was the third time he'd been addressed. "What?" he asked stonily.

"Do you have anything you'd like to say?"

With one final scan of the men around him, Desmond wondered if there *was* anything he could say. He could proffer their theory about the Varons. He could tell them that all of this was a setup. He could admit that everything he'd done, every action he'd taken, it had all been out of his love for Cait. Would they listen to him? Would they care to hear his side of the story? Would they believe him?

Brett rested back in his seat, sure of his victory. Kenneth Greene frowned at his hands, clasped on the table. Ryan smirked knowingly at his father's side. And Desmond knew they wouldn't listen. They'd been planning this for months. Maybe even years.

And his irreverent, rebellious behavior had given them all the evidence they'd needed.

With a scoff, Desmond stood. He scanned the entire table, leveling his fiercest glare at the ones he knew were involved. He drew in a breath, the council members drawing up to hear his words.

Infusing every ounce of fury he possessed into his voice, he held Brett's gaze. "You can all go to hell," he said.

Then, he swiftly left the room.

# CHAPTER THIRTY-THREE

# Desmond

Over the next several hours, Desmond grew increasingly numb. Once he'd left the council meeting, he'd driven around Porthaven, eventually winding up at the old factory. Seething, he sat silently in his car until his stoicism finally gave way under the crashing waves of his emotions. He wasn't sure how long he'd screamed and railed. His eyes burned, and at last, he couldn't fight the tears.

He'd tried so hard. Over the eighteen years of his life, he'd tried so damn hard to be perfect, to live up to the expectations of his parents, his peers, and the Warden. Every rebellion and misdeed had only been to cover just how desperately he wanted their respect. He fought to hold in all the fear, to stave off all the doubt, to prove himself to be above it all.

And he'd still failed to save her.

Desmond didn't know how long they had until the Warden made their move. With his dad's dismissal, there would be other, more pressing arrangements to be made. But they knew Cait was the Vessel now. They'd want to ensure their control of her.

Worse, Cait's birthday was next week. She'd be eighteen in a matter of six days, an adult in the eyes of the law and the Warden.

They had six days at the most.

Six days to prepare.

Because once she came of age, the Warden would follow protocol to the letter.

The sky turned black by the time Desmond fell back into apathy. He stared into the darkness, slowly caging his rage. His face was still stained by tears, and his hands hurt from how long he'd held them curled into fists. But finally, he descended into the cold numbness of detachment that frequently protected him from how much he felt.

Desmond glanced at the clock. It was already past nine. It was a school night. Usually, his dad would be pissed if he didn't make it home by ten. Tonight, he didn't think it would matter.

Climbing out of his car, Desmond walked into the woods. He didn't know how long it would take, but he knew that if he kept walking a straight path, eventually, he'd run into Cait's neighborhood. The frigid October night wormed its way into his bones, the black sky oppressive above him. He didn't bother to summon Hades. He wanted to be alone with his emptiness.

When Desmond arrived at the edge of Sinker Street, he slipped again into the woods, winding his way around to the back of Cait's house. He sat in the darkness, watching her window. The yellow light of her bedside lamp glowed softly. He waited until she appeared, silhouetted as she closed her curtains.

Desmond considered turning back then. Wouldn't it be kinder to leave her in ignorance for as long as possible? Why ruin what little time of freedom she had left? He had no alternatives to offer her, no solutions that could fix the problems he'd created.

No. Desmond wouldn't let his selfishness get the better of him. She deserved to know, and he wouldn't keep this from her to mitigate his own pain.

Desmond snuck across the backyard to the large tree. He climbed it easily, carefully working his way onto the roof and to her window. Her sister's light wasn't on in the room next to Cait's, but that didn't mean she wasn't home.

Before he could even knock on the panes, the curtain lifted, and Cait peered out at him. His heart almost broke at her bright smile. She shouldn't be happy to see him. Yet, the instant she opened the casement window to let him in, he felt a sudden surge of desperation.

Desmond nearly tumbled off the window seat as he rushed into the room. The moment his feet hit the floor, his arms locked around her, crushing her to him. He buried his face in her neck and breathed in the relief of her nearness. She smelled like the softest flowers, sunshine, and salty air. And he wanted to hold her forever.

Her hands rested soothingly on his back, her embrace filling him with an overwhelming mix of comfort and sorrow. "What are you doing here?" she whispered, her breath tickling his ear.

Not ready to admit the full truth yet, he murmured part of it into her hair. "I just needed to see you."

Cait relaxed into his embrace. They stood there for untold minutes, holding one another. He began to count her inhales and exhales, cherishing each one as her chest expanded and contracted in his arms. He relished every second he had left with her.

Eventually, Cait's grip loosened. Desmond reluctantly pulled back as she extricated herself from him. "You know you can't stay, right?" she said, affection in her blue-gray eyes.

Mutely, he nodded. His lungs were too tight to speak.

Cait twisted her fingers in the oversized graphic tee that hung around her bare thighs.

The image jolted him out of reality, and he drew in a sharp breath. "Are you—" He cleared his throat around the hoarseness of his voice and gestured toward her. "Are you not wearing pants?"

"What? Oh—" She looked down and laughed nervously. Then, she lifted the hem of her shirt, revealing small, pin-striped shorts. "Yeah, sorry. I wasn't expecting you, or I would have covered up more."

Desmond pursed his lips. "Remind me not to ever let you know when I'm coming by."

She grinned even as she tried to appear reproachful.

A thought struck him. "How *did* you know I was out there?" he asked, motioning to the roof. "Did I make that much noise?"

Cait's eyes widened for a fraction of a second before she shook her head. "You were perfectly quiet."

"So . . . you just happened to look out the window?"

She bit her lip. "I kind of—I just—" She floundered for a few more seconds before shrugging. "I could feel that you were there."

Desmond considered that. The pause as she struggled to come up with an answer told him that she wasn't telling the whole truth. But as he'd done the same to her moments ago, he decided to let her keep her secrets.

He reached across to tug on her shirt. "You just have a sixth sense for me, huh?"

"Something like that," she muttered.

He stepped closer. "I like it."

Cait's breaths came out in small puffs of anticipation. "You should probably go."

Desmond rested his hand on her hip. "I have to talk to you first," he said, unable to stop staring at her mouth.

"Then, you probably shouldn't touch me," she whispered.

"You're probably right."

She began to move away, but he caught her hand.

Desmond forced himself to ignore every desire he felt. Slowly, he donned the numbness once more, pulling it over his shoulders like a jacket. No more feelings, just plain facts.

"Sit with me?" he asked.

Watching him curiously, Cait allowed him to draw her onto the window seat beside him. He threaded their fingers, allowing himself this one tie to emotion. She would be his anchor, keeping his words gentle as he spoke the truth, throwing them into the storm-tossed sea of the future.

A thin beam of moonlight fell onto the side of Cait's face, a contrast of silver in the dim golden light of her room. Her icy gaze held steadily with his. Her expression was placid, calmly waiting for him to speak.

Waiting for him as he prepared to destroy her life.

Unable to face her, he stared at her knees on the light blue bench, her legs curled up beneath her. "They know," he said vacantly. "The Warden knows."

Her fingers flinched around his.

"Hunter told them."

A painful second passed before Cait's voice came out in a broken whisper. "Why?"

"I don't know."

Desmond gathered up all his bravery then and met her tear-filled gaze. It broke his heart to see the first drop fall. He reached over to cup her cheek, brushing the tear away with his thumb. "I'm so sorry, Caity," he whispered. "It's my fault."

"How could it be your fault?" The question was hollow.

A thousand reasons flew through his head. He settled on the only one that mattered.

"I couldn't save you."

She gripped his hand, which still held her face. Her eyes closed as though savoring his touch. "I never expected you to," she whispered.

That hurt almost more than if she'd yelled at him.

He drew her closer, pressing his forehead to hers. "I *wanted* to."

They sat frozen, too frightened to pull apart, knowing what they'd face when they did. All their disappointment and pain bound them together. It felt as though their physical contact could translate every unspoken word between them.

But eventually, they had to let one another go.

Cait released him first, shifting back on the seat and moving away from his touch. "What happens now?" she asked, voice devoid of emotion.

Knowing she'd donned the same protective numbness he wore, Desmond spoke with brutal honesty. "They'll probably show up in the next few days," he said, staring at his hands in his lap. "First, they'll check on your block. They'll try to tighten it and probably fail. Then, they'll research how to fix it, and once they figure that out, they'll come back. The block will eventually cause damage to your brain, and you'll probably wind up with severe dementia in your sixties."

He looked up, checking to gauge the impact of his words. Tears freely flowed down her cheeks, but she sat silent and devoid of expression.

Voice catching on the thickness in his throat, Desmond held her gaze as he continued, "As soon as you turn eighteen, they'll begin making plans for after graduation. You'll be required—" He stumbled then, struggling to voice what he'd feared for the last ten years.

"You'll be required to choose a husband from a pre-approved list of candidates," he gathered the courage to explain. "There's a chance someone from Porthaven will volunteer, but as the only single men under the age of thirty include Ryan Greene, Dustin Edgars, Brady, Garrett, Hunter, Scott, and myself..."

He paused, seeing the blankness in her stare.

His words were hollow when he said, "I wouldn't count on that."

She didn't ask why he wouldn't volunteer, and that cut him more deeply than he thought it should.

He answered the unspoken question anyway. "After what's happened—now that they know that I knew about you and lied—they wouldn't accept me as an option."

Her chin dipped in silent understanding.

Desmond hesitated, a painful solution in his mind. "I could probably talk Brady into it—"

Her grimace brought an end to the idea.

"Which means that your choices will be men from other Warden towns," he said. "They'll let you choose two or three to bring here so you can meet them first. But they'll want it all decided within a month. Whoever you pick will move here so you can get to know one another, but they won't make you get married until after you graduate. After that, they'll require that you have a kid, then do whatever surgery is necessary to be sure you don't have any more than that."

As she showed no sign of a response, Desmond concluded his report. "And you'll live the rest of your life in Porthaven however you wish."

A long, excruciating silence stretched between them. Cait blinked, staring out the window into the darkness. And Desmond stared at her.

He hated everything about the situation. For his entire life, he'd disliked the Warden's procedure for the Vessels. He'd always thought the life they forced on the Faulks was wrong. But it hadn't ever really meant anything to him until he met Cait. Until he fell in love with her.

That word had started creeping up in Desmond's thoughts over the last few days: Love.

He loved Cait. He'd known it for a long time now. He was just finally admitting it to himself.

He loved her, and he was going to lose her.

"I turn eighteen on Wednesday," Cait mumbled.

"I know."

"This will all start in less than a week."

"Like I said," Desmond murmured, the words cracking, "they'll probably come sooner than that."

Cait finally looked at him. The lamplight had turned menacing on her pale skin, almost acrid in its yellow hue. "Thank you for telling me," she whispered.

He didn't have anything he could say.

A disheartened sigh escaped Cait. Then, her fingers found his once more. "I'm grateful," she said. "Even if it couldn't be forever, I'm grateful we had what time we could."

That was the worst thing she could have said. It ripped through Desmond's chest like a wolf's teeth as it tore through sinew and bone. She'd relegated them to the past. But he wasn't done with her yet.

Desmond didn't care if it would hurt more tomorrow or if it would prolong their pain tonight; he leaned across the bench and kissed her. He kissed her with every emotion tied up in his chest, with every feeling he'd hidden over the past ten years, with every passion he'd denied, and with every promise he'd ever wanted to give her.

Cait's arms wound around his neck, returning his fervency. He could feel all her secret dreams for them, all her constancy through the years, all she'd wished they could be, and all she'd never dared to say bound up between them.

And he was suddenly aware of how dangerous those feelings were.

This was the end of them. They both knew it now.

Well, he determined, he would hold onto this final moment for as long as it would last.

Throwing what little caution he had left to the wind, Desmond slipped an arm under her legs and tugged, drawing her to half lean, half lie on the bench. When she wound her fingers around his jacket collar to keep him close, he knew she'd decided to let go of reason as well. They lingered in long, intimate kisses they never should have shared. Their hands traveled carelessly where they never should have wandered. And Desmond whispered the one thing he never should have confessed.

"I love you."

Cait sucked in a sharp breath as he kissed her again. Then, she set a hand on his chest and pushed. "What?" she gasped.

Hovering over her in their tangled embrace on the window seat, Desmond stared into her attentive blue-gray eyes. They made him think of the sea at the cove.

He brushed some of her silver-blonde hair from her cheek. "I love you," he repeated, surprisingly not embarrassed to say such a vulnerable, cliché thing.

Joy and heartbreak played across Cait's face.

"I know it's horrible of me to say that," he admitted. "It's selfish. I shouldn't let you know how impossible it is for me to accept that this is it. I shouldn't say how desperately I refuse to let you go. I shouldn't tell you that if I could do anything—"

He pressed his palm to her cheek. "Absolutely *anything* in this world . . . I'd marry you."

Cait gripped his arm, but she didn't speak, and she didn't stop him.

Desmond smiled, brushing his thumb over her lips. "I'd spend the rest of my life kissing you until you forgot every terrible thing you've had to endure."

She closed her eyes, leaning into his touch.

So, he closed his eyes, too, resting his head on hers. "I shouldn't tell you that," he whispered. "Because it'd be easier for you to forget me—to forget us—if you thought I didn't care at all."

Cait didn't say anything. She didn't have to. She just wrapped herself tighter in his arms, both of them soaking in their last few moments together.

Shifting on the bench, Desmond curled up beside her, holding her close. He found himself planting small, almost comforting kisses along her temple, cheek, and jaw. If he was about to lose her to some other man, if he had to abandon her to someone who didn't and *couldn't* love her the way he did, then he'd let himself love her as long as their lives would allow.

She deserved that much. If she couldn't have a husband who'd chosen her because of his undying love, then he'd do what he could to make her feel cherished, if only for a moment.

"Des," she whispered.

"Hm?"

Cait wove her fingers through his, their hands floating in the air above them. "I love you too."

He pressed his lips to her silky hair. "I know."

They lay there a long time, their fingers running back and forth along each other's, enjoying the temporary closeness. Her skin was as smooth as a pearl, nearly as pale as one too. He'd always like that about her. It made her feel precious and rare. Like the gemstone itself, built into a strong, beautiful thing from the pressure enforced upon it.

Would any of the men on the Warden's list feel that way about her? Would any of them figure out how wonderful and impressive she was? He didn't think he could watch her resign herself to anything less. What would he do if the man she chose didn't love her well?

Unsolicited, Brady's words from weeks ago whispered in his memory.

*"There is another option,"* he'd said.

Desmond remembered being confused by his friend's suggestion and further baffled when he said, *"You could marry her before anyone else got the chance."*

But now, the idea didn't sound so stupid.

Looking down at Cait, her eyes heavy as she stared at their hands twisted together, Desmond smiled. "You should go to bed," he told her.

"I don't want to," she whispered back.

"You're going to fall asleep eventually."

A sleepy grin brightened her face. "No. I'll stay awake with you forever."

He tightened his fingers around hers. "Because I'm that wonderful?"

"Because I don't want to let you go."

That decided it.

"You won't have to," he promised.

"Des—"

He took her face in both of his hands. "Trust me, Caity. I'm going to find a way."

Doubt filled Cait's eyes, but she nodded.

Desmond kissed her one last time. Then, he forced her to sit up with him. They parted reluctantly, but soon he was back out in the cold. He'd been there longer than planned. But after their confession of love, he walked through the woods with a renewed determination.

He was going to marry Cait.

He just had to figure out how.

# William

William stared at the whiskey tumbler on his desk. He'd skipped dinner, coming into his office and pouring two fingers of the liquor, intending on dulling the inner voice of his father's disapproval. However, the glass remained untouched, his thoughts stuck on the same line, repeated in his head over and over.

*"You're soft, William. You'll lose our inheritance if you don't toughen up."*

Those were the last words Charles Simon had ever said to him. As he lay on his deathbed mere months ago, he'd scowled at his son, calling him a failure. *"You'll lose our inheritance,"* he'd kept saying.

And he was right.

William cleared his throat, attempting to clear the emotion caught there. He held the Varon signet in his hand, the gold ring biting into his closed fist. His father was right, and now he'd lost their place at the Warden's head.

A soft knock rapped on the open door of his home office. Robin stood in the doorway, her expression thoughtful. "You know," she said, her keen eyes falling on the untouched whiskey glass, "my dad always said I was better at deduction than Rick. Something to do with womanly intuition making me a natural cop."

Looking up at his wife, William couldn't fight the small smile that crept onto his lips. "It's one of your most alluring traits," he replied.

Robin laughed and moved into the dimly lit room. The faint golden lamplight made her honey-brown hair shimmer as she stepped up to the desk. She'd always had a striking beauty, and even in her forties, she was still one of the most attractive women he'd ever seen.

Taking a seat on the desk, Robin picked up the tumbler. She jiggled it, making the whiskey swirl. "You've been brooding for the last five hours," she noted. "Explain."

William drew in a deep breath. He'd intentionally kept the meeting's results to himself. He wanted more time to process it, to deal with the knowledge that he'd ruined everything before he came clean to Robin. But he refused to lie to her, even if it hurt to face the truth.

"Effective this afternoon," he said, holding her bright blue gaze, "I'm no longer the leader of the Warden in Porthaven."

Robin stared at him for several seconds. Then, she sighed and knocked back the whole glass of whiskey. "What happened?" she demanded.

"I was caught in a lie."

"How bad of a lie?"

William tilted his head in response.

"That bad, huh?" Robin set the tumbler on the desk. "Care to tell me what it was?"

"There were several," he admitted. "Most importantly, I knew which Lewan girl is the Vessel, and I didn't tell anyone."

Robin's eyebrows drew together in disbelief. "*That's* enough to fire someone?"

"You know how important Vessels are, Robin," he said. "Amongst my other lies, I would have fired myself."

"Then, why did you lie in the first place?"

William dropped his gaze to the desk. "For Desmond."

Robin drew her shoulders back. "What does he have to do with this?"

Holding the Varon ring between his fingers, William considered whether to keep his son's secrets. After everything, though, he thought Robin deserved to know. "He's in love with her," he stated blankly.

"The Vessel?" she said.

He nodded, still staring at the ring.

Robin huffed. "Caitriona."

He looked up then.

With a sweep of her hand, she dismissed his surprise. "He brought her over last week to study. Which, astoundingly, actually meant studying. But it wasn't hard to figure out how he felt about her," she said. "Our son is frighteningly obvious when he's trying to play it cool."

A humorless smirk came to his lips. "He comes by it honestly," he said, remembering how poorly he'd hidden his interest in Robin all those years ago.

"So, she's the Vessel?" Robin prompted.

"She is."

"And how does she feel about him?"

William raised his brow. "I haven't exactly asked her."

"But we can surmise that they're involved," Robin said. "After all, he was an hour and a half late to his birthday dinner due to 'dropping her off.'"

"From what I understand, that's a recent development."

That caused Robin's eyes to widen. "Wait, is . . . is he talking to you about this?"

"Yes."

"How'd you manage to get him to do that?"

William grinned wryly at her shock. "I told him I'd help him save her."

Robin frowned. "Does she need saving?"

"If he wants to be with her, then yes." William sighed. "And now, it's even more important. If we can't find a way to remove the spirit-being from its tether to her, then they can't . . ."

"William," she said as his words trailed off. "Are you telling me our son wants to marry this girl?"

"Maybe not today, but ultimately, I believe that's his hope."

Robin's lips parted in something between awe and compassion. "He's *actually* in love with her?"

He just nodded.

Robin held the whiskey glass back out to him. "I'm gonna need another of these," she said.

He smirked and picked up the bottle resting on his desk.

"So, without you as the Warden leader, that means Desmond's no longer in line to lead either," she surmised as he poured the liquor.

"Correct."

"But wouldn't that make him a better candidate to marry her? If he doesn't have to lead, then it wouldn't matter if their children were potential Vessels."

William shook his head. "First, they'd only be allowed one child. Second, they would never approve of Desmond as a viable spouse because *he* lied as well. Besides, he's the Varon heir," he concluded, lifting the ring. "They wouldn't want a true Varon and a Vessel together. That's too unpredictable, too powerful."

Robin's eyes darted to the gold signet. "They can't take that title from you, can they?"

"True Varon?" William shook his head. "It's a birthright, not a job description. No one can fire you from your family."

"Then, the Varons still have to listen to the Simons?"

"Technically," he confirmed. "But I don't believe they will."

"They don't have a choice," Robin said sharply. "You're the true Varon. You are their ultimate leader. Whether they like it or not, that's a fact. *You* carry the power of the Varons. They can't take that from you."

William supposed she was right, but that didn't change the problem at hand. "I was fired," he reminded her. "I'm no longer in charge of what happens in Porthaven."

"Bullshit," she quipped with a smirk.

He raised his chin at the uncharacteristic expletive.

Robin pointed at his chest. "You're the true Varon. And you're still the mayor, aren't you? You may not run the Warden here any longer, but you still run this town. And you will show them that they made a mistake replacing you. You've dedicated your entire life to protecting this town. You won't stop now."

Holding his wife's fierce gaze, hearing the conviction in her words, William found himself filled with unquenchable hope. She was right. Jun had removed him from his position as the leader of the Warden, but he couldn't take his job as mayor. Not until his term was over, at least.

So, William would take what time he had left in office to prove his worthiness for the job.

"Do you know," he said, smiling at her, "you're the most impressive woman I've ever met?"

Robin smirked. "Hyperbole isn't flattering, dear."

"How's this, then?" He leaned forward, taking her hand. "I love you. And I'm a better man because of you."

She winked at him, a sly glint in her eyes. "That's pretty good."

"Yeah?"

"Mm-hm. I'd almost consider marrying you after that," she teased.

These moments were what he'd always liked best about their relationship. Before Robin, his life had been fraught with demand and responsibility. His wife lightened his heart and made him feel loved just as he was.

Lacing their fingers together, William rose to lean closer. "Any way I could improve my odds?"

"Gross," Desmond deadpanned, drawing their attention to the doorway.

Robin laughed, and William straightened as they turned to look at their son. William glanced at the clock. "It's past curfew," he noted.

"So, ground me again," Desmond retorted.

William didn't rise to his snark. "Did you need something?"

Desmond glanced at his mom, then nodded. "It's kind of . . . sensitive," he said.

"Warden sensitive?" Robin asked, lifting her brow with a knowing look. "Or girlfriend sensitive?"

He blinked, nervously scanning her. "The, uh—the second one."

"Mm." Robin leaned over, kissed William quickly, and moved for the door. She patted Desmond's cheek teasingly. "I like her," she said. "She seems sweet."

Desmond kept his head down, shifting awkwardly on his feet. Robin slipped through the door, closing it behind her, leaving father and son alone.

"What is it?" William asked.

Desmond crossed the office to stand before his desk. "I've made a decision," he said, dark eyes steadily holding William's. "And I need your help."

With a swift assessment of his son's seriousness, William took a deep breath. Whatever this decision was, he expected it would require more lies. "Go on," he instructed.

Hands clasped before him, Desmond was clearly trying not to fidget. "Cait turns eighteen next Wednesday," he said.

Memory refreshed, William nodded. The date was on his Warden calendar. "Yes, and . . . ?"

Desmond swallowed, then continued in an even voice, "I want to marry her."

Surprised at how unsurprised he was by the announcement, William sat down slowly. He slipped the Varon ring back onto his right ring finger.

"Due to our situation," he said, "I assume that means you want to marry her without the Warden's knowledge and before they can begin the process of marrying her to someone else."

"That's exactly what I mean."

"And how do you intend to pull this off?"

Desmond opened his mouth but only grimaced. "I'm not sure."

William pressed his lips together around a smile. "And that's why you're coming to me?"

"Pretty much."

"Mm-hm." William picked up the whiskey glass his wife had left behind. He took a sip, letting the amber liquid warm his chest. "All right."

Desmond gaped at him. "Yeah?"

William nodded. "Yeah."

"Just like that?" Desmond said. "I don't need to convince you? Or tell you why I think getting married while I'm still in high school isn't an insane idea. You're just cool with it?"

"I can't say I'm 'cool' with it," William replied. "If you want me to play devil's advocate, then sure, getting married while you're in high school isn't great. You don't have a job. You can't afford a ring, let alone a house. You just lost your future job, thanks to me. And the Warden will consider it a power move when they find out. If you have children, they're going to be Vessels unless we figure out a way to remove the spirit-being from your future wife, which is impossible by all accounts. And . . ."

William paused, noting the wide-eyed, overwhelmed expression on Desmond's face.

With a smile, William set his hands on the desk. "And you have no idea what the future holds," he concluded. "But if you know this is the woman you want to face that future with, then forget all that."

"She is," Desmond said quietly. "I can't let her go."

"Then, I'll help you marry her."

If his son had come to him at any other time, on any other day, William might have balked at the idea. He might have used all those excuses and helped Desmond see that marriage wasn't the answer. Their futures would be too fraught with difficulty for it to be the right choice. But in the wake of losing everything, William realized what really mattered. Having Robin by his side—having a wife who made him a better man—was more important than anything. And if he could help his son find that same happiness, if he could keep him from losing the woman who could make him the best man possible, he would do whatever it took to make it happen.

A cautious smile brightened Desmond's face even as he continued to fidget. "Okay, cool. Uh, so how do we do this?"

William chuckled, pushing the whiskey glass across to him. "First, calm down," he instructed. "Your anxiety isn't going to help anything."

"The Warden is about to take my wife away from me," Desmond said, ignoring the liquor. "I think I have a reason to be anxious."

"She isn't your wife yet," William reminded.

Desmond frowned in response.

William waved off his nerves. "I'm going to call Ben," he said. "I'll bring him up to speed, and we'll get everything set in place. By next weekend, you'll be married."

"Her birthday is Wednesday," Desmond repeated. "Why don't we just do it then?"

"That's fine," he promised. "Now, sit down. We have some details to figure out."

# CHAPTER THIRTY-FIVE

# Cait

She wanted to believe Desmond. But even though he'd promised to find a way for them to be together, she knew there wasn't one. The Warden knew her secret, the block was breaking, and her dreams were getting worse.

For years, Cait had woken in the middle of the night, gasping and desperate for air after choking on the smoke in her dreams. Since Desmond had started showing up in them, she woke with tears on her face, her lungs burning, and her throat tight. Once the dream shifted to the tree, she'd startled awake as though struck by lightning, an ache in her limbs and a sneaking suspicion that she was missing something. Then, the strange flash and the sense of power brought her to consciousness with a tingle on her skin and lungs full of air as though about to speak.

Those reactions would be disconcerting enough on their own. But worse, even in the daylight, she couldn't shake the image of Desmond being torn from her, dragged away in the sea by the tendrilled monster.

The image felt like an omen, as though her dreams were reminding her that he wasn't hers and never would be.

Still, something strange had happened to Cait when Desmond told her that he loved her.

When she rose the next morning, she felt an unexpected sense of acceptance. She knew the truth of her condition now. She was the Vessel for the Wolf, the Warden was preparing to come for her, and her time with Desmond was up. Yet, it was as though she didn't care anymore. She knew Hunter had betrayed her to the Warden, but she couldn't find it in herself to be angry with him. Whatever his reasons for outing her, this had always been her fate. But she had Desmond's love. Even if she lost him, she could face anything knowing that he loved her.

So, Cait kept the betrayal to herself. She let Matt and Genni believe nothing was wrong, going through the school day like she always would. She didn't treat Hunter differently, even when she noticed him staring at her nervously throughout the morning. She smiled at him as she did the rest of her friends because Cait saw no point in losing the only friends she'd ever had to his bad choice.

After all, she'd probably lose them next week anyway, when the Warden began the process of securing her as an official Vessel. Why speed up that loss? Why not enjoy the last week of freedom and happiness she would ever have?

Cait had relegated herself to carrying this curse—and it was a curse even if Hunter insisted that it was an honor. She would accept her fate with grace. No protesting, no fighting, no regrets. This was her burden to bear as it had been her da's before her. She would carry it just as well as he had. And oddly, that reawakened a sense of closeness to Owen Lewan that she hadn't felt since his death.

Rising from their final class, Matt and Cait joined their friends on the journey through the halls and to the parking lot. Early in the day, Hunter and even Sterling seemed uneasy with Cait's presence (she assumed that Hunter had admitted the truth to Sterling, causing their distance). But as the day went on and they found she wasn't acting differently toward them, they relaxed. It began to feel like any other day. And Cait was able to pretend that the betrayal hadn't happened.

She was grateful for the small mercy. Perhaps she should be angry or hurt. Perhaps she should confront Hunter. Instead, she let herself be free from worry and pain. She let herself be happy, if only for a moment.

"So," Liz said as they worked their way to the exit, "I know we said we'd do your party on Saturday night, so it's not a school night and all that, but . . . Shouldn't we do something *on* your birthday? Like, what if we all went out for burgers or something?"

Cait's heart warmed at her kindness. "I'd love that, really, but my nan always makes a special dinner for our birthdays. I couldn't skip out on it."

"Aw, that's precious." Liz nodded. "All right. And you're sure you want to keep it as just a girl's night on Saturday? We could have the guys come and play games or something."

Though Cait actually thought a game night with everyone would be fun, she shook her head. "Let's keep it as us girls only."

Liz shared a smile with Melissa at her side, then slipped her arm through Cait's and gave it a squeeze. "Sounds good to us," she said.

When they stepped out into the bright sunlight, she released Cait. They all said their goodbyes, preparing to head their separate ways. Matt and Cait started on their way to his truck. Genni was spending the evening with Alexis and Jared again, so they would head home alone.

"I've been thinking," Matt said as they walked. "It's been a while since we've hiked, and soon it'll be too cold for that. What if we went back to that beach we found—ya know, the sketching place?"

Cait blanched, gripping her backpack straps more tightly. "Uh, yeah," she replied weakly. "I remember it."

"Yeah," Matt nodded with excitement, "it was great, right? We should go back there and just hang out. Maybe tonight?"

"Oh, Matt . . ." Cait sighed. She turned toward him as they neared the truck. "I don't want to lie to you anymore. I already knew about the cove."

He blinked, confused.

"That's sort of where . . ."

A light dawned in Matt's eyes, and Cait knew she didn't need to explain anymore. "Oh," he said flatly. "You guys meet up there?"

Cait shrugged apologetically.

He sighed, staring at his toes. "No wonder there was a trail."

"I couldn't tell you before," she explained in a quiet tone. "We couldn't let people know."

Matt glanced up at her, a cautious look on his face. "Are you two—?"

Before he could get the question fully out, they were interrupted. "Hey," Hunter said nervously, approaching with Sterling just behind him. "Could I, uh—could we talk for a second, Cait?"

Cait and Matt stared at the boys wide-eyed with shared surprise, though she knew their reactions were for different reasons.

"Of course," Cait said, tucking some hair behind her ear. She passed an uncertain glance toward Matt.

Hunter caught the look. "Matt can stay if he wants," he said. "He . . . well, he should probably know too."

Raising her chin, Cait decided to let Hunter deliver the news rather than inform him that she already knew what he intended to say.

Anxiously, Hunter's feet shuffled, and Sterling kept his chin dipped with obvious regret. This was why Cait had decided to let it go. Somehow, she'd known the betrayal hadn't been malicious.

With a heavy sigh, Hunter began. "Cait, I messed up," he confessed. He met her eyes as though forcing himself not to flinch away from responsibility. "I—Wednesday night, after your meeting, Sterling came to me and told me about your theory. About my family. And it freaked me out, so . . ."

Taking pity on him, Cait spoke when he paused. "I know."

Hunter winced, and Sterling frowned.

"It's okay," she promised.

Hunter's brow furrowed. "It's not," he said tightly. "I broke my promise, and now—"

"What's going on here?"

The hum flared as Desmond jogged over, a look of indignation hardening his expression. Cait's heart dropped, recognizing that protective glint in his gaze.

Brady hurried up behind him, reaching out to grab his arm. "Desmond, let it—"

Desmond jerked out of his grasp, stepping between Cait and Hunter. Beside her, Matt frowned.

"I asked you a question, Hunt," Desmond said sharply.

Hunter bristled, but it was Cait who responded. "Des, it's fine," she whispered.

He hardly glanced over his shoulder at her. "He told on you, Cait," he said, back to glaring at Hunter. "That's far from 'fine.'"

"It wasn't intentional," Hunter insisted.

Desmond let out a caustic laugh. "Oh, well, it's all okay then," he sniped. Reaching over, he mockingly patted Hunter's shoulder. "You didn't mean to run to Daddy, is that it? Throwing Cait under the bus was an unavoidable accident, huh?"

That caused Matt's jaw to drop. Hunter flinched as though he'd been slapped.

Desmond took a threatening step closer. "I knew she shouldn't trust you."

Cait saw the danger in the flash of anger in Hunter's eyes, but she was too unsteady, the hum thrumming too furiously in her head, for her to do anything about it as Hunter snapped, "Like she can trust you?"

Desmond's shoulders stiffened.

"You tell her about the prophecy yet?" Hunter demanded indignantly. "Or were you waiting to do that until after you got her into bed?"

Cait's heart stalled at his words, too mortified by the insinuation to question whatever prophecy he referenced. But Desmond didn't hesitate. His fist collided with Hunter's jaw with a vicious *smack*. Matt, Brady, and Sterling all called out in alarm as Hunter stumbled back, holding his face. His blue eyes were wide, and a bead of blood welled at the corner of his mouth.

A few straggling students in the lot stopped to look over at the disturbance. Cait shrank back, frightened at what conclusions they'd make.

"You son of a bitch!" Desmond shouted without an ounce of regret in his voice. "You sold her out!"

A look of righteous indignation spread across Hunter's face. "I have nothing to say to you," he spat coldly.

"Then, I'll make you say it," Desmond said, tightening his fist and stepping forward again.

But Brady was already on him, gripping the back of his collar with one hand and his arm with the other. "I suggest," Brady said, voice sharp yet hushed, "that we make this conversation a little less *obvious*."

The parking lot was unnaturally silent for a few heartbeats. Only a smattering of cars remained, but several students and teachers had begun to cluster together. None of them or their families were members of the Warden. Likely, the only reason the adults weren't approaching was because it was Desmond, and no one dared question the mayor's son— even in a moment like this.

Hunter backed away, swiping at the blood on his lip. "Like I said, I've got nothing to say to *you*." He paused, then turned back to Cait. His expression softened. "But I do want to apologize to you."

Seeing the adamance in his gaze, Cait took a deep breath. The boys all stared at her, waiting for her response. She met Brady's gaze. "Get him out of here," she said, barely glancing at Desmond but seeing that his brow was pinched together in agitation. "And can you try to clear this crowd?"

Brady gave her a nod, then tightened his grip on Desmond.

"Cait," Desmond began, but she shook her head.

"Go, Desmond," she insisted. He looked ready to argue, so she leveled him with a glare. "Hunter insulted you, so you punched him. It had nothing to do with me."

Logic broke through Desmond's impulsivity, and he slumped in Brady's grip. "He's wrong," he said brokenly.

Cait sighed, knowing what he meant. Whatever secrets Desmond held back, whatever lies he still harbored, none of them had been under the guise of sleeping with her. Whatever Hunter saw in their relationship, he didn't understand it.

Cait wished she could reach out and take Desmond's hand to reassure him physically. Instead, she gave him a weak smile. "I know," she promised. "Go."

With a terse nod and one last glare at Hunter, Desmond turned with Brady, heading off across the lot. In silence, they watched them go. Brady called toward some of the stragglers, and they began to break up.

Cait released a breath, the tightness subsiding from her lungs.

She turned back to Hunter, expectant. He looked truly repentant, his features drawn down and his head dipped. Keeping his voice low, he began, "I didn't mean to say anything, Cait. It just sort of happened."

At her side, Matt crossed his arms, clearly still confused but coming to conclusions. "What's that supposed to mean?" he demanded. "Betraying someone doesn't just *happen*, Hunter."

"This is my fault," Sterling interjected, stepping forward. "After our meeting on Wednesday, I . . . I was upset. I didn't like the idea that Hunter or his family was a part of something so messed up. So, I asked him about it."

"He was trying to be a good friend," Hunter said.

It didn't make Cait feel any better, but she kept listening.

"I told him," Hunter continued, "I had no clue what he was talking about. My family has nothing to do with the Veil's damage. And we aren't staging some coup."

"Tell that to Desmond's dad," Cait said flatly.

"Yeah, about that—" Hunter scrubbed a hand over his face. "Sterling's questions kind of riled me up. I knew it wasn't true, but . . . it was all convincing enough to make me worry that maybe it was. So, I went to my dad and asked him, point blank: 'Are you trying to take the leadership of Porthaven back from the Simons?'" Hunter shrugged. "He said yes."

Cait closed her eyes around the truth.

"But," he added, "then I asked him about everything else, and he had no idea what I was talking about."

"And you believed him?" Matt asked bitterly.

"Why wouldn't I?" Hunter said. "After he admitted to the coup, why wouldn't he admit to the rest too? My family may want our rightful place back, but we wouldn't do something like that. The Varons vowed to protect the spirit world five centuries ago. We aren't going to break that promise now."

Sterling watched warily as though aware the argument had its faults.

Cait pulled in a deep breath, accepting the answer anyway.

Matt wasn't as forgiving. "That doesn't explain why you told on Cait."

"He—" Hunter paused, sucking in a tight breath. "After I asked my question, he asked why I'd ever think that, and I had no choice. I had to tell him."

"You didn't *have* to tell him that Cait was a Vessel," Matt argued.

Hunter frowned. "He kept asking things. If I dodged the questions, he'd know something was up."

Matt raised a brow, glancing toward Sterling. "And what about Sterling? Did you tell on him too?"

To *that* question, Hunter had no response.

Matt scoffed, but Cait held up a hand to forestall whatever biting words he'd say next. She turned back to Hunter with what she hoped was a forgiving, if hurt, look. "It's not okay, Hunter," she said, refusing to fully absolve him even if she wouldn't hold his actions against him. "What you did . . . It's not okay. My life is not mine anymore because you decided to break your promise."

"I know." His whisper was filled with shame, but he held her gaze steadily, facing the consequences of his actions. "And I don't deserve your forgiveness, but please, don't think that Liz or Mel or Sterling or even Scott had anything to do with this. None of them knew. It was all me."

A cold breeze swept through the parking lot. It whipped Cait's hair across her cheek, and she reached up to pull it down even as she shivered. This was why she hadn't intended to say anything to Hunter. His choice was his, and it wasn't fair that if she wanted space from him, she'd lose her other friends in the process.

Taking a fortifying breath, Cait looked up at him once more. "I can't trust you anymore, Hunter," she said. "It's up to you to fix that. But I'm not losing my friends because you decided to be a jerk."

Hunter raised his brow, and Sterling snorted at her unexpected candor.

Cait stepped back toward Matt's truck. "You have to fix this," she charged again.

With an understanding nod, Hunter promised, "I will."

Though Cait knew what he'd set in motion could never truly be fixed, she believed his sincerity. She turned and nodded to Matt, then moved for the passenger door. She heard Matt mutter something under his breath, but he climbed into the truck after her. Hunter and Sterling moved toward their own vehicles, a visible weight on their shoulders.

Cait played with the strap of her backpack, watching them walk away.

"Do you *really* want to hang around them still?" Matt asked quietly, his voice taut with agitation.

Letting out a heavy sigh, Cait felt as though she'd never clear her lungs of the pressure that had built within them. "We all make mistakes," she muttered.

"Not *this* bad," he countered.

Cait pressed her lips together, passing him an appreciative smile. "You're a good friend, Matt. But sometimes, you demand too much of people."

He deflated.

"I'm not forgiving Hunter because he deserves it," she explained. "I'm doing it because I'll only hurt myself if I don't."

Matt's head dropped, but he turned the key in the ignition, the truck rumbling pleasantly when the engine turned over. "And what about Desmond?" he whispered so softly she almost didn't hear him.

Cait furrowed her brow. "What about him?"

"Was Hunter right?"

Cait set her jaw, knowing what Matt was asking. Were she and Desmond a couple? Were they involved?

"No," she said, knowing it wasn't a lie anymore. Because no matter what they'd become a week ago, they'd already returned to what they'd been: nothing. And that's all they could have ever been.

# Desmond

**"I** wondered when you'd be back."

Desmond stared at Lilith through the screen door. He hadn't bothered hanging around after the scuffle at the school. He let Brady calm him down as they walked to their cars, knowing all the while that no matter what Cait said, Hunter's apologies could never be enough.

He'd hated watching as Cait let Hunter get away with his deception and betrayal the entire day. She'd just let him go with no repercussions. He deserved to pay. *He* deserved to be the one whose life was turned upside down.

Yet, she'd gone through the school day acting as though nothing was wrong.

It agitated Desmond. And then, he'd seen Hunter and Sterling approach her after school. Brady had tried to talk him out of inserting himself, but his efforts had been useless. Even as Desmond knew it would only make things worse, he couldn't stop his feet from carrying him across the macadam lot and straight to Cait's side.

Then, he'd punched Hunter, caused a scene, and drew the attention of the school to their group. Desmond could hear the truth in Cait's tone as she'd said, *"Get him out of here."* He'd screwed up. He'd let his emotions get the best of him, and it had just been another of the terrible, impulsive choices that had brought him to this place—futureless and devoid of hope.

But he wouldn't give up.

With a hollow feeling in his stomach, Desmond shrugged lazily as Lilith pushed the screen door open for him to enter. "Things got a little complicated," he said.

"Does that complication explain why my protection detail has been recalled?" she asked, leading him back into the house.

"Yeah, most likely," he admitted. Though he hadn't known that Jun pulled the watch from Lilith and her house, it didn't surprise him.

"Tea?" she asked.

"No, thank you. I can't stay that long."

Lilith moved to sit on a couch, a half-empty teacup already on the coffee table. "How can I help you, Desmond?"

He took the seat across from her, the same seat he'd been in when the nyct attacked. He tried to ignore the tear on the cushion as his chest spasmed reflexively, remembering the pain of the beast's claws. The five white marks had indeed left scars, highlighting Lilith's weaker healing powers.

"I'd like more information," he said.

Lilith raised an eyebrow.

"More *specific* information," he clarified.

"About what?" she asked, her white-blonde hair glowing in the low-hanging sunlight.

"Like I said, things are complicated. There are choices that need to be made, and I'd like to have all the information before I make them."

Her gaze narrowed. "Spirit world complicated?"

"Warden complicated."

"Mm." She tipped her head to the side and picked up her teacup. "I'll do my best to facilitate."

Desmond leaned forward in his seat. "There's someone I care about," he told her. "Someone I need to protect."

"Protect . . . from the Warden?" she surmised.

Desmond dipped his chin in acknowledgment.

Lilith hesitated, taking a sip of tea. Then, she crossed her legs and rested the cup on her knee. "I'm going to take a wild leap," she said wryly, "and guess that the questions you asked the other day pertain to this young woman."

Desmond paused, shocked by her assumption. Then, he realized it wasn't strange at all. Lilith was a perceptive woman. She'd always read him easily. She clearly saw how he felt about the individual he wanted to protect.

Feeling on the verge of betraying Cait, Desmond shifted in his seat. Was this really his best option? Trusting a Druid? But who else did he go to? His dad couldn't help. Not only did he lack the answers, but he'd also lost his job. All his previous access to the Warden's knowledge would be revoked or, at best, severely limited.

He had nowhere else to turn.

Desmond set his jaw and decided to trust Lilith. "They do."

She heaved an almost apologetic sigh. "She's a Vessel?"

He nodded.

"An *attached* one?"

Again, he nodded.

"What help would you like me to give?" she asked with kindness.

Desmond settled into his decision, knowing he would lose Cait if he didn't get answers, even if those answers came from a Druid. "I want to know how it works," he said.

"How what works?"

He held Lilith's dusty-blue gaze, unflinching in his resolve. "Tell me how to keep her safe."

Lilith uncrossed her legs, resettling herself on the couch. "By telling you what?" she asked. "Desmond, what do you want me to say about this? The Warden has their way of doing things. I can't interfere. The best I can do is tell you what I know of Vessels and how they sometimes work in tandem with their kindred. I can teach you about their power, about their history, about the legends surrounding them. That's it."

Desmond had anticipated her reaction. She didn't understand what he was looking for. She'd assured him that separating Spectral and Vessel was impossible, but he refused to believe that. And he *would* find a way.

Deciding to try a different approach, Desmond said, "Do you have any experience with blocks on a person's spirit?"

She drew back in her seat. "Not personally. It isn't a standard practice amongst Druids. We prefer to embrace our power."

"But you know about them?"

"Theoretically," she confirmed. "There were some in my faction who utilized them, either as a means of punishment or as a way to keep their adversaries from fighting back. But I was never involved in such pursuits."

"Do you know what happens when they're in place long-term?" He had the information from the Warden's research, but he wanted to see if Lilith's knowledge from the Druids lined up.

"From my understanding, they're highly damaging to the individual's psyche. Being cut off from your spirit is a harmful thing."

Desmond raised his brow. "But you don't have experience with that?"

"No. Most of the blocks I've witnessed in action—which admittedly were few—were temporary."

He frowned. "I didn't know they could be temporary."

"Oh, yes. To impose a lifelong block would require regular upkeep, strengthening the block over time. From my limited understanding, it's how the Warden keeps their Vessels from accessing their kindred."

Desmond didn't bother confirming the practice, focusing on the other, more important issue. "So, if a block is damaged, it *can* be fixed?"

Lilith's expression pinched with uncertainty. "I don't know about that. I've never heard of a damaged block."

"You just said they require upkeep, though."

She nodded as though seeing why he might be confused. "Think of a block like a rope. You tie a knot, binding up the individual's spirit like you would their hands. Over time, they might work the knot loose, and it could slip free. So, you tighten it, ensuring the knot holds."

Desmond found himself wringing his hands between his knees. "And what if the rope was damaged—frayed?"

"Then, you'd have a frayed block."

"Could you tighten it?"

She gave him a humorless grin. "You could. But you'd risk severing the already weakened rope."

"And if it breaks?"

"At that point, your prisoner is free."

Desmond sucked in a disappointed breath. "So," he concluded, "if a block is broken, there's no fixing it?"

"Not to my knowledge."

"But could you replace it?" he asked.

"Potentially." She grimaced. "But as it's never happened, I don't know what that would do to an individual. After breaking the first block . . . A new one may require a stronger hold, and that could cause greater damage."

"Great," Desmond grumbled, deciding to move on. "Next question: What do you know about the rumors on how to separate a Vessel from its Spectral?"

Lilith pressed her lips together. "I've already told you it can't be done."

"Forgive me if I don't take your word for it," he said without a hint of apology, then pressed again, "What do the rumors say?"

Lilith tapped her fingers against her thigh. "There are a few. None of them have been successful."

"Based on your knowledge: What do they say?"

Her irritation was plain on her face, but Desmond didn't care. "Well, there's one that suggests you can carve out the kindred by splitting the Vessel's heart in two. Would you like to try that one?"

"This isn't a game to me," Desmond replied sharply. "I'm trying to protect someone."

"And I'm trying to mitigate your expectations," she returned. "The very concept of dividing the Spectral and their host is like suggesting you flay a person's spirit from them. The two are bound together. It isn't something you remove like a bandage. It's extracting an intrinsic part of who the Vessel is. You could more easily strip them of the blood in their veins."

The imagery was successful in causing Desmond's chest to constrict and his grip to tighten. Yet, he wouldn't be deterred. Not if it would save Cait's life.

"But it's possible?" he prompted.

Lilith's expression shuttered. "Possible? Maybe. But is it worth attempting?" She narrowed her cunning gaze at him. "If you want to protect this girl, protect her from the fate of losing a part of her soul."

"She didn't ask for this," he insisted. "She doesn't want it."

"It's too late," Lilith said. "If she's bound to the kindred, her fate is sealed. Trying to part them will only endanger her more."

"How do you know that for sure? What if there's a way?"

Lilith stared at him.

Desmond was too desperate, too hopeless, to let go of this one last hope. "I *have* to save her from this."

Something like compassion pulled Lilith's expression down. "Being a Vessel isn't some horrible fate, Desmond," she said softly. "If our previous conversations haven't convinced you of that, then I don't know what will. She's been given a gift. If she would only accept it, she would find freedom in that."

"I don't believe that," he said, the knowledge of the prophecy and his lifelong training belying whatever Druidic rhetoric she held firm to.

"Or is it that you don't *want* to believe it?"

Desmond supposed she had a point. If they lived anywhere else, if they worked for any other organization, he might not feel so opposed to Cait's connection to the Wolf. In Bushmills, the Warden hadn't treated her father with such confinement. He'd been free to live as he pleased. There'd been no block, no regulations, no restrictions—which was part of the reason the Druids found him. Rumors spread easily, and the stories of Owen Lewan's power had worked their way across the globe.

That danger was nonexistent in Porthaven. In two centuries, they'd never had a breach. Their secrets were secure.

Here, Cait was safe but imprisoned. Elsewhere, she was free but in danger.

And even in Bushmills, they wouldn't have wanted a Varon heir marrying a Vessel.

He'd heard people talking over the years. In five centuries, a Varon Vessel had never existed. They claimed it was for good reason, that too much power could never be a good thing, God would never give a Varon something that could make them so dreadfully unstoppable. The Varons claimed that it was because God had given them strength enough.

He didn't particularly hold an opinion, nor did he care. All he knew was that if the Warden found out that he intended to marry a Vessel, that he intended to have a family with her, they'd stop him at all costs because they'd never want a Varon carrying the power of a spirit-being too.

"There has to be a way," Desmond insisted. "There's *always* a way."

"None that I know of," Lilith said, but she paused. "None that are safe, at least."

Desmond sat up straighter. "And those that are unsafe?"

Her brow furrowed with doubt. "You'd be willing to risk this girl's life to set her free?"

"I risk her life if she *doesn't* get free," he said.

Lilith considered this. "Because of the Warden?"

He nodded.

She took a deep breath, looking toward the terrarium in thought. "You could leave with her," she suggested in a whisper. Her sharp eyes drifted back to meet his gaze. "You could run."

"And go where?" Desmond returned. "The Druids and the Warden want her. If I take her out of Porthaven, she'll be chased down. That puts her in even more danger."

Lilith pursed her lips. "I could send you to the people I know," she offered. "The good ones."

Desmond gave her a flat stare. "I may not trust the Warden anymore, but that doesn't mean I trust Druids. Not even your 'good' ones."

"So, you're dead set on separating them?"

"It's the only way to truly protect her."

Lilith sighed. Silently, she looked off to the side again. Desmond didn't know what internal debate she was having, whether it was to consent to help him or whether it was *how* she could help him. But he waited patiently, determined to get an answer from her.

"I'm not an expert," Lilith began at last. "I've been told little in my lifetime and had no reason to study it. But there are people I know who are more versed in the subject. I could contact them, perhaps. See if they have any wisdom to impart."

"No." Desmond's reply was immediate. "No one can know she's here."

"I wouldn't have to tell them—"

"Even if you said it was purely for intellectual study, it'd be cause for speculation. That's not an option."

Mockingly, she tipped her brow up. "You want answers, but you don't want me to get them for you. How am I supposed to help?"

"Tell me what you already know," he insisted.

"Nothing," she returned. "The theories I'm aware of have all been proven false. The rumors aren't viable. You can't separate a Spectral from its Vessel unless you kill the Vessel."

Desmond shook his head. "I can't accept that."

"Then, you'll have to leave Porthaven and obtain the answers yourself," she said. "Because I don't have them."

Desmond sat back, put off by the suggestion. He couldn't leave. Not when he planned to build a future with Cait.

But maybe . . .

Desmond pushed off the couch. "I've gotta go," he said, knowing there'd be no more information to glean from the woman.

Lilith rose as well, her sharp gaze still watching him uneasily. "I'm sorry I couldn't be more helpful, Desmond." She sounded genuine. "I really am."

"It's fine," he said, giving her a half-hearted smile. "Thanks for trying."

"If there's anything else I can do . . ." she offered.

He gave a brusque nod in acknowledgment before turning to leave. Lilith walked with him to the door, shutting and locking it behind him. He trekked across the gravel to his car, thoughts churning.

No, Desmond couldn't leave Porthaven. Not yet, at least. He had to ensure Cait's freedom here, graduate, and begin their lives together first.

But after that, there was a chance . . .

He could travel—going for short trips at a time and gathering information where he could. Maybe he could visit that "good" Druid town that Lilith knew. If she vouched for him, perhaps they'd be willing to help. He wouldn't have to give them his real name. He could even pretend to be a Druid, too, doing academic research. That wouldn't be suspicious, would it?

Perhaps he couldn't free Cait immediately. Maybe it would take years. But for now, he'd secure her future. He'd protect her from the Warden's plans for the present and free her from the prophecy later.

# CHAPTER THIRTY-SEVEN

# Cait

It happened on Sunday.

Cait spent the weekend at home. She and Desmond couldn't meet up—not when the Warden was watching them so closely—and the Tridents had a travel basketball game. It was a six-hour drive, so the team left early Saturday morning and didn't return until Sunday afternoon. Matt had offered to stay home to keep her company, but Cait insisted he go.

"I need some time alone," she'd told him.

Though she could tell he didn't want to, Matt had accepted her request.

So, Cait sat at home, expecting the Warden representative Desmond had mentioned to show up on her doorstep at any moment.

Instead, they called Maeve.

"Girls," she'd said to them Saturday evening, "we'll be having some company tomorrow after church. Reverend Lavigne and a gentleman from the Warden would like to come talk with us."

Having expected as much, Cait took the announcement in stride. Rese and Genni, however, were shocked.

"Why?" Rese asked with indignation. Her gaze darted to Cait worriedly. "What could they possibly want?"

"Yeah," Genni chimed in. "The reverend was here, like, two months ago for his annual weirdness."

Maeve scolded Genni, then said, "They didn't tell me the specifics but mentioned this new gentleman—Jun, I believe—wanted to meet yeh girls because he's helping with the leadership of the Warden here in town. That's all."

Cait knew perfectly well that wasn't all. But she kept her mouth shut and internally prepared for Sunday afternoon.

Through the night and another dark dream, Cait resigned herself. The door bore a lengthening tear. Desmond was ripped from her in the water, reminding her of their fate. A storm brewed as she gazed upon the fractured sycamore, where the ash and the aspen twisted their way out of its trunk. As usual, she attempted to discover the identity of the figure shrouded in shadow. And then the tree exploded in amber light, leaving her body alight with a sense of unprecedented power and relief.

It was as though the dreams were trying to tell her something. But Cait couldn't quite decide what that something was.

Throughout the church service, Cait found her mind returning to its ominous omens. In the margins of the bulletin, she sketched the three trees growing together. Her eyes regularly drifted to the front of the church, where William and Robin sat. It was odd seeing them without Desmond at their side. It was odder still to be in the church without the hum steadily pulsing with his presence. She didn't think she liked it much.

Cait thought about going up to William and apologizing for her shortness two weeks ago. He was trying to be kind, and she'd rudely rejected his goodness. She wanted to tell him that she forgave him. She wanted to thank him for what he'd tried to do for her. And she wanted to tell him that she accepted the blame for his loss of the Warden's leadership. After all, he'd only lost his job because he'd lied for Desmond and her.

But even as she thought about doing so, her stomach clenched. She couldn't bear speaking to Desmond's parents, not now that she'd ruined their family so thoroughly. She couldn't fathom the way they'd look at her, the hurt and anger in their expressions. She didn't want to face that.

So, she stayed in the back of the chapel with her nan, sisters, and Penny Davis.

Then, Liz approached.

"Hi, Cait," she said, worry in her tone. Her posture was slumped as though expecting Cait's wrath. "Do you have a second?"

Rese furrowed her brow, watching as Cait slipped past her to go with Liz toward a secluded part of the sanctuary. Keeping their voices low, the girls talked.

"I just wanted to say," Liz's words were hurried as she wrung her hands, "I'm sorry for everything with—with Hunter. I didn't know—"

"I know," Cait promised.

Liz's nerves didn't ease as she shuffled her feet. "Okay, well, I need you to know he came clean to me Friday night, and I'm freaking pissed at him." Her eyes shone with the hint of tears, but she didn't let any fall. "We're on a break for now because I—I—I can't believe he'd do that to you."

Cait grabbed Liz's hands, keeping her from squeezing them anxiously. "Liz," she said with a sad smile, "please, don't break up with Hunter because of this. He was trying to do the right thing, and he screwed up. We all do that from time to time."

A faint, affectionate whimper came from Liz as she pulled Cait into a hug. "You're too good, Cait," she whispered, her voice sounding strained. "I'm so sorry I didn't see that before. I'm so sorry it took me this long to be your friend."

Cait returned the hug, fighting off tears of her own. Not because she'd been alone for so long. Not because she was still hurt by Hunter's choices.

Because in such a short time, she'd found a true friend in Liz. Something she hadn't ever hoped to have.

After a long embrace, Liz pulled back. "Okay, so—" She sniffled around her unshed tears. "We don't have to do the whole girls' night birthday thing anymore if you don't want to. Like, it's totally understandable if you hate us now."

"Why would I hate you?" Cait smiled, feeling it deeply in her heart. "You and Mel haven't done anything wrong. And I'd love to celebrate my birthday with you both."

Liz returned the smile, though hers almost looked like a grimace with the way her face scrunched with emotion. "Good. I'll, uh—I'll see you at school tomorrow?"

"Nothing has changed," Cait promised.

After another hug, the girls parted. Cait returned to her family feeling lighter. Perhaps her life would be dictated to her. Perhaps she'd be caged in Porthaven. At least she wasn't alone anymore. If anything, Hunter's actions had revealed that. He might have made a mistake, but he'd owned up to it and clearly wanted to make it up to her. Sterling hadn't rejected her either. She had friends. She had Matt, Genni, Liz, Melissa, Sterling, Scott, and, yes, even Hunter.

If she was going to lose Desmond, at least she had them beside her.

When the Lewan women returned to their home, they moved into a flurry of activity, changing and preparing for their after-lunch guests. The reverend and the Warden representative were to arrive in thirty short minutes, so they hurried through lunch. Maeve put out a hasty meal of leftover fish and colcannon. Genni grumbled the entire time.

"Why does our day have to be disrupted because *they* want to come over?" she said before shoving another bite of the potatoes in her mouth.

Rese didn't complain, having been abnormally silent the whole morning. In fact, she'd been especially reserved the last few weeks, Cait realized. She hadn't noticed because Rese had remained naturally aloof from their family ever since they'd arrived in Porthaven. It was as though she'd erected a barrier between her present life and her life in Ireland. And as they'd been part of her childhood, she'd left them in the past as well.

But lately, things felt different. Rese still interacted with them, even if it was often stilted and reserved. But over the last two weeks, Cait couldn't remember her sister intentionally starting a conversation with her once.

She didn't have long to dwell on the curiosity of Rese's behavior before a knock sounded on the front door. Cait offered to answer.

They so seldom used the front door that it felt odd walking through the living room to unlock it. She felt strangely out of place, even in her own home. A dreamlike sense swept over her as she opened the door to find two men standing on the porch. Reverend Ben Lavigne looked so much like his son that Cait could almost imagine it was a grown-up Brady smiling down at her. However, the man at his side, Cait didn't recognize.

"Good afternoon," the stranger said, holding out a hand. "I'm Kevin Jun, Municipality Analyst for Sheraton Corporation."

Cait shook his hand, introducing herself. "I thought you worked for the Warden," she said meekly.

Jun glanced at Ben with an amused look. "I do," he said. "Sheraton Corporation and the Warden are synonymous."

While Cait had never heard of the other organization, she nodded and invited the men in without asking more questions. Maeve, Rese, and Genni had moved into the living room, and a round of greetings were made. Maeve offered the men drinks, which they politely declined before they took their seats on the outdated and threadbare couches.

"We hope not to take up much of your afternoon," Jun said simply. He had an oddly detached way of speaking, keeping his voice calm and measuring each word.

His gaze fell on Cait then, and she drew her shoulders back, preparing for what was to come.

"Miss Lewan," he said to Cait, "are you aware of our purpose for coming here?"

Her nan and sisters whirled to stare at her.

Cait swallowed down her nerves and nodded. "I am," she admitted.

"Mm." The smallest twitch lifted the corner of Jun's lips before his stoicism resumed. "I take it by the reaction of your family that they do not?"

"No."

Jun addressed Maeve and the girls. "It has come to our attention that the burden of your son and father, Owen Lewan, has fallen to your granddaughter and sister, Caitriona."

Maeve blanched, Genni gaped, and Rese blinked.

"As such, the Warden's policy is to ensure her absolute safety," Jun continued while the women struggled to process the news.

"Cait," Genni whispered brokenly, "who—"

"It doesn't matter, Gen," she whispered back.

Seeing the short exchange end, Jun continued, "Your lives will not change, but she will be required to submit herself to regular check-ins and follow some daily guidelines."

"All for her safety, right?" Rese said, unexpectedly sharp.

Jun didn't appear to hear the bitterness in her tone. "That's correct," he confirmed, then turned back to Cait. "Miss Lewan, we have a few things we'd like to discuss with you privately. However, as you are a minor, you are welcome to have your grandmother remain with you."

A hollowness had settled into Cait's heart, the feeling somehow bolstering her. "No, that's all right," she replied, not wanting her nan beside her while she accepted her impending fate.

Maeve looked hurt and frightened all at once. "This—how do yeh know?" she demanded. "There've been no signs. The block—"

Cait closed her eyes, accepting that her nan had known—all along, she'd known the Warden was suppressing them—and she'd chosen not to say anything.

"We have adequate evidence," Jun said, but he offered none in support.

Maeve didn't like that. She turned to Ben, who'd been silent the entire time, with agitation. "Where's William?" she demanded.

"Mayor Simon is no longer employed by the Warden," Jun answered. "I will be taking his place as Supervisor of the town until such a time as a suitable replacement can be selected."

Ben shifted awkwardly in his seat as Maeve's lips parted in shock. "Why?" she asked.

Jun hesitated, and for a moment, Cait thought he might answer truthfully. Then, he looked up with that impassive dark gaze of his and said, "That's classified at present, ma'am. Reverend Lavigne and I need to have a word with your granddaughter if you'd be so kind as to give us a minute."

With the dismissal in place, Maeve merely blinked a handful of times before turning to Cait. "Yeh knew?" she murmured.

Cait dipped her chin. "I did."

Maeve's expression pinched. "And yeh didn't tell me?"

Cait had nothing to say to that.

Suddenly, Genni rose, her form shaking with anger. "Who told?" she demanded.

Maeve gaped up at her, undoubtedly realizing that Genni knew too. But it was Jun and Ben who faced the young girl's wrath.

Unperturbed, Jun replied with a simple, "I'm not at liberty to discuss that."

Genni's eyes narrowed, but Ben cut off her sharp retort. "It was Brett Varon," he said in the same casually blunt manner that his son shared. When Jun frowned at him, Ben shrugged. "Fire me too if you want, but I'm not going to lie to appease your sense of control. They deserve to know."

Cait forced down a smile. She decided she liked the Lavigne men.

During the exchange, Genni had figured out the truth. She looked at Cait with blatant hurt in her blue eyes. "Hunter?" she asked weakly.

Wanting to get the meeting over with, Cait offered Genni a small smile. "He didn't mean to," she reassured, then hurried on before her sister could reply. "We'll talk about this later, Gen. I need to talk with Mr. Jun and the reverend alone for a bit."

With a reluctant scowl, Genni moved toward the stairs. Maeve rose next, hands clasped nervously before her. "Yer sure yeh don't want me to stay, *a leanbh*?"

"I'm sure, Nan."

Maeve let out a heavy sigh, glanced at the Warden men, then motioned to Rese, who sat stock-still in the corner of the couch. She didn't respond to Maeve's prompting, so their nan reached over to set a hand on her arm. Rese jerked as though woken from a dream, and that's when Cait saw the glimmer of tears in her eyes.

Abruptly, Rese stood and rushed from the room without a word.

Cait frowned as she looked over her shoulder, watching her sister stomp up the stairs. Her bedroom door slammed a second later.

Maeve exited with more grace, leaving Cait alone with the men.

Jun sat forward, but Ben spoke first. "I want to assure you, Miss Lewan," he said kindly, "that we'll do *whatever* we can to protect you."

Cait met the reverend's stare, intending to thank him, but paused as she caught an odd glimmer within that adamant expression of his. His eyes flickered to Jun, and Cait caught the warning. Ben was here as an employee of the Warden, but he was like his son—he was dedicated to the Simons. Which meant his assurance was offered on the Lavigne family's behalf, *not* the Warden's.

"Thank you," Cait said quietly, hoping he caught her understanding but that Jun did not.

She turned back to the Warden agent, her shaky hands clasped on her lap. "I know that I'm the Vessel," she said. "As my friend—nothing more, I want to be clear about that—Desmond kindly prepared me for what's expected of that role. I will happily comply with whatever the Warden deems necessary for my protection and the protection of others."

Something like curiosity lifted Jun's brow. "It was good of him to prepare you," he said, and Cait couldn't tell if he believed her insistence regarding their platonic relationship or not.

"It's a shame," he continued sincerely. "I truly believe that Desmond is a good kid and could become a great leader. He has the heart for it. But he lacks the discipline."

Though Cait wanted to disagree, she found she couldn't. Desmond would make a good leader *if* he could let go of his selfish resolve to live free of authority. That had always been his problem. He rebelled not because he didn't want the role he was set to inherit but because he didn't want others to tell him how that role needed to look.

"Now," Jun said, "there are a few things we need to address today, starting with checking on your block. It seems that it may be slipping, allowing you to wield. Generally, we don't like to suppress people's abilities to connect with the spirit world, but for you, it's particularly dangerous. If you connect with the spirit world, you *will* connect with the spirit-being. And that could have devastating effects."

Though Cait didn't know how much to believe this man, she could hear that *he* believed what he was saying. And she had no trouble accepting the truth of it. The creature connected to her was dangerous. By extension, she was dangerous. They both needed to be controlled.

So, Cait let Ben step forward to check the block. "The location isn't important," he said dryly just before laying his hands on her crown. "But the touch is necessary. I just find the head to be the least awkward option."

Cait couldn't help her small smile, grateful to discover that Ben and Brady shared a personality. No matter how little she knew Brady personally, she'd become familiar with his character through Desmond. And over the last two weeks, she'd come to discover that if they had had a chance, she would have happily been friends with Brady too.

When Ben pulled back, he was frowning.

"What is it?" Jun asked, seeing his worry.

Ben sank back into his seat. "Her block isn't slipping. It's breaking.

It's . . . it's like the binding of a book that's been abused for years. It's hanging on by a thread."

The frown spreading across Jun's face drew his brows low. "Can you fix it?"

Ben scoffed. "I tried," he said. "That's not something you fix easily. If a book's binding breaks, you tear away the old binding and create a new one."

Cait didn't like the sound of that. If the block was removed in order to be replaced with a new one, wouldn't that release the Wolf in the meantime?

By his tightening expression, Jun didn't seem pleased with the sound of it either. "I'll contact the archivists," he said blandly. "They may have an alternative for us."

Jun turned back to Cait. "Do you understand what happens if your block fails?"

Cait nodded but didn't bother to speak.

He returned the nod. "We will work with speed to find a way to recover its hold," he promised. "In the meantime, try to stay away from anything that might induce the spirit world's pull."

"I don't do anything like that," she told him.

"Hm." Jun looked contemplative for a moment as though unsure how to advise her. Then, he decided to move on. "We have some other things to discuss. First, let us explain to you what it means to be a Vessel with the Warden."

Over the next hour, Jun walked Cait through all the same things Desmond had told her. He was more thorough, but in the end, everything he told her was something Cait already knew. Her life would be limited to Porthaven's township, but she'd be allowed to live whatever life she'd like within its borders. Her day-to-day would look little different than any regular woman's, aside from the check-ins and protocols. She would bear the block (though they didn't mention the risk of dementia), and she would be required to have one child with a spouse of her choosing from amongst the Warden to ensure the bloodline.

When she asked about Rese and Genni, if they would be required to follow any protocols as potential Vessels too, Jun explained, "Now that we know you are the Vessel, they are free to live as they choose, so long as they remain within a Warden town, in the event that your line is broken. However, once you have a child of your own, the odds of their inheritance decreases exponentially."

They didn't tell her anything about the spirit-being. They didn't even mention his name—the Wolf. But they let her ask questions when she had them, and in the end, when they left (stating that they'd return next Saturday) and Cait shut the door behind them, she felt the same hollow resignation she'd felt the last three days.

Cait was the Vessel; she'd inherited her da's curse, and she couldn't have the life she wanted. Her sisters would get to go on and live however the desired. They could marry men they loved and have large families. They could even leave Porthaven, should they desire. All while she was leashed like a dog, forced to marry someone she'd never met and relegated to rigid protocols.

But Desmond loved her.

In her life of sacrifice and captivity, Cait decided that memory would be enough.

# Rese

She waited until the Warden men left. Then, Rese enacted her plan.

Hurrying out the door, she dropped into the rusty sedan the Lewan ladies shared and backed out of the driveway. Her tears had long ago dried up in the resolve of her anger. She didn't fully understand what had happened—how had Hunter Varon learned about Cait's connection to the Wolf in the first place?—but she didn't care.

Rese didn't bother calling; she simply showed up at the Greene family house, parked beside the four-car garage, and headed along the hexagon paver path to the side door that belonged to Ryan's space. It was ridiculous really. When Ryan graduated from high school, his parents had been stupid enough to renovate and give him a separate entrance, like he had his own apartment within their home. He'd exploited it numerous times from the stories he told. But in this situation, Rese found herself grateful for the Greene parents' foolishness.

Knocking on the door, Rese only had to wait a few seconds for Ryan to answer.

"Reese's Puff," he said with fond surprise. He leaned against the doorframe, a bright smile on his handsome face. "What're you doing here, babe?"

Bristling at the endearment, Rese tried not to let her agitation show on her face. "May I come in?" she asked.

"Of course." Ryan stepped back, letting her walk past him into the large space. It was a predictable bachelor's pad, though with much more expensive pieces than the average college-aged man's belongings. The plush gray couch had a smattering of clothes draped across the back, the coffee table bore days' worth of dishes, and the bed in the far corner was clearly not made. The TV thrummed with an ESPN newscast.

After shutting the door, Ryan slipped an arm around Rese's waist and kissed her quickly. "So," he said, still holding her close, "you miss me or something?"

Gently extracting herself from him, Rese gave a weak smile. "Obviously," she lied, then let her worry show. "But I also need to talk to you."

Ryan's expression clouded as he stepped back. His sharp gaze scanned her as though looking for the cause of her anxiety. "Well, you're definitely not pregnant," he muttered.

Rese rolled her eyes. Did he think about nothing but sex? She fought off the urge to huff. "Why would you even say that?" she demanded sharply.

"Well, typically, when a girl comes over acting all freaked out and saying, 'we need to talk,' it's either 'cause she's pregnant or she's breaking up with the guy," he said, then paused. His brow furrowed. "Are you breaking up with me?"

He said it with such worry, like he thought she might actually leave him, that Rese almost felt bad. But then her mind stuck on his earlier statement. "Wait," she said, gaping up at him, "have you gotten a girl pregnant before?"

"No!" he exclaimed in shock.

Though Rese's cynical side didn't want to believe him, she couldn't deny his genuine bafflement at the mere suggestion. Pressing her hands to her face, she paced farther into the room. This was off to a bad start. If she couldn't convince him to help her, then everything she'd done over the last twelve years would be pointless. Her efforts to protect her sisters would be moot. And Cait would be lost.

"Rese." His concerned voice filtered through her thoughts, and then he was there, gently resting his hands on her arms. Though he was shortsighted and lazy at times, the care in Ryan's gaze couldn't be denied. "You're kind of scaring me, babe. What's going on?"

Drawing in a short breath, Rese let her plea whisper out. "I need your help."

"Anything," he replied immediately, and she could tell he meant it.

Rese smiled sadly. This was why she'd chosen Ryan. He might not be a white knight, but he did care about her. And deep down, he had a sincere, if spoiled, heart.

"Cait's the Vessel," she said.

Ryan's demeanor shifted instantly, visibly closing off. "How do you know that term?"

Rese frowned at the change. "My da taught me about Vessels when I was a girl," she explained.

"You were seven when he died."

"And he started teaching me when I was six."

His face screwed up with something like horror. "You were a kid."

Rese shrugged out of his touch. "Yeah, and I was supposed to inherit," she returned. "But that damn Wolf decided to target the weakest of us. He picked Cait, the sweetest, quietest, most gentle person this world has ever seen. And he's going to destroy her if we don't do something."

Slowly, Ryan backed up as she spoke. He watched her with a worried expression, clearly put off by her knowledge. "You're not supposed to know this," he said.

"Did you not hear me?" Rese demanded. "We have to save Cait."

He stared at her for several seconds before sighing. "There's nothing we can do," he said. "The spirit-being chose her. It is what it is."

Rese gaped at him. How could he say that? How could he be so unfeeling?

Because he didn't know Cait.

Giving him the excuse, Rese tried a new tactic. She'd make him understand. She'd make him help her. "Look," she began, forcing her tone to soften as she presented her case logically, "Cait isn't going to make a good Vessel. She's not strong enough to hold him."

Ryan's brow pulled together as though the suggestion sparked a thought.

"For her sake and the sake of the town," Rese continued, then shook her head and made the implication grander. "For the sake of the *Warden,* she can't remain the Vessel."

"The thing made its choice years ago, Rese."

"What if we could get it to change its mind?" she asked.

Ryan drew back in shock.

Rese lifted her hands, begging him to understand. "My da offered himself to the Wolf as a boy," she explained. "The Wolf had gone for centuries without a host because the bloodline was lost. But my da found him and offered himself. The Wolf saw a kindred spirit in him and accepted. He saw his strength and his loyalty, and he knew they were the same."

Pressing her hands to her chest, Rese made her case. "I can offer myself," she said. "It was meant to be me from the start. I'm the firstborn, and my da prepared me. I'm strong. I'm loyal. I can hold him."

Ryan averted his gaze in thought.

Rese knew she had to keep pushing; she had to make him see. She stepped closer, setting her hands on his arms, letting them glide to his chest, gently drawing on his affection for her. "Ryan," she whispered his name, "I can take on the Wolf. And you can help me."

His jaw twitched. "They have protocols, Rese," he murmured.

"Like what?" she asked, unconcerned by whatever they might require of her.

He looked down at her, his fingers brushing along her sides before his hands rested on her hips. "They'd want us to marry," he said quietly as though considering the idea. "Probably immediately since you're nineteen. Then, they'd want us to have a kid right away."

Rese bit the inside of her cheek. Though they'd only been dating for a month, she'd already planned to marry Ryan and have his children. It was a fate she'd resigned herself to months ago. "Would you want that?" she asked, inflecting the words with a gentle desire for it herself.

He hesitated, then gripped her more tightly. "I'd happily marry you, Rese," he murmured, though he didn't sound sure. "I just didn't anticipate it so soon."

A mix of relief and resignation filtered through Rese's chest.

"But," his gaze shuttered as he looked up at her, "this is all assuming that you could take the spirit-being from your sister. And you can't."

Rese tensed under his touch. "Why not?"

"It's not possible. Never in centuries has it happened. The spirit-being makes a choice, and that's that. You can't separate them."

Rese's heart squeezed painfully. "You don't know that."

"It can't happen, Rese," he said without remorse. "It's a nice thought, but it's a waste of time. Your sister is the Vessel. And maybe we'll get married, but it won't be until I'm done with medical school."

"That'll be five years from now," she said, realizing that her plans to elevate her sisters and give them security had been faulty from the start.

Ryan shrugged casually. "The good news is that you're not the Vessel, so you could come with me to Portland."

"And do what?" Rese asked coldly. "Work in a coffee shop while you go to school and wait for you to finally commit?"

He scoffed. "What do you want from me, Rese? Do you want to get married now? Fine. We'll get married, and I'll take you with me to medical school. Would that make you happy?"

Rese glared at him, realizing she'd come to the wrong person. He wasn't going to help her. He wouldn't even give her answers without something in exchange. What had she expected from him? He liked her—he might even believe he was in love with her, though he hadn't said so—but he didn't truly care about her happiness. He cared about what made *him* happy.

Shutting out the last of her emotions, Rese refused to feel the weight of that realization. She ignored the hurt and pressed down the dejection. "You know what, Ryan?" she began sharply. "No, that wouldn't make me happy. And maybe you'd already know that if you'd actually bother to learn something about me."

Without waiting for his response, Rese turned on her heel and headed for the door. She heard him call her name, but she didn't stop. She got in the rusty blue car, drove off the Greenes' property, and wound back through the streets of downtown Porthaven.

The gray clouds reflected her dark mood. The clogged sky withheld its rain, mimicking Rese's feelings as she forced them to stay bottled inside. Her throat closed tightly as she drove down Lawrence Avenue. She eyed the town hall, thinking of the Warden and its tight hold over their lives. Beyond the government building, she saw the barest glimpse of the old white houses of the founding families. Her gaze flickered toward the chapel's bell tower, hanging in the sky in the distance.

Maybe Ryan wouldn't help, but she would help herself. She'd return home and read the entirety of the book Brady had given her. But first, she'd talk with her sister.

Rese forced her gaze back to the road. Her fingers twitched on the steering wheel, her mind made up. She'd put off the conversation with Cait for too long. It was cowardly, but Rese hadn't felt she had a right to confront her sister. Especially when she had nothing to offer but a menial, "I'll fix it somehow."

Whatever Cait and Desmond's relationship, Rese didn't approve. She couldn't let her sister let that boy drag her down with him. But it was even more important for Cait to know Rese was on her side. She had a sister who was going to save her, one way or another.

When Rese arrived back at the house, she found Cait in the kitchen, helping their nan make dinner. The yellow glow of the overhead light was dreadfully dim. Only one working light bulb remained in the fixture, and the additional outdated bulb from the range did little to help brighten the space.

It grated on Rese's already testy mood. How was it that the Simons, Greenes, Lavignes, and all the rest of the Warden members got cushy, beautiful homes while they had to live in this dump?

Rese dropped the car keys on the kitchen table, eyeing her sister and their nan. "Where'd yeh go, *a leanbh*?" Maeve asked lightly. She didn't sound suspicious, but it still irritated Rese that she always had to explain herself.

"I went to see Ryan," she replied tersely. She forced herself to take a deep breath. "Sorry, could I borrow Cait for a minute?"

The two women looked up at her. Cait's hand stilled over the carrots and leeks she was pushing into the pot on the stovetop. Her sharp blue eyes looked so much like their da's; sometimes, the sight of them made Rese's stomach twist.

Cait glanced over her shoulder at Maeve, who nodded approvingly.

After pushing the last of the veggies into the pot, Cait set the cutting board on the counter. She kept her head ducked as Rese suggested they go out on the porch. Nowhere in the house was exactly private. The entire downstairs was open enough to listen in on conversations, and the walls were thin enough to be heard from room to room at times. And while the closed-in porch was on the other side of the kitchen, at least it offered an exterior wall to suggest a hint of seclusion.

"Hey, so," Rese began, crossing her arms against the chilly breeze that cut through the porch's screens. "I've been wanting to talk to you about something. For, like, three weeks now."

Cait stood before her, an innocent expression on her face. Her shoulders were slumped, and in the dull afternoon light, her skin looked paler than usual. "Okay," she said softly.

Rese ground her teeth. This was the problem with talking to Cait. She was so compliant—so docile. It was like trying to have a serious conversation with a kitten.

She drew in a tense breath through her nose. "Where were you that Monday night?"

Cait's expression flashed with something between shock and bald-faced confusion. "What—?"

"I get it, Cait," she interrupted, not giving her the chance to lie. "It was the anniversary. We were all having a rough time, but you don't get to act out just because you're sad."

That caused Cait's lips to part. "You're accusing *me* of acting out?"

"What is that supposed to mean?" Rese demanded.

Cait shook her head. "It doesn't matter," she mumbled regretfully. When she met Rese's eyes again, she wore a submissively pleading look. "Rese, I don't know what you're talking about. I was home that night. *All* night."

Rese stared at her sister. A part of her believed that Cait meant it. Perhaps she'd been completely unaware of Desmond Simon's presence. Maybe she really wasn't involved with the boy at all.

But Rese knew what she'd seen, and Brady had even confirmed Cait and Desmond's strange relationship in his own way.

Yet, Cait's lie was so convincing.

"Since when did you become a liar?" Rese asked coldly.

Hurt drew Cait's lips into a frown. "What is wrong with you?" she spat. "Why would I lie about that?"

"I saw you, Cait," Rese accused. "He carried you into your room while you were completely unconscious. I wanted to give you the benefit of the doubt, but seriously? You snuck out to get drunk with Desmond Simon?"

A sharp exhale swept out of Cait like a scoff. "You're the one who got plastered at the Greenes' party. You're the one who made out with

Ryan in front of the entire town."

"He's my boyfriend," Rese defended. "And he actually cares about me. What? Is Desmond working to complete the circuit of the senior class? Is that why he's finally paying a shred of attention to you?"

Something like a snarl lifted Cait's lips. "You don't know what you're talking about."

"I know enough."

"Whatever you *think* you understand," Cait said angrily, "you're wrong. I didn't go out that night to get drunk. I didn't even go out of my own volition. You heard the reverend and Mr. Jun: I'm the one with the curse. And *it* took me out that night. Desmond only brought me home because he happened to be there. He and I aren't anything to each other. But you wouldn't know that because even *he's* more present in my life than you are."

Rese gaped at Cait, unaccustomed to the sharpness in her sister's voice.

"No matter what you want to pretend, you stopped caring twelve years ago," Cait said in a low rumble, her old accent slipping in. "You shut me out like you shut out every other part of Ireland. So, don't try to pretend like you're some caring big sister. For all the attention you've shown me the last decade of our lives, you may as well be dead too."

Without another word, Cait shoved past Rese. She ran off the porch, the screen door rattling against the frame with the reverberation of her fury.

Rese stood frozen in place. Tears welled in her eyes, but she shoved them away. "I do care," she whispered, even though her sister wasn't there to hear. "And whether or not you believe me, I'm going to save you."

# CHAPTER THIRTY-NINE

# Cait

**"They came."**

Cait sent the text to Desmond the moment Ben and Jun left that afternoon. She knew he wouldn't be able to respond right away. He was on his way back to Porthaven from the basketball game, surrounded by students and coaches. But he'd want to know.

Hours later, he finally responded.

*"Meet me at the cove tomorrow morning. 6:30."*

Cait smiled at her phone, sitting tucked under the blankets, ready for bed early. She'd spent the afternoon explaining everything the Warden told her to her nan. Though Maeve had cried openly, needlessly apologizing for Cait's plight, she had managed to get through the exchange with a hold on her own emotions. Genni had demanded a private recounting of what had happened with Hunter. And Rese . . .

The argument with Rese rankled in Cait's heart. It startled her to hear that Rese had seen Desmond return her to her room that night. It scared her that her sister might have uncovered their relationship. And after a whole day filled with too much emotion, Cait had snapped.

She felt bad, but after walking the streets of their neighborhood, she finally calmed down.

All the talking, all the weeks of secrets, had left Cait spent and devoid of emotion. She'd taken dinner in her room (something that Maeve never approved of normally but had allowed, given the circumstances), then readied for bed, planning to sketch within the comforting embrace of her blankets.

Then, her phone vibrated.

Cait stared at the screen as though she could see Desmond through it. It had only been two days since she'd seen him, yet it felt like a lifetime, knowing that their time was coming to an end. She had three days left until her eighteenth birthday. Three days during which she would allow herself to enjoy Desmond's company. After that, she'd have to let him go.

But tomorrow, she'd meet him at the cove. It was Columbus Day, which meant school was out. They could spend hours together with no one the wiser.

*"Okay,"* Cait texted in reply. Then, she paused, considered, and sent two others.

*"I know I shouldn't text this, but . . ."*

*"I miss you."*

Several minutes passed, and Cait plugged her phone in, planning to lie down and sleep at last. She reached up to turn off the light when the phone buzzed, the vibration jostling it an inch across the nightstand. She picked it up as it vibrated a second time.

*"Delete this as soon as you receive it,"* Desmond's first text read.

The second made her smile grow tenfold.

*"I miss you too."*

Cait didn't delete it. She set the phone down, turned off the light, and burrowed under her blankets, all the while smiling despite knowing she would dream of Desmond being taken from her again. It didn't matter. They would be parted, yes, but she'd always known that. And moments like these, moments like their day at the cove tomorrow, would get her through whatever the future held.

~

Rising in the early morning, Cait dressed quickly, thoroughly layering for the cold, though she made sure to wear her blush pink blouse with the tie on the collar that Desmond had complimented a month ago. She took extra care with her makeup, too, but settled for pulling her hair back in a ponytail to keep it away from the wind's untamable fingers. All in all, she thought her look was practical yet pretty. Perfect for a secret rendezvous with the boy she loved.

Once she was ready, she grabbed her backpack and headed downstairs before anyone else was awake. She scribbled a note to tell her nan where she'd gone, leaving it on the table when she escaped out the back door with Red.

The morning sky was still a deep gray as she pedaled toward the woods. The cold wind nipped at her cheeks. She smiled anyway, her fingers steady on the rubber handles of her bike. The tires bumped off the macadam onto the grass.

Stowing the bike inside the trees, Cait unleashed Red early. Then, she took off running.

She breached the tree line within minutes. Red jolted past Cait, paws carrying him across the beach with jittery speed. In the predawn light, the cove was an eerie reminder of her dreams. The rocky cliffs loomed, penning in the sea. The dark water rumbled, its waves tugging at the pebbled shore. And there, with his back to her, Desmond stood, waiting.

The hum pulsed at the back of her skull, but she shook away the uncanny image. Her heart filled at seeing him even from this distance.

The smallest beam of golden sunlight seeped over the horizon. Her sneakers crunched over the pebbles and sand, announcing her arrival.

Desmond turned, eyes wide in alarm. "Oh, uh—okay, you weren't supposed to be here yet," he said, hiding his hands behind his back.

Cait smiled, half-attempting a glance at what he was hiding. "You said six-thirty," she reminded him.

"I'd hoped you'd be late."

"Then, you should have said to be here later." She looked behind him, taking in the scene he couldn't hide.

The seafoam-blue striped blanket lay spread out. They usually weighted the corners with clusters of rocks from the shore, but today, he'd used vintage books with small votives on top. Hades perched on the log, tails drifting lazily. A smattering of blue aster flowers dotted the blanket, haphazardly placed in uneven clumps. A wooden serving platter sat in the middle, empty.

Amused that she'd caught his romantic offering early, Cait smiled. "What is this?" she asked.

Desmond scratched the back of his head, one hand still behind his back. "A date?" He said it like it was a question.

It felt as though her smile had taken over her face. "I've never been on a date before."

"Good." He frowned after he said it as though he'd confused himself. "I mean—" He finally revealed his hand, and she saw more blue asters in his grasp. "Not like, 'good, you've never been on a date,' but 'good, I'm glad I get to be your first date.'"

Cait had never seen Desmond so nervous. It was oddly cute. "I'm glad too," she replied.

They stood there, staring at each other for a moment.

Suddenly, Desmond's body jerked as though realizing how awkward he was being. He gestured to the blanket. "Do you want to sit down? You should sit down."

Laughing, Cait did as requested.

"Um, here." He offered her the flowers. "I'm not very good at this."

Taking the bunch and twirling one of the stems between her fingers, Cait asked, "Should I continue to spread them out?"

"Sure," he said, then held up a finger. "Wait—"

He took one flower back from her, carefully and gently placing it behind her ear. "There," he said, smiling. But his expression dropped immediately. "Is that dumb? It's dumb, isn't it? I'll take it out."

"Des—" She grabbed his hand, halting him. "Stop being weird."

Hands falling back to his sides, Desmond let out a huff. "I am being weird, aren't I?"

"Yeah."

"Sorry."

"That's okay." She lifted the flowers. "I'm going to spread these out. You keep doing whatever you were doing."

They went about their separate tasks. She laid out the flowers in a prettier and more logical manner—surrounding where they would sit rather than across it—and he unloaded his backpack and a cooler, filling the serving tray with breakfast. Red's nose carried him over, but Desmond shooed the terrier away. Finally, he lit the votive candles.

When he was finished, he sat beside her, tossed a berry to Hades, and poured coffee from a thermos. He held the first cup out to her, and Cait hesitated.

"What?" he asked. "I brought cream and stuff if you don't like it black."

Cait bit her lip, not wanting to disappoint him. "I don't like coffee," she admitted.

His face went slack. "Who doesn't like coffee?"

"I'm more of a tea person."

He looked out at the sea. "How did I not know that?"

"We've never talked about it," she said. "I didn't know that you *did* like coffee."

"Everyone likes coffee."

"No, they don't."

His pursed lips indicated he disagreed. "Well, I have water too," he offered.

"That's perfect," she promised.

The rest of the breakfast was filled with things Cait *did* like: blueberry muffins, cinnamon-spice doughnuts, strawberries and blackberries, ham and egg bites, and sausage patties. He'd even brought little plates and silverware—real ceramic and metal ones.

"Be careful with those," Desmond said, pointing to the blue and white floral-printed plates. "Mom'll kill me if one of 'em breaks."

"Did you make all of this?" Cait asked, amazed.

"What? Oh, no. I'm shit in the kitchen."

She frowned at his language.

He smirked, tapping her nose. "I bought it all. Well, all except the egg things and sausages. I made those last night."

They watched the sunrise as they ate. The sea reflected bronze and gold, slowly shifting to an icy blue. While the sky lightened, they talked, choosing inconsequential topics. An unspoken agreement stood between them not to discuss the spirit world, the Warden, or the creature breaking free in her dreams.

"If you could go anywhere in the world," Cait said, setting her plate down, "where would it be?"

Desmond considered it, finishing off a muffin. "To visit or to live?" he asked after he'd swallowed.

"Either. Both."

He nodded thoughtfully. "Ireland," he said, meeting her gaze. "But you'd have to come with me."

The answer made Cait feel blissfully happy and devastatingly sad. "Really?" she asked.

"Really."

"To visit or live?" she repeated his earlier question.

His smirk was dangerously adorable as he replied, "Either. Both."

The sea breeze cut across the shore, tickling Cait's ears and neck. She held Desmond's intense gaze, the hum thrumming in her head. The sunlight caught in his brown eyes, highlighting the green flecks hidden within them.

He meant it, she knew. He hadn't chosen her homeland to flatter her. If he could go anywhere—live anywhere—he'd go to Ireland with her.

Cait felt the overwhelming urge to kiss him.

"I have something for you," he said, suddenly turning to his backpack. It brushed Hades when he lifted it, and the cat-beast jumped off the log to saunter toward the trees.

Drawing a deep breath, Cait tried to clear her head even as the hum urged her to inch closer to him. "You do?"

He faced her again, holding out a small, rectangular black box, a lavender ribbon tied around it. "Consider it an early birthday present," he said.

Pleased and surprised, Cait took the box. It was thin and light, and something rattled softly inside. "You've never given me anything before."

"That's absolutely not true," Desmond objected. "I've kissed you the past four years, which is the greatest gift you could receive."

Laughing softly, she lifted the box. "So, you're not going to kiss me this year?"

"I can't tell you that," he said, pretending offense. "It'd ruin the surprise."

Shaking her head, Cait looked between him and the gift. "Should I open it now?"

He pulled in a breath. "Yeah."

She tugged the lavender ribbon free. "Did you know purple is my favorite color, or did you just guess?"

"Caity, I've seen your room," he said. "It wasn't hard to figure out."

Cait smiled, lifting the lid of the box. She looked down to find a necklace resting on a velvet cushion. The silver chain and pendant flashed in the morning light. Delicate swirls and florals were etched into the oval pendant's face.

She lifted it free from the box, the pendant filling most of her palm. "It's beautiful," she said, her voice light.

"I'm glad you like it," Desmond replied, his own voice shaky.

"I do. Thank you." She closed her fingers around the necklace, preparing to give him a hug.

But he pointed to her hand, a strange expression on his face. "It's, uh—it's a locket."

"Oh." Cait lifted it again, looking for the hidden closure. She grinned at him teasingly. "Did you put your picture in it?"

He gave a half-hearted chuckle. "Something like that."

Figuring out the latch, Cait managed to get the locket open. And immediately, she froze.

Instead of a picture, there in the metal casing lay a ring.

The hum surged, filling her head with eager anticipation. Numbly, Cait tilted the ring out onto her palm. Three diamonds graced the simple gold band. None of them were large, but they refracted the light with a radiance that made Cait's eyes sting with recognition.

"It's your mom's," Desmond said, confirming her thoughts. "When the Warden moved your family here, they gave all of your parents' stuff to my dad. He gave most of it to your nan for you guys, but he put the valuables in a safety deposit box."

Cait tore her eyes from the ring to look up at him. His head was dipped as though in reverence. "It was my dad's idea," he admitted. "Using this ring. At first, I thought it was weird, but then I realized how much it would mean to you to have it back and that it was kind of perfect. Because I can't ask your dad for his blessing, but I can still include both your parents in my proposal."

"Desmond—"

"I want to marry you, Cait," he interrupted, stalling her objection. "I don't care if the Warden approves. I'm not volunteering to keep your bloodline alive or to fulfill some obligation. I want to marry you because I love you. And I want to spend the rest of my life loving you."

Under any other circumstance, Cait wouldn't have hesitated to say yes. In any other life, she would never have questioned it. But in this life, she couldn't believe that it was possible.

"We can't," she whispered even as the hum whispered that they should.

He scooted closer. "We can."

"How?"

"I've already worked it out." He took her hands in his, the ring pressing into her palm. "You'll be eighteen on Wednesday, so legally, no one can stop you. My dad has access to the marriage licenses at the town hall. He'll fill out the information and submit the paperwork himself."

"He's okay with this?" she asked incredulously.

"Yeah. And he's convinced Ben to marry us."

Cait's eyes went wide. "Why would he agree to that?"

"Because he's my dad's best friend and my best friend's dad."

Cait remembered Ben's words from yesterday, his promise to do whatever he could to protect her.

She blinked away the thought, struggling to fathom that Desmond was truly offering this to her. "Where—when would we—?"

"At my house on your birthday."

He really had worked it all out. And Cait was struggling to find more excuses.

"Desmond, we're in high school."

"Which isn't ideal, I know. But I've got that figured out too."

"You do?"

"Uh-huh." His thumbs brushed the backs of her hands. "Obviously, things will be kind of complicated at first, but since I'm not a minor anymore, I can officially start making money from my internship, so I'll get something from that. And when we graduate, my dad's gonna get me a full-time thing at the town hall."

"What about college?"

"I'm not going."

Cait started pulling away in protest, but he tightened his grip. "I never cared about college, Cait," he said. "I was only ever going because it was what was expected of me."

"Your parents won't be okay with that," she argued.

"They've already approved."

Cait blinked in shock. "Where would we live?"

He grimaced at that. "Well, temporarily, we'd have to live separately."

"What?"

"For now, you'd stay with your family, and I'd stay with mine."

"Would we—" Cait chewed on her lip, too embarrassed to ask about their more intimate sleeping arrangements during that time. Instead, she said, "It'd hardly feel like we're married."

"It wouldn't be forever, Caity," he promised. "Only until the situation with the Warden is resolved."

At first, Cait thought he was talking about the Wolf and the Veil, but then she realized there was more. "What situation?"

Desmond grimaced. "Right, I didn't get to tell you. Uh . . ." He hesitated, his hands loosening around hers. "So, my dad was fired as the Warden leader in Porthaven. Which sort of means I got fired too—from my future job. Once the Warden finds out that we got married, they'll be pretty pissed."

Cait drew in a deep breath, his words from the other night coming back to her. "Because you lied?"

He nodded. "They want Vessels to marry people they can control. They'll be mad that I went behind their back, but they'll also likely question if our marriage was an attempt to maintain power."

"So, we have to keep it a secret?"

"Only for a little while."

Cait slumped. "I don't want to keep lying, Desmond."

"I know, and I don't want to either." He squeezed her hands. "But, Caity, if we don't do this, they'll make you marry someone else."

"What if I refuse?"

He hesitated as though he hadn't even considered it as a possibility. "Then, you'll live the rest of your life alone, and when you die, the spirit-being will pass to one of your sisters or their kids."

Cait stared at their hands, the hum vibrating around his touch. Her heart stuck on that final word, and she managed the bravery to whisper, "Would we have kids?"

"If you want to," he said.

"But the Wolf would pass to them."

"Not if we find a way to free you first."

It was all too much. The hum rumbled like the waves of the ocean beating against her heart. The ring bit into her palm, giving her too much hope, and her heart hurt, knowing she should say no. She shouldn't let him sacrifice his life and future to marry her. If she truly loved him, she'd let him go.

Desmond's hand cupped her cheek, the warmth of his palm pulsing into her. The hum rose to muddle her senses as he leaned in. She looked up into his handsome face, his dark brow pulled low, and his lips quirked up in the corner, drawing her attention to the two freckles that formed a line from his cheek to his mouth.

"Stop arguing with me, Cait," he said. "And just listen."

She was frozen in compliance, and Desmond reached for her hand. He pried open her fingers, extracting the ring from her grip. Then, he held it between them as he moved to kneel on both knees before her. She held her breath as he spoke.

"Caitriona Lewan," he began, "you are the strongest, most beautiful, and most incredible girl I've ever met. I couldn't deserve you in a million years. You're too good and too kind to be with someone as selfish and insecure as me. Yet, in the past ten years, you've seen me—more than anyone else—and you've never asked me to change. You've loved me despite how unlovable I am. And if you'll let me, I'll spend the rest of my life working to be worthy of your love."

Desmond captured her left hand. "Will you marry me, Cait?"

The hum vibrated through her skull with the pressure of the deepest ocean floor. The world stopped as her mind stilled, focused on the one word she was desperate to say. She stared into his green-flecked brown eyes and knew she was hopeless to refuse him.

But instead of giving her "yes," she heard herself say, "I have plans on my birthday."

It took a moment for Desmond to realize she wasn't rejecting him. He smirked. "Then, we'll get married the next day."

Cait's body relaxed, and the hum fell to a gentle sigh at the back of her mind. "All right," she breathed.

His brow rose, a nervous gleam entering his eyes. "So, that's a yes?"

"Yes."

A relieved huff slipped from Desmond. "Thank God!" he exclaimed. "I thought I'd have to spend the rest of the day convincing you."

Cait laughed even as he slipped the ring onto her left hand. The gold band fit loosely on her finger.

"I know you can't wear it," Desmond said apologetically, despite the smile on his face. "Not yet. But that's what the locket's for. We may be a secret for now but consider it a promise that it won't be for much longer. Soon—"

He paused to swallow. "Soon you'll be my wife, and we won't have to hide, and no one—*no one* will be able to separate us."

Cait didn't bother with words after that. She kissed him, arms around his neck and the delicate weight of the ring on her finger. Their joy wove them into an unbreakable tangle, snuggled on the blanket. They stayed that way, laughing and kissing and talking about how they'd spend the rest of their lives together in Porthaven. They made plans and promises. And under the gentle sunshine of the cove, Cait had never been happier.

# CHAPTER FORTY

# Cait

After school the next day, Cait joined Liz to shop for their girls' night. They went downtown to the grocery and picked out snack after snack to fill their cart. While they'd already planned the party, Cait could tell Liz was going overboard as if to prove her friendship after Hunter's mistake. Though Cait felt he'd paid an adequate price due to the guilt he clearly felt and the bruise that lingered on his jaw from Desmond's punch.

"Cake or ice cream?" Liz asked, then gave her a dramatic look. "Or both?"

"Ice cream," Cait said with a quiet laugh.

"Not both?"

Cait shook her head.

Liz shrugged and headed for the frozen goods aisles. Nervously, Cait followed.

During their time at the cove, Desmond and Cait had made all the final plans for Thursday night. The wedding would take place at six, giving plenty of time to prepare after school. William and Robin were leaving for a long weekend out of town after that, which meant that Desmond and Cait would have the house to themselves. They'd carefully avoided the topic of *why* they'd want the house to themselves and moved on to the other details.

Of course, they'd have to find an excuse for Cait to be gone all evening and night. She could sneak out, but Maeve or one of her sisters would certainly check in on her if she skipped dinner. Beyond that, Cait didn't want to climb off the roof in a dress (regardless of whether it was white or not). So, they needed a reason for her to stay downtown all evening without rousing the suspicions of Maeve, her sisters, or Matt.

And thus, Cait's nervousness around Liz.

Desmond had taken care of everything else. This was *her* task.

As they rounded the corner, rows and rows of colorful ice cream containers surrounding them, Cait took a breath and forced herself to say, "Hey, Liz?"

Liz glanced over her shoulder, a look of concern on her face. "Yeah?" she asked, clearly hearing the anxiety in Cait's tone.

Trying to ease her friend's worry, Cait smiled shyly. "I kind of have a favor to ask of you."

Liz's expression softened. "Anything," she said, and Cait believed her.

Cait took another deep breath and prepared to lie once again. It was almost becoming second nature at this point. "I need your help with something," she said. "Thursday night, I . . . I have a date."

"A date?" Liz's green eyes were wide, and her smile was instantly excited. "With whom?"

With an internal grimace, Cait muttered, "Brady Lavigne."

That surprised Liz. "Really? Hm. I never would have guessed."

"Yeah, me either." She tucked some hair behind her ear. "Anyway, my nan is kind of weird about us girls dating. You know how Ryan had to come over before he and Rese could make it official?"

Liz's mouth quirked, and a disapproving glint entered her eye. "Yeah."

"Well, Nan would probably want to meet him and ask all kinds of questions before we went on our date," she explained. "The thing is, I don't want to make a big deal out of this. We sort of agreed to just go out once to see if anything was there. If not, we can go our separate ways, no hurt feelings. But Nan won't understand that. And I can't tell Genni because she'd tell *everyone*."

"Mm, I think I understand," Liz said knowingly. "You need some place to get ready and an alibi. No worries." She patted Cait's arm. "You can come over after school, and he can pick you up from my house. If anyone asks, we were hanging out all night."

"Thanks," Cait said, genuinely grateful for her friend's help. "Also . . ."

Liz raised her brow, curious.

Cait wrung her hands. "Could I tell my nan I'm spending the night with you?"

Her brows rose even higher.

"Not like—not because I'd be spending the night with *him*," she hurried to clarify. "But Nan has a pretty hard and fast curfew on weeknights. If I don't say I'm spending the night with you, she'd want me home by nine at the latest. And what if it goes well? I don't want to have to cut the evening short because of that."

"Okay," Liz said with a shrug. "Sure. When you get done, just come back and stay with me."

Cait hadn't thought of her being anything but an excuse, so her heart jolted, and she rushed to add, "Oh, well, I'll probably just have him drop me off and tell my nan I decided against it."

Liz's expression pinched in confusion. "Won't she be suspicious of you being all dressed up?"

"She'll be in bed by the time I get home," Cait lied.

Liz bought it and shrugged. "If you're sure? You're welcome either way."

Cait felt her chest ease. "If I change my mind, I'll let you know."

"Good." Liz moved down the aisle. "Now, chocolate or vanilla. And just know: The wrong answer to this could destroy our friendship."

With a light giggle, Cait slid up to her favorite brand of ice cream and pulled out her favorite flavor. "Chocolate *with* caramel swirl and chocolate chunks," she said, proffering the pint toward Liz.

Liz took the ice cream with a huge grin. "I was right," she said merrily. "We should have been friends years ago." Then, she paused. "Wait, what are you going to wear?"

Cait blinked. "What do you mean?"

"On your date."

That caused Cait to flush. What would she wear? She kept imagining herself in a white dress, but she didn't have any that were pretty enough, and she couldn't ask Rese to let her borrow the one she'd worn to the Greenes' party.

At a loss, Cait shrugged sadly. "I don't know."

"Hm." Liz gave her a wry grin. "I guess we'll just have to go shopping then."

~

When Cait woke on her eighteenth birthday, her body trembled with the leftover spike of power from her dreams and a name lingering on her lips. She couldn't remember the name; she just knew it was there, waiting to be spoken, and it unsettled her.

The dreams had been growing more intense each night, that pressure increasing at the base of her skull, right where the hum originated. She didn't know what it meant, but it frightened her along with the fissure in the door. The crack now reached the handle. And somehow, Cait knew if they didn't seal it soon, the Wolf would break free.

But Cait didn't know what to do. No one knew how to fix it. Not Desmond, not Hunter, not even William.

So, she sucked in an uneven breath and rose to get ready for school.

She told herself to focus on tomorrow, focus on the wedding. Tomorrow, she'd marry the boy of her dreams. They could figure out the problem with the Wolf after.

Still, Cait moved through the school day, trying to remember the name that died on her lips when she awoke. All morning, she'd tried forming the word, hoping her subconscious would bring it back, hoping beyond reason that it would be the answer. If it was a name, perhaps it was the name of the redhead or even the shadowy figure. Perhaps one of them held the answers they sought. But no matter how hard she tried, she couldn't remember.

The fact that it was her birthday was both a benefit and a nuisance. While Cait's brain was busy shuffling between thinking about her impending wedding and the unknown name, everyone kept wishing her a happy birthday, asking her how it felt to be an adult (she learned she was the oldest in their friend group) or questioning how she planned to celebrate. Part of her was grateful. The social interactions helped keep her mind occupied on something else. The other part of her—the frightened part—wanted to tell them all to leave her alone.

It didn't help that Sterling pulled her aside the instant they got to the school. "Happy birthday, or whatever," he said, then got to the point. "Weird dream last night?"

"Yeah," Cait whispered. "Well, I mean, the dream was the same, but when I woke—"

"You were about to say a name. Then, it disappeared?"

"Exactly!"

Sterling pressed his lips together, glancing around as they huddled out of the way by the bike rack. "I don't like this, Cait," he said. "Things are getting too serious, too real. And I'm worried. Have you seen how the crack is almost across the whole door?"

Cait nodded, sucking in a deep breath. "Yeah. Yeah, and I'm worried too. But what can we do?"

"I don't know, but we've gotta do something." Sterling ran a hand through his hair. "My mom woke me the other night because she heard me call out in my sleep. She came to check on me, and I don't know what to do because if my parents find out about this, they'll tell the Warden."

Cait understood his concern. So long as the Warden didn't know which Faulk member carried the spirit-being, they'd give Sterling longer to sort out his life. They'd potentially even let him choose a spouse if someone caught his eye in Porthaven. But if they knew for certain that it was him, they'd want to establish a firm control of his lineage like they did hers.

"Do you really think your parents would do that?" Cait asked.

"Look, my parents are great," Sterling said. "Genuinely. But they're fanatics. They'd do whatever the Warden said, no questions asked."

She frowned compassionately.

"I have to find a way to end this," he said.

Holding his intense stare, Cait nodded. "I know. Me too."

Of all people, Sterling could feel the sincerity of her words. The stakes were the same for them both.

"What about the name?" Cait asked.

"What about it?"

"Don't you think it means something? Whoever's name it is . . . Maybe they know something. Maybe they can help."

Sterling shrugged dejectedly. "Maybe. But what? Do we just wait around until we figure out the name? What if the door splits by then?"

Cait chewed on her lip. He had a valid point. One that Cait had no answer for.

So, they went on to class and made their way through the day as best as they could. Cait tried to be thankful to her friends for their distracting chatter just as she tried to take comfort in the subtle hum that reminded her of Desmond's constant presence within the school. They'd made eye contact early in the day, though they hadn't spoken a word to one another.

Cait had to admit she felt slightly irritated with him. He hadn't texted her in two days. And while she knew he was being cautious, it was her birthday. He should have said something already. Instead, after that first look, he didn't even glance at her the rest of the day.

After the long, emotionally exhausting day, Cait struggled not to sulk. Her nan had invited Matt and his mom to join the birthday dinner. Everyone expected her to be in a pleasant, cheerful mood when all she wanted to do was crawl into bed and daydream about tomorrow night.

Why had Cait put off the wedding until Thursday? Why hadn't she found some excuse to get out of dinner tonight? Or why hadn't she thought to sneak out after and get married late in the night? Now, she was left shaky in anticipation of having to make it through yet another day.

Their dinner party was pleasant enough. Her gifts contained more art supplies from Maeve and Genni, a handful of cute, thrifted tops and dresses from Rese, and a leather sketchbook from Matt.

"I, uh—I bound it myself," he told her when she opened it.

"I didn't know you could do that," she said in surprise.

He shrugged, his ears pink.

She ran her thumb over the soft leather cover where he'd embossed her initials: CAL. "How did you know my middle name?" she asked.

"Genni told me."

"Right." She smiled at her sister, then thanked Matt for the gift a second time despite wanting to give it back. He'd gone to too much trouble and done something far too nice for a girl he liked who was getting married in secret tomorrow.

Cait found herself playing with her locket. (When her nan asked where she'd gotten it, she'd said it was a gift from Liz.) Was she making a mistake in marrying Desmond? She'd ruin his life, no matter what he said. Their relationship would mean him giving up everything he'd worked for. Could she really claim to love him and let him sacrifice everything for her?

Life without Desmond would be hard, she knew, but it wouldn't be impossible. If the Warden made her choose someone else, she *could* choose Matt. He clearly liked her enough. He was kind, attentive, and loyal. Desmond hadn't even wished her happy birthday. Matt had taken the time to make her a sketchbook.

That could be enough.

Couldn't it?

The hours dragged by while Cait waited for the night to end. They played cards, laughed, and ate ice cream. But she couldn't enjoy any of it.

When the door shut behind Matt and his mom, she thanked her nan for the birthday dinner and passed around hugs. Then, she trudged up the stairs, thoughts muddled. In less than twenty-four hours, she was supposed to get married, and she was starting to question her sanity. Why had she agreed to it? Yes, she loved Desmond. No, she didn't want the Warden to force her to marry someone else. But she didn't want to live in secret either. She didn't want to lie to her family and friends anymore. And most of all, she didn't want to carry the Wolf.

Cait was so lost in her thoughts that she didn't recognize the rumble in her head until her fingers were on the knob of her door. Her lips parted, and all doubts fled as she carefully pushed it open. Her heart stuttered when she looked inside. There, on the window seat, sat Desmond, waiting for her.

"Don't look so thrilled to see me," he said, keeping his voice low. "It might give me a complex."

Carefully shutting the door behind her, Cait couldn't take her eyes off him. "You already have one," she replied, then practically flew across the room.

He rose, his arms ready to surround her as she crashed into his chest. He was perfect and steady and *there*. And it was her favorite moment of the day.

"Happy birthday, Caity," he whispered into her hair.

She pulled back to slug him in the shoulder. "You could've texted me."

Desmond's expression grew serious. "I absolutely could not," he said. "You can only say 'happy birthday' once, and I wanted it to be in person. Plus, I had to give you your present."

"My—?"

Before she could finish, he kissed her. It was a long and slow and far more romantic kiss than on any of her previous birthdays.

"Okay," Cait whispered. "I forgive you."

Desmond's eyes widened. "I didn't realize I needed forgiving."

"You didn't text me," she repeated. "And you ignored me at school."

"I *have* to ignore you at school," he replied gently. Then, he smirked. "Though not for much longer. Once we get things figured out—once Dad and I show the Warden that we can still be trusted—then you won't be able to get rid of me at school."

Cait let out a half-felt chuckle. "How long do you think that will take?" she asked.

Knowing what she meant, Desmond lifted his shoulder in a shrug even as he continued to hold her. "Hopefully? Only a month or so. We're both going to work hard to resolve things. We intend to prove ourselves by fixing the Veil and saving you. If we can do that . . . there's no way they'll be able to doubt us."

Desmond pulled her onto the window seat then, settling his arms around her waist. "I'm not going to stay long," he said. "I just wanted to see you and tell you that I won't be at school tomorrow."

"Why not?"

He played with her hair, twisting it around his finger. "I've heard something about bad luck when you see the bride before the wedding."

Cait felt her cheeks warm.

"Are you ready?" he asked quietly.

"I think so," she whispered back. "I went shopping with Liz yesterday, and I found a dress. She's excited about helping me get ready for my 'date.'"

"Your date?" he asked in surprise. "You didn't tell her *we* were going out, did you?"

Cait shook her head, face heating.

His eyes narrowed. "Then, who?"

"Brady," she admitted.

His expression twisted with disgust. "You told her you were going out with my best friend?"

"He was the only person I could think of," she said apologetically. "Besides, he can pick me up from her place, and it won't seem weird."

"I don't want people thinking my best friend is dating my wife."

She rolled her eyes. "*People* won't think anything. Liz will think we went on *one* date. I'll tell her neither of us felt anything was there, and no one else has to know."

"She's already told Hunter, I guarantee it."

Cait couldn't help her amused chuckle at his irritation. "Fine. The two of them will think I went on one date with Brady, and at the end of it, we mutually determined we didn't want to pursue it. We could even make it sound like he was thinking of volunteering to marry me, like, as a friend."

Desmond considered it. "I still don't like it."

She tugged on the string of his hoodie. "But you want to marry me, right?"

He smirked, pulling her closer. "Obviously."

"Then, you'll deal with it?" she asked, leaning in.

"I don't have much of a choice, do I?" he said. But instead of kissing her like she expected, he drew back. "How do you feel about cake?"

Cait blinked at the sudden question. "Cake?"

"For our wedding."

The thought of their wedding made her insides squirm nervously. It sounded so wrong. They couldn't be getting married. They were just kids.

"Oh, uh—" Cait shrugged. "I mean, it isn't like a real wedding."

Desmond's brow furrowed. "It's very much a real wedding."

"No, I mean," Cait sighed, "we aren't doing real wedding things, like having a reception where we'd cut a cake and dance or any of that stuff."

"Just because no one's there doesn't mean we can't do those things."

Cait hesitated. "Do you *want* to do those things?"

Now, Desmond hesitated. "If *you* want to," he said uncertainly.

Why hadn't they talked about this? In all their planning, they'd discussed the logistics, but they'd never even talked about typical wedding details. Suddenly, Cait didn't feel ready. Did she want cake and dancing? Did she want a bouquet or a veil? And who was going to walk her down the aisle?

The thought crashed into Cait. She'd never considered walking down an aisle, be it in a home or a church. She'd never imagined that she'd marry. And now, she realized how disappointed she was that she'd never get that moment with her da.

She dropped her head onto Desmond's shoulder. "No," she whispered. "I just want to marry you. I don't care about anything else."

Though Desmond couldn't know the reason for her sudden somberness, he held her gently. His fingers trailed through her hair, brushing along her back. Cautiously, he murmured, "What if my mom already made a cake?"

Cait paused. "Did she?"

"Kinda."

Smiling, she snuggled closer. "What kind?"

"Chocolate with buttercream frosting and strawberries on top."

Cait chewed on the inside of her lip even as she enjoyed the comfort of Desmond's embrace. "Is she upset with me?" she whispered.

Desmond looked down at her. "Does cake usually mean someone's upset with you?"

Cait laughed weakly. "No, I just—she doesn't know me," she explained. "And you're her only son. Isn't she disappointed that you aren't going to marry someone like Liz in the chapel?"

He snorted wryly. "Mom thinks Liz is a know-it-all. And no, she doesn't care about that stuff. She's the least snobby person I know."

"You're sure?"

"I'm completely sure." Desmond loosened his grip on her. "So, you're good with cake?"

Smiling up at him, Cait nodded. "Yeah, I'm good with cake."

He returned her nod, his eyes locked with hers, and she could tell he was fighting the urge to kiss her. "I should probably get going."

Cait didn't bother to reply. He was right, but she didn't want him to be.

Desmond took her left hand, brushing his thumb against her bare ring finger. "I'll see you tomorrow," he said. "Right at six."

"At six," she promised.

Steadily, the hum pulsed through her as if it were anticipating the day as much as they were. Cait rested her forehead against Desmond's. Why did it feel so difficult to part when tomorrow they'd be bound forever? Perhaps it was because of that knowledge. Perhaps knowing made the separation even harder.

"I'm not gonna kiss you again, okay?" Desmond whispered.

"You're not?" Cait tried not to be disappointed.

He shook his head, forehead still pressed against hers. "Because if I start, I don't think I'll be able to stop."

"Then, you'd better not."

"Nope."

Painfully, Cait pulled away, kissed his cheek, and rose off the bench. "Goodnight, Des," she whispered.

With a deep inhale, Desmond stared at her. He reached up behind himself to unlatch the casement window. "Goodnight, Caity."

# CHAPTER FORTY-ONE

# Cait

Cait blinked, staring at herself in Liz's floor-length mirror.

"You look perfect," her friend exclaimed, surveying her work. She'd curled Cait's hair, applied her makeup, and even let her use one of the elegant perfumes on her vanity. "You were right. Blue is a good color for you."

"Thanks," Cait said, smoothing the folds of her skirt. Though she'd have preferred something white, she'd struggled to find one in the meager offerings at the store. Instead, she'd settled for this ice-blue knee-length dress that billowed softly below the empire waist.

She might not look like a traditional bride, but it made her feel strangely grown and beautiful.

"All right—" Liz rushed to grab Cait's bag, shoving her phone into the side pocket. "He's waiting out front, so you'd better hurry up."

Together, they rushed to the front door. Liz gave her one more spritz of perfume and brushed down some flyaway hairs before giving her a thumbs-up. "Have an amazing time," she said with a hug. "And let me know if you decide to spend the night."

Cait thanked her again, then dashed out the door. The last time she'd been at the Greene house, the long gravel driveway had been filled with cars. Today, it only held Brady's white sedan waiting at the foot of the steps. He stood at the passenger door, holding it open for her.

"Uh, hi," he said, reaching out to take the overstuffed backpack from her. "I'll put that in the back. You look nice, by the way."

Once they were in the car, Cait kept fussing with the folds of her skirt to be sure it didn't wrinkle. The radio played some indie rock song that she didn't recognize. Brady didn't say a word as he drove.

"I appreciate you doing this," she said to break up the awkward silence.

He glanced at her. "Picking you up? Or pretending to be your date?"

She blushed. "Both."

"It was a joke," he said with a grin. "I'm just glad to be invited."

Cait played with her locket. "Desmond wouldn't do this without you. And I'm happy to have you there too."

"You don't know me," he said, then added, "Yet. After this, we'll practically be family."

"Is that—is it weird for you?"

"What? You marrying my best friend?" He said it so casually that it almost sounded normal.

"Your best friend being married," Cait clarified.

He lifted his chin in thought. "Nah. It *was* my idea."

Cait felt her brow furrow. "It was?"

"Oh, yeah. I told him to marry you the day after I found out about you two."

"Why?" she asked, unsure what else to say.

"Because I saw the way he protected you on the island," he said matter-of-factly. "Desmond doesn't care about anyone like he cares about you. And if he's gonna be with anyone, I figure it should be *you*."

Cait pressed her lips together, then remembered the gloss that Liz had applied and worried she'd smeared it.

Brady glanced at her again. "You should probably put your ring on." He nodded toward her hand, which was absentmindedly playing with the locket.

"Oh. Right." Carefully, she opened the locket, slipping the ring out. She placed it on her finger, letting the evening light glitter in the triad of diamonds. She smiled, remembering Desmond saying that it represented her parents. Her da might not be able to walk her down the aisle, but both he and her mum would be with her anyway.

Brady cleared his throat. "Your, uh, your sister . . . sisters—" He tapped the steering wheel. "Do they know about this?"

"Oh, no," Cait said. "No, if Genni knew, she'd immediately tell our nan. Mostly because she wouldn't want me to make a mistake."

"And Rese?"

Cait shrugged as they pulled into the Simon family's driveway. "Well, Rese kind of hates Desmond, so . . ." She passed him a dry smile. "I think she'd try to put a stop to it too."

"Mm." Brady parked and gave her a close-mouthed smile. "Well, we're here. I had a nice time, but I'll be honest, I don't think it's gonna work out between the two of us."

"We gave it a shot," Cait replied, amused.

As they got out of the car and walked through the meticulous backyard, Cait's stomach began to spin. She stared at the beautiful white house, certain she was living in a dream. In no reality could she actually be about to marry the boy set to inherit all this grandeur and the responsibility that went with it.

Brady entered the house like it was his second home. He moved through the kitchen, calling out, "We're here."

Within seconds, Robin Simon turned the corner. "Try not to yell, Brady," she said lightheartedly. "It isn't befitting the occasion."

"Right," Brady said, accepting the woman's affectionate pat on the cheek. He hefted Cait's bag. "Where should I put this?"

"Desmond's—" Robin corrected herself. "*Their* room."

Cait blanched at the thought.

"That's not weird," Brady muttered, heading for the door. "He up there?"

"He's with William in the office. Your dad's running late."

"Got it."

With Brady gone, Cait faced Robin alone. Her insides squirmed. "It's nice to see you again, Mrs. Simon," she said meekly.

The woman's elegant navy dress brought out her crystal-blue eyes. "It's Robin," she said, then hesitated. "How do you feel about hugs?"

Cait's eyes widened. "Oh, uh—they're . . . nice."

Robin smiled. "Would it be terribly awkward of me to hug you?"

Swallowing down the sudden swell of emotion within her, Cait didn't know if it was gratitude, relief, or joy she felt most profoundly in that moment. She'd lost her mum twelve years ago. And while Robin Simon couldn't ever be the same to her as Sabine Lewan, her affection unable to replace the loss of her mum's, this was the closest she'd ever come.

"Not at all," Cait whispered, afraid that if she spoke too loudly, she'd wake from this dream.

"Good," Robin said, then gently pulled Cait into a hug. She smelled like daisies and comfort. Her steady embrace was the most heartwarming experience, like being wrapped in a blanket straight from the dryer.

When she pulled back, Robin's smile lit her whole face. She took Cait's hands in hers. "I very much look forward to getting to know you, Caitriona."

"Me too," Cait murmured, struggling to find her voice.

Robin squeezed her hands. "While we wait for Ben to get here, I have something I'd like to show you," she said, moving toward the hallway.

Cait followed, noting the woman's bare feet on the plush runner over the hardwood. They walked through the short hall, and the hum steadily filled her head, wending into her limbs. Her eyes habitually sought Desmond's presence, her heart pattering in her chest.

She jumped as Robin called, "Door, William."

At the end of the hall, William Simon appeared in an open doorway, the light of sunset warming the office behind him. He gave Cait a smile and a nod before shutting the door. Robin turned into an adjacent room. Cait lingered in the hall, listening to the muffled tones of Desmond's voice on the other side of that closed door.

"In here, dear," Robin beckoned.

Cait forced her gaze away, the hum vibrating through her whole being. She stepped into the bedroom, her lips parting as she took in the space. A vaulted tray ceiling held a beautiful yet understated chandelier. A large four-poster bed rested on the far end. Chocolate brown velvet curtains draped floor to ceiling, the amber sunset streaming through the windows.

Robin shut the door, then moved across to the antique white dresser. "Here," she said, picking up a striped box. "Now, I don't want you to feel obligated, so feel free to tell me no. But you have your something old and something new." She motioned to Cait's locket and ring, then brushed the flowing sleeve of her dress. "And your something blue. So, if you'd like, it would be my honor to contribute your something borrowed."

Taking the proffered box in an unsteady state of awe, Cait mumbled her thanks. She lifted the lid to find white gauzy material lined in lace folded around a thin satin headband.

"It was my veil," Robin explained. "I know it's out of fashion. The late eighties aren't known for being the height of wedding couture. But I pride myself on having enough sense to choose a timeless style even then."

Cait cautiously pulled the veil free, finding its simple design decidedly sophisticated. "It's beautiful," she breathed.

Robin's chin dipped. "Does that mean you'd like to wear it?"

"Yes." The word came out in a rushed breath. "I—I'd love to."

The kindest smile filled Robin's whole face. Her eyes twinkled with joy. She drew Cait closer to the dresser and directed her to face the large mirror attached. With the tenderest care, she set the veil in Cait's hair.

Cait stared at her reflection. Her curls had already begun to droop, her expression was wildly startled, and she was too young to look like a true bride. But as Robin tucked the veil to lay flat, she suddenly felt like one.

"There," Robin said, draping Cait's hair around her shoulders. A glimmer of tears rimmed her eyes. "You're stunning."

Cait chewed on her lip, certain she was too nervous to be stunning.

With a wink, Robin's mouth turned up in a smirk so very much like Desmond's. "My seabird isn't going to know what hit 'im."

Spinning to face the woman, Cait was suddenly sure she needed to apologize. "This isn't right," she said. She touched the ends of the veil. "I—you shouldn't let me wear this. I don't deserve to."

Surprise softened Robin's expression. "Why not?"

"Because we lied to you," she said. "And you just met me. It isn't right. You—you should know the girl who's going to marry your son. She should be normal. He should bring her over for dinner and—and you should have months or years of history. He shouldn't—he can't—I'm not—"

Robin grabbed Cait's hands, which flailed between them. She had to lean down slightly to hold her gaze. "Desmond has never been an easy child," she said firmly but with kindness. "He's too clever and too strong-willed for that. Will and I didn't always channel that well. We tried, but . . . no parent knows exactly the right way to raise their child. We do our best, and we make mistakes in spite of it."

She stepped closer, expression softening. "I never expected him to choose a 'normal' girl," she said. "I wouldn't have wanted that for him. 'Normal' is boring. It wouldn't challenge him. And while I may not know you yet . . ."

Robin stood straight, her blue eyes like the clear sky above the cove.

"I know that if my seabird chose you, then you're everything he needs you to be."

Cait struggled to believe her. What mother didn't want her son to marry a perfect, normal girl? One who wasn't haunted by curses and dreams. How could Robin or any mother accept Cait with so little acquaintance? She was the mayor's wife. She had to know the rumors; she had to know the truth. It shouldn't matter what Desmond thought he wanted; his mother should be skeptical of Cait.

But she could see by the affectionate lift to Robin Simon's smile that she meant every word.

A *click* and voices in the hall drew both women's attention. Reverend Lavigne had arrived, and he was speaking with William. Then, she heard Desmond's voice. The hum brayed gently against her chest. Muffled laughter and movement signaled the men moving down the hall.

Robin squeezed Cait's hands again. "Is there anything you need?" she asked. "Water? A bite to eat?"

Cait shook her head, her stomach too tight to accept food or drink.

"What about the ceremony? Desmond said that you weren't particular, but if there's anything you thought of, it's no problem. I have Pachelbel's *Canon in D* lined up for your entrance, but I can have Brady change it."

Cait didn't recognize the song's title but assured her it was fine.

"We kept the proceeding short," Robin explained, "but I have candles in case you wanted to do that, or we have crackers and wine if you'd like communion."

"Um, that'd be nice, I guess."

"Candles or communion?"

"Communion."

Robin nodded and then picked up her phone. "I'll tell William." She typed as she continued, "There are lemon halibut and rice in the oven and a small cake in the refrigerator. If you need anything else, don't be shy; this is your home now too. Will and I leave straight after to go to the cabin—"

"You have a cabin?" Cait heard herself ask.

She grinned. "It's yours, too, dear. We'll head out immediately and stay the whole weekend. If there's anything you need, feel free to text or call."

Cait thought about telling her she couldn't spend the entire weekend in the house with Desmond but was too uncomfortable discussing the idea of *staying* with Desmond to speak.

"We're about ready to begin, so do you need to use the restroom or freshen up your makeup?"

"I don't think so," Cait murmured.

A knock sounded at the door.

"Yes?" Robin called.

"I've been sent on behalf of the seabird," Brady said on the other side.

Robin chuckled and invited him in.

Opening the door, Brady took a second to survey Cait's veil. "Fancy," he noted. He stepped forward, awkwardly holding out a small bouquet of white roses. "These are from Desmond."

"Thank you," Cait said, the stems cold in her hand and her heart warm in her chest.

"Sure thing." Brady rocked back on his feet. "You good to go?"

Breath caught in her throat, Cait could only nod.

Robin slipped into some flats, then caught Brady's arm before he raced out the door. She turned back to Cait. "One last thing," she said. "We're set up in the living room. I'll be standing with William, but would you like Brady to stay and walk you to the room?"

"I don't think—" Brady protested, but Robin interrupted.

"Not to walk you down the aisle," she assured, pausing. "Unless you'd like him to?"

Cait shook her head, and Brady looked relieved.

"Then, just to show you the way, if you need," Robin said.

Appreciating the offer, as Brady knew the house far better than her,

Cait decided against it. She wanted a moment to herself. One final minute to convince herself that this was reality. One final chance to be Caitriona Lewan, the outcast of Porthaven, before she became Caitriona Simon, the secret future matriarch of the town.

"I'll be fine," Cait promised.

Brady practically ran from the room while Robin lingered a second longer. "Take your time," she said, and then she was gone too.

Cait stood in the master bedroom, the subtle lilt of classical music reaching her ears. So *that* was the "canon" song Robin had mentioned. It was decidedly more stuffy than expected, but she supposed it sounded matrimonial.

Cait looked at herself in the mirror one last time. Adjusting her bouquet, she tried to look bridal rather than anxious. The sunset was fading, the room turning a deep shade of rust. With her ice-blue dress, ivory veil, white-blonde hair, and pale skin, she stood out like a ghost.

Her eyes caught on her ring—her mum's ring. Would Owen and Sabine have been happy today? Would they accept Desmond the same way that Robin accepted her? Or would they be disappointed in her for marrying in secret?

A comforting hum spread from the base of Cait's skull across her shoulders. She looked at the door hanging ajar, expecting Desmond to appear. The hum remained, but he didn't come.

Cait took a step, and the hum pulsed as though summoning her forward.

With another step, it grew louder.

Gripping the roses more securely, Cait left the room behind, the hum filling her body with reassurance. She paced down the narrow hallway, each step giving her strength. She smiled, knowing that her parents would not only be happy for her but also would have proudly taken Desmond as a son. They would have been overjoyed that she'd found someone who made her heart soar and her spirit feel free. They would have stood with William and Robin, gladly witnessing the union of their children.

Cait passed the kitchen and turned under the arched entry to the living room. She'd timed it poorly—the music ended as she entered, a momentary silence preceding the loop. Candles filled the space, lighting it with a romantic, ethereal flicker. Most of the furniture was missing, leaving the middle of the room open. Rose petals and blue aster flowers dotted the floor to create an aisle. William and Robin stood to the side, hand in hand. Brady fidgeted across from them. And at the far end, the reverend stood with Desmond at his side.

The hum kicked up, filling her head like the howl of the wind.

Desmond raised his head when she entered, shoulders easing back. To her surprise, he wore a full suit: a white shirt, black jacket, slacks, and even a thin lavender tie. He'd combed his hair, taming its usually unruly waves. His mouth was pulled in a tight, barely contained smile.

Their eyes locked, and instinct told Cait to run to him, to wrap her arms around his waist and sink into his touch. But the presence of the others kept her gait steady as she crossed to him. Her lungs were full, and her head was dizzy.

Desmond held out his hand as she neared, drawing her to him. He didn't speak, but she could see in the keen attentiveness of his gaze that it wasn't for lack of emotion. Like her, his voice was tangled up in every promise they were about to make.

"Shall we begin?" Ben said, an encouraging smile on his lips.

Fingers entwined and hearts full of hope, Cait and Desmond turned to face the reverend.

Ben held a small, leather-bound book in his hand. "Good evening," he said. "I can safely say this is the smallest wedding I've ever officiated but probably the most significant." He paused, then added dryly, "At least, until Brady finally finds himself a wife."

Desmond chuckled while Brady muttered, "I'm not rushing it."

Ben's grin was identical to his son's. "As it is," he continued, "I'm honored to lead you into matrimony. Desmond, you have been a second son to me. And no matter the circumstances leading to this marriage, it proves what a good and honorable man you've become. The troubles of life will press you down, but you've got to stand strong despite them with God and your wife beside you."

Desmond's fingers twitched around Cait's, their hands hanging at their sides between them. She brushed her thumb along his index finger, thinking Ben was right. Desmond had become a good man. No matter his flippancy and rebellion through the years, he'd never truly veered from the right path. And he was choosing to be brave, righting the wrongs he'd done and marrying her rather than cowering before the opinions of others.

"Cait," Ben said, directing his attention to her. "Of course, I haven't had the opportunity to get to know you as I would like. But after speaking with Desmond and through the years of our limited interactions, I have discovered one clear truth: You are a strong, courageous young woman."

Cait blushed at the compliment, sure it couldn't be true. Desmond squeezed her hand as though to emphasize the point, bolstering her hope that it might be.

"You don't shy away from difficulty. Instead, you accept the responsibilities laid upon your shoulders, determined to care for those around you. If there is anyone who can help Desmond be the man he's meant to be, it's you."

Cait found herself glancing at Desmond, who stared at her with a nervous affection.

"Now," Ben concluded with lighthearted enthusiasm, "let's get on with the ceremony, shall we?"

The reverend led them through the declaration of intent, to which they both said, "I do." He read a few verses from the Bible, discussing the gift of marriage, keeping his words short and to the point. As he began to guide them through the vows, Cait realized she'd never actually been to a wedding. While her family might have attended one in Bushmills, she couldn't remember, and they didn't have close enough friends in Porthaven to be invited to one. Desmond repeated the vows easily, but she had to ask Ben to repeat a couple of the lines a few times to be sure she said them right.

"I'm sorry," she muttered after the second time.

Ben smiled and shook his head. "It isn't a problem."

After the vows were complete, Brady stepped forward to hand Ben a small velvet box. The reverend pulled a ring out and handed it to Cait. She took it numbly. Ben instructed her to place it on Desmond's finger, and she pushed it all the way on before she realized she was ahead of herself.

"Sorry," she said again.

"It's fine, Caity," Desmond said, smiling brightly. He clasped her hand instead of letting her fix her mistake.

Ben smirked knowingly at their awkwardness. "Just repeat after me," he said and gave her the line.

Staring into Desmond's eyes, Cait repeated, "With this ring, I thee wed."

It was Desmond's turn next. Gently, he settled the ring on her finger, holding it by the knuckle. "With this ring," he guided the band to rest against the triad of diamonds, holding her gaze all the while, "I thee wed."

The hum rumbled in approval. Cait's stomach churned like the sea while Ben led them through the sacrament of communion. It wasn't possible. This moment had been an unattainable dream. Yet, here she stood before Desmond as he claimed her as his wife.

In the background, Ben was offering a prayer, but Cait couldn't hear it past the howling in her ears and the thrumming under her skin. She and Desmond stared at one another as though realizing the same incredible fact: They were married.

When Ben said "amen," she blinked, attempting to clear away the overpowering hum enough to hear his next words. "By the power vested in me by God and the state of Maine, I now pronounce you man and wife. You may kiss the bride."

Neither of them moved.

They watched one another, dumbfounded. They were *married*.

A slow, relieved smile came to Desmond's face, and the truth settled into Cait with equally joyous liberation. *They were married.* No one could separate them. They wouldn't be taken from each other. They had the rest of their lives to be together.

No longer *nothing* as they'd so often pretended. As husband and wife, they were the most profound *something* in the world.

Suddenly, Desmond reached for Cait. He kissed her deeply. Probably too deeply, considering they were in front of his parents, his best friend, and the reverend. But Cait didn't care. She threw her arms around his neck, reveling in the truth: They were married, and they *were* real.

# CHAPTER FORTY-TWO

# Rese

"So, I was thinking about it," Ryan said, leaning on the pastry case while Rese dismantled the espresso machine for cleaning. They hadn't exactly made up, but he had taken the initiative, coming to visit her at the coffee shop.

Marcy had instituted a "Coffees and Crochets" night on Thursdays years ago. Since the woman was a member of the crochet club, Rese generally didn't have to work. But her boss inevitably caught the sniffles at the turn of the seasons, so she'd asked Rese to cover tonight while she got some much-needed R&R.

Looking up from dumping the grounds' bin, Rese met Ryan's gaze. He grinned fondly and apologetically. "You were totally right," he said. "I haven't taken the time to learn what would make you truly happy. And I'm sorry about that. And because I'm sorry . . ." he dipped his chin penitently, "I want to take you on a proper date."

Rese raised her brow, uncertain of his sincerity. "Oh, yeah? You wanna take me to dinner at the diner?" she asked with a tinge of bitterness.

"We do have nicer restaurants in Porthaven," he countered. "But no, I was thinking of something better than that."

"Like what?"

"Like," his eyes twinkled in the setting sunlight, "there's this fancy place in Portland that you have to wear a tie to get into."

"You hate ties," she noted.

Ryan shrugged. "But you don't."

A girlish joy spread through her chest at the idea, though an underlying worry tempered her smile. "Portland is four hours away."

He gave her a knowing smirk. "I can afford a hotel room." At her wary look, he quickly added, "Separate beds, I promise."

Still unsure, Rese studied Ryan. He seemed genuine, but she couldn't believe he didn't have an ulterior motive. "That is a pretty big trip for a simple date," she said.

"It isn't a simple date," he said, his eyes locking with hers. "It's a chance for me to get to know you. The *real* you. It's a chance for me to learn every last thing about you."

Rese pursed her lips. She glanced over his shoulder to the front of the shop, where the crochet club women greeted one another enthusiastically. Most were well over fifty, but a handful were in their twenties or thirties. Sometimes, she thought about joining them. They all seemed so happy and content together, making blankets and beanies and sweaters for charity and the new babies in town.

She couldn't help wondering if she'd ever have the chance to experience a community like that. Even as Ryan's wife, would she be accepted into such a wholesome group of supportive women? Or would she be destined to play the role of the snobby, pretty girl who couldn't quite keep any friendships?

Unable to fully accept Ryan's goodness, Rese shifted closer. She lowered her voice as she asked, "And what do you get out of this date?"

His expression dropped for a moment as though disappointed that she thought he wanted something from her. Then, his smile returned, softer than usual. "A happy girlfriend," he said. "Which is pretty important from what I understand."

Holding his gaze, Rese tried to detect any hint of duplicity. Yet, she didn't find any. Ryan was entirely, surprisingly, sincere. He wanted to take her on a fancy date because he knew she liked fancy things. He wanted to get to know her heart because he wanted to be a good boyfriend. Full stop.

Rese felt herself warm from the inside out. Maybe life with Ryan Greene wouldn't be so bad after all. But that didn't mean she could accept this overnight trip to Portland.

"Nan won't approve," she said.

Ryan quirked a brow derisively. "You are an adult. Your grandma can't tell you what to do anymore."

"It isn't about that," she replied gently. "I have two little sisters, Ryan. I don't want to be a bad example."

The way his eyes narrowed said he thought it was too late, but she chose to ignore that.

Rese reached across the counter to grab his hand. "Thank you," she said. "I love the idea, but I can't leave town like that. Just . . . take me on a picnic or something. And you can still wear a tie."

"It could snow any day now, Rese." He squeezed her fingers. "A picnic is a great way to freeze."

"We'll bundle up," she said.

"Then, you can't see my tie."

Rese laughed and pulled away. "Come up with something better then. I've got to finish cleaning this before these women all order flat whites."

Ryan looked incredulous. "They all order the same thing?"

"More or less," she said, then shrugged. "Makes my night easy."

He chuckled, leaning across to kiss her. "Have fun then. I'll see you after?"

"Maybe," she said, unwilling to promise anything. After her visit to the chapel, with its Gothic arches and columns, she'd had an urge to reread Jane Eyre, and tonight would be her first chance. But Ryan wouldn't understand that, so she simply added, "I have some things I've got to get done."

Though he looked mildly disappointed, Ryan gave her a smile and a final goodbye.

With a warning to the crochet women, Rese took the espresso machine parts into the back for cleaning. She moved as quickly as she could, knowing the women would be lining up to order their beverages soon. Once the machine was back together, she wiped her hands on her apron and moved to the register. Ten of the twelve women ordered flat whites. The other two chose tea.

Rese created an assembly line of the drinks, making them with rote familiarity. Her thoughts drifted to the book Brady had given her. It was filled with useless information. She would have considered that his goal was to send her on a wild-goose chase, except that it actually was solid information on wielding. If she could access the spirit world, if she didn't have the block his dad had placed within her, then she might've benefitted from its study.

Instead, she was no closer to figuring out how to save Cait.

Rese kept the book in the faux leather backpack she carried as a purse. She had it ready and waiting to return to the reverend's kid, hoping he'd have a better book to offer in the future. But finding opportunities to talk with him wasn't as easy as he'd made it seem.

Most days, she worked while Brady was at school, getting off before he might potentially come in. When they were around one another in public, Ryan was there too. As she didn't care to hear what he'd say if he saw them talking, she pretended not to notice Brady at all.

Which meant she'd been lugging around an impossibly heavy backpack all week.

Rese wished she'd just traded phone numbers with the boy. Now, she was stuck in a holding pattern with no surer means to save Cait.

Was her fate even that bad? Their da had taught Rese that the Warden was trustworthy and its purpose pure. She'd believed him until they moved to Porthaven. The structure of the organization here was different than in Bushmills. She'd known the members there, and she remembered liking them all. They weren't self-seeking or haughty. They didn't try to stifle the truth or put a limit on who could and couldn't wield. They were cautious, yes, but not closed off.

And they'd never suppressed Owen's ability to connect to the spirit world. Not even with the Wolf at his side.

Rese's thoughts drifted to Cait. Could her sister handle that? Could she walk through life with a monster as a pet? The timid, fearful child she'd become couldn't, of that, Rese was sure. But if Ryan was right, there was no way for Rese to convince the Wolf to take her as his host instead.

She still felt bad about their argument the other day. It went exactly the way she expected. No matter how hard Rese tried to get her sister to understand, no matter how many ways she tried to show her love, it always backfired. Yet, somehow, she had to find a way to make up with Cait.

The café bell chimed, and the women all chirped like birds, cooing flirtatiously with the newcomer. Rese turned to find Donna Lavigne, the eldest member of the crochet club, tugging on her grandson's sleeve, pulling him down to kiss his cheek. Brady didn't appear the slightest bit embarrassed by the exchange, returning her hug and greeting the women casually.

"Come to join us, birdy?" Donna asked playfully.

Rese raised her eyebrow at the nickname but averted her gaze when Brady glanced her way. "Sure thing, Gram," he said. "Just give me a few minutes, and I'll let you teach me."

Donna had caught his surreptitious look and gave him a wink. "Oh, take your time, sweetie. We'll be here when you get done."

Brady pretended not to hear the insinuation, just as Rese pretended to be reorganizing the tea jars as he approached.

"Let me guess," she said by way of greeting. "Drip coffee, black."

He stared at her in that stoic way of his. "It's seven in the evening."

For some reason, Rese felt the inexplicable urge to tease him. "And your grandma's drinking espresso, *birdy*. What, you can't handle caffeine better than Donna?"

His thick eyebrows drew together. "You know my grandma well enough to call her by her first name?"

"She's a regular," Rese said casually. She tipped her head to the side. "You want something or not?"

"I didn't just come here to crochet," Brady replied. His delivery was so dry she didn't realize he was joking at first.

She found herself laughing softly. "What do you want then?"

"I have it on good authority that you can make more complicated drinks than drip, so . . ." He gave her a pointed stare, placid as ever. "Surprise me."

Rese picked up a cup, considering him. "But no cinnamon, right?"

"Right."

"Mm-hm." Rese turned, picking up the Sharpie pen on habit. Deciding what she wanted to make, she marked the side thoughtfully. Then, she set about making his drink, keeping her back to him the whole time.

Surprisingly, he didn't try to engage her in conversation. She was almost disappointed, amused by his wry sense of humor. But she told herself not to care.

When she turned around to deliver his drink, he was missing.

"Over here," he called, sitting at the bar along the side of the counter.

Setting his cup down, Rese intentionally spun it so he'd see the nickname scrawled on the side in her cursive. "Enjoy, birdy."

He grinned, then motioned to the cup. "What is it?"

"Americano with heavy cream and toffee." She gave him a look that dared him to complain. "Try it before you send it back, Mr. I-Take-It-Black."

"I told you to surprise me," he noted, then sipped it. His bland expression gave nothing away. "It's good."

Rese doubted he liked it and took a strange satisfaction in that. "Why does she call you 'birdy'?" she asked without meaning to.

"She says it's cuter than Brady," he replied. "I think it's her way of telling my parents she hates my name."

Rese smiled sweetly. "It is a pretty stupid name."

"Thank you." He said it so seriously that it sounded like he meant it.

Shaking her head, Rese smirked, feeling a tinge of exasperation. "You're being pretty obvious, you know," she said.

"About what?"

She leaned against the counter, crossing her arms. "As you so kindly pointed out, I'm not stupid. And you aren't that subtle."

Brady eyed her blandly. "I believe my exact words were that you're smart. But seeing as how you spend time with guys like Ryan, I can see why you wouldn't be used to compliments."

Noting that he didn't deny his interest this time, Rese arched an eyebrow. "I'm brave enough to admit that you're cute, Brady. Both physically and surprisingly in personality. But you're not my type."

"That's right," he said with a nod. "You like douchebags."

She narrowed her eyes. "Your best friend is the king of douchebags, and I'd rather kiss a seagull."

He pursed his lips, raising his drink. "That'd be interesting to watch."

"What do you want, Brady?" she asked, the exasperation leaking into her tone now.

He reached into his jacket pocket. "I have something for you."

"You're bringing me gifts now?"

"I wouldn't call it a gift." Brady pulled out a thin book with a marbled paper cover and leather spine. "But I am giving it to you for free."

Gingerly taking the book from him, Rese peeked under the cover. The title read, *Epistolary of Ariane Valente & Gabriel Varon.* She looked up at him, confused. "What is this?"

"Uncle Will gave it to me," he said. "He's helping Desmond and me find some answers for Cait."

Rese felt her expression go slack, baffled at what he was revealing. "You're—" She straightened, regarding him with what felt like new eyes. "You're helping her?"

Brady nodded. "I know you don't want to believe it, but she makes him better. And he's my brother, if not by blood, then by choice. So, I'll do whatever it takes to help her because it helps him."

Rese didn't know how to take that. It had been twelve years since she'd had someone who cared for her that way. Maeve was a good caretaker, but the loss of her husband and son had broken her. She couldn't provide the same sense of security. And Cait and Genni were her little sisters. *She* was supposed to care for them.

What must it be like to have a friend who regarded you with so much kindness and consideration?

"Do you know how to save her?" Rese asked, her voice cracking.

Brady's stoic expression finally softened. "That's what we're trying to figure out."

"By reading letters between some woman and a Varon?"

"Among other things," he said.

"And you're doing this because Desmond cares about her?" she asked dubiously, remembering the moment he'd so affectionately taken care of her that night weeks ago.

"Believe it or not, yes."

Rese grimaced. "Does he . . . *like* her?"

He tapped the side of his coffee cup, a sly grin on his lips. "Ummm— you could say that."

She shivered and made a face like she'd tasted the most bitter coffee on the planet. "Disgusting," she muttered. She composed herself and faced him again. "Fine, whatever. I'm in."

Brady was smiling, brighter than she'd ever seen before. "Yeah?"

"She's my sister," she replied. "No matter what—even if she likes your freaking jerk of a best friend—I'd do anything for her. I'd do anything to *save* her."

"I know," he said, and it sounded like he really did.

Rese held his gaze for a few moments, unsure what she was getting herself into. But she thought, whatever it was, it must be for the best.

"I have your other book," she said suddenly, uncomfortable with the sweet way he was looking at her. "It's in the back."

"You finished it already?" he asked with genuine surprise.

"I'm a fast reader."

"Okay, valedictorian, whatever you say."

"I wasn't—" She paused, eyes narrowing. "How did you know about that?"

"My aunt's the principal."

She huffed. "So, how does this work?" she asked. "You give me books to read, and I report back with my findings?"

"Something like that," he admitted. "For now, at least. We also—" He made a face. "We kinda have this weird team thing going. You could join if you wanted."

"Sounds adorable." She tapped the new book he'd given her against her palm. "Sure. I'll talk to Cait about it."

"Great."

"Do you want the other book?"

"I guess." He lifted his cup. "Let me know what I owe you."

She backed up, preparing to retrieve the book. "Crochet night is on the house."

He gave her an amused look. "I'm not actually crocheting, Rese."

"Then, consider it a trade," she said, brandishing the thin book in her hand.

When she returned from exchanging the books, Brady rose from his seat. He propped the large tome under his arm and lifted the coffee cup. "You know," he said thoughtfully, "this isn't half bad. You should put it on the menu."

Rese couldn't help grinning at him. "I'll run it by Marcy. We can call it The Birdy."

Brady blinked in that stoic way of his. "Nah, it should be named after its creator," he said, eyes locking with hers. "Maybe call it the Irish Rose or something."

A momentary flutter swept through Rese's stomach. He couldn't know. "Rose" had been her mum's nickname for her. Outside of her family, no one in Porthaven knew that.

Regaining her composure, she rolled her eyes. "Roses are cliché," she said.

He shrugged. "It's the flower of *your* birth month, but whatever."

Rese stared at him, open-mouthed. He *couldn't* know. And yet, he knew her birth month flower and chose to attribute the nickname to her himself.

"Have a good night, Rese," Brady said, then walked away, stopping to give Donna a hug before heading out the door.

# CHAPTER FORTY-THREE

# Cait

Cait and Desmond stood in the kitchen, staring at the back door.

Ben and Brady were the first to leave, their congratulations in place. The reverend had said some rather kind things to Cait, wishing her happiness and promising he would support the Simon family to whatever end. Brady's goodbye was less eloquent but equally kind. Then, he'd slugged Desmond's arm and muttered slyly, "Have fun, seabird."

Cait's face burned for the next ten minutes.

William and Robin's departure was only slightly delayed. With the veil safety tucked back into storage, Robin kissed Desmond's cheek—he grimaced but didn't wipe it away—and whispered something in his ear, which made him flush a very deep red. She patted him on the shoulder, a wry grin on her lips, and turned to hug Cait for several long seconds before slipping out the door.

After squeezing his son's shoulder, William turned to Cait.

He opened his mouth to speak, but Cait's words rushed out first. "I'm sorry," she said. "When you came to my house—when we spoke before—"

William cut her off with a raised hand and a smile. "I told you then, Caitriona," he said kindly. "No matter what, I will protect my son *and* you."

Cait drew in a sharp breath, suddenly understanding the weight of expectation that Desmond always felt from his dad. William Simon had a peculiar way of impressing his regard on a person. Held in his dark gaze, Cait could feel the devotion deep within him. He *would* protect her, no matter what. And that placed a strange burden on her to return such unshakeable loyalty.

William's smile was small but sincere. "One day, I hope to earn your forgiveness," he said. "But today, I thank you for loving my son better than even I could."

Gaping up at him, Cait didn't know what to say. So, she watched silently as William nodded to her and left. The Simons' SUV backed out of the driveway, leaving Desmond and her alone.

That had been two entire minutes ago.

Desmond cleared his throat. "So," he said, turning to her, "you hungry?"

The bright scent of lemon and herbs filled the kitchen. Cait's stomach still felt too tight to consider eating, but she didn't want him to eat alone. "Yeah, dinner sounds good," she replied.

A flicker of some unreadable emotion tugged down his expression for one moment before it resolved to a neutral state. "If you want," he said, moving to the oven, "we can eat down here. Or we can take it up to my room and, uh, watch a movie . . . Or something."

Thinking a distraction would be nice, Cait nodded. "A movie sounds great."

"Great," he repeated, retrieving the plates.

With a stilted awkwardness, they worked their way up to his room— *their* room, per Robin's pronouncement. What a strange thought, imagining herself living in the Simon home. It wasn't as though she could move in. And once they made their marriage public knowledge, wouldn't they get their own place? Maybe they could purchase one of the small houses in her neighborhood, giving them distance from the prying eyes of the townspeople.

Stepping back into the mossy green of Desmond's room was like entering the woods. The bedside lamps lit it dimly. The scent of him overwhelmed her once again. She felt infinitely more awkward, glancing at the bed, still incapable of believing she'd spend the night there.

Desmond shut the door with his foot. Being alone in the house was one line crossed. With his bedroom door closed, it felt like another boundary knocked down.

Watching as he set their plates down on the coffee table—he'd insisted on carrying them—Cait brushed her fingers over her new rings. If the engagement ring hadn't been enough, Desmond had purchased an official wedding band to match his. Simple but special, with a Celtic pattern etched into the sterling silver face.

Desmond shrugged off the suit jacket, and they both kicked off their shoes before settling onto the couch. Cait accepted her plate with a faint "thank you." She stared at the fish and rice distractedly. Her body felt peculiar—not ill, but off in some way—almost unsteady, as though she were lightheaded. She chalked it up to nervousness and tried to ignore the sensation.

Desmond turned on the TV, oblivious to her uneasy state. "I was thinking," he said. "You said you've never seen *Star Wars*, so we should probably rectify that crime."

"Isn't that, like, a space movie?"

Desmond snorted but managed to keep from smirking too derisively. "Yeah, something like that."

"Is it—well, does it fit the occasion?" she asked shyly, uncertain why she felt so shy when this was *Desmond*.

He furrowed his brow, and then understanding hit him. "Oh, you mean, is there a romance? 'Cause . . . wedding, right?"

"Right."

"Well, yeah," he confirmed. "Yeah, I mean, it's probably got one of the greatest love stories of all time."

"Really?" she asked, surprised.

"Sure. You kind of have to watch all of 'em to get the payoff, but yeah, it's got the whole . . ." He waved a hand through the air, searching for the word before settling on, "Deal."

Without any better suggestion to offer, Cait agreed.

Once he got the movie going, Desmond sat back, his side pressed into hers. They ate slowly, picking at their full plates. Cait couldn't say that she found the movie all that interesting but thought it had more to do with how flustered she felt. She was alert to Desmond's every movement, keenly aware of her arm brushing his every time she took a bite. She found herself eating just for the pleasure of touching him.

What was more, Cait still felt strange. Something nagged at her, telling her that something was off. Not between them. She felt the same toward Desmond as she always did, even if there was a new tinge of awkwardness between them.

No, it was within her. *She* felt odd, her mind strangely light.

When Desmond set his mostly empty plate down, she followed his lead. He loosened his tie and undid the top buttons of his shirt. Then, they settled deeper into their seats. The young man in the movie had been attacked by people in creepy masks, only to be saved by an old man. She didn't understand what was happening in the least, and her level of confusion was made even worse when Desmond put his arm around her.

They snuggled closer on the couch. Cait wished she had a blanket but tucked her feet underneath her. His fingers brushed along her arm, playing with the loose fabric of her sleeve.

"This is a nice dress, by the way," he said over the movie. "I should have told you before, but you look really beautiful."

Cait felt her face flush. "Thanks. Liz did most of it." She tugged on his loosened tie. "Lavender is a good color for you."

He chuckled. "Glad to hear it," he said, pressing a kiss to her temple.

When he pulled back, their eyes met, breath caught between them. Then, he kissed her mouth. Soft and slow, like the waves kissing the shore on a clear day.

With reluctance, Desmond drew away. "You're not beautiful because Liz dressed you up, Caity," he whispered. "Without this dress, without the makeup or the fancy curls, you'd still be the most beautiful girl in the world."

Cait kissed him that time. What could she say to such a sweet declaration? What could she do but wrap her arms around his neck and kiss him deeply?

One kiss turned into dozens before he set his hands on her arms. "Did you want cake?" he asked.

Mind fuzzy, it took a moment for Cait to remember the cake Robin left for them in the fridge. "I'm not very hungry."

Desmond's arm slipped around her waist, tugging her closer until she was practically on his lap. "Good. Me either."

The movie was forgotten after that. It felt much like their first kisses in his car, heated and desperate. Only this time, there was no fear of separation. There was no need to question the other. They were wholly free to touch and revel as much as they desired.

Over time, Desmond jerked his tie free and shut off the movie, and they wound up twisted together on the couch. He lay atop her, both of them exploring readily. Cait wasn't certain how long they went on like that. But it was in the utter silence of the room around them that she realized what was so strange.

Cait listened closely to be sure, only hearing the sounds of their equally ragged breaths, their kisses, and the rustling fabric between them. And she knew the answer.

For the first time in her life, the hum had gone silent around Desmond.

Cait panicked at first, her heart seizing. What did it mean? Desmond was the only one who brought that hum to life, and now it was suddenly gone. But fear gave way to peace as she considered the gentle silence in her head.

Cait felt fully herself, fully of sound mind, in Desmond's arms. She'd never realized how loud the hum had been. There was no magical pull, no overwhelm of her senses. She was wholly and completely free to respond without the dizzying magnetic tug in her core. With the hum gone, giving herself to Desmond didn't feel like a compulsion but a choice. She had control for once in her life, and she knew without a doubt that she wanted this.

Their kisses slowed, and Desmond paused. "Caity," he murmured, lips brushing hers.

"Mm?"

"Would it be okay if we took this to the bed?"

Nerves blossomed in her stomach. But she realized how ridiculous that was when his hand was already on her thigh, and her skirt was practically around her waist.

Looking up into his rich brown gaze, Cait said, "I'd like that."

Things progressed quickly then. Desmond was up, pulling her with him. They were across the room, leaving a pile of clothes next to the bed. They were bound in the softness of the sheets, enfolded in an intimate, eager embrace. And despite her earlier anxiety, Cait found that she wasn't embarrassed at all when he saw all of her or when they gave themselves to each other. Because this was Desmond, and what could she fear from him? This wasn't some foolish, reckless act. There could be no reproach for their desire or their vulnerability.

It was trust that kept their union leisurely and their hearts secure. Beyond anything or anyone else in the world, Cait and Desmond trusted one another with every part of themselves. Bared and stripped of everything else, they were of one soul now. As they lay in each other's arms, drifting into the solace of each other's touch, they whispered promises of forever.

And without the knowledge of either young heart, the fissure within

Cait grew until a mere fragment remained to hold back the creature that lurked inside.

~

Moonlight and smoke filled the room. Cait stood, staring at the door, scarred by the jagged line that tore from the uppermost hinge almost to the latch. The Wolf paced behind the damaged barrier, the hum a deep rumble in her head.

Cait took a step back, her heart hammering. She couldn't take comfort in the memories of her childhood. The quilts, dried flowers, crayon artwork, and stuffed animals didn't carry their soothing charm. Not even thoughts of her da's stories gave her hope.

The low padding of the Wolf's stride, its nails scratching against the floorboards, reverberated with menacing patience. Time was running out. The block was breaking down. And the Wolf was breaking through.

*Thud.*

Cait jumped as the Wolf threw itself against the door. The smoke twisted higher. The silver moonlight refracted off the swirling clouds. The hum rose to a whine, piercing her ears. Her breathing came out ragged and panicked as the creature crashed into the door again. The wood lurched in its frame, the fissure bulging.

Tears filled her eyes. The dreams were so different now. The fear, the pain, the sorrow—it was all still there. But the suffocation, the beasts, the brutality of her parents' murdered forms—they no longer came. Now, she faced the panic of the growing fissure, the horror of having Desmond ripped from her arms, and the plaguing mystery of the island tree.

Why couldn't she have one night? Cait wanted just one night of sleep without this aching dread haunting her. One night, when her throat wouldn't burn with fear and sorrow, when she didn't fight for every breath in her lungs.

Another fierce *crash*, and then the raven flew in. Its wings cast aside the coiling smoke, brushing it back like a curtain. The bird perched gently on the dresser, crooning its eerie greeting. "Caw."

After all this time, Cait still didn't know how to feel about the raven. While she welcomed the reprieve from the hovering beasts, her mother's heartbreaking scream, and suffocating in the smoke, the bird brought other horrors to her dreams. And she hadn't decided if it was an omen of good or ill repute.

Warily, Cait watched the raven, her hands curled into fists. The Wolf paced the hall once again, no longer attempting to break through. The temporary respite didn't settle her heart rate or temper her anxiety.

The moonlight caused the raven's ebony-sapphire feathers to shimmer as it spread its wings. It let out another cry and took flight, sailing over Cait's head.

Cait didn't turn. Instead, she stared at the door and its fractured wood. The rumble of the Wolf's growl vibrated in her core. She could feel its desperation, its rage, its need to break through. It wanted her with a fury that she'd never felt before. It wanted to consume her.

Unable to bear the oppressive need of the Wolf, she abandoned her childhood room. Cait turned on her heel to stand on the edge of the cove. A black sky churned with violent storm clouds, the full moon peeking through the seething mass above her. Lightning flashed. The dark sea raged, its waves curling in on themselves. The cliffsides of the cove loomed. And Desmond stood on the shoreline, oblivious to the world around him as he stared at the horizon.

The hum reverberated in Cait's chest with an aching pain unlike ever before. This wasn't just the boy she secretly hoped for any longer. This was the young man she'd married, the one she'd given herself to, heart and soul. She couldn't bear to have him ripped from her arms to drown in the onyx black depths of the ocean yet again.

The sand and pebbles crunched under her boots as she sprinted for him. Cait wouldn't lose him again. She wouldn't wait; she wouldn't say a word. She'd save him however she could.

Cait crashed into Desmond's back like the waves at his knees. Her arms looped around his waist, tugging him backward, determined to get him away from the water and the grasp of that tendrilled monster of the sea.

"Cait?" Desmond's hands gripped her wrists. He tried to turn, but she held on tight.

She planted her feet and pulled. The waves tumbled higher.

"No," Cait said with determination, tightening her hold on him.

Unknowingly, Desmond fought her as he angled to meet her gaze. "What are you doing here?"

Tears broke from Cait's eyes, but she gritted her teeth, tugging him away from the sea. "We have to get out of here, Desmond," she said sharply.

Struggling against the aggressive waves now swallowing up their legs, Cait slipped. The sand gave way under her boots, betraying her attempts to save him. "No," she ground out again.

Desmond caught her, bringing them face-to-face. His arms were sure and steady, his expression concerned and adamant. "What's going on, Caity?"

"No!" Cait shouted, fiercely grabbing his jacket. She tried yanking him back with her, but the waves pulled them deeper. "No!"

"Cait," Desmond whispered, his hand on her shoulder.

She tugged and pulled and struggled and railed, trying with all her might to save him from the ocean's pull, all the while crying, "No!"

Desmond stumbled under the waves at his back. He held her tighter, saying her name again and again, worry making his voice tender.

Cait shut her eyes, tears coursing down her cheeks. The water sucked at their feet, the waves threatening. She couldn't save him. She pressed her head against his chest, even as she tried to back up, one step at a time. *But she couldn't save him.* The waves would overtake them, the monster would rip him from her arms, and she'd lose him for good.

"No," she sobbed.

"Cait!" Desmond shouted and began to shake her.

The wave slammed into them, the dark ocean swallowing them whole, and then . . .

Cait gasped for breath, suddenly out of the sea and her dream. The wan light of Desmond's bedroom surrounded her as he gripped her shoulders. The moment her eyes flew open, he stopped shaking her and let out a sigh of relief. He hovered over her while her breaths puffed out in short, choppy bursts. Her muscles were coiled tight, aching as though she'd been fighting the ocean. She felt weak and exhausted, emotionally spent as she stared up at the shadowed angles of Desmond's face.

"Des?" she murmured, then remembered.

She was in the Simon house, sleeping in the soft gray sheets of his bed. The moonlight cast a hazy line above his blackout curtains, barely giving her enough light to see him propped on one arm above her. But she could feel him, his hand on her shoulder, his nearness at her side.

After their marital exchange, they'd readied themselves for bed, often sharing shy, affectionate looks in the process. She'd made sure to text Liz to say that she was returning home and told herself not to feel guilty for another lie. Then, she changed into her frilly pink pajamas and joined Desmond back in their bed. They'd curled up under the blankets once more, snuggling close and kissing until they'd drifted off, too tired to stay awake any longer.

And through everything leading up to sleep, Cait had forgotten about her dreams.

Desmond stared down at her now, worry teetering close to fear in his dark eyes. "Cait, what—?"

"I'm fine," Cait promised, clinging to him for his comfort as much as her own. "It was just a dream."

"Your dreams," he muttered in sudden understanding. "I didn't realize they—you were shaking, Cait. You were crying and—and struggling to breathe, and I thought you were dying."

She pressed closer to him, taking solace in his warmth. "I'm fine," she whispered again.

He held her close, doubt still pinching his expression. "Is this what it's always like?" he asked. "Is this what they do to you?"

Cait pressed her face into his shoulder. "Yes," she murmured.

"Every night?"

"Yes."

"Oh, Caity." His arms were around her then. He held her so closely she couldn't truly tell where she ended and he started.

"I'm sorry." Her words were muffled against his neck. "I should have warned you."

"No," he sighed, pausing. "Well, maybe. It would have kept me from freaking out so much, but . . . *I'm* sorry, Cait. How do you ever sleep like that?"

"Barely," she admitted. She relaxed, her body softening in his embrace. His fingers gently tugged through her hair, a physical lullaby slowing her heart rate. His familiar scent draped over her like the warmest blanket. The hum had returned, rumbling soothingly across her skin.

Desmond's lips pressed against her forehead. "I'm sorry," he said again.

Comforted by his touch, Cait was already slipping back to sleep. "It's okay. This is better."

"What is?"

She looped her arm around him, her fingers tracing his bare back. "This," she repeated. "You. I've never had someone with me."

"Never?"

In the recesses of Cait's brain, she knew that Rese had been with her in the earliest days after their parents' deaths. But she was too tired to explain it.

With a restful exhale, Cait nuzzled closer into Desmond's embrace. "Thank you," she murmured. "For waking me."

She could feel his nod. He remained tense even as he held her. "Were you . . . You said my name," he whispered. "Were you dreaming about me?"

"Mm-hm."

"You kept saying 'no.' Why?"

In her daze, all she could think to say was, "Because I can't lose you."

Desmond sighed, somehow finding a way to hold her closer. "You won't, Caity," he said. "I promise. I'll never leave you."

Cait smiled and fell asleep, believing deep in her heart that he was right.

# CHAPTER FORTY-FOUR

# Desmond

"**W**ell?"

Desmond practically jumped out of his Doc Martens at Brady's sudden arrival. He fumbled with his textbook, catching it before it tumbled from the locker. "Have you lost your mind?" he said with a scowl.

"Possibly," Brady replied, leaning against the lockers. "You gonna answer my question?"

"What question?"

"Well . . . ?"

Though Desmond understood his friend's meaning with the suggestive inflection of the one word, he wasn't altogether sure he intended to answer it. "Well, what?" he asked, stalling for time.

Brady tossed a surreptitious glance over his shoulder. Students milled through the halls, caught up in their own conversations. Still, he lowered his voice. "Was it worth it?"

Zipping up his backpack, Desmond tossed him a mildly perturbed glance. "You're gonna have to be more specific, Brade," he said.

"Dude."

Desmond didn't relent.

Brady sighed, his jaw tense. "Fine," he grumbled. "Was it worth waiting until . . ." Another glance around the room, and another ten decibels lower. ". . . marriage to . . . ?" He emphasized the final silence with a beckoning gesture, begging Desmond to fill in the blank.

Amused by his friend's avoidance of the word "sex," Desmond screwed up his face in mock confusion. "What are you talking about?"

Brady glared at him. "Just answer the question."

He shut his locker, then slung his backpack over his shoulder. Until that moment, he hadn't been sure what he'd say when Brady asked—and he'd known that Brady *would* ask. Growing up, they'd gone through all phases of life together, from the days when girls were gross and annoying to the ones where neither could stop thinking about them.

As the reverend's son lined up to inherit the position, Brady did everything by the literal Book, unlike most kids in school. And while Desmond wasn't as devout as his friend, he'd never tolerated the idea of going to bed with any girl. Not when he knew he'd only be thinking of Cait.

Though they kept the identities of their true interests a secret, the boys often discussed the subject, questioning the validity of abstaining beyond religious purposes. Desmond expected Brady's curiosity now, knowing he'd be just as curious were their roles reversed. So, he decided to answer him honestly.

"Yeah," Desmond said somewhat wistfully. He thought of Cait and the wonderful, baffling, heart-stopping reality that she was now his wife. "It's definitely worth it."

Brady's shoulders relaxed visibly. "Good."

With a smirk, Desmond shoved his friend, moving down the hall toward class. "Never ask me about it again," he said.

Brady snorted. "If I wanted details, I'd ask Garrett."

He scoffed. "I wouldn't trust Garrett to know the first thing about making a woman happy."

"Exactly," Brady said. "I'd take what he says and do the opposite."

"Huh." Desmond considered it. "That's not a bad idea."

"It wouldn't be worth it."

"Why not?"

"He'd probably make stuff up just to sound experienced." Brady passed him a conspiratorial look. "I'm still not convinced he and Whitney have actually gone that far."

Knowing that Desmond had started similar rumors about himself, he thought Brady might be onto something.

They continued through the school, winding to class. Garrett was back with Whitney on the stipulation that he walk her to class every day. Their towheaded friend was already in his seat when they arrived, holding hands with his girlfriend at the desk beside his. Whitney was talking nonstop while Garrett stared at her with a glazed-over look.

The couple greeted Desmond and Brady offhandedly. But Desmond didn't notice.

Cait sat at the back of the class, her blue-gray eyes already finding his.

His heart expanded to devour his chest. It'd only been a handful of hours, and somehow, he felt desperate enough for her to cross the classroom and pull her into his arms. Instead, he took his seat.

In the early morning hours, he'd taken her home using his dad's sedan since his muscle car could be heard a mile away. Desmond hadn't realized how hard it would be, parting from her after only one night together. He felt like she was taking a piece of him with her. It left him hollow and unsettled the entire drive home.

Now, seeing her across the class, he nearly felt whole again.

Desmond adjusted his wedding ring. He wasn't used to wearing jewelry of any kind, and he found himself oddly aware of its presence. He'd transferred the ring to his right hand. With its Celtic etching, it masqueraded as a fashion piece rather than a symbol of matrimony. And he was rather certain that in a matter of weeks, half the guys in the school would be wearing rings, too, just as they'd done when he started wearing baseball tees back in his freshman year.

As Penny Davis started their history class, reminding them that their Fisher's Festival essays were due next Friday, Desmond absentmindedly began to play with the ring. He worked it off and on his finger, feeling the ridges of the engraving, thinking of Cait. They'd never finished their essay, he realized. They should find a time for that. Maybe this weekend. She could come over tomorrow. They could spend the whole day together, finishing up the essay, cuddling on the couch, and watching movies . . . amongst other things. But then he remembered that she had her girls' night scheduled to celebrate her birthday tomorrow.

So, maybe they couldn't spend *all day* together. But all morning and into the afternoon . . . after he snuck her back into his house tonight.

He still hadn't figured out how to work that out yet. After school, they had a basketball game, and she would have to go home so as not to make her nan suspicious. But Desmond was determined to find a way. Even if he had to drive to her neighborhood, wait for her nan and sisters to fall asleep, and help her sneak out. Now that he'd slept beside her once, he didn't think he could ever sleep without her again.

And then there were those dreams.

Desmond could still feel the panic that flared through him, watching Cait writhe, tears on her cheeks as she muttered through short breaths. He'd genuinely thought she was dying at first. Then, he'd begun to fear that the Wolf was breaking through, hurting her in the process.

When she woke, alert and gasping for air, he'd found a way to breathe himself. And when she'd told him it was a nightly occurrence for her, he'd decided then and there that he'd never let her face it alone again. No matter how difficult it was, he would find a way to be there to wake her, to hold her, and to banish away those frightening dreams.

The whole day, Desmond was stuck in a loop of those thoughts. He saw Cait at a distance—only ever at a distance. He'd texted, asking to disappear to the roof with her and plan their late-night rendezvous, but she'd been unable to break away from her friends. It was a bittersweet thing to see her with others. He was glad that she finally had friends, and yet he was jealous of her time.

He saw Sterling pull her to the side after leaving class at one point. The guy's expression was serious and almost frantic. It worried Desmond, but he let it go, knowing he could talk to Cait about it tonight.

Somehow, Desmond made it through the school day in his distracted state. He left the last class and headed to the locker room to get ready for their final drills before the game.

Desmond had never enjoyed basketball the way everyone thought he did. Sure, he was reasonably good at it. That's what happened when you were afraid of disappointing everyone around you. You *found* a way to be good at whatever it was they wanted you to be good at. And then you acted like a douchebag to pretend that you weren't desperate for their approval.

But in the end, Desmond wished he'd never let his dad talk him into it. Sports weren't his thing. Books were. Science fiction and horror, where the stories were adequately thought-provoking, and he could escape to another world.

Only Cait and Brady knew that about him, though. (And his mom, but she didn't count 'cause she was his *mom*.)

So, Desmond played basketball in the fall and baseball in the spring. He practiced in the summer and made sure he had enough skill to maintain his captaincy over both teams. And tonight, he led them to another win for the season. No thanks to Sterling, who'd been so distracted that Coach benched him after the first period. Which was annoying because Sterling was notorious for his three-pointers.

When the game was over, and they were all in the locker room getting cleaned up and ready to go, Desmond checked his phone. He had a few missed calls from his dad and a voicemail, but he got distracted by Cait's text waiting for him.

*"I'll be ready."*

He'd messaged her earlier, giving her a detailed plan and then instructing her to delete the text. He promised to pick her up just outside her neighborhood. She only had to leave a note for her nan saying she'd gone for an early morning walk. He'd even suggested she bring Red to sell the idea.

Gathering his things, Desmond walked out the door with Brady and Garrett at his side. They exchanged goodbyes and talked about meeting up tomorrow night for video games. Then, they went their separate ways.

Desmond got in his car, started the roaring engine, and looked up to see Sterling Faulk's ancient Honda turn right out of the school.

Desmond frowned.

Sterling had turned *right* toward the docks instead of left toward his home.

Normally, Desmond wasn't bothered by other people's business. He let them live their lives how they wanted and lived his own how he wanted. Who cared why Sterling was going toward the docks at night?

Yet, after the way the guy had pulled Cait aside and after his distracted performance during the game . . . Desmond had the strongest urge to follow. Something was off. He felt it in his gut.

So, with a low muttered curse, Desmond turned onto Lawrence Avenue and followed Sterling toward the pier.

He was just making sure the guy was okay; that's what he told himself. He'd follow, ensure that Sterling wasn't up to something nefarious or dangerous, and then he'd turn around and head toward Cait's.

But when Sterling parked by the rock bridge that led to the island, Desmond knew he couldn't ignore it.

Turning into the lot, Desmond watched anxiously as Sterling headed for the bridge. "Don't do it, man," he muttered. "Get back in your car and let me go see Cait."

Sterling didn't listen.

The guy stepped onto the bridge and began to walk across to Aster Island. "Shit."

Desmond parked and sprinted after him. There was only one reason Sterling would head to the island. Every kid in Porthaven knew the island was off-limits. They didn't bother trying to get on it because if Fish caught them, there'd be hell to pay.

It was obvious to Desmond: Sterling was going to the Veil.

The full moon glittered like silver confetti on the black slate sea as Desmond stepped onto the rock bridge. It reflected off the white stone lighthouse, lighting it up like a beacon. A midnight blue sky stretched overhead, not a cloud in sight.

Sterling was halfway across the bridge when Desmond was close enough to call out. The boy stopped, turning warily to face him. "What do you want?" he demanded.

Slowing to a stop, Desmond worked to keep his footing against the slick rock. "Why are you going to the island?" he asked.

"That's where the Veil is, right?" Sterling said, not bothering with pretense.

Desmond's lack of response was confirmation.

Sterling angled to face him more directly. "Something's wrong," he said. "My dream last night—something's happening to the tree. I tried to talk to Cait about it today, but she said something woke her before she got to that part."

Knowing that *he* was what woke her, Desmond furrowed his brow. He'd always relegated these dreams of Cait's to her brain's strange way of processing the trauma in her life. Ever since Sterling began to share them, he knew it had to do with the spirit-beings—the Spectrals. And that worried him more than most things.

"What happened to the Veil?" Desmond asked.

Sterling hesitated. "I don't know for sure. But . . . I think it's dying. In the dream, after the explosion, the tree split into two. Then, I heard a voice. I don't remember what it said, but when I woke, I said a name."

Desmond's skin prickled. "What name?"

"Phylius."

Though it meant nothing to Desmond—he'd never heard that name before—somehow, he knew it was the name of Sterling's Spectral.

"I think—" Sterling swallowed. "I think he's breaking free."

"And how will going to the Veil help stop that?"

"What else am I gonna do?" he demanded. "It's either sit around, waiting for him to take over, or go to the Veil and try to stop it."

"I can't let you do that."

"Desmond—" He glared at him with a determined glint in his eyes. "This isn't just about me. If this thing in me gets free, so does Cait's."

Cold dread raced up his spine. "We don't know that."

"We're having the same dreams. Do you really think the two aren't tied together?" Sterling shook his head. "Cait managed to make a seal. Maybe I can too. Maybe with both of them, it'll fix it."

"But the Veil on the island is only attached to you," Desmond said. "Even if we figure it out, it won't help Cait."

"If we figure it out, then you can find her Veil and fix it too," Sterling countered. "I know how you feel about her, Desmond."

He bristled.

"And that means you'll do whatever it takes to protect her."

Though Desmond wanted to deny it, to protect their secret, the hope that he could save Cait stopped him.

Taking a step forward on the bridge, Desmond gestured to the island. "Let's go."

They crossed the remainder of the rock bridge, stepping onto the tall grass of Aster Island. The wind bit at their cheeks and noses. It whirled, rattling the forest ahead of them. Desmond cast a glance toward the lighthouse and the cottage beside it. Warm amber light filled the windows, but there was no sign of Fish or his wife.

Placing a hand on Sterling's shoulder, he pushed him forward toward the tree line. They had to be quick. While there weren't any more Warden members patrolling the forest, he didn't care to explain himself to Fish if they got caught. And he'd promised to meet Cait in—he checked his phone—ten minutes.

Sending a quick text to let her know he'd be late, Desmond took the lead, guiding Sterling deep into the trees. He'd gone to the Veil several times now. Even in the darkness, he could remember the path. His mind stilled as they grew near, the preternatural calm settling over him.

The sycamore sat in the center of the hollow, moonlight cascading over its skeletal branches. Decaying leaves covered the ground. A light fog swirled in the air.

Sterling took an immediate step toward the tree, his movement appearing almost unconscious. "It looks exactly the same," he muttered.

Desmond gritted his teeth. "Come on," he said. "Let's get this over with."

They crossed the clearing, winding around to face the jagged tear in the trunk. Mottled brown and gray bark spread open around amber, the resin coursing all the way to the ground.

Sucking in a sharp breath, Desmond hurried forward. "It—this isn't right," he said. "Last time I was here, it was, like, a third of the size."

Sterling narrowed his eyes. "Well, it's always been like this in the dreams," he said. "Just not with the amber on it."

"Wait, it doesn't have the seal in your dream?"

Sterling shook his head, gaze locked on the tree.

Desmond ran a hand through his hair. "That's not terrifying," he murmured. Then, he knelt to inspect the fissure. The sycamore had no roots above the ground, allowing him to crouch right next to the trunk. Like a stream, the amber trailed down, stopping barely an inch from the dirt.

Whatever Cait had done, it may have stopped the beasts, but it hadn't fixed the Veil's damage.

"Uh, okay." Desmond rose, backing away. "You got any ideas on how to fix this thing?"

Sterling stared at the tree, his head tilted to the side as though listening. His lips moved, but no sound came out.

"Sterling," he prompted.

When the guy didn't respond, he shoved him.

Woken from his creepy reverie, Sterling scowled. "What?"

Desmond threw his arms to the sides. "You're the one who brought us here. How do you plan on fixing it?"

Blinking as though coming out of a dream, Sterling shook his head. "I dunno."

"Fantastic."

Desmond turned back to the tree. "I don't like this," he said. "I think we need help. Maybe . . . maybe someone in the Warden will know what to do."

As much as he was loathe to go to Jun, he didn't see any better options. After all their attempts to uncover what was happening to the Veil, none of them had come up with any answers. It was clear they no longer had time to research and plan. They needed a solution now. And Jun was their only hope left.

Except . . .

Desmond chewed on the inside of his cheek. What if he went to Lilith? She clearly knew more than most of the Warden. Though she still considered herself a Druid, she'd said she didn't have any interest in pursuing the evil path of her most volatile compatriots. There were good Druids, just as there were bad Warden members. She'd saved his life. He could trust her.

"We should go back," Desmond said. "There's nothing we can do here."

Sterling frowned. "No. There—we *have* to do something. I'm not losing myself to some freaky monster."

"That's not what it is," Desmond said.

"How would you know?"

Not willing to reveal his source, he brushed it off. "I'm the Varon heir," he said. "I know everything."

Sterling rolled his eyes but moved closer to the tree. "Says the guy with no idea how to fix the Veil."

"Hey," he defended, "I tried. It didn't work. There's something seriously wrong with it if *I* can't fix it."

"Humility," Sterling remarked, scanning the tear. "That's what I like most about you."

"Funny," Desmond replied. "I've always admired your optimism."

Ignoring the quip, Sterling pointed to the amber. "This was Cait?"

"Yeah," he said reluctantly.

"Have you ever heard of someone creating physical substances through wielding?"

Desmond shrugged. "It's not common, but yeah, there are some stories about it. Mostly Varons or other powerful Sages."

"Vessels too?"

"I guess."

"I wonder what its purpose is."

Desmond furrowed his brow. "What do you mean? She sealed the Veil to keep the beasts from coming through."

"Why is it growing then?"

"What do you mean?"

"She didn't seal it," Sterling said, gesturing to the tree. "The amber is growing. *It's* what's spreading the tear."

Desmond blinked, realizing he was right. "Oh, hell."

"Yeah. She may have stopped the beasts, but the Veil is breaking apart. It's as though whatever she did is encouraging the tear to expand."

Ruffling his hair again, Desmond tried to figure out what to do. The fissure was almost all the way to the earth. At the rate it was spreading, there was a chance it'd reach the ground before they could get back with help. He had to do something to stop it.

Taking a step closer to the tree, Desmond set his jaw. He would find a way. Last time, he'd known little about Spectrals and Vessels. Now, with Lilith's teaching, perhaps he could find some connection between the two. Whatever was causing the damage to the Veil, it was the reason Cait and Sterling's blocks were breaking. If he could stop the damage to Sterling's Veil, then he could spend the rest of his time finding Cait's and fixing the damage there.

After all, hers didn't have amber ripping it apart.

Reaching out a hand to the tree, Desmond gathered his will, channeling the spirit world. He could almost feel it brushing over his skin, the power rippling, waiting for him to take hold of it. A gentle whisper of sound rushed through his ears.

Then, Sterling gasped.

Desmond's hand snapped back to his side. "What?" he asked, turning to find Sterling doubled over, head in his hands.

Panic raced up Desmond's spine. "What's happening?"

But Sterling couldn't answer. His face contorted, his eyes squeezing shut. A low moan slipped from him, and he dropped to his knees.

"Sterling!" Desmond moved to offer whatever help he could when a sudden whistle of wind, like a sharp inhale, cut through the clearing. And then the amber on the tree shattered in a spray of glittering shards and rusty-orange light.

Desmond raised his hands to cover his face, the shards pummeling him. One sharp edge sliced the back of his hand. A ground-shaking rumble filled the air, and a deafening *crack* echoed through the forest. Then, the world fell into silence.

Carefully, Desmond peeked through his fingers at the Veil.

Shock rolled through him. The sycamore's trunk was fully split in two now, either side lolling languidly as the aspen and ash trees finally broke free. The two trees were fully twisted together, winding out of the split. Crisp white and ashen gray bark contrasted against the mottled brown of the sycamore. Unnatural and sudden, it looked as though the three had grown together all at once.

Heart pounding, Desmond didn't know what to make of the disaster.

"Who—who are you?" Sterling said.

Desmond whirled, worried that the boy's mind had been destroyed by the Veil's damage. Had the dementia from the block taken hold early?

But Sterling wasn't looking at Desmond. He was staring at the clearing before him as though someone else stood there.

A gentle breeze pushed through the shadowed forest.

"No," Sterling muttered. "No, no."

Desmond took a cautious step toward him. "You okay, bud?"

Head in his hands once more, Sterling kept muttering. "I didn't want this. I didn't ask for it. My dad—he's—he was ready. He was willing. Why would you pick *me*?"

When he said the last words, Sterling looked up, his expression adamant and pleading with the open air before him. And that's when Desmond knew the Spectral had been freed.

Jerking around, Desmond stared into the forest toward Porthaven's shore. It didn't mean anything. The Veils were separate—the Spectrals were separate. Sterling's might have broken free, but that didn't mean . . .

"Cait." Her name slipped as a desperate prayer from his lips.

# William

Stepping out onto the porch, William moved to stand behind Robin. He wrapped his arms around her waist, watching the sun sink into the bronze waves on the horizon. The beachfront cabin had been in his family for the past sixty years, on the mainland and down the coastline near Portland. They'd regularly vacationed there through the years, an easy getaway from the tensions of Porthaven.

William and Robin arrived late last night, then spent their Friday walking the beach, talking about their next steps, and planning for the future. And in the midst of it all, William was finding that he didn't mind having the leadership of the Warden taken from him. For the first time in years, he didn't feel the oppressive weight of responsibility on his shoulders. He was still the mayor, but he was beginning to wonder if he'd like to give that up too. Perhaps he could pursue another career. One that wouldn't demand so much from him and his family. One where they could live the rest of their lives in peace, enjoying life together.

Robin rested her head back against his shoulder. "I think they'll be happy," she said. "Even if things will be difficult for a time."

William smiled. She kept finding ways to bring the conversation back to Desmond and Cait. "I think you're right," he said.

"And she's so sweet." Robin pursed her lips. "Maybe too sweet. Do you think she'll let Desmond get away with too much?"

"No," William replied with ready humor. "I don't know her much personally, but from what I understand, she doesn't let him get away with anything."

Robin chuckled. "Good. He needs someone to give him a hard time."

"Seems she's up to the task."

Resting her hands on his arms, Robin squinted into the sunset. "Can we save her, Will?" she whispered.

"I don't know," he answered honestly. "I hope so."

Robin pulled back to look at him. They were practically the same height, with her sporting the Edgars' family height and him representing the Varons' characteristic shortness, so they easily held one another's gaze. "I want to help," she said. "In whatever way I can."

William nodded, then began to tuck her back into his arms.

She drew away, setting a hand on his chest. "Now, William," she insisted. "I want you to bring me up to speed. Tell me everything you know, and let me see if I can spot something you haven't."

"Now?" he asked with disappointment.

She smiled dryly. "Yes, now."

William sighed, giving up his thoughts of a romantic evening. However, as he led her back into the house, he realized that a night discussing the spirit world with his wife wasn't that unappealing. Robin was right; getting an outside perspective might be the key to understanding what was going on. And he always loved watching her mind work out problems like this.

While he gathered what few things he'd brought in his work bag, Robin poured glasses of wine. Then, they settled on the couch, and he spread the papers onto the coffee table. The rusty sunlight streamed through the large windows, mixing with the golden lamplight. It warmed the cool blues and whites of the furnishings and decor.

Slowly, William walked Robin through everything that had happened in Porthaven over the last two months. While he'd told her about the damaged Veil and the beasts at the outset, he went into more detail now. He presented it to her like a police case, knowing her investigative mind would latch onto the finer details.

When he showed her the heavily marked map of where he'd searched for the second Veil, she frowned. "You searched the entire peninsula?"

He nodded. "I couldn't find a thing."

"Is it possible Tim was wrong?"

"Of course, it's possible," he admitted. "But the reverend from Bushmills said their Veil disappeared a year after the Lewans came to Porthaven."

"So, we should have it?" she said.

"Seemingly."

"What if it just combined with the Veil we already had?"

"I assumed that too," William said. "It seems like the only reasonable explanation at this point."

Robin considered it, then picked up the picture of the Veil he'd printed, the amber seal covering the tear in the trunk. Fish had taken the photo for him. He'd hoped it would help him research similar effects on other trees. He'd had no luck.

"Cait did this?" she asked, pointing to the amber.

"After she sent seven beasts back into the Veil," he confirmed.

Robin frowned. "I thought the block made it so that she couldn't access the spirit world."

"It does," he said, then corrected himself. "It *did*. But when the Veil was damaged, so was the block."

"Which is another reason we can safely assume that her Veil is tied to this one."

William tilted his head, the idea new to him. "I suppose so. I thought that perhaps the second Veil had been damaged as well, but Desmond said that the beasts stopped appearing in her dreams, so perhaps when she sealed it, she removed the danger of the beasts altogether."

"Wasn't she dreaming of beasts before the damage?"

"Yes, but the dreams are changing, apparently," he said. "Seemingly, in conjunction with the increasing damage to the Veil."

"And we're still searching for who or what caused this damage?" she said.

At his confirmation, she asked, "Who are your suspects?"

"Originally, it was the Vessels and Lilith. Then, we began to consider that the Druids are finally coming for the Vessels. Now, Desmond proposed the theory that it could be the Varons, attempting to point fingers at my inept leadership."

Robin hummed thoughtfully. "They all sound plausible."

"The problem is," he continued, "we haven't found any evidence to support any of those theories. While the Varons *used* the situation to depose me, nothing has convinced me that they caused it. And aside from the attack at Lilith's house, there's nothing that suggests Druidic activity."

Robin's jaw tensed. "I still don't like that you kept that from me."

"I admit that my integrity has been questionable the last several weeks."

She moved on, scanning the papers spread across the glass tabletop. "We're missing something. If it isn't the Vessels, or the Varons, or the Druids, then . . . we're overlooking something obvious."

"Such as?"

She was silent, hand over her mouth as she thought. She tapped the photo of the Veil again. "What could cause a tear like this? One so rapidly expanding too."

William shook his head. "Desmond said that there are two trees growing through the sycamore."

"Trees?" Robin raised her brow. "That sounds Druidic."

"Yes, but the Veil is a tree itself."

Robin met his gaze. "Two more trees, you said?"

"An aspen and an ash."

"Two *different* types of trees?" She pressed a hand to her temple. "Is that even possible?"

"Not from our research."

"So, it's definitely supernatural," she concluded. "And in whatever manner it got there, it involves the spirit world."

"Which brings us back to all the same suspects," William said.

"Not necessarily." Robin tapped her chin pensively. "The beasts were created by the Veil itself, right? They weren't tethered to an individual, meaning no one was summoning them."

"Right."

"So . . ." Robin held her hands out as though that solved the problem. "What if the damage was the same?"

William stared at her in confusion. "I don't understand. How could the damage just happen?"

"The same way the beasts 'just happened,'" she said. "Something in the spirit world is off, and it's causing the problem. That's why you haven't found any evidence of tampering. There *is* no culprit."

Sitting back, William looked at the pages with new eyes. Could it be that simple? If she was right, and something was inherently wrong in the spirit world, then they had no secret enemy lurking in their town. Simply a problem with the spirit world itself. But what could cause a problem like that?

William stared at the image of the sycamore, studying the amber encasing the aspen and ash beneath its resin. "Why two more trees?" he murmured.

"What?" Robin asked.

"If the damage is caused by a problem in the spirit world, what are the trees about?"

Robin sat silently, considering his question.

Three trees. A sycamore, an aspen, and an ash. What did they signify?

He knew the Veils didn't necessarily represent the spirit-being tied to them. They could mean anything. The sycamore didn't symbolize the Leviathan. The reverend in Bushmills had told him that the Wolf's Veil was a specific portion of the ocean that met the Giant's Causeway. Before that, it was in Amesbury, attached to Stonehenge itself. So, when they moved, they didn't necessarily take the same form they'd had before. Now, they'd all but concluded that the Wolf's Veil had joined the Leviathan's within the sycamore.

The thought crashed into William like the stormy sea.

He cursed under his breath. "Robin, we've got to get back," he said, rising and gathering the pages.

Staring at him wide-eyed, Robin asked, "Why?"

"You were right. It *is* obvious. And we overlooked it this whole time."

"What are you talking about?"

"It's the same Veil," he said, waving the picture at her. "That's the problem."

Robin shook her head, not understanding.

He pointed to the amber. "It's the same Veil," he repeated. "Two Veils connected to two spirit-beings, both fighting for dominance."

Robin's expression fell, her skin paling. "The Veil is splitting itself," she breathed.

William held her panicked stare, his heart thundering dangerously. "And if it splits entirely . . ." He paused, the words catching. "It'll release them both."

Robin stared from the picture to William and back. "But . . ." She shook her head. "Why three?"

"What?"

"William," she said, taking the photo from him. "The sycamore represents the Leviathan. It's been here all two centuries. If the other two trees are breaking through, then what do they represent?"

He frowned, unable to come up with an answer.

Robin's expression tightened with fear as she said, "If each tree is a Veil, then how are there three?"

# CHAPTER FORTY-SIX

# Cait

Stuffing the last of her things into her backpack, Cait did a mental pass back through her packing list: pajamas, a change of clothes, sketchbook, and her phone. Desmond had purchased a toothbrush for her to leave at his place, and he already had face wash and a surprising amount of other hair and skin care products, so she didn't need to take any toiletries beyond her makeup. She'd teased him about his collection last night, but he leveled her with a serious stare and said, "Do you like how I look or not?"

Admitting to herself that she very much *did*, she chose not to make fun of him again.

Cait had told her nan that she intended to go for a walk early in the morning to paint the sunrise using the new watercolors Genni had given her for her birthday. That allowed her to avoid taking Red and excused her absence in the morning. But it also meant that she'd need to paint the sunrise so she could show her work.

After adding the watercolors to her bag, Cait was satisfied. Her packing was complete. Now, all she needed was to sneak out of the house in—she glanced at her phone—ten minutes.

A knock came on Cait's door.

Grimacing, Cait hid her full backpack by the side of her bed. "Come in," she called.

Rese entered, her expression hesitant. "Hey, Cait," she said with a strangely gentle inflection. "Could I talk to you for a minute?"

Knowing she didn't have long before she needed to leave, Cait forced herself to smile. "Uh, sure." She took a seat on the bed. "What's up?"

Shutting the door behind her, Rese moved to join her. "I, uh—I wanted to apologize," she said.

Cait blinked in surprise. Her phone buzzed on the bed beside her, but she ignored it as she listened to Rese.

"Obviously, when we talked the other night, I . . ." Rese stared at her hands while she spoke. "I handled it poorly. Whatever is going on with you and Desmond—well, I can't say that I approve of it, but I understand that you haven't exactly had reason to confide in me about stuff like that. And I didn't handle that conversation correctly."

Though Cait couldn't argue, her sister's evident guilt nudged her compassion. "Neither did I," she admitted. "It was a lot that day—with Mr. Jun and Reverend Lavigne coming by. I shouldn't have said what I did."

"You were right, though." Rese played with a loose string on Cait's comforter. "I haven't been there. I shut you and Genni out because I was trying to protect you. I thought if I kept it to myself, I would make your lives easier."

Cait couldn't understand quite what her sister was trying to say. "Kept what to yourself?"

Rese's gaze lifted to hold hers steadily. "I remember everything about Ireland. And Da . . ."

Cait stared at her sister, a longing filling her chest.

Rese looked truly contrite, tucking some of her golden waves behind her ear. "He told me some things," she said. "Secret things about his . . . his connection."

"To the Warden?" Cait asked uncertainly.

"To the Wolf."

Cait's heart stuttered.

"I always thought it would be me," Rese said adamantly. "On my sixth birthday, Da told me about it because he said it was almost always the firstborn who inherited. He was intending to teach me more, to help me prepare. Then. . . ."

She didn't need to finish the thought. They both knew what happened next.

"Why didn't you tell me?" Cait asked.

"I thought it was going to be me," she repeated. "There was no reason to worry you or Gen because neither of you would have to deal with it. But when I figured out that it was—it was you . . ."

Cait's breath caught.

Rese grabbed her hand. "I've been trying to find a way to free you, Cait. My whole life, I've been preparing for this. It's *my* burden to bear, not yours."

Though Cait appreciated the sentiment, and a part of her wanted it to be true, she couldn't accept it. "It chose me, Rese," she whispered sadly.

"It shouldn't have."

"But it did."

"Fine, yes," Rese sighed. "It chose you. But I think maybe there's a way to get it to change its mind."

The hum began the faintest rumble at the back of Cait's mind. Desmond must have arrived. Yet, she couldn't move, gaping at her sister, sure that it couldn't be possible but hoping beyond hope that it was.

Rese reached over and took Cait's other hand. "I talked to Brady," she said. "He told me that you guys are working to figure this out, and I want to help. I think if we can find some way for me to talk to the Wolf, then I can convince him to choose me. Then, you wouldn't have to worry about it anymore. I'm already—I can get Ryan to marry me, so I'll be taken care of. And with our marriage, there won't be any reason for you or Genni to worry. You've seen the Greenes' house. Ryan stands to inherit all of it, so I can take care of you guys, and you can—you can marry whoever you want. And the Warden will be thrilled to know that the Wolf is secured."

Cait stared at her sister, trying to understand everything she was saying, everything she was offering. Was it possible to convince the Wolf to go to Rese? Cait didn't need to feel bad about giving her the creature— she was ready and willing to take it on. And she and Desmond could be free, never having to live in secret again.

The hum gave a little jolt of agitation, and Cait's thoughts tripped over the rest of Rese's words.

Cait frowned. "Do you even *want* to marry Ryan?"

Rese blinked as though the question had never occurred to her. She shrugged. "Yeah."

Scooting closer, Cait squeezed her sister's hand. "Do you *love* him?"

Rese's silence said more than a thousand words.

"Why would you want to marry him then?"

Rese pulled away. "Love isn't practical, Cait. I like Ryan just fine. I find him attractive, and while he isn't exactly driven, he is smart in his own way. He'll provide for me and my family, and that's enough."

"It's not," Cait insisted, the hum thrumming through her head now, reminding her of just how important love was.

Shaking her head, Rese moved to brush off the subject. "I've worked it all out, Cait. I'll take the Wolf from you, marry Ryan, and the Warden won't have any hold on you or Genni anymore."

"But they'll control *you*."

"I've spent the last twelve years of my life planning this," Rese said. "The Warden may think they're controlling me, but I've chosen this. I've played them to *my* end goal. While they get a subservient Vessel, I get everything I ever wanted."

Cait wondered if her sister fully understood what the Warden would require of her. But then she realized that Rese had already taken care of the loveless marriage part herself.

Suddenly, her sister's eyes narrowed as she looked toward the floor. "Why is your backpack stuffed?" she asked as though she already knew the answer.

Cait's throat thickened as Rese met her gaze. "Cait," she said tightly, "please tell me you aren't sleeping with him."

The hum pulsed furiously, causing Cait to grimace. She glanced at the window, worried that Desmond was there, about to knock. "No," she stuttered nervously. "What are you—why would you—?"

Rese groaned with disappointment. "Cait, you are so much better than this—than him!"

Feeling defensive of her husband, a current of anger lanced through Cait's chest like the lightning in her dreams. The hum whirled through her head like a torrent of wind. Pinpricks of frustration tickled her skin.

"You don't know the first thing about him," Cait returned.

"The entire town knows about him. He has a reputation a mile long. He's made out with every girl at the school, and at least half of them have confirmed that they've slept together too."

Despite the fact that Desmond had started those rumors himself—the girls just perpetuated it because it made them look "good" to have caught the most popular boy's attention—Cait couldn't stop herself from momentarily wondering if they were true.

She shook her head against the thought. She *knew* it wasn't. Though she wasn't exactly knowledgeable in the more intimate parts of romance, Desmond had very clearly been as new to the experience as she had the previous night, both of them fumbling through some of the more intricate details of the moment.

Cait glowered at her sister, preparing a sharp retort, but her phone began to vibrate earnestly on the bed beside her.

Rese instinctively glanced down, her face scrunching with surprise. "Why is Brady calling you?" she asked, inordinately curious.

"I don't know," Cait said, picking up the phone, worried something was wrong. The hum grew louder, making her head swim. "Hello?"

"Hey, Cait." Brady's voice came through deeper and more tense than usual. "Have you heard from Desmond recently?"

Remembering that she had a notification waiting from when Rese first entered, Cait said, "I'm not sure. Maybe. Let me check."

She pulled her phone away from her ear, finding an unread text from Desmond. *"Running late. Be there in twenty."*

"Yeah, he texted me like fifteen minutes ago," she told Brady. Then, she glanced at Rese, who sat with her arms crossed, watching her intently. "Why?"

"What'd he say?" Brady asked.

"Just that he was running late."

"He didn't say why?"

"No."

Brady cursed under his breath. "Look, Uncle Will is trying to get in contact with him. He called him, like, ten times and left a voicemail about thirty minutes ago, and he hasn't responded. Obviously, if he texted you, he's okay, but even I tried calling, and he's not answering. Do you think you could try?"

Eyes flashing back to Rese, Cait tried to figure out how to inform Brady that Desmond was waiting outside her window without letting her sister know too. The hum pressed against her skull, causing her thoughts to muddle. "Uh, sure, but . . . I mean, can I just tell him to call you back?"

"Evidently, he doesn't want to talk to anyone but you."

Cait sighed. She rose and started to pace. Rese's gaze followed her through the room.

"Okay, yeah, I'll—I'll talk to him and see what's going on. Does he need to call his dad?" Cait asked.

"Yeah, Uncle Will figured out some stuff with the Veil," Brady said. "And it's, like, super important that we get it handled tonight."

"Tonight?" Cait asked, shocked. "Why—?"

She broke off, gasping as the hum grew to a near-painful howl, ricocheting through her head. The phone dropped to the floor, and she doubled over, hands to her ears, as she fell to her knees.

Rese leaped off the bed, calling out. But Cait couldn't hear her.

The hum grew and grew and grew, deafening her. Her eyes squeezed shut, not so much in pain as in concentration. She could sense Rese at her side, but the sound encompassed every thought. It filled her whole body, vibrating with determination to break free like the sea straining against the cliffside. Eventually, the rock would give way to the pressure— breaking, cracking, eroding.

Abruptly, the hum ceased.

Cait's mind stilled, and a tension she hadn't known she held in her chest released. A pressure settled at the base of her skull.

She sucked in a breath, opening her eyes. Rese knelt before her, hand on her shoulder, calling her name. Behind her, a shadow loomed.

Cait opened her mouth, ready to warn her sister of the beast's presence. But then the figure became clear, and her heart stopped.

A man stood there, tall and narrow-framed. He had dark blond hair, cropped close, and the short growth of a beard, threaded through with rusty orange. His fierce but kind blue eyes were like the sky at the horizon line. A strong forehead and jawline defined his face, which was marked by a tender yet wry smile.

He wore a charcoal gray jumper with a white and navy Fair Isle pattern, knitted by one of the women from their church. Cait could practically smell the malt and tobacco from the pub in its weave. She wanted to press her face into his chest and let the memories wash over her.

Tears sprang to Cait's eyes as she held his gaze. "Da?" she whispered.

Rese flinched, turning to follow Cait's stare.

Owen Lewan smiled, then spoke in a voice decidedly unlike the one she remembered. It didn't carry the same warmth and lightheartedness, nor was it accented in his Irish lilt. Instead, it was low, like a growl, and resonant, like the hum that filled her head.

"Hello, wolfling."


*Cait and Desmond will return*
*in book seven of Archives of the Warden*

*Also Available from V.K. Dixon*

ARCHIVES OF THE WARDEN
*Lake of Glass*
*Vault of Stone*
*The Raven's Cry*
*Veil of Mist*
*The Wolf's Howl*
*Of Spirit & Ether (Spring 2026)*
*Book Seven (Fall 2026)*

WARRIORS & MAGES
*Fire & Night*
*Sword & Shadow*
*Relics & Thrones*

*Places to follow my author journey:*
*Newsletter:* vkdixon.substack.com
*Instagram:* @v.k.dixon
*TikTok:* @vkdixon

# Glossary of Terms & Names

**Advocate** — Classification of Wielder, able to interact with ghosts and tether phantoms

**arachne** — *[ar—ack—nay]* — Arachnid-like beast from the spirit world

**artio** — *[ar—tee—oh]* — Bear-like beast from the spirit world

**Aster Island** — Island off the coast of Porthaven that houses the lighthouse and the Veil

**aughisky** — *[ahg—is—key]* — Horse-like beast from the spirit world

**beast** — A creature summoned from the spirit world to work on behalf of a Wielder

**Benjamin Lavigne** — *[Lah—veen]* — *aka 'Ben'* — Reverend; Brady's father; Warden member

**Brady Lavigne** — *aka 'Brade'* — High school senior; son of the reverend; best friend of Desmond

**Brett Varon** — Hunter's dad; Warden member

**Caitriona Lewan** — *[Kuh—trina Lew-en]* — *aka 'Cait'* — High school senior; originally from Bushmills, Ireland; middle Lewan daughter

**Charles Simon** — Father of William; previous mayor and true Varon of Edmond's line; deceased

**Cleric** — Classification of Wielder, able to interact with ghosts and summon beasts

**Corva** — *aka 'the Raven'* — Prophetic spirit-being

**Desmond Simon** — High school student and Warden member

**drake** — Lizard-like beast from the spirit world

**Druids** — *aka 'Children of Gaia'* — A cult of Wielders intent on releasing the spirit world upon the physical world

**Elizabeth Allard** — Past Vessel of Corva

**Elizabeth Greene** — High school senior; daughter of town doctor

**Fischer Lavigne** — *aka 'Fish'* — Lightkeeper; Warden member

**Gabriel Varon** — The first Varon connected with the Warden; considered the father of the Varon line

**Garrett Edgars** — High school senior; second son of the sheriff; cousin of Desmond

**Gary Lavigne** — Retired reverend; Brady's grandfather; Warden member

**Genevieve Lewan** — *aka 'Genni'* — High school sophomore; youngest Lewan daughter

**George Faulk** — Father of Timothy Faulk

**ghost** — The lingering spirit of a dead Wielder with unfinished business in the physical world

**Gregory Varon** — Hunter's grandfather; Warden member

**Hades** — A sith beast; summoned by Desmond Simon

**hellhound** — Hound-like beast from the spirit world

**Herald** — Classification of Wielder, able to see ghosts

**Hunter Varon** — High school senior; Desmond's rival

**hydra** — *[hi—druh]* — Snake-like beast from the spirit world

**Kenneth Greene** — Town doctor; Elizabeth's father; Warden member

**Kevin Jun** — *[Juhn]* — Municipality Analyst for Sheraton Corporation

**the Leviathan** — A spirit-being under the guard of the Warden

**Lilith Drake** — Owner of the tea shop; ex-Druid

**Ludus** — Cait's dog in present day

**Lyndon Simon** — Christopher Varon's heir; great-grandfather of William Simon; deceased

**Maeve Lewan** — *[May—vuh]* — Grandmother of the Lewan sisters

**Marcy Yates** — Owner of Sea Beans, the coffee shop

**Martin Varon** — Great-great uncle of William Simon; deceased

**Matt Davis** — High school senior; new to Porthaven

**Melissa Porcher** — Friends with Hunter Varon and Elizabeth Greene; dating Scott Edgars

**nyct** — *[nicked]* — Bat-like beast from the spirit world

**Owen Lewan** — Father of Cait; Warden member; deceased

**Penny Davis** — History teacher at Porthaven High; Matt's mom

**Peter Varon** — Writer and Warden member from DeVerre, WA; true Varon of Matthias's line

**phantom** — A ghost that has been tethered to a specific location in the physical world

**Porthaven, ME** — Small, Warden-run town in northeast Maine

**ratatoskr** — *[rah—tah—toss—ker]* — Rat-like beast from the spirit world

**Raymond Edgars** — Fire marshal; Scott's dad; Warden member

**Red** — Lewan family terrier

**Richard Edgars** — *aka 'Rick'* — Sheriff; Garrett's dad; Warden member

**Robin Simon** — Wife of William and mother of Desmond; Warden member

**Ryan Greene** — Son of Kenneth Greene; brother of Elizabeth Greene; dating Therese Lewan

**Sabine Lewan** — Mother of Cait; Warden member; deceased

**Sage** — Classification of Wielder, able to speak to ghosts, summon beasts, and wield the essence of the spirit world.

**Saliha Faulk** — Mother of Sterling; Warden member

**Scott Edgars** — High school senior; son of fire marshal; cousin of Desmond; best friends with Hunter

**scylla** — *[sky—luh]* — Cephalopod-like beast from the spirit world

**sith** — Cat-like beast from the spirit world

**Spectral** — *aka 'spirit-being,' 'the kindred'* — A creature of the spirit world that attaches to a Vessel with unknown qualities and abilities

**spirit world** — A parallel world that exists alongside the physical world

**Sterling Faulk** — High school senior; best friends with Hunter

**Sydney Bellerose** — High school senior

**Sylvia Lyons** — Past Vessel of Corva

**Therese Lewan** — *aka 'Rese'* — Barista; eldest Lewan daughter; dating Ryan Greene

**Timothy Faulk** — *aka 'Tim'* — Carpenter; father of Sterling; Warden member

**valravn** — *[val—rah—ven]* — Bird-like beast from the spirit world

**Veil** — Specific locations around the world where the boundary between the spirit world and the physical world is thin; connected to the Spectrals

**the Warden** — An organization of Wielders dedicated to protecting the spirit world from the control of the Druids

**wendigo** — *[when—de—go]* — Deer-like beast from the spirit world

**Whitney Toussaint** — *[Too—sawnt]* — High school senior; Garrett's girlfriend

**Wielder** — A human with the ability to wield the spirit world

**William Simon** — Mayor and leader of the Warden in Porthaven; father of Desmond

# Acknowledgments

This story feels as though it was such a long time in the making. Cait and Desmond have been in my heart and mind for more than a decade, and finally getting to tell their story is wildly surreal.

Thank you to all my amazing readers! You're kindness and support for this story has truly kept me going.

To my beta readers, Alexandra, Anna, Brooke, Kaitlynn, Lydia, Rachelle, and Stevie: Thank you all for your wonderful insight and notes. You're amazing!

To my editor, Brittany: As always, you take my words and make them everything I hoped they'd be. Thank you for your keen eye, clarity, and encouragement!

To my husband, Josh: You will forever be the best!

And thank you, God, for planting this story in my heart all those years ago, and for giving me the strength to keep writing through every moment life sends. May every word bring you glory!

# About the Author

V. K. Dixon writes fantasy and romance novels filled with found family, lasting love, and unique magic. She believes that the extraordinary gives us a deeper desire for the things beyond us—the things of God.

www.ingramcontent.com/pod-product-compliance
Lightning Source LLC
Chambersburg PA
CBHW031159010826
48971CB00013B/953